Hal Sp
Second Course

Book Two in the Hal Spacejock series

Stay in touch!

Author's newsletter:
spacejock.com.au/ML.html

facebook.com/halspacejock
twitter.com/spacejock

SECOND COURSE

SIMON HAYNES

Bowman Press

Works by Simon Haynes

All of Simon's novels* are self-contained, with a beginning, a middle and a proper ending. They're not sequels, they don't end on a cliffhanger, and you can start or end your journey with any book in the series.
Robot vs Dragons series excepted!

The Hal Spacejock series for teens/adults

Set in the distant future, where humanity spans the galaxy and robots are second-class citizens. Includes a large dose of humour!

Hal Spacejock 1: A robot named Clunk
Hal Spacejock 2: Second Course
Hal Spacejock 3: Just Desserts
Hal Spacejock 4: No Free Lunch
Hal Spacejock 5: Baker's Dough
Hal Spacejock 6: Safe Art
Hal Spacejock 7: Big Bang
Hal Spacejock 8: Double Trouble
Hal Spacejock 9: Max Damage
Hal Spacejock 10: Cold Boots (2019)

Also available:
Omnibus One, containing Hal books 1-3
Omnibus Two, containing Hal books 4-6
Omnibus Three, containing Hal books 7-9
Hal Spacejock: Visit, a short story
Hal Spacejock: Framed, a short story
Hal Spacejock: Albion, a novella

The Robot vs Dragons Trilogy.
High fantasy meets low humour!
Each set of three books should be read in order.

1. A Portion of Dragon and Chips
2. A Butt of Heads
3. A Pair of Nuts on the Throne
4. TBA (2019)

The Harriet Walsh series.

Set in the same universe as Hal Spacejock. Good clean fun, written with wry humour. No cliffhangers between novels!

Harriet Walsh 1: Peace Force
Harriet Walsh 2: Alpha Minor
Harriet Walsh 3: Sierra Bravo
Harriet Walsh 4: Storm Force (2019)
Also Available:
Omnibus One, containing books 1-3

The Hal Junior series

Written for all ages, these books are set aboard a space station in the Hal Spacejock universe, only ten years later.

1. Hal Junior: The Secret Signal
2. Hal Junior: The Missing Case
3. Hal Junior: The Gyris Mission
4. Hal Junior: The Comet Caper

Also Available:
Omnibus One, containing books 1-3

The Secret War series.
Gritty space opera for adult readers.

1. Raiders (2019)
2. Frontier (2019)
3. Deadlock (2019)

Collect One-Two - a collection of shorts by Simon Haynes

All titles available in ebook and paperback. Visit spacejock.com.au for details.

This edition published 2012 by Bowman Press

Text © Simon Haynes 2011
Cover art © Simon Haynes 2012

ISBN 978-1-877034-03-9 (Ebook)
ISBN 978-1-877034-09-1 (Paperback)

Previously Published 2006 by Fremantle Press
First Published 2003 by Bowman Publishing

NATIONAL LIBRARY OF AUSTRALIA

A catalogue record for this book is available from the National Library of Australia

Dedicated to my family

The interstellar freighter *Volante* powered through space, her streamlined flanks speckled with pinpoints of light from distant stars. In the flight deck, Hal Spacejock was studying the main viewscreen from his customary stance in the pilot's chair - hands clasped behind his head, boots up on the flight console and a cup of coffee at his side. He was watching a planet on the main screen, an aquamarine pearl rotating slowly against a rich backdrop of twinkling stars. It was a welcome sight after several intense hours flying the bulky ship through the vast emptiness of space, and Hal was looking forward to a couple of days rest and recreation. Particularly the recreation.

Without warning a comet tore across the screen, missing the planet by the thickness of its atmosphere.

'I bet that woke them up,' said Hal, as the glittering trail faded. He watched the display for a few moments longer, then frowned at a recessed camera. 'Navcom, are we moving?'

'We're at optimum cruising speed,' said a neutral, female voice.

'So why isn't that planet getting any bigger?'

'Planet?'

'You know, the big round things we land on.'

'I know what a planet is,' said the computer patiently.

'However, I don't know which one you're referring to.'

Hal gestured at the screen. 'That one!'

'I think I understand your confusion. You see, that's not a planet.'

'What is it, then? A weather balloon?'

'Negative. It's an animation I display when the viewscreen is on standby.'

Hal looked down at the controls. 'Are you telling me I just spent four hours flying the Volante through a screen saver?'

'You weren't flying anything. The ship is on autopilot.'

'All right, get rid of that thing and show me Ullimo.'

'But –'

'Don't argue!'

The screen changed to show a pinpoint of light against a sea of solid black.

'Is that it?'

'Sort of.'

Hal frowned at the camera. 'Yes or no?'

'No,' admitted the computer. 'Additional jumps are required before I can display a real-time image. This simulation is the best I can do.'

'It's not much of a simulation.'

'Ullimo isn't much of a planet.'

'And what's all this about additional jumps? Why didn't you get closer in the first place?'

'The Ullimo system is thick with dust and debris. Navigation is difficult and . . .'

'One of these days I'm going to take the controls. Then we'll really go places.'

'I cannot cede control of the ship until you've finished the flight manual. Would you like to read it now?'

2

'All right, put it up.' Hal crossed his arMs. 'It's just a refresher, though. I know all this stuff.'

A slab of ten-point text appeared on the main viewscreen. 'Owner's handbook, chapter one,' said the Navcom. 'I've marked the second paragraph, which is as far as you got last time.'

Hal gazed at the dense text for several seconds. 'I don't have time for this,' he said at last. 'I've got things to do.'

'Actually, there is something you can help with,' said the Navcom. 'I've calculated the import duty on our cargo and I need you to authorise the payment.'

'Oh yeah? How much?'

'Two thousand credits.'

Hal jerked upright, spilling his coffee on the console. 'That's over half our fee!'

'You promised FIS delivery.'

'What does that mean?'

'Free into store. We pay all the charges.'

Hal cursed. 'I thought the customer looked happy.'

'Will you authorise the payment?'

'Are you sure you haven't made a mistake?'

'I do not make mistakes,' said the computer coldly. 'Even a human could calculate ten percent of twenty thousand.'

'Ten percent! That's robbery!'

'It does seem a little high. Incidentally, there is liquid dripping into my circuits.'

Hal mopped up the spilt coffee with the sleeve of his flight suit. 'What's the duty on robot parts?'

'Two percent. And it won't work.'

'What won't?'

'You can't declare the cargo as something else.'

'What about something related?'

'Such as?'

'Bed sheets.'

'Twelve percent.'

'Curtains?'

'Fifteen.'

Hal examined his coffee-stained sleeve. 'What about cleaning rags?'

The Navcom hesitated. 'There is no duty on rags.'

Hal beamed. 'There you go then! Change the manifest to cleaning rags and submit the forms.'

'But our cargo consists of brand new fabric on rolls.'

'So change the manifest to brand new cleaning rags on rolls.'

'But –'

'Navcom, what are cleaning rags made out of?'

'Fabric,' said the computer unwillingly. 'But ...'

'No buts. Change it.'

'Alterations complete. Next item: twelve boxes of fruit.'

'Any duty?'

'Negative. Unprocessed food is not subject to tariffs.'

'Good. Anything else?'

'We have to declare Clunk.'

'He's part of the crew!'

'They'll issue a refund when you leave the planet. In the meantime, you have to pay two percent of his total value.'

'Two percent of nothing is nothing. Even a computer could work that out.'

'Are you saying Clunk has no value?'

'He's not worth anything in a money sense.' Hal glanced over his shoulder. Fortunately the flight deck was clear. 'Don't tell him I said that. I mean, he might not understand.'

'I daresay he wouldn't, what with being a worthless robot.'

'That's not what I said!'

'You said he had no value.'

'All right, put him down for five hundred credits. Anything else?'

'We have to declare everything of value.'

Hal grinned. 'Like me, you mean?'

'No, everything of value.'

Hal's grin slipped. 'Surely I'm worth something?'

'Not unless you learn to navigate.'

'All right, I can take a hint.' Resigned to the inevitable, Hal settled down to read the flight manual. He'd managed two sentences when the lift doors hissed open.

'Mr Spacejock!'

'Not now, Clunk.'

Footsteps approached. 'Mr –'

'Wait!' Hal's lips moved as he struggled with the dense text. 'What's a clutch?'

'Mr Spacejock, I must speak with you.'

Hal sighed and spun his chair around. A battered bronze robot stood before him, its squashy, furrowed face arranged into a look of concern. 'All right, what's up?'

The robot opened its mouth to speak, and a split second later the words came out. 'I would like to discuss an engineering matter. During my rounds I discovered that the main generator is running warm.'

'Can we fix it?'

'No. We'll have to schedule an inspection when we land on Ullimo.'

'What's that going to cost?'

'Nothing. It's covered by warranty.'

'Good.'

'Unless they discover the missed services.'

'Eh?'

'I faked the maintenance logs as per your instruction, but an investigation could uncover inconsistencies.'

'But –'

'You know, if you hadn't wasted all that money on advertising we wouldn't be experiencing such problems.'

'Now wait just a minute. We wouldn't have any work without advertising.'

'True. However, your choice of media outlets was somewhat questionable.'

'What do you mean? I got a banner ad into twenty thousand ebooks!'

'They were picture books. As a rule, three-year-olds don't move a lot of freight. Still, at least you didn't order any more fridge magnets.'

'Now you mention it, I've got four cartons in the hold.'

'Really? Why don't you hand them out?'

'They don't work properly,' mumbled Hal. 'I stuck one on the AutoChef and it zipped off again. Almost took my eye out.'

'How odd.' Clunk frowned. 'Where did you store them?'

'That cupboard in the engine room.'

'There are no cupboards in the engine room.'

'Sure there are. Big grey things with silver handles.'

'Mr Spacejock, are you telling me you put four cartons of magnets inside the gravity generator?'

'If that's the grey cupboard, then yes. There was loads of room once I moved a few wires and things out the way.'

Clunk stared at him.

'Okay, so the fridge magnets aren't very attractive. But what about my fast food sponsorship? I got our vouchers on every soft drink container for a month!'

'With a company that only supplies prisons.'

'There's no such thing as bad publicity.'

'And you're doing your best to prove it.' Clunk sighed. 'Mr Spacejock, it'll be a miracle if any of your ill-conceived campaigns earn back the money you spent on them. In the meantime, we can't afford to service the ship.'

'We have to advertise to get a better class of client. I'm fed up with dodgy businessmen. We need someone who'll give us a bit of prestige.'

'Like pre-schoolers and convicts? Anyway, nobody judges you by your clients.'

'Oh yeah? Why do spaceports always give us landing spots around the edges?'

'They're afraid you'll destroy the buildings. Now, if you'll excuse me I must tend to the generators, and I have to reseat the manemol flange on the hyperdrive.'

After Clunk left, Hal turned to the screen and frowned at the cramped text. 'Oh yeah, clutches.' He read for a few moments, then shook his head. 'I need caffeine.' Standing up, he walked to the back of the flight deck and extracted a mug of coffee from a dispenser. As he sipped the brew, he gazed across the flight deck. The text on the screen was too small to read, but the paragraphs made an interesting checkerboard pattern. 'Hey, when's the last time we played chess? Do you remember?'

'Only too well,' said the computer.

'Let's have a game now.' Hal returned to the console with his coffee. 'Set the board up. I'll be black.'

'According to my logs, you're supposed to be white.'

'Yeah, but you know what happens whenever I move first. That upgrade Clunk installed makes every game a joke.'

'Nevertheless, it's only fair to swap sides.'

'It's not, it's a waste of time.'

The Navcom was silent.

'Oh, quit sulking,' growled Hal. 'You can play black if you want to.'

A chessboard appeared in mid-air, rotated so that the rows of white chess pieces were nearest to Hal. He indicated one of the pawns, then tapped the square two spots ahead of it. The pawn darted across the board and stopped.

'I resign,' said the Navcom.

Hal groaned. 'Come on, make a game of it.'

'It's pointless. You will beat me in fifteen moves.'

'I won't!'

'You will. I have already calculated the sequence of moves leading to your victory.'

'That's amazing, because I haven't.' Hal replaced the pawn and moved another. 'What if I start like that?'

'Sixteen moves,' said the Navcom. 'You have me in a hopeless situation.'

Hal replaced the pawn and moved a knight.

'A very cunning start. Checkmate in fourteen moves.'

'Where's your competitive spirit?' demanded Hal.

'Fighting lost causes is a waste of energy.'

'You don't see me quitting when I'm behind, do you? I don't chuck it all in when the going gets tough.'

'No, you always fight to the bitter end,' conceded the Navcom.

'Thank you,' said Hal.

'It wasn't a compliment,' said the computer. 'I was just stating facts.'

Hal sighed. 'Do you have anything else we can try? Something where you don't quit after two seconds?'

'My library of games is somewhat limited, although I do have one involving mines.'

'Really? What does it do?'

'You select squares until you pick the wrong one, at which point the game ends.'

'And that's entertainment, is it?' Hal sighed. 'Stick the flight manual back up. Even that's better than this rubbish.'

◆

Clunk limped along the lower deck corridor, lost in thought as he made his way to the engine room. He wasn't overly concerned about the generator, since modern ships issued warnings for the most trivial temperature variations. No, he was worried about all the regular services they'd skipped. Should anything serious go wrong with the *Volante*, the manufacturer would discover the faked service records and refuse to fix it under warranty. Mr Spacejock, not having any money, would be forced to sell his ship. And Clunk, with nowhere else to go, would be consigned to the scrap heap.

So, trivial variation or not, he resolved to keep an eye on the generators until they landed.

Clunk navigated a narrow staircase just inside the cargo hold, and once at the top he opened the heavy access door to the engine compartment. The bulk of the drives lay behind the shielding, leaving a narrow service tunnel which led to the generator compartment at the rear. Clunk squeezed between the roaring engines and opened a small door, revealing a cramped, stuffy alcove where two bulging cylinders whined in tandem, sucking fuel and cooling fluid through thin metal pipes and feeding the ship's electrical circuits through thick insulated cables. Above the neat tubing, a screen displayed half a dozen gauges and a page full of scrolling text.

Stepping over a patch of grease, Clunk approached the nearest cylinder to begin his inspection. Modern robots carry a range of testing equipment which allows them to download log files and parse error reports while simultaneously engaging the bridge crew in witty repartee. Unfortunately Clunk wasn't a modern robot, so he pressed the side of his head to the generator and rapped the curved metal with his knuckles. Satisfied, he repeated the process with the second whining cylinder. Inspection complete, he peered at the gauges. All of them were in the green, although one was flickering slightly.

Clunk reached out to tap the screen, slipped on the patch of grease and fell head first into the cooling pipes, which groaned and creaked as they supported his weight. He lay motionless for a second or two while his internal diagnostics verified he was okay, then extracted himself from the tubes and stood up.

Immediately, he became aware of two rather worrying developments: The alcove was much hotter, and the cylinder beside him was making a strange growling sound.

Clunk stared at the status panel. He didn't have a swallowing reflex, but he did his best. Half the needles were in the red, and the rest were dancing like heartbeat monitors. He was just bending to examine the pipes when Hal's voice burst from the intercom.

'Clunk, I've got red lights all over the console. Temperature warnings, lubrication alerts, pressure indicators - you name it, it's flashing. And what's that funny rumbling noise?'

'I'm just carrying out a minor repair,' shouted Clunk, raising his voice over the growling generator. He reached for the panel and yanked a handful of fuses, blanking out the gauges.

'Ah, that fixed it,' said Hal. 'For a minute there I thought you'd broken something.'

'Over and out,' said Clunk, hurriedly cutting the connection. He set the fuses aside and inspected the damage to the cooling pipes, wincing as he saw the twists and kinks. Using his fingers like pliers, he worked the flattened metal into its original shape. The growling ceased as the coolant flowed, and before long his sensors told him the air temperature was dropping.

Breathing a sigh of relief, he grabbed a rag and wiped the patch of grease from the floor. Once it was clean, he hung the rag over the damaged pipes and sniffed the air. Thank goodness - it was back to normal.

Clunk was just about to leave when a horrible thought struck him. What if a repair team noticed the buckled cooling pipes when they examined the generators? If they questioned him about it, he would have to tell the truth: that he'd damaged the tubes himself. They'd blame him for everything, including the original temperature variation, and Mr Spacejock would lose his ship!

If only he could lie like a human! Unfortunately, he wasn't programmed for it. All he could do was report events exactly as they were stored in his memory banks. If he refused they'd connect him to a computer and force it out of him.

Clunk left the generator room deep in thought. What if the memories weren't there in the first place? All robots lost data from time to time - particularly when their operating systems crashed. As he left the engine room, Clunk paged through his short-term memory until he found the spot where he'd slipped on the grease. Moving forwards, he found the segment where he'd mopped the grease up. Next, he snipped everything in between, entered a file error into his log and rebooted.

There was a moment of darkness, and when he recovered he was facing the lift in the Volante's lower deck corridor. He shook his head, annoyed at the waste of time. The generator fault had been nothing but a false alarm!

Hal was sitting at the console with a fresh cup of coffee, doggedly working his way through the Volante's flight manual. There was a tin of biscuits at his elbow, and after struggling through a particularly dull passage on rocket fuel he selected one and took a large bite. 'Who wrote this junk, anyway? It's terrible!'

'They don't have to write well,' said the Navcom. 'They just have to impart knowledge.'

'I bet it was written by a robot,' said Hal, his voice muffled by the biscuit.

'I resent that.'

'Name one great work of literature written by a computer.'

'Name one spaceship designed by a human.'

'That explains a lot.' Hal took another bite. 'This is stale.'

'It was cheap.'

'If I wanted cheap I'd dunk toilet paper.' Hal inspected the biscuit suspiciously. 'Unless I already am.'

'No, it's definitely not toilet paper.'

'How can you be sure?'

'The organic material in that biscuit is entirely insect in origin.'

'Ugh!' Hal peered into the tin. 'I thought those were raisins!'

Buzz!

'Incoming call,' said the Navcom.

'Who is it?'

'Central Bank. They have a freight job for you.'

'Central, eh? Now that's the sort of customer we need.' Hal brushed the crumbs off his flight suit and ran his fingers through his hair. 'Okay, put them on.'

There was a crackle from the speaker and a short, balding man appeared on the viewscreen. He was wearing a dark suit, and in the subdued lighting his pale face seemed to float in mid-air. 'Are you Hal Spacejock?'

'Sure am,' said Hal. 'How can I help you?'

'My name is Cecil Fish. I am the Services Procurement Officer for Central Bank.'

'Really?' Hal looked impressed. 'What does one of those do?'

Fish ignored the question. 'I understand you're en route to planet Ullimo. Correct?'

'We're some way out, but my computer will get us there eventually.' Hal wiped his forehead. The air in the flight deck was normally kept at a steady twenty degrees, but for some reason it felt much hotter.

'I'm glad to hear it,' said Fish, oblivious to Hal's discomfort. 'I have some important files which must be taken to our branch on Ackexa. I would like to employ your services.'

'Files? Can't you upload them?'

'At Central Bank we do not entrust valuable documents to electronic media,' said Fish primly. 'In any case, every page is signed and witnessed.'

'You're paying the bill,' said Hal with a shrug. 'If it was me, I'd post the things.'

'Which is why you're not running a bank,' said Fish. 'Now,

the consignment consists of thirty-six pallets. Estimated weight is seventy-two thousand kilograms, allowing for a moisture content of five percent.'

Hal pursed his lips. 'That much?'

'Five percent isn't high.'

'No, I mean thirty-six pallets. That's a lot of freight. It could be expensive.'

Fish held up a wrinkled paper cup. 'According to this voucher you are seven point five percent cheaper than the opposition.'

'Hey, that's my prison drinks advert! Where'd you get hold of it?'

'I was visiting my accountant.' Fish regarded Hal with pale eyes. 'Is this voucher not good?'

'That offer was some time ago. Fuel is more expensive now.' Hal wiped his sleeve across his forehead. 'You know how it is.'

Fish crumpled the cup. 'Very well, I shall contact Curtis Freightlines. They have a modern fleet and their prices are –'

'No, don't!' said Hal hurriedly. 'I'll take the job. And this isn't some bucket of bolts, either. The *Volante* is brand new.'

'Most encouraging. Very well, the cargo is yours. Oh, one final thing. It must be delivered by close of business tomorrow.'

'On time every time, that's us. As long as there aren't any hold-ups, of course.'

'You'll be on time, hold-ups or not. We have severe penalties for late delivery.' Fish gestured at the screen, cutting the call.

Hal brushed away a bead of sweat. 'Navcom, what's happening to the air?'

'Nothing.'

'It's hot.'

15

'No it isn't.'

'You could've fooled me.' Hal squinted at the small white dot on the viewscreen. 'How long now?'

'ETA about twenty minutes.'

'What do you mean, 'about'? Is everything okay?'

'I am completely operational and ...'

'A simple yes will do,' interrupted Hal.

'Fine,' said the computer, sounding miffed. The screen changed to display chapter three of the flight manual. 'Don't forget your reading.'

'It's upside down. And what was the 'about' about?'

'Nothing, nothing,' said the Navcom promptly. 'I am comple–'

'Navcom, it's like an oven in here. Stop telling me everything's all right.' At that moment the lift arrived, and the normally silent doors opened with a loud grinding noise. 'Clunk, how much do we make with this seven percent discount lark?'

'It's seven and a half, and we don't make anything,' said the robot. 'If you recall, I advised against it.'

'You advise against everything. Lucky I never listen, because Central Bank just hired us.'

'Central Bank?' exclaimed Clunk.

'Yes. They want us to take some paperwork to their branch on Ackexa. Not to rub it in, but they saw my voucher on a soft drink cup.'

'Ackexa, did you say?' Clunk looked thoughtful. 'Mr Spacejock, what do you know about Outsider planets?'

'They're outside Union space?'

'A fairly safe deduction. Watch this.' Clunk brought up a navigation chart and zoomed in on a sparsely populated area. 'You can see the division between Union and Outsider space,' he said, pointing to a thin red line. 'Beyond that line you're at the mercy of a legal system with a perfect record.'

'What's so bad about that?'

'To achieve that perfect record they jail all suspects without trial. Some areas are worse than others, of course. In the outer reaches they shoot first and incarcerate your remains.'

'You mean incinerate.'

'I know what I meant.'

Hal mopped his forehead. 'So where are the dangerous bits?'

'This planet is the worst,' said Clunk, pointing to a blue dot.

'No sweat. We'll just stay clear of that one.'

'Oh yes?' Clunk zoomed in until the dot was a fat blue planet. 'That's Ackexa, our destination. Overcrowded, polluted and completely lawless.'

Hal eyed the screen, shaking his head. 'You're exaggerating.'

'I am?'

'Sure you are. You're just annoyed because I got this job.'

'You've arranged delivery to the deadliest part of the galaxy, and you want me to be happy?'

Hal shrugged. 'We don't have any choice. If I turn this job down they'll never offer me another.'

'Don't say I didn't warn you.'

Hal pulled at the neck of his flight suit. 'Is it just me, or is it getting hot in here?'

'It's thirty-seven degrees,' said Clunk.

Hal turned to the console. 'Navcom, get the temperature down. Now!'

'Comply cannot,' said the computer. 'I see icy.'

Hal heard a movement, and turned to see Clunk hurrying towards the lift. 'Where are you going?'

'There's a temperature warning on the main generator. I'd better check.'

17

'Again?'

Clunk frowned. 'What do you mean, 'again'?'

'You just checked it.'

'I did?'

'Yes! You said you had to reseal the manny-thingy on the army-whatsit.'

Clunk looked surprised. 'I said that?'

Hal patted his pockets. 'Silly me, I've misplaced my handy-dandy conversation transcriber. Look, I don't know exactly what you said, but that was the gist of it, okay?'

'How strange, I have no memory of the conversation.'

'You're serious.' Hal stared at the robot. 'We'd better get you serviced.'

Clunk nodded. 'Loss of memory can be very dangerous. I shall retrace my steps while you continue with your reading.'

'With my ...?' Hal looked at the viewscreen. 'What's that?'

'It looks like the flight manual,' said Clunk. 'Why is the third sentence highlighted?'

'That's as far as he got before he lost interest,' said the Navcom.

'I did not lose interest. I was conducting a business meeting with an important client.' Hal glared at Clunk. 'What happened to retracing your steps?'

'On my way.'

As the doors closed, Hal turned back to the screen. 'I'm going to make a real effort this time. It can't be that complicated.'

'Incoming call,' said the Navcom suddenly. 'Rex Curtis, priority one.'

'Rex who?'

'Curtis,' repeated the computer.

Hal shrugged. 'Put him on.'

A scene appeared: a plush office with wood panelling, pure white carpet and a huge desk. Behind the desk sat a large, dark-haired man in an immaculate suit. 'Mr Spacejock?' he demanded in a gravelly voice.

'That's me,' said Hal.

'We need to talk about freight.'

'What kind of freight?'

'Paperwork. Thirty-six pallets for Ackexa.'

'Sorry, I'm already booked. We can talk when I've delivered the first lot.'

'You're not delivering anything,' snapped Rex. 'Curtis Freightlines has a contract with Central Bank. You'll just have to turn them down.'

For a moment Hal was tempted. According to Clunk, Ackexa was a powderkeg and the *Volante* was a lit match. On the other hand, he didn't like this Curtis character, and they'd won the job fair and square. 'Sorry, I've already taken the job.'

'It's a simple choice, Spacejock. Cancel that pickup or suffer the consequences.'

Hal shrugged. 'Do your worst.'

'You're going to regret this.' Curtis leaned across the desk, his face looming in the camera. 'I've had it up to here with two-bit throttle jockeys, rust bucket freighters and slack deliveries. The whole bloody lot of you should be rounded up and thrown in jail.'

'Rust bucket?' Hal waved airily, encompassing the pristine flight deck. 'I don't know what kind of clapped out ships you're used to, but the *Volante* is brand new.'

'You must have stolen it.'

'No, I earned it with hard work. Speaking of which, I'm busy

'...so get lost.' Hal brought his fist down on the disconnect button. 'Navcom, if he calls again you can tell him to get –'

'I don't think that's wise,' interrupted the computer. 'Mr Curtis is a very powerful man. You can't tell him to ... well, you can't say what you were going to say.'

'Put him through again and I'll prove you wrong.' Hal turned to the screen, and had barely scanned the next sentence when a klaxon whooped. His feet slipped off the console and the tin of biscuits went flying as he fell to the deck, arms and legs flailing. 'What the –'

'Emergency!' screeched the Navcom, as biscuits rained down all over the console. 'Main generator failed. All hands on deck!'

There was a splutter and the lights winked out.

'Navcom?' Hal stared into the darkness. 'Hey, quit screwing around!'

There was no reply.

'Navcom?'

There was total silence. The console was dead, the air purifiers were still and even the distant roar of the main drives had ceased. Life support gone, shields down, no power ... only an experienced pilot could save the ship now.

Hal squared his shoulders and cupped his hands to his mouth. 'Clunk!' he shouted. 'Help!'

◆

'You took your time,' growled Hal as the lift doors grated open.

'I was inspecting the generators.' Clunk entered the flight

deck, blinking owlishly in the emergency lighting. 'What happened?'

Hal tried to construct a suitable answer from his store of technical language. 'There was a buzzy noise and the lights went out.'

'That's not very illuminating,' remarked Clunk as he approached the console. He felt under the front edge for the catch, and the entire surface rose with a hiss of compressed air. The robot secured the lid with a metal rod and peered inside.

Hal looked over the robot's shoulder. 'Well?'

Clunk turned round slowly. 'Well what?'

'What went wrong?'

The robot straightened. 'Mr Spacejock, ten minutes have passed since you called for my help. During that time, your sole contribution was to reactivate the coffee machine.'

'Caffeine helps me think,' said Hal defensively.

'Really?' Clunk gave him a hard stare. 'You should drink more of it.'

'Very funny.' Hal crossed his arMs. 'Now get on with the repairs before I become the proud owner of a flute.'

'Flute?'

'It's a hollow tube full of holes.'

'I know what a flute is,' said the robot patiently. 'I fail to see the connection.'

'Well you won't find it talking to me.' Hal jerked his thumb at the console. 'If anything, it'll be in there. You know, a loose wire or something.'

Clunk looked over the controls. 'Did you touch anything?'

'Only that big red button marked 'Initiate self destruct sequence'.'

The robot turned his back, muttering under his breath. His

elbows moved vigorously for a few minutes, then . . . 'Ah-ha!' he said. There was a click, and the overhead lights came on.

'Clunk, you're a marvel,' said Hal. 'Navcom, can you hear me?'

'Loud and clear.'

'Start her up. Let's get going.'

'Don't be so hasty, Mr Spacejock.' Clunk unhooked the stand, letting the console sink down onto its base. His expression was that of a mechanic with a long list of unpaid bills and a short list of customers.

'Why not? What's the problem?' demanded Hal.

Clunk tried to arrange his face into a reassuring look, but it plainly said 'the big end's gone'. 'Well, I don't know whether to . . .'

'Come on, I can take it. What's up?'

'I'll see whether I can explain the problem in simple terMs. You see, the windings on the armature have delaminated, and –'

'Simple, Clunk. Simple.'

Clunk spread his hands. 'Mr Spacejock, unless you understand these matters you'll never gain entry to the Spacer's Guild.'

Hal snorted. 'Why would I want to join that stuck-up bunch of hot air merchants?'

'Right. That's why you've been studying their application forms, measuring yourself for the ceremonial uniform, making little replicas of the membership badge –'

'Hey, who said you could go through my stuff?'

'Go through your stuff? There are scraps of gold-painted plastic all over the ship!'

'Yes, well maybe we could discuss the great clean-up operation later. Right now I want the *Volante* fixed.'

'There are two problems with that. First, the main generator has failed.'

'I got that bit from the Navcom.'

Clunk held his hand up, displaying a wet palm. 'This is the second issue.'

'So grab a towel.'

'This came from the console.'

'Condensation?'

Clunk shook his head and offered his hand. Reluctantly, Hal sniffed it. 'Doesn't ring a bell.'

'It's coffee, Mr Spacejock. The console is awash with it.'

'Burst pipe?'

Clunk shook his head. 'Careless human.'

'You always blame me!'

'You're right, it could have been any of the numerous coffee drinkers aboard this ship.'

'Never mind the witch hunt. What's the plan?'

'We must land. Quickly.'

Hal jerked his thumb at the screen. 'Ullimo's just a few jumps away.'

'We won't make it. We need something closer.'

'Is there anything else around?'

'Ask the Navcom,' said Clunk, heading for the lift. 'I have to check the secondary generator.'

Hal swung his chair to face the console. 'Navcom, what's the nearest planet?'

'Inhabited, habitable or any old rock?'

'We'll need an atmosphere,' called Clunk from the lift, just before the doors grated to.

'Did you hear that, Navcom?'

'Affirmative,' said the computer. 'I have a target. Uninhabited, but otherwise suitable.'

'Okay, hit it,' said Hal. 'Not literally,' he added hastily, as the lights flickered.

'Jump complete,' said the computer. 'Oliape directly ahead.'

Hal drummed his fingers on the console. 'I should be doing something.'

'Would you like a game of chess?'

'No, I would not like a game of chess. I meant something useful.'

There was a long silence before the Navcom replied. 'Gamma class freighters are self-sufficient, and human interaction is actively discouraged. Since the introduction of this policy, fatalities have fallen thirty-five percent.'

'Spare me the sales pitch and give me a visual on the planet.'

The viewscreen blinked into life, showing a whirling confusion of green and blue.

'We're getting a bit close,' said Hal. 'Where are we going to land?'

A cursor appeared on the screen. 'Right here,' said the Navcom. A dotted line appeared, ending in a large green cross. 'After impact, a large part of the ship will settle in this location.' A lot of smaller crosses appeared. 'And this is the estimated location of the rest.'

Hal blinked. 'I'm not a hundred percent behind you on this one. What do you mean, 'the rest'?'

'Hull fragments,' said the Navcom.

Hal swallowed. 'Get me Clunk.'

'Complying.' The speakers crackled, and a horrible wail filled the flight deck.

'Clunk?' shouted Hal. 'Clunk, are you there?'

'Yes, Mr Spacejock.'

'Are you busy?'

There was a long silence. That is, there was as much silence as could be expected with the secondary generator screaming itself to destruction. 'Just a little,' said Clunk finally. 'Why?'

'I may need you to handle the landing,' said Hal.

3

Curtis Freightlines had its headquarters in the Ullimo commercial district, a sprawling area which relied on the spaceport for most of its trade. A stream of employees bustled in and out of the twelve-storey building: humans and robots of all shapes and sizes making their way to and from their place of work.

Every individual stopped for a scan at the entrance. Robots leaving the building were scanned for company information, so that anything deemed sensitive or private could be wiped. Robots entering the building were scanned for malware: infections picked up during visits to other firms, or trojans planted deliberately by competitors and corporate regulators. Now and then an alarm would sound, and a hapless robot would be dragged away for a wipe and reinstall. Most passed through unhindered.

Humans were also scanned for infections and viruses, but of the biological kind. Those with symptoms were sent to work in the quarantine wing, away from the healthy employees. At Curtis Freightlines, to qualify for sick leave you had to be on life support.

A young woman in a grey business suit entered the building. Her fair hair was styled in a bob, with a fringe almost touching the frame of her sunglasses. As she approached the barriers, she removed the glasses, revealing grey eyes and straight, dark eyebrows. Several men glanced at her. Most looked again.

Sonya Polarov ignored them. There was only one man she was interested in: Rex Curtis himself. Not that she'd ever met him, of course. Mid-level managers weren't allowed beyond the eighth floor, and Curtis had an office on the twelfth.

She tucked the sunglasses into her pocket and held still for the retinal scanner, forcing her eyes open as the harsh blue light passed over them. Once the scanner had finished she blew into a metal grille, and seconds later the turnstile clicked, ushering her into the foyer.

Sonya made for the lifts, her shoes clacking on the polished marble. She passed a number of co-workers on the way, none of whom said a word to her.

When the lift arrived, she was the last to enter.

'Floors please,' said the lift.

People called out their numbers, none of them higher than six. As they spoke, the corresponding digit on the control panel lit up.

'Nine,' said a deep voice. Everyone glanced at the speaker, a heavy-set man dressed in an expensive suit. There were one or two curious glances, but the man stared them down with easy confidence.

'Twelve,' said Sonya, in a clear voice.

There was a gasp, and everyone stared at her. Including the man in the suit.

'I'm sorry,' said the lift. 'You're not authorised.'

'I have an appointment,' said Sonya firmly. Her Outsider accent was faint but noticeable, and if any of the other occupants hadn't been staring intently before, they certainly were now.

'Please hold.'

There was a lengthy delay and the other workers began to fidget and mutter amongst themselves. Someone laughed, and Sonya's lips thinned as she imagined the nature of the joke. A young woman visiting Curtis on the top floor? Some appointment, ha ha. She felt her fingers straighten, felt her muscles tense. One more laugh . . .

'Clearance approved,' said the lift, breaking the tension. The doors closed and the car shot upwards, stopping to dispense passengers on each level. Finally, there were just two occupants: Sonya and Mr Level Nine.

The man cleared his throat. 'Care for a drink after work?'

'Care for a broken wrist?'

The lift stopped on the ninth floor, and the man hurried out before the doors were fully open. Sonya allowed herself a smile as the car took off again. She was just warming up.

The doors parted on the twelfth floor, revealing a sumptuous waiting room dominated by the reception desk: a huge construction of dark lacquered wood, with 'Curtis Freightlines' inlaid in gold lettering. Behind it sat a middle-aged woman with short grey hair and a welcoming smile. 'You must be Ms Polarov,' she said warmly. 'I'm sorry, but Mr Curtis is running behind schedule.'

Sonya nodded and looked around, absorbing the rarified atmosphere.

'If you take a seat I'll fetch you a drink. Coffee?'

'Please.' Sonya chose an armchair and almost vanished into its embrace. When the secretary returned with a coffee she found Sonya perched on the front edge, her elbows dug deep into the arms to stop herself falling backwards.

'These chairs are a nuisance,' confided the secretary. 'I swear we lost the finance minister down the back of one. And just look at the state of the economy!'

Sonya smiled, grateful for the woman's good humour. She took her cup and breathed the aroma, then took a sip. Excellent.

'Mr Curtis shouldn't be much longer. Call me if you need anything.'

Sonya nodded. She was prepared to wait all day.

◆

Rex Curtis gazed out of his office windows, lord of his domain. Twelve stories below, freighters and cargo haulers were dotted around the landing field, their angular shapes blurred by the rain. Wind howled, rain lashed the huge expanse of glass, and Rex frowned as he spotted mechanics and riggers huddling under nearby ships. The rest of them were probably lurking in the canteen, he thought. Time wasters.

For months now, the company had been suffering from dwindling freight business, and a falling economy had led to a squeeze from their largest accounts. Some of them had sued to break off their contracts, and the legal costs had been horrendous. Rex's lips thinned as he thought of Central Bank. Loyal clients for almost ten years, they'd just stiffed him over a few thousand credits. What happened to thrashing out a contract over a business lunch?

Then there had been a couple of highly publicised incidents where company ships had failed to emerge from hyperspace. The Transit Bureau had been through Curtis Freightlines like a disease, souring relations between ground staff, pilots and management. The last nails were being pounded home by the proliferation of freelancers - desperate losers carting freight in rust buckets. You wouldn't trust them with an important cargo unless you were looking to claim the loss on insurance, but enough got through to make them an acceptable risk for less valuable freight.

Curtis stared out the window. He couldn't drop his prices any further; they weren't covering costs as it was. And new servicing regulations meant half his ships were undergoing inspections or trivial repairs at any given moment, thanks to which he was no longer able to handle rush jobs - which were often the most lucrative. He looked down at one of the stationary ships and cursed. According to the job sheet, the ship was in dock to replace a cracked toilet seat. As if that wasn't enough, they were paying a competitor to fetch the replacement part.

Curtis returned to his desk, where his gaze fell on a scale model of a spaceship. It was a detailed effort depicting a Rigel class freighter configured for deep space. His expression softened as he remembered his early years. Those were the days, he thought. He'd criss-crossed the galaxy at his leisure, picking only the best freight jobs. No commitments, no staff and nothing to tie him down. Idly, he wondered where the Aurora had ended up. Then he grimaced. She was probably in the hands of a bloody freelancer.

His intercom buzzed, breaking into his reverie. 'Yes?'

'Mr Curtis, it's Mac. Engineering.'

'Put him through.'

'And Ms Polarov is here to see you.'

'What for?'

'You agreed to an interview. Cost savings.'

30

'All right, give me ten.' Curtis pressed a button. 'Mac? What is it?'

'We need some spares for the Morgana. The depot's out, and you told me to clear these purchases with you.'

Rex pulled up a job sheet on his terminal. He scanned the schedule and cursed. 'That ship's supposed to be halfway to Plessa by now.'

'The Transit people won't release her.'

'What do we need?'

'The air purifiers have gone. It'll take a compressor and half a dozen filters.'

'How long?'

'Two days.'

Rex cursed. 'This is killing us. You know that?'

'We need more spares in stock, Mr Curtis.'

'Just get it fixed.' Rex cut the connection and switched his terminal to accounts. 'What are we supposed to buy spares with?' he muttered, as columns of red figures filled the screen. He gestured at his terminal and watched it drop silently into the surface of his desk. Sinking, just like his company.

His intercom buzzed. 'Mr Curtis? I have a Tom Sqrew from Garmit and Hash on hold.'

'I've gone to lunch.'

'He says it's important.'

'To me or to them?' Rex sighed. 'All right, put him on.'

'Sqrew here,' said a deep voice. 'Mr Curtis, I've been going over your accounts and I'm afraid I have some bad news for you.'

'Go on.'

'I understand you lost Central Bank?'

'We're in negotiations,' said Curtis. 'It's a delicate matter, but –'

'I've already spoken to Fish. You've lost the account. And furthermore, based on your remaining clients and projected trading levels, your company will be insolvent in six weeks. Therefore, Garmit and Hash are revoking your finance.'

'Run that by me again?'

'Your company is going broke, Mr Curtis. We want our money back.'

'Now listen to me, sunshine. I've been your biggest customer for twenty years. Trading conditions aren't good right now, but the whole economy has –'

'The economy is not my concern. Incidentally, I discovered a number of suspect transactions relating to the refurbishment of a property in your wife's name. If I were you, I'd make sure I was absent when corporate regulators start investigating the collapse.'

'What collapse? We're still trading!'

'Not for long. We begin wind-up procedures in twenty-four hours. Good day to you.'

'Sqrew, listen to me. Sqrew?' Curtis stared at the intercom in shock. There was no question of finding another lender. With his balance sheet he'd be laughed out of town. He spotted the wastepaper bin and lashed out with an immaculate, handcrafted shoe. The bin flew across the pure white carpet, scattering paper before smashing into the panelling.

The intercom beeped. 'Are you all right, Mr Curtis?'

Curtis leaned over his desk. 'If I want a health check I'll hire a nurse.'

'Yes sir,' said the voice calmly.

Curtis pulled his chair up and sat down. The model of the Aurora caught his eye and he imagined the vessel soaring through space, heading for freedom and a new beginning. And why not? he thought. I can start again. He shook his

32

head as he recalled his conversation with Spacejock, who was coming to Ullimo with a brand new freighter to snatch Central Bank from right under his nose ...

Rex sat bolt upright. A new freighter. A new beginning. What if ...? He reached for the intercom. 'Is that Polarov woman still waiting?'

'Yes, Mr Curtis.'

'Send her in.' Rex released the intercom and sat back in his chair, mentally preparing himself for his visitor. If his judgement was correct, Sonya Polarov could hold the key to his future.

◆

It was late afternoon and the setting sun cast a weak light through the forest canopy. The trees were festooned with creepers, straggly green tendrils that hung like wet hair. Nearby, a tiny stream bubbled over mossy rocks, ran down a narrow channel and disappeared under a fallen tree.

Beside the log a small furry creature sat on its haunches, sniffing the breeze. Satisfied, it bent to the stream and lapped at the water with a tiny pink tongue. Once it was done, it sat up and wiped its whiskers with its paws, curling each long hair through tiny delicate fingers.

Suddenly it froze, staring into the middle distance with a look of intense concentration on its pointed face. An ear twitched, and a split second later the creature was gone.

There was a distant rumble of thunder, then another. The rumble became a roar, and the creepers shivered as the noise turned into something physical. Leaves fluttered to the ground, followed by showers of rainwater shaken from the branches.

Small stones cascaded down the muddy slope, choking the stream, and as the noise reached a tearing crescendo several trees gave up the struggle and fell over. Billowing smoke tore through the undergrowth, turning creepers into party streamers and leaves into soggy confetti.

There was a splintering crash and a huge white shape descended through the canopy. Trees collapsed as the ship forced them apart, and wide metal feet groaned as they sank into the soft ground.

The howling subsided and the billowing smoke cleared. All was still.

The furry creature peered out from its log to survey its surroundings. Steam rose from blasted, shattered vegetation, and the picturesque stream was now a series of muddy, rock-strewn rivulets moving sluggishly over the torn earth. A hiss filled the clearing, and the creature fled in terror as a gleaming doorway opened in the side of the huge white shape.

Humans had arrived on planet Oliape.

◆

Hal leant out of the *Volante's* airlock to examine their surroundings. It was not an impressive sight: thick gloomy forest, a muddy stream and fallen trees. 'And no shops,' muttered Hal in disgust. He returned to the flight deck, brushing drops of water from his overalls. 'Don't buy any real estate, whatever the brochures say.'

'I'm sorry?'

34

'Nothing. How long will it take to fix that generator?'

'It's hard to say. I'm afraid it's a dockyard job.'

'You might not have noticed, but this isn't a dockyard.'

'Tell me, have you been in the generator room lately?'

'You're joking. I don't even know where it is.'

Clunk held his hand out. 'I found these on the floor.'

Hal saw three or four miniature cylinders nestled in the robot's palm. 'What are they?'

'Fuses for the warning circuits. That's why the generator failed.'

'Could they have fallen out?'

'I doubt it.' Clunk sighed. 'Look, I may be able to jury-rig the secondary generator, but it'll take time.'

'How long?'

'Unknown. While I'm busy, you should look around outside to ensure the ship is not in immediate danger.'

Hal glanced at the airlock. 'What if the immediate danger is out there?'

Clunk shook his head. 'There's nothing to worry about. This planet is barren.'

'What about the trees?'

'There are no trees here.'

'In that case they've got the biggest weeds I've ever seen.'

'There are no weeds either. I told you, this planet is barren.'

'No it isn't.'

'It is! The Navcom's database is explicit. No trees.'

Hal led him to the airlock and pointed out the towering greenery.

'How extraordinary,' said Clunk.

'You don't think we've landed on the wrong planet?'

'You doubt my abilities?'

'You're always telling me to look at the facts, and the fact is we've landed in a forest on a barren planet. Face it, you might just have stuffed up.'

'Robots don't make mistakes,' said Clunk stiffly.

'All right, calm down. It just looks odd, that's all.'

Clunk crossed his arMs. 'Do you want me to debate our location or fix the generator?'

'Go for the generator,' said Hal.

Clunk turned to enter the lift, then stopped. 'By the way, I suggest you find a place to sleep tonight.'

'I'll be sleeping aboard, surely?'

'I'd advise against it. There's no air circulating and the build up of fuel toxins can be fatal.'

'What about here in the flight deck? I can leave the door open.'

Clunk shook his head. 'Fatal, Mr Spacejock. You must stay outside.'

'But it's wet and muddy!'

'Your ancestors lit fires for warmth. You'll need something to heat food on anyway.'

'You're taking this very seriously.'

Clunk nodded. 'It's a very serious situation. All your food is deep-frozen and you can't use the AutoChef without power. It could be a week before I complete repairs.'

'A week!' exclaimed Hal. 'I thought we'd be lifting off in an hour or two!' He eyed the dripping greenery through the airlock. 'A week,' he muttered. 'What about our cargo? What about Central Bank?'

Clunk spread his hands. 'Let's get off this planet first.'

'But –'

'I suggest you cease worrying about it.' Clunk lifted the

console and poked about inside. 'There's not much I can do up here. I'll be in the engine room if you need me.'

— 4 —

'Ms Polarov?' The secretary gestured towards the panelled door. 'You can go in now.'

Sonya retrieved her document case and strode towards the door. It opened smartly at her approach, and she stepped through into the inner sanctum. Rex was sitting at a desk with his back to a wall of glass. He was working at a terminal, and Sonya studied him with interest as she crossed the carpet. He was younger than she'd expected, mid-forties she guessed, with dark hair and a weather-beaten face. As he looked up she noticed his eyes had the calm assurance of a space pilot. 'Mr Curtis,' she said, taking a seat.

'They tell me you've identified some wastage. Using too many paperclips, are we?'

Sonya felt a flash of irritation. 'You don't want to save nine million credits?'

Rex coughed. 'You've been with this company three months, right?'

'Correct.'

'You work on the third floor?'

'Second.'

'And you can save me how many millions?'

Sonya held up her document case. 'Everything's in here.'

Rex put his hand out.

'I need something in return.'

'I should have known. Go on.'

'I'm on a short term contract here. I enjoy my work, and I'd like to . . . I'd like a permanent position.'

'You're an Outsider, aren't you?'

'You noticed.'

Rex smiled. 'It's in your records. Nobody gets through that door without a thorough check.' He gestured at his screen, and Sonya's photo appeared above several columns of text. 'Says here you did six months in the armed forces.'

Sonya nodded.

'Four years at university. Electives in computing and navigation. High marks all round.'

'Where I come from education is still important.'

'And you saved enough money to escape.'

Sonya frowned. 'To emigrate.'

'Why do you want a job in accounts?'

'It's rewarding. It, er –'

'Bullshit.' Rex laughed. 'Come on, out with it.'

Sonya felt her face redden. 'You know enough about me. I'm sure you know my problem.'

'You need a full time job so you can get residency. After three years you can apply for Union citizenship, and once granted you'll be free of your Outsider roots forever.'

Sonya leaned across the desk. 'Without residency, they will send me back. One month, perhaps two. Back to the factories or the armed forces.' She gestured around the office. 'If I return to my home planet and tell them what the Union is like it will only make things worse.'

'Why do your people want you back?'

'No, it's your people who want to send me. The Union is only too happy to repatriate us, to seed dissent and rebellion amongst Outsiders.'

'Oh, come on. Rebellion?'

'Perhaps too strong a word. However, those returning from Union space bring with them tales of wealth and comfort. Envy can topple governments, Mr Curtis.'

'And you can stop all this if I employ you?'

Sonya snorted. 'No, if you employ me I'll live here and enjoy my life.'

'Self interest, eh?' Rex grinned. 'Now that's a Union trait.' Suddenly he pointed at the model on his desk. 'Do you know what that is?'

Sonya stared at it, wondering whether she was being tested. 'It's a Rigel class freighter,' she said at last.

'Correct, and it was my very first ship. I built this business off the back of it.' Curtis frowned. 'And now the entire company is at risk.'

'It is?'

Rex glanced at the intercom. The light was off. 'I suppose you're wondering why I brought you in?'

'We had an appointment. My figures –'

'I don't care about your figures. And I was going to cancel the appointment.'

Sonya felt cold. 'Cancel?'

'Relax, something came up. Something you can help me with.' Rex gestured at the wall of glass behind him. 'Take a look outside. What do you see?'

Sonya rose in her chair and saw sunlight glistening off half a dozen freighters. 'Ships.'

'Exactly. Lots of ships. Pilots. Support staff. Money going down the drain day by day, week by week.' Rex warmed to his theme. 'I'm competing against a bunch of cowboys hauling freight in dangerous, unstable freighters at half our best prices. The authorities won't lift a finger as long as they get their kickbacks.'

Sonya nodded politely, wondering where he was leading.

'Well they're not bringing Curtis Freightlines down,' said Rex firmly. 'I spent twenty years building this business up and I'm not letting scum like that tear it down again.' He paused to take a breath. 'So, we're going to turn up the heat.'

'You want me to look at their accounts? Find illegal deductions?'

'Er, not quite.' Rex glanced at the screen. 'I was more interested in your military talents. Tell me, are you prepared to walk the fuzzy line between legal and not exactly legal?'

'I don't understand.'

Rex sighed. 'It's like this. Rust buckets I can handle. They're just bottom-feeders moving the shoddiest kind of junk.' He raised a finger. 'However, there's a freelance pilot called Hal Spacejock who's really got it in for me. He's flying a brand new Gamma class freighter, and he just snatched my biggest account. A better ship, lower prices . . . the rest of our customers could flock to this guy. Before you know it he'll be buying ships and hiring pilots, and I'll be looking for a new line of business.' Rex hesitated. 'There's another thing. I understand he was involved in smuggling. Refugees - some of your lot. There's a case you might remember, something about half a dozen families abandoned on an uninhabited planet.' Rex shook his head. 'They were left to fend for themselves with no food, no water, no medicine or shelter. By the time the authorities found them they were ready to eat each other. A man who could do that . . . '

'You want me to break his legs? Kill him?'

'Hell no. We're going to be a touch more subtle than that.'

'A disappearance, then.'

'No! I don't want him harmed.'

'It would solve the problem.'

'And the investigation would create a whole lot more. Look, I just need to send a message to Central Bank: hire these unreliable freelancers and it's anyone's guess where your precious cargo will end up. All I want to do is hold Spacejock up for a while, so he's late for the delivery.' Rex tapped his intercom. 'My tech guy has some equipment for you. He –'

'You mean Dent? They say he's got a piece of equipment for everybody.'

'Hugh's a harmless old fool, nothing more.'

'That's not what I heard. Some of the girls said he –'

'Can we focus on the job here?' demanded Rex, waving her objections away. 'Go and see Dent, get the equipment and go to the spaceport. After Spacejock lands you'll go aboard his ship and gather certain information.'

'How?'

'Dent will explain.' Rex turned to his terminal. 'Spacejock will be landing soon, so if there's nothing else . . . '

'What about my permanency?'

'Let's see how this little effort works out first, eh?' Rex studied his terminal. 'Close the door on your way out.'

◆

After Sonya left Rex took out a bulky envelope and tipped the contents onto his desk, riffling through the folded paperwork and half-completed forms until he found what he was looking for: a sturdy booklet embossed with the Outsider coat of arMs. When he opened the navy cover, Sonya's expressionless face stared up at him from the full-colour hologram.

He flipped through the pages, noting the smart chips printed directly onto the heavy paper. Sonya had taken a circuitous route from her native Outsider planet, every stamp representing passenger fares, customs checks and hefty bribes. The very last page held the most impressive stamp of all: an entry permit for Union space. Unlike the others it was impervious to crackers, wrongdoers and crooks alike. In fact, Union IDs had been foolproof for years, which was why this low-tech Outsider passport was so valuable.

Rex turned back to the hologram. The image was fused to the paper, but with the right skills and equipment it was possible to substitute one face for another.

Rex lifted his commset and dialled a number.

'Yeah?' said a sleep-laden voice.

'I need some paperwork edited.' Rex tapped Sonya's passport on the edge of his desk. 'I want my face on the letterhead.'

'You know I can't do that.'

'This paperwork is outdated. Some Outsider firm went bust.'

There was a pause. 'I can't make any promises.'

'You never do,' said Rex, hanging up. He dropped Sonya's ID into the envelope, scrawled an address on the front and activated his intercom. 'Get me a courier,' he said. 'Single envelope. Secure delivery.'

'A local address?'

'Yes. And get Mac on the line.'

'Which one, sir?'

'Ullimo ground.'

'Putting you through.' The line went dead for a moment, then crackled into life with a burst of static.

'Mac speaking.'

'I want something done.'

'What's that, Mr Curtis?'

'There's a ship coming in today. The *Volante*. If she looks like leaving I want her held up for an hour or two.'

'Hold the *Volante* for an hour or two. Got it.' There was a pause. 'Any reason?'

Rex frowned. 'Because I said so.'

'I mean, should I give the pilot a reason?'

'Just your everyday delaying tactics. Weather's bad, ground crew on their lunch break ... use your imagination.'

'Will do, Mr Curtis.'

Rex cut the call, pleased with himself. Everything was going to plan.

◆

Sonya took the lift to the basement, where Hugh Dent had his lab complex. Mysterious smells and muffled explosions greeted lost souls who stepped off at the wrong floor, and mischievous receptionists often directed door-to-door salesmen there, watching in barely concealed glee as they fled the building, scattering remaindered books and plastic toys in their wake.

Sonya stepped into a concrete-lined room just as the glass door in the opposite wall opened. Dent entered the room and Sonya eyed him warily. He was a hunched-up fifty-year-old with a bald head, red-rimmed eyes and hands that seemed several sizes too big. Sonya stared at them. She'd heard all about Dent's hands.

'Ah, Sonya m'dear. Come in, come in,' said Dent genially, stepping back and waving her through.

Sonya grabbed Dent's hand with both of hers, shaking it hard. 'Curtis called you?'

'Ah-hmm.' Dent looked at her shrewdly. 'Surveillance, intelligence gathering and disguises? Come in, come in.' He led her to a frosted glass door and touched a contact pad. 'Through here,' he said, as the door swished open.

'You first,' said Sonya.

They made their way along the passage to another door, this one made from a slab of steel.

'Impressive security,' said Sonya.

'Can't have helpless young women wandering around on their own,' said Dent, raising his large hand to the pad. 'Anything could happen to them down here.'

'So I've heard.'

The heavy door rumbled open and Dent hurried in. 'Follow!' he called over his shoulder.

They entered a large room with shaded lights hanging over cluttered workbenches. There was a desk heaped with exotic computer equipment, and alongside it stood a sinister-looking cabinet emblazoned with warning signs. Sonya's eyes widened at the sight of a huge grey robot standing in its packing crate, and opened further still when she spotted a row of missile launchers leaning against a stack of ammunition boxes.

'Come on, come on,' called Dent, who was making straight for the cabinet.

'What is that thing?' asked Sonya.

'Coffee maker.'

'Is it safe?'

'I hope not,' muttered Dent. He retrieved a dirty mug and began filling it with steaming black liquid. 'Want one? It's real caffeine.'

'Not right now.' Sonya picked up a missile launcher and aimed it at the back of Dent's head. 'Who are we invading?'

Dent spun round, slopping his coffee. 'Put that down, woman! You think these are toys?'

'Range eighteen kilometres, blast radius five hundred metres ... this ain't no toy.'

'You know your weapons,' Dent said grudgingly.

Sonya swung the tube off her shoulder and propped it up with the rest. 'What's Curtis doing with all this stuff?'

'Trade war,' said Dent. 'Very hush-hush. Can't discuss it.'

'What do you have for me?'

Dent put his cup on the workbench and retrieved a wooden box. 'I designed this myself,' he said, snapping the catches open.

Sonya looked inside. 'A gun?'

'No ordinary gun.' Dent took the weapon out and held it up to the light, which shone right through it. 'A glass gun.'

'I see. And the advantage is?'

'It's invisible in water. I had a devil of a job perfecting a transparent battery, I can tell you. Here, take a - Oops!' Dent grabbed for the falling gun but it struck the edge of the desk, tumbled onto the floor and shattered. Dent swept the pieces aside with his foot. 'As you can see, it's easy to dispose of the weapon in an emergency. Now, Curtis tells me you have to get aboard a ship for a recce. Correct?'

Sonya nodded. 'Unarmed, from the look of it.'

'I've had some items delivered to the landing pad. There's a hazard suit, a sprayer, that kind of thing. You can go aboard

46

the ship to fumigate, and the helmet will hide your face. I've also been working on a device which will suck everything you need from the ship's computer.' Dent reached under the bench and brought out a silver case with a large smiley face on the side. 'Meet Bobby the Briefcase,' he said, setting it on the worktop.

'Bobby the ...' Sonya blinked. 'You expect me to carry this in public?'

Dent looked surprised. 'Of course. This is the most sophisticated, the most advanced, the most ...'

'Dumb-looking,' supplied Sonya.

Dent ignored her. 'The most powerful and the most intelligent portable computing device ever.'

'And you called it Bobby the Briefcase. Is it the air down here, or what?'

A cooling fan began to blow through a vent in the side of the case, sending a stack of paperwork fluttering. 'I called myself Bobby,' said the case in a jolly voice. 'It creates a bond of friendship and understanding with my users.'

Sonya stared at the briefcase. 'You thought this up for yourself?'

The briefcase made a throat-clearing sound. 'Mr Dent, you still haven't entered a serial number.'

'Oh, yes.' Dent patted his pockets. 'I just have to find the codes,' he said. 'Won't be a moment.'

'What codes?' asked Sonya.

The briefcase piped up. 'This software product has not been unlocked. You have six days before self-destruction. Do you wish to enter an activation code now?'

'No!' called Dent from behind the workbench. 'Damn it, where did I put that stupid packaging?'

'Activation cancelled,' said Bobby. Another fan cut in and Dent's cup began to slide towards the edge of the bench.

Sonya watched Dent up-ending wastepaper baskets and tipping out drawers. 'Can you not crack it?'

'That's a negative,' said the briefcase. 'Do not discuss such matters or I'll be forced to report your illegal activities to the nearest authorities.'

'You do that and I'll teach you to smoke,' said Sonya.

'Impossible. I could never do such a thing.'

'Data socket plus mains voltage. You'd smoke all right.'

Dent returned empty-handed. 'I can't find it anywhere. Never mind, I'll dig it out later. Plenty of time.'

Sonya hefted the case, which was surprisingly heavy.

'Hey, mind the equipment,' said Bobby.

'What do I do with it?' asked Sonya, putting the case back on the bench.

'Connect the lead to any data socket aboard the ship and you'll have the whole thing in minutes.' Dent lowered his voice. 'Even a Gamma class freighter can't stand up to my persuasion for long.'

'Why's it blowing so hard?'

Dent tried to look modest. 'That's my patented cooling method. It's a miniature reactor powered by nitrogen.' He pointed to a grille on the side of the case. 'There's no fuel - it takes what it needs from the air.'

Sonya reached for the grille to feel the suction.

'No!' said Dent, striking her hand away. 'Never, ever cover the inlet. Without a constant source of fuel the reactor will ... ' he swallowed. 'It's still experimental.'

Sonya saw the fear in his eyes. 'It's not dangerous?'

'Absolutely not, I put it together myself.' Dent hesitated. 'Of course, if something did happen the explosion could knock a planet out of orbit.'

'You mean a spaceship,' corrected Sonya.

'No, I mean a planet.' Dent laid his hand on her arm. 'Now m'dear, how about a little drink before heading off? A celebration perhaps?'

'Pass,' said Sonya, pushing his hand away.

'I have a bottle of fine wine I've been saving. We could –'

'No we couldn't,' said Sonya firmly, resisting the temptation to break one of his fingers.

Dent's face fell. 'Oh, very well. Come, I'll show you out.'

Sonya picked up the briefcase and followed Dent through the giant steel doors. They walked down the hall to the frosted glass door, where Dent began to type in numbers. Suddenly he stopped. 'That reminds me, Bobby is also a versatile cracker. Get him within range and he can open anything.' He leered at her. 'Almost anything.'

'Is that so?' Sonya nodded at the door. 'Can I try with this?'

'I fear my security will be more than a match for Bobby,' said Dent with a laugh. 'But you're welcome to try, m'dear.'

With a fluid movement Sonya swung the briefcase at the door, shattering the glass. 'Not bad,' she said, as thousands of glittering fragments cascaded to the floor. 'It could use a thicker grip.'

— 5 —

Rain lashed the Volante, running off the ship in thick, twisting streaMs. Leaves fluttered in the wind, sticking briefly to the curved metal hull before washing away in the heavy downpour. Inside, Clunk was sitting in the pilot's chair, busy at the console. Having done his best with the generators, he was now running tests with the Navcom's diagnostic suite.

A particularly heavy squall hit the Volante, rocking the ship on its landing legs and drawing Clunk's attention to the airlock. Through the opening he saw trees bent double in the wind. The driving rain was almost horizontal. There was a beep, and Clunk switched his attention back to the console. 'Navcom, let me know when the diagnostics are complete.'

'Estimate nine minutes longer.' There was a pause. 'Where is Mr Spacejock?'

'He's building a camp fire,' said Clunk, eyeing Hal's biscuit tin.

'According to my calculations, ambient moisture precludes such activity.'

'Correct,' said Clunk, glancing at the airlock. 'And if he does manage to light something, the wind will blow it straight out again.'

'Shipboard environment is now back to optimal. Can't he

come in?'

'Give him a bit longer.' Clunk opened the tin and selected a biscuit, sniffing it to savour the aroma.

'He's not going to be very happy,' said the Navcom, as another squall rocked the ship.

'Mr Spacejock needs a little lesson from time to time. Particularly if he's going to accuse me of basic navigation errors.' Clunk replaced the biscuit, sat back in his chair and linked his hands behind his head. 'Now, tell me about this planet.'

◆

Hal spent a lot of time searching the forest for a dry piece of ground to sleep on, discarding one swampy hole after another until he finally came across a clearing. It wasn't much more than a gap amongst the trees, but the ground was firm and it was better than the muddy ground near the ship.

Now it was dark, and the green wood on Hal's diminutive campfire generated more steam than smoke as it spluttered and hissed to itself. The rain had put it out several times, and Hal turned his collar up as drops began to fall again.

There was a rustle from the bushes, and Hal stared into the darkness. Was Clunk bringing a nice hot meal from the Volante's galley? Better still, was he coming to say the repairs were finished? 'Clunk, is that you?'

A twig snapped, but nobody answered.

'Clunk, stop messing about.' Hal stared into the gloom, but the spluttering flames had wrecked his night vision. He picked up a solid branch and threw it onto the fire, which promptly went out. 'Damn,' said Hal. He took out a flamer and held it to the steaming pile, playing the jet onto the singed wood at the centre. The fire burst into life, and Hal added a handful of leaves. The flames grew bigger so he added some twigs, then the large branch, followed by several bushes and a tree trunk. When he'd finished the flames were ten metres high and the clearing was lit up like a stage on opening night.

Satisfied, Hal returned to his tree stump to watch. Now and then he added more fuel, stirring up sparks which rose into the cool air and vanished against the cloudy sky.

There was another sound, a rustling noise which gradually grew louder and louder. Hal turned to stare into the shadowy undergrowth. 'Clunk?'

The robot entered the clearing, his alloy skin scratched and oily and his face smudged with grime. 'How are you, Mr Spacejock?'

'Never mind me. How's the ship?'

'Almost ready. It's a slow job.'

'It'll be even slower if you keep coming out here to tell me how slow it's going to be.'

'I've rigged a light in the flight deck. Perhaps you'd like to come aboard now?'

'What about the toxins?'

'They're dispersing rapidly.'

'Forget it.' Hal nodded at the fire. 'I've only just got this going. I want to enjoy it.'

'Nevertheless, you'll be comfortable aboard the Volante. Safer, too.'

'What do you mean, safer?'

Clunk hesitated. 'While I was waiting for some tests to finish I decided to look up the information on this planet.'

'You already did that before we landed. There's nothing

here but trees, and the atmosphere is fine.' Hal laughed. 'You think the bushes are going to reach out and grab me? Is that it?'

Clunk shook his head. 'Not the bushes.'

Hal picked up a solid-looking branch.   'If I see any threatening foliage, I'll whack it. Happy now?'

Clunk lowered his voice.   'I just discovered there's a quarantined planet in this system. It's called Oliape II.'

'Why tell me about it? I mean, we landed on Oliape.'

Clunk shook his head. 'This is Oliape II.'

'Really?' Hal looked around. 'It's still a dump.'

'It's also inhabited. Oliape II has several species of mammals, a number of reptiles, that kind of thing.'

There was a rustle from the bushes.

'Large ones?'

The robot nodded. 'The dominant life form is a carnivorous ape, about so high.' He held his hand out at shoulder height, then raised it until he was at full stretch.

'Okay, before I batter you into scrap with this branch, kindly explain how we ended up on the wrong planet.'

'It's a complex matter involving celestial navigation and orbital mechanics.'

'You screwed up, didn't you?'

'The planetary orbits intersect! When we approached Oliape II it was closer to the primary than Oliape. The planets are very similar, there are no beacons and ... '

'And you screwed up.'

Clunk hung his head. 'I was under pressure. I'm sorry.'

'Hey, don't sweat it. To err is human and all that.'

'Quite.'

'All we have to do is leave before these creatures find us.'

He'd barely finished speaking when a large orange shape leapt from the bushes and threw itself on Clunk, knocking the robot into the mud. The creature fastened its jaws around the robot's neck and bit down, hard. There was a splintering sound, and the creature howled, shaking its head and pawing at its muzzle.

Hal took one look at the giant ape, tossed his lump of wood aside and ran full-tilt for the ship. Clunk scrambled to his feet and followed.

They ran through the darkness, crashing through wet bushes and leaping over fallen trees. Behind them, a tortured scream echoed around the clearing.

'What was THAT?' gasped Hal.

'I think it just discovered fire,' puffed Clunk.

Hal pushed through a dense bush and found himself at the foot of the Volante's ramp, where a light cast a soft glow on the churned-up mud. He pounded up the metal ramp and entered the airlock, where he reached for the controls. Then he realised Clunk wasn't with him. Looking down, he saw the robot halfway up the ramp, waving his arms like a hyperactive windmill.

'What is it?' called Hal.

'Behind you!' screeched Clunk.

'What do you mean –' Suddenly Hal felt hot breath on the back of his neck, and what the robot meant became all too clear. He turned to face the threat, and froze as he saw the enormous creature behind him.

The shaggy orange ape was over two metres tall, with long, muscled arms, multiple rows of serrated teeth and beady, red-rimmed eyes.

Hal turned to flee, only to see another of the creatures burst from the forest and leap onto the foot of the ramp.

They were trapped.

Hal looked over the side of the ramp, wondering whether to jump. It was a long way down, but the soft earth might cushion his landing. Of course, while he was struggling to stand up the other ape would probably bite his head off.

'Wowlf?' The huge ape raised a hairy finger and scratched the side of its head. The gesture was so human Hal almost laughed. Almost.

'Oof!' he said, as the creature prodded him in the chest. He heard thudding footsteps and risked a quick glance. Clunk was running up the landing ramp towards them.

The ape batted Hal aside and ran down the ramp with a low-slung, sideways gait, covering the distance with astonishing speed. Clunk saw it coming and threw himself face down as it leapt. The creature sailed over him, landed on its chin and began to roll head over heels. It collected the second ape and both of them tumbled down the ramp, landing in the mud at the bottom.

'Quick!' yelled Hal, as Clunk scrabbled for purchase, hands and feet slipping on the slick metal. At the foot of the ramp the apes regained their feet and sprang towards Clunk, mud splattering from their pumping legs.

Clunk took one look at them and bolted up the ramp on

all fours, striking sparks in his haste. Hal stood with a hand poised above the airlock controls as the robot approached, and as Clunk hurled himself into the ship, Hal slammed his hand on the button.

Nothing happened.

Hal stared at the oncoming creatures, watched the lightweight metal ramp swaying and bouncing as the slavering beasts ran towards him.

'The door won't operate without full power,' said Clunk calmly.

'Well don't just stand there, help me push the damn thing!' Hal threw himself at the heavy slab of metal, his feet slipping and sliding on the deck. Clunk joined him, and the door began to move. Hal strained, Clunk whined, and the thudding feet got closer.

There was a thump as the door closed. 'Lock?' demanded Hal, panting hard.

Clunk shook his head.

They dived for the inner door and fell into the flight deck in a tangle of arms and legs. There was a crash as the outer door burst open, and Hal threw himself at the inner door, sealing it just as the creatures rammed it from the other side. There was an angry howl, followed by a flurry of heavy blows.

'That was close,' muttered Hal.

Suddenly there was a terrific squeal, followed by the thunder of departing footsteps.

'What the hell was that?'

Clunk got to his feet, dusting himself down. 'I sent a high-pitched tone through the airlock's intercom. Our guests didn't like it.'

'They didn't like you, either. Something about you really set those guys off.'

'In my experience, semi-evolved simians are highly sensitive to variations in external appearance.'

'Do what?'

'I don't think they liked my colour.'

'Why would that make any difference?'

The robot shrugged. 'With a primitive life form like that, who can tell? The point is, he didn't attack you when he had ample chance, and –'

'He? How do you know it was male?'

Clunk's eyebrows creaked up. 'I assure you, from my viewpoint there was no doubt.'

Hal sniffed. 'What's that stink?'

The robot examined the underside of his feet. 'Oh dear.'

Hal took a rag from a locker and handed it to him. While Clunk was busy cleaning up, Hal glanced over the banks of instruments. 'At least it didn't touch anything.'

'I'd better finish the status reports. We'll be leaving shortly.'

'Really?'

Clunk nodded. 'The repairs should see us through to Ullimo. We can have the generators checked there.'

'And it's under warranty, right?'

Clunk hesitated. 'Technically, no. I found several crimps in the lubing system. It was well done - very hard to prove it was deliberate.'

'Deliberate?' Hal's mouth fell open.

'Yes. I found evidence of tampering.'

'Are you saying we were nobbled?'

'Yes, Mr Spacejock.'

'But ... who?'

Clunk shrugged. 'One of our competitors, perhaps? On the other hand, it could have been accidental. I recall something similar on a vessel I once shipped with. One of the cleaning robots fell across the battery terminals and fused the flight computer.'

'We don't have any cleaning robots.'

'I do my share,' said Clunk stiffly.

Hal's eyes narrowed. 'And if the damage is deliberate I have to pay for the repairs?'

Clunk nodded.

'What if I did it?'

'You!' The robot looked startled.

'I mean, what if I accidentally twisted this pipe thing when I was checking the oil?'

'Then it would be an accident.'

'And that's covered by the warranty?'

'Actually, by the insurance.'

Hal sighed. 'Clunk, I have a confession to make. When I was checking the oil I accidentally bent this pipe thing.'

'Mr Spacejock, someone tried to kill you. We can't cover that up!'

'Tell you what. You show me who did it and I'll have them arrested.'

'I don't know who did it.'

'Right. Therefore it was me, and the damage will be fixed for free. And next time we're in port, I want you to keep a very close eye on anyone who comes aboard. If they so much as breathe on the wrong pipe, I want you to brain them with a spanner. Got it?'

Clunk looked doubtful. 'I don't know whether I can perform violent acts, Mr Spacejock. Not against humans.'

'Just smack them in the head with a spanner, Clunk, and I'll do the violent acts afterwards. Now go and finish the generator so we can get off this miserable little planet.'

'On my way,' said Clunk.

As the doors closed on the robot, Hal sat at the console. 'Navcom?'

'Yes, Mr Spacejock?'

'Next time you land on the wrong planet I'll have you wiped.'

'It was a mistake,' said the computer. 'Unavoidable, given the circumstances.'

'I bet I'd have landed on the right planet.'

'Not without this.' There was a beep, and a page full of text and diagrams appeared on the main viewscreen.

'What the hell's that?'

'Basics of navigation, chapter one,' said the Navcom. 'I've highlighted the section concerning celestial mechanics.'

Hal stared at the screen. 'What are those squiggly lines?'

'Probability matrices.'

Hal was quiet for several minutes as he studied the densely packed information. He tried tilting his head to make sense of a particularly complex diagram, but it only made things worse. 'Navcom?'

'Yes, Mr Spacejock?'

'Do I really have to know all this stuff to join the Spacer's Guild?'

'You need a basic understanding, yes.'

Hal sighed.

'Incidentally, did you enjoy your lesson on Oliape?'

'What are you talking about?'

'While you were outside, Clunk said he was going to teach you a lesson.'

'He what?' There was a swish as the lift doors opened, and Hal turned to stare at the robot. 'Clunk, what do you know about teaching me a lesson?'

The robot blinked. 'I'm sorry?'

'Just now, the Navcom asked me whether I enjoyed my lesson.'

'Oh, the Navcom meant experience. Whether you enjoyed your experience.'

Hal looked from Clunk to the console and back again. 'If I thought for one minute ...'

Clunk wiped the guilty look from his face and replaced it with one of hurt innocence. 'Would I do something like that?'

'I don't know. Would you?'

There was a slight pause. 'Do you think so?'

'Yes or no, Clunk.'

'I'm sorry, what's the question again?'

Hal pointed at the airlock. 'Did you send me on that little camping trip to teach me a lesson?'

'Well, I ...' Clunk looked over Hal's shoulder at the viewscreen, which was displaying the navigation manual. 'Oh, look at that! Navcom, there's an error in line seventy-three. Correction: do NOT press this button, instead of DO press this button.'

'Complying,' said the computer.

Hal looked from the robot to the screen and back again. 'What do you mean, 'error'?'

Clunk shrugged. 'They get humans to transcribe these manuals from legacy copies. It's hardly surprising there are mistakes.'

'You mean I could memorise all this crap and bits of it might be wrong?'

'Very likely.' Clunk reached across the console and flipped a small red switch. The manual vanished from the main viewscreen, replaced by a display of celestial bodies spinning around the sun at breakneck speed.

'Which one are we on?' asked Hal.

'That's just a splash screen,' said Clunk, without looking up.

Hal's eyes followed the spinning planets, faster and faster. Finally they vanished, but Hal's eyes kept circling. He put a hand out to steady himself, missed, and fell across the console. Clunk helped him into the pilot's chair, where he sat with a glassy expression on his face.

'Navcom, we're leaving,' said the robot. He crossed to the airlock to check their unwanted guests had left, then returned to the console. 'Complete pre-flight checks, retrieve the ramp and seal the exits.'

'What happened to Mr Spacejock?'

'He studied the screen a little too closely.'

'Why are his eyes going round and round?'

'Round and round,' repeated Hal. 'And round.'

'I think he's hypnotised,' said Clunk. 'I'll revive him later. Right now, we have to leave.'

Hal's expression didn't alter as the main drives fired. The distant roar grew louder as Clunk ran the engines up prior to lift-off. Then he reduced the thrust and strapped himself securely into the co-pilot's chair. 'Ready, Mr Spacejock?'

'Round and round,' mumbled Hal.

'Okay, Navcom. Take us up.'

The ship trembled as the lifters fired. The main screen altered to show a top-down view, and Clunk saw a maelstrom of dust, stones and shredded vegetation as the Volante lifted off. The ship rose rapidly, until their temporary landing place was just a cloud of dust and dirt. Air whistled past the hull as they gained height, tailing off as they reached orbit, until there was nothing but the distant rumble of the engines to break the silence.

Sonya tugged the heavy sweater over her head and threw it on the couch. She ran her fingers through her hair, grimaced, then unclipped the portable commset from her waist and placed it on the polished table. The lights in the kitchen came on as she walked in, gleaming off a spotless wooden table and sleek modern chairs. She took a drink from the cool box and activated the pickup on the wall.

'How may I help you?' said a soft voice.

'A plate of pasta with a side salad, thanks. And coffee. White.'

'Confirmed.'

Sonya released the button. A buzzer sounded from the lounge and she cursed as she saw her commset blinking. She strode across and picked it up. 'Yes?'

'Ms Polarov, why do you not return my calls?'

Sonya's heart skipped a beat. 'Who is this?'

'Immigration.'

'Really?' Sonya glanced at her watch. 'Still in your cage at this hour?'

The caller sighed. 'You know, much as we welcome our delightful visitors from the Outsider planets, we cannot have them staying here indefinitely.'

'I'm not a visitor!' said Sonya sharply.

'True. You found casual employment. Temporary, alas.'

'They offered me a permanent position today. I spoke to Rex Curtis himself.'

'I find that hard to believe.'

'Take my word for it.'

The caller laughed. 'Of course, your letter of employment will be on file.'

Sonya frowned. 'They're just organising it.'

'So it's not confirmed?'

'Only verbally.'

'Ms Polarov, I realise your Outsider worlds treat paperwork as an afterthought, but here in the Union we do not operate on a verbal basis. Therefore, I must put you on notice. I'm officially revoking your right to work in Union space, you will be deported unless you obtain permanent employment in the next twenty-four hours. Is that clear?'

'I told you. I've got a job!' There was a loud knock on the wall. Sonya raised her middle finger at it. 'Just a few more days,' she said, lowering her voice.

'Ms Polarov, we had the same conversation last week. You're out of time and I'm closing your case.'

'No, wait! I'll get an employment letter!'

'No obvious forgeries?'

'A real letter, signed by the head of Curtis Freightlines.'

'You have twenty-four hours, Ms Polarov. Good evening.'

Sonya hurled the communicator at the wall, prompting a fresh bout of knocking from her neighbour. She yelled back and stalked into the kitchen, where she was calmed by the delicious aroma of the waiting food. She'd just carried her plate to the table when the lounge room commset chimed.

'Who is it?' called Sonya.

'Sender's ID suppressed,' said the machine.

Sonya sighed. 'Put them on.'

A man's voice crackled from the speaker. 'Ms Polarov? Are you alone?'

'I am indeed, Mr Curtis.'

'Sorry to call you like this. I tried your portable but it rang out.'

Sonya glanced at the litter of black plastic on the carpet. 'It's being serviced.'

'I have something for you.' The speaker clicked, and seconds later a printed message spooled out.

Sonya tore the sheet off and scanned it.

'*Volante* disappeared. Await instructions. C.'

Sonya cursed. Instead of an employment letter, her boss was sending cryptic messages. Annoyed, she crushed the paper into a ball. Curtis wasn't the only game in town - what if she found another job?

She sat at the terminal and tapped into Galnet. When the employment page came up there were thousands of positions available. Sonya entered her qualifications and the list shrank to half a page. Then she entered her planet of origin and all but two positions disappeared. Sonya scanned the entries and made a face - she wasn't that desperate.

'Where am I?'

Clunk glanced around and saw the empty pilot's chair. Then he looked down and gave a guilty start as he saw Hal lying flat on his back. He'd forgotten to strap the human in.

'What's going on?' demanded Hal. 'Why am I lying on the floor?'

'You had a dizzy spell,' said the robot. 'I was busy with departure.'

Hal sat up, rubbing his head. 'I don't remember anything. No, wait. I remember something going round and r–'

'I'm sure it will pass,' said Clunk hurriedly.

'I need caffeine,' muttered Hal, struggling to his feet. He got a cup of coffee from the dispenser and returned to the console. 'How's the generator?' he asked, sipping the steaming liquid.

'Good,' said Clunk, remembering that he was supposed to be monitoring it. 'Excellent. Top condition.'

'What's that flashing light, then?'

'Where?'

'The one labelled 'generator'.'

Clunk looked at it. 'Just a warning, nothing to worry about. I should probably check it though.'

As Clunk headed for the lift, Hal lowered himself into the pilot's chair. 'Navcom, give me a sit rep.'

'I don't understand your command.'

'Sure you do.' Hal took another sip of coffee. 'Situation report.'

'We're approaching planet Ullimo with a cargo of textiles. Vision on main screen.'

Hal examined the image, which was completely dark except for a blue dot in the centre. 'Is that really Ullimo?'

'Yes,' said the Navcom.

'Not a simulation? Not a screen saver?'

'No, it's the real planet.'

Hal watched it for a moment or two. 'It's not getting any bigger.'

'That's because we're not moving very fast.'

'Speed up, then.'

'Not possible. We must obey local traffic rules.'

Hal made a rude noise. 'I'll obey traffic rules when they start enforcing them. Hit it.'

There was a rumble below decks and the ship leapt forward.

'Speed increased.'

Hal watched the blue dot grow into a planet. 'That's more like it. We're really shifting now.' He looked down as a two-tone alarm sounded. 'What's that?'

'Ullimo traffic enforcement. They just issued an infringement.'

'Eh?'

There was another ping from the console. 'That's two. Shall I continue to increase speed?'

'No! Stop!'

Thrusters fired to slow the ship, but not before three more pings rang out.

'It's going to take us forever to get there,' muttered Hal, taking a swig of coffee.

'Not forever. Our ETA is three days.'

Coffee sprayed from Hal's mouth with an explosion of compressed air. 'What do you mean, three days?' he spluttered. 'The planet's in sight!'

'Thirty minutes until arrival, plus seventy-two hours for quarantine clearance.'

'But we're carrying rags!'

'It's not the fabric, it's the boxes of pango fruit.'

Hal snorted. 'That was just a last minute filler. Dump it and reapply for clearance.'

'Dump . . . ' began the Navcom.

'Open the cargo doors and blow it out. I'm not hanging around here for three days.'

'That fruit was a special order for the President of the Ullimo Horticultural Society.'

'I don't care if it's a bribe for the head of the Peace Force. Get rid of it!'

'Complying.' There was a whine below decks, followed by a whoosh of air.

'Take an entry for standing orders,' said Hal. 'No fruit.'

'Complying. Now contacting ground for clearance.' There was a pause. 'Ullimo Customs wish to speak to you.'

'Put them on.'

A young man in a peaked cap appeared on the screen. His uniform jacket was buttoned up to his neck, and his epaulettes looked like they were polished on the hour. 'Am I addressing the captain of the *Volante*?'

'That's me,' said Hal. 'How can I help you?'

'I am Phillip Farquhar, assistant head of Ullimo Customs.' The man held up a form. 'This is a shipping declaration we

68

received from your port of departure.' He held up a second form. 'And this one just arrived.'

Hal's heart sank. 'I thought you people liked everything in duplicate.'

'We do. However, these are not duplicates. In fact, they're not remotely similar.'

'That's probably my robot,' said Hal with a nervous laugh. 'Always messing things up.'

'How could a robot turn rolls of brand new fabric into bales of rags?'

'You haven't seen Clunk loading cargo.' Hal spread his hands. 'Look, there's obviously been a mix up. Last time this happened I made a little donation to the office slush fund. What do you say?'

'I say you're already facing a hefty fine for smuggling. Let's not add a jail term for bribery.' Phillip tapped one of the forMs. 'You've listed your robot here. Is it really this old?'

'Oh yes. Ancient.'

'In good working order?'

'He can walk and talk, if that's what you mean.'

'You see, I need a robot rather urgently.'

'Clunk's not for sale,' said Hal firmly.

'I don't want to buy him. It's just a loan.'

'Sorry, but no. Clunk's an integral part of my crew. We go everywhere together.'

'Even to jail?'

Hal pursed his lips. 'When do you need him?'

'Today.' Phillip leant closer to the camera. 'My aunt is a director at the Ullimo Museum. They're setting up a 'Life in the Past' exhibition which opens at ten this morning. They have a lot of exhibits but she still hasn't found a suitable robot.'

'Come on, there must be hundreds of them around.'

'Yes, but their owners are worried about public liability. The museum doesn't have any cover, and should the robot fall on one of the guests ... well, let's just say it could be an expensive exercise.' Phillip smiled. 'You, however, do not have a choice.'

'Why is this important? Why a robot?'

Phillip shrugged. 'My aunt wants a robot, and it's my duty as a loving nephew to acquire one for her.'

'Say that again with a straight face.'

Phillip grinned suddenly. 'She's wealthy, and if I don't play the dutiful nephew she'll leave all her money to the museum. I don't want to be sitting at this desk in twenty years time, which means I do what I'm told.'

'Clunk's not going to like it. He can be funny.'

'So much the better. He can entertain the customers.' Phillip held up Hal's form. 'Call the museum the instant you land, and once the robot is on display I'll file this in last year's register.'

'It's a deal.'

'Good day, Mr Spacejock. I trust we won't speak again.'

The screen went blank.

'Well, that's a turn up,' remarked Hal. 'We should pull this stunt more often. We saved thousands in duty.'

'And shopped Clunk to a museum,' said the Navcom.

'You let me do the explaining. I don't want him getting the wrong idea.' Hal glanced over his shoulder as the lift doors swept open. 'Ah, Clunk. How's the generator?'

'It'll hold together until we land.'

'Good. Excellent. Listen, I was reading up on Ullimo and I discovered they have a museum.'

Clunk's eyebrows rose. 'Do you know what a museum is?'

'Of course I do. It's a place where they stick old stuff nobody

. . . ' Hal tried again. 'It's where they display valuable antiques, so that people can appreciate their origins.'

'What is your interest?'

'Well, I thought we could use a bit of culture.'

'We could?'

'Sure! We're always dashing around, flitting from one planet to the next. We should take our time and soak up the history of these places.'

'Are you feeling all right, Mr Spacejock?' asked Clunk in concern. 'I've never heard you speak like this before.'

'I just think we should enjoy every planet to the full.'

'So we're going to this museum?'

'Absolutely.'

'What about repairs to the ship? Unloading the cargo?'

'Oh, the ground staff can do those while we're gone.'

'This museum. Are they paying people to visit?'

'Well, let's not stand around chatting,' said Hal. 'Oh, that reminds me. Can you call the guy who wanted the pango fruit? Tell him it missed the pick-up.'

'It's in the hold.'

'Not any more.'

'Is that why you opened the cargo doors?'

'Yup. Customs wanted three days for clearance, so I spaced the lot.'

'Did you tell them we had a certificate?'

'A what?'

'A quarantine certificate. I organised it with the forwarder before we left.'

Hal's eyes narrowed. 'Did you organise anything else?'

'Yes, I sent our manifest ahead. It saves time on arrival.'

Hal closed his eyes. 'Clunk, did I see a jetbike in the hold the other day?'

The robot nodded.

'Good. I want you to go out and fetch the boxes of fruit.'

Clunk raised one eyebrow. 'All of them?'

'No, just the red ones with bows on. Of course all of them!'

'But the contents will be frozen solid!'

'We've got twenty minutes before we land. Defrost them.'

'How?'

'I don't know - stick 'em under the generator or something. Use your head.'

The robot returned to the lift.

'Clunk,' called Hal.

'Yes?'

'Next time you organise something, how about letting me know?'

The lift doors swished to, cutting off the robot's curt reply.

◆

Clunk threaded his way between the large reinforced cages containing huge rolls of fabric. Near the back of the hold there was an empty space where the fruit had been. Clunk tutted to himself at the sight, and he was still clucking disapproval as he walked past the back doors to a waist-high enclosure in the corner. It was a large box with rounded corners, built into the rear bulkhead, and when Clunk opened the door he saw a gleaming white spacebike inside, clamped upright in its cradle. KleenAir Corporation had once been a mighty conglomerate with manufacturing standards second to none, but a cursory glance told him their ZoomMaster 4000 jetbike was a hastily conceived product designed to look good in glossy adverts. The swept-back windscreen was patently useless in a vacuum, and the padded leather seat was hardly necessary in zero gravity. However, the bike did have a tracker, and the oversized 3D display fitted neatly between the handlebars and the shield.

Clunk lifted the access flap and stepped into the enclosure. There was barely enough room to get a leg over the bulky jetbike, and how anyone was supposed to get aboard wearing a spacesuit ... Clunk shook his head. All that room in the cargo hold, and they had to cram the bike into a tiny little launch tube.

He clipped his feet into the stirrups, then reached up and closed the flap. The instruments lit up and Clunk scanned the status displays: Fuel levels were fine, hydraulic pressure was optimal and the brakes were off. He gunned the motor, twisting the throttle to maximum, and the bike emitted a deafening roar as thrust poured from the jets.

It didn't move.

There was a treble-boost button alongside the throttle grip, for use in dire emergencies. Clunk pressed it.

For a split second it was like sharing his personal space with a box of exploding hand grenades. Thrusters belched in the small enclosure, and the heat was incredible. Through the shuddering vibration Clunk felt the bike lurch, and when he looked down he discovered it was still latched to the cradle. This was a safety mechanism to prevent over-eager pilots from gunning the throttle and ramming the jetbike straight into the thick door sealing the end of the tunnel. The thick metal ribs holding the bike down were bending forwards under the extreme forces, and even as the STOP impulse travelled from Clunk's brain to his thumb, they gave way.

From a standing start the bike took half a second to travel

the first five metres towards the airlock door. By this time Clunk had released his thumb, reversed the throttle, applied both air brakes and stuck his legs out the sides to try and stop the runaway machine. The next four metres took a quarter of a second, with the bike slowing from over two hundred kilometres an hour to just under fifty. The final metre was a relatively pedestrian affair, as he brought the heavy bike to a stop in a whirling cloud of smoke and dust only millimetres from the inner door.

Clunk glanced back up the tube. Through the exhaust haze he saw a large scorch mark and bits and pieces of cradle, and he was suddenly glad that Mr Spacejock didn't inspect the ship very often.

He operated the inner door, eased the jetbike into the compact airlock and waited for the outer door to open. The haze thinned out, and then he was facing a jet-black disc of space, dotted with distant stars. He fired the engine and shot out of the tube, then activated the tracker. Immediately the display lit up with a dozen small blips and a huge area of solid green. Clunk aimed for the furthest crate and the bike leapt forward, leaving the freighter behind as it streaked towards the first target.

— 8 —

Sonya strode along the maintenance corridor at the Ullimo spaceport, heading for the landing field. A heavy rucksack swung from her hand, with Dent's briefcase computer crammed inside. Not that it was necessary to hide the thing - it was just that she hadn't been able to peel off the inane smiley sticker.

She came to a security door, which opened smartly as she touched her palm to the contact. Outside there was a U-shaped collection of buildings surrounding half a dozen landing pads. The buildings were connected by covered walkways, their inward-facing windows heavily shuttered against the arriving and departing spaceships. There were two vessels nearby - a small flyer and a towering Delta class liner. A crane was busy with the latter, removing a section of hull over the right-hand engine while half a dozen mechanics lounged around watching.

A siren wailed and the mechanics downed tools and ambled away from the parked ships, chatting to each other and paying not the slightest attention to a growing rumble in the sky above them. They reached a door and filed inside, and there was a series of bangs as the shutters facing the landing field slammed shut.

Sonya darted back into the maintenance corridor, closing the door even as the panes darkened against the glare. The rumbling got louder, and through the black glass she saw a dim glow high in the sky. The building shook from the noise and the glow became a flare, then a flaming torch, then a rising sun, before it was obscured by billowing smoke and dust. The walls shook as the spaceship hovered above the landing pad, engines howling, and there was a solid thump when it set down. The engine noise tailed off, the shutters re-opened with a series of crashes and the glass turned clear again, driving bright daylight into Sonya's eyes.

The Volante was an impressive ship, with sleek lines and a pure white hull. Hot air from the jets made the tailplane shimmer like a mirage, and a ramp began to extend from the airlock.

A door opened in the building opposite and several mechanics made for the ship. One was pushing a trolley with catering logos, another was dragging a length of fuel pipe and a third carried a large mallet over his shoulder.

Sonya donned her sunglasses, hefted the rucksack and went outside. As she approached the ship, one of the mechanics took his mallet and tapped it on the landing leg. He tilted his head to listen for the echoes, then nodded to himself and set the mallet aside. Pulling a grease-stained rag from his equally grubby overalls, he wiped his hands and approached the mechanic dragging the fuel pipe.

'Going to the game, Nat?'

'To see our lot hammered again? Gotta be kidding, Sam.'

Sam sighed. 'Gonna bet on the Woritans?'

Nat screwed up his face and spat on the rough concrete. 'You see the odds, man? I'd rather chuck the money down a sewer.' He stood back and stared at the landing leg through half-closed eyes. 'You finished that fatigue test?'

'Yup.'

'Swap, then.'

As the men changed places, Sonya cleared her throat.

'Whatcher want, miss?' demanded Sam.

'Mr Curtis sent me to fumigate this vessel.'

It was Sam's turn to spit on the concrete. 'Curtis, huh? Okay, sprayer's in the shed.'

Sonya resisted the urge to spit right back, turned on her heel and marched towards the door Sam had indicated. Inside she found a hazard suit which smelled like a football team, a helmet that smelled like a football team's socks and a large oval canister covered with warning labels. Sonya put the rucksack on the floor next to the canister and went to work with a screwdriver.

A few minutes later she was ready. Clad in the suit, wearing the helmet and with the canister strapped to her back, she went back outside, where she found Sam and Nat standing in a puddle of fuel, arguing over the fuel hose. 'Excuse me!' called Sonya. 'Can one of you call the ship and tell them I'm coming aboard?'

'Do it yerself,' said Nat.

Sonya walked up to him. 'I'm sorry, I couldn't hear you through this helmet.'

'I'm busy, call the ship yerself.'

Sonya's knee flashed up, and a split second later Nat was rolling on the ground. Sonya turned to the second man. 'Sam, isn't it?'

'I am, miss. I'll just call the ship for ya, miss.'

'Thank you so much.'

Hal leant back in his seat and took a deep breath. Although the computer controlled every aspect of landing with ease, he still got nervous each time the ship fell towards a tiny concrete landing pad. What if something went wrong? What if the thrusters failed? He reassured himself with the thought that modern spaceships were hand-built by robots, then caught sight of Clunk sitting next to him and immediately felt worse.

'Did you say something?' asked Clunk, who was busy scanning instruments.

Hal shook his head and gripped the armrests.

There was a bump and Clunk started throwing switches, cutting the engines and preparing the ship for a lengthy stay on the ground. The overhead lights flickered as the ground crew switched the Volante onto mains power, supplied by one of the assortment of cables, pipes and tubes now attached to the ship like oversized umbilical cords.

'I'm going to top the tanks up,' said Clunk. 'The gravity here is a fraction higher than standard, and we'll burn more fuel than usual when we leave.'

Hal frowned. 'I've always wondered - where does standard gravity come from?'

'Earth.'

'What, the stuff you stand on?'

'No, Earth the planet.'

Hal laughed. 'Get away. Next you'll be telling me there's a moon called Moon.'

'There really was a planet called Earth,' said the robot firmly. 'It was the birthplace of humanity.'

'Really?' said Hal. 'Where is it?'

'Nobody knows,' said the robot. 'There was an expedition once, but nothing came of it. Didn't they teach you anything in school?'

Hal shook his head. 'I spent all my time making paper planes.'

'Pity you didn't learn more about planets.'

'Why?'

'Because it's not unheard of for spaceship pilots to learn a little about celestial mechanics and the laws of physics.'

'Whoa!' Hal raised his hands. 'Laws of physics? That crap's for the boffins.'

The robot stared at him. 'It's part of the training!'

'Negative, Clunk. They make the ship, I fly the ship.'

'You don't fly the ship at all. You just tell the computer what you want.'

'Something wrong with that?'

'It's not flying, is it? You might as well be ordering food from the AutoChef.'

Hal frowned. 'Don't talk to me about that thing. Anyway –'

A chime rang out from the console. 'Incoming call,' said the Navcom. 'Orbit ground crew.'

'Put them through,' said Hal.

'Ground here. We gotta deconta - docan - dacci - er, we gotta spray yer ship. You need to git down here.'

'Is that normal?'

'Sure. We do it all the time. Bugs 'n' stuff.'

Clunk leaned forward. 'I'd like to finish our landing procedures first.'

There was a muttered exchange. 'Okay, but you got to make it quick.'

'We'll need at least ten minutes.' Clunk cut the connection and continued working on the console.

'Where do they get these people?' asked Hal, who was still shaking his head in disbelief.

'Ex starship pilots.'

'And I don't like the idea of them spraying gunk around.'

'A quarantine sweep is probably just as well after our visit to Oliape II.'

'Listen, I want you to forget we ever went there. In fact, I want to forget we ever went there.'

'How can I forget anything? I'm a robot.'

'I don't know. Erase bits of your memory.'

'I can't ...' Clunk frowned. 'I don't think I can do that.'

Hal laughed. 'Sure you can. You've just forgotten how.'

'Incoming call,' said the Navcom. 'Orbit ground.'

'Again?'

'This call is from the office.'

'Okay, put them on.' Hal gestured at Clunk. 'Go and tidy yourself up.'

'What for?'

'You can't turn up to the museum looking like that.'

'Volante, ground here. Please advise how you wish to pay for your fuel.'

'On account. Didn't my computer send the details?'

'Yes, but the payment was declined.'

'There must be a mistake,' said Hal. 'That's my trading account. There should be enough to cover it. Check it again.'

'One moment, sir.'

Hal waved Clunk towards the lift. 'Go on, go and polish yourself.' He brushed biscuit crumbs off his flight suit. 'Personal appearance is important if you want to create a good impression.'

'What's wrong with my appearance?'

'You're all dull. Now get moving.'

Clunk opened his mouth to reply, but at that moment a voice came through the speakers.

'I tried to process the transaction again, sir. It was declined.'

'Okay, charge it to my ship.'

'Certainly, sir. What's your Spacer's Guild number?'

'One two three four.'

'One moment.'

Hal waved Clunk away, and after a long, thoughtful look the robot departed.

'I'm sorry, sir. That number is invalid.'

Hal tutted. 'I must have misplaced my card.'

'Then I'm unable to extend credit. How do you propose to pay?'

'How much do I owe you?' Hal turned pale as the operator told him. 'What did you fill it with, mineral water?'

'Standard, sir.'

'Last time it was half that.'

'I don't set the prices sir, I just collect the money.'

'Okay, okay. Navcom, give this guy my savings account number.'

'Confirmed. Transaction processed. Your balance is now –'

'I don't want to know!' interrupted Hal.

'Minus seven hundred and thirty-three,' finished the Navcom. 'I have an incoming call.'

'Who is it?'

'Pilots First Bank. Overdraft department.'

'Get rid of them,' said Hal hurriedly. 'And get me the museum. I want to speak to the manager.'

'Complying.' The main screen showed a pair of rotating cogs beneath a company logo.

'Welcome to the Ullimo Museum,' said a male voice. 'How may I help you?'

'I need to speak to someone about an exhibit.' Hal lowered his voice. 'They're borrowing my robot.'

'Can I say who's calling?'

'Hal Spacejock, from the Volante.'

'You want Arlene. I'll just find her for you.'

There was a slight hiss from the speakers, and a few seconds later an elderly woman appeared on the screen. She had a large, cheerful face and a mass of grey curls piled up on her head, held in place with a clip shaped like a clam. 'Captain Spacejock?'

'That's me. Are you Phillip's aunt?'

'Arlene, please. Phillip told me all about your robot, and we're simply thrilled. It's so kind of you.'

'It's nothing, really.'

'Don't be so modest! Phillip told me about you, too. The rugged starship captain, the lone entrepreneur fighting red tape, the successful businessman –'

'I do my best,' said Hal modestly.

'And then there's your legendary generosity.'

'Eh?'

'Shall we discuss your donation over dinner this evening?'

'No!' Hal stared at the screen. 'I mean ... I can't. I've got a cargo to deliver. Central Bank. Paperwork. You know how it is - we entrepreneurs never stop.'

'Such a pity. Never mind, we can discuss the matter when you deliver the robot.'

'How do you want me to get him there?'

'I suggest a cab. They'll deliver to the door. See you soon!'

'And, er, about the fare ... '

But the screen was blank.

9

Hal and Clunk emerged from the Volante's airlock and stepped onto the passenger ramp. Together they strode towards the ground, enjoying the early morning sunshine. The Ullimo spaceport was set into a valley between majestic snow-capped mountains, and in the clear morning air Hal felt he could almost reach out and touch them. Closer to the ship a large passenger liner was being serviced, and the spaceport buildings beyond it were designed to blend in with the wooded slopes.

A flock of birds burst from the trees, cawing loudly as they whirled in tight circles.

'Black gulls,' said Clunk, watching them.

Hal smiled. 'They fly better than mine ever did.' The birds settled, and Hal continued down the ramp, his breath frosting in the crisp air. 'I'd rather be out here than inside getting sterilised.'

'Decontaminated,' said Clunk.

'Hey, that was good. You can coach the guys on the landing pad while we wait.'

They were almost at the foot of the ramp when a figure in a hazard suit and reflective mask emerged from a nearby shed, carrying a large cylinder with a sprayer nozzle as big as the

Volante's landing jets. Hal stood aside to let the figure past, but it stopped and looked up at him.

'Hal Spacejock?' said a female voice.

'That's me.'

The worker patted her cylinder, which was plastered with warning labels. 'This stuff disperses in five minutes. Keep out of the ship until then.'

'Is this really necessary?'

'Our laws are strict. You go to jail if you bring unauthorised organisms to this planet.'

'Don't let us keep you.'

The woman slung the cylinder over her shoulder and strolled up the ramp. Hal watched, admiring her easy gait until Clunk's delicate cough drew his attention.

'Yeah?'

'The museum closes at four,' said Clunk.

'How'd you know that?'

'I looked it up. Did you know they're running a 'Life in the Past'exhibit?'

'Fancy that,' said Hal. 'Are they really?'

'They've got some old robot as their chief exhibit.' Clunk sighed. 'Probably scooped the poor thing's guts out so they could use it as a novelty waste bin.'

'It won't be that bad.' Hal looked around. 'Come on, let's supervise the unloading.'

They crossed beneath the ship, emerging near the lowered cargo ramp. There was a whirr overhead and a cage full of fabric appeared at the top of the ramp, driven by hydraulics under the decking. It stopped, and a large crane lowered a hook, lifting the crate and swinging it over Hal's head. The crane whined as the boom descended towards a flatbed truck, then fell silent as the heavy cargo made contact.

'One down, thirty to go,' said Clunk.

Hal yawned. 'Okay, let's get a cab.'

'What about supervising the unloading?'

'They look competent enough.'

'But they have access to the ship!'

'Only the hold, and the Navcom will keep an eye on them. Come on.' Hal led the way across the landing pad to the blast barrier, where he lifted a handset from its cradle. The screen flickered, and a young man appeared.

'Good afternoon, sir. How can I help you?'

'I need a cab for the local museum.'

'Certainly sir. Which ship?'

'The *Volante*.'

The man glanced at his terminal. 'Mr Spacejock?'

Hal nodded.

'Your cab will be there momentarily. Have a nice day.'

Hal dropped the handset back in the cradle. 'Momentarily,' he muttered, shaking his head. He looked back at the ship, where the crane was moving another crate onto the waiting truck. 'How many's that?'

'Two,' said the robot.

Hal looked around, trying to spot the cab. There was no sign of it, and his gaze lingered on a row of concession stands nearby, selling everything from sweets and magazines to giftware. One stand caught his eye: much larger than the others, it contained a pair of battered wardrobes and a podium.

'Where are you going?' asked Clunk, as Hal set off towards the display.

'I want to know what they're up to.'

'What about the cab?'

'Don't worry, we'll see it.'

As they approached the stand they noticed the wardrobes were festooned with wires and plastered with circuit boards. At the rear of the display an elderly man was checking connectors and touching various components with a probe, oblivious to passing traffic. Next to him, a young man was sitting on an ordinary kitchen chair, reading a dog-eared paperback. He was well built, and his red skivvy so tight it could have been painted onto his barrel chest.

The elderly man spotted Hal out the corner of his eye, and he beamed as he looked up from his work. 'I spy curiosity!'

'Just looking,' said Hal quickly.

'Come, come and look closer.'

'I was just wondering what you're doing.' Hal gestured at the wardrobes and the wiring. 'Is this a sculpture?'

The man's face twisted. 'Sculpture? Nein, not that. It is a revolutionary transportation device, the likes of which have never before been seen.'

'Even in those old vid programs?' asked Clunk innocently.

The man ignored him. 'This, sir, is the most revolutionary idea since Comfort Corporation began putting seams on the outside of their underwear.'

'You mean they used to be on the inside?' Hal looked surprised. 'Wasn't that uncomfortable?'

'In the extreme. Someone got fed up with wearing underpants inside out, and revolutionised the industry.'

'What's that got to do with this old junk?' asked Hal, gesturing at the display.

'I was pointing out that innovation is everywhere, mein herr.' The old man straightened. 'And this is not junk. This is my MTD, or Matter Transfer Device.'

'And what does it do?'

The man frowned. 'I just said what it did. It transfers matter.'

86

'Teleporter,' murmured Clunk, tapping his forehead with a finger.

'Teleporter!' exclaimed Hal.

'No, this word is not what I said. The word you used does not adequately explain my device.'

'Plus it's trademarked,' said the robot.

'You would perhaps like me to demonstrate?' The man eyed Clunk with distaste. 'Perhaps with your robot ...'

'Sorry,' said Clunk. 'I'm allergic to conmen.'

'Conman! My dear metal friend, this device will be huge. It will be bigger than ... than ...' Realising he was never going to impress the robot, the scientist addressed Hal instead. 'Sir, you look like an intelligent man.'

Clunk coughed.

'Perhaps you would care to view a demonstration?'

Hal gazed at the tangled wires and sparking electrical components. 'Is it safe?'

'Oh, yes. Most certainly.'

'Why have you set it up here?'

'Funding. I cannot get past the small-minded lackeys that stifle the lower levels of government and big business.'

'Why don't you teleport into the upper levels, then?' muttered Clunk.

'What do you mean, funding?' asked Hal.

'Sir, I am a scientist. Imagine the value of my invention. Imagine the value of a company which develops it properly. Therefore, I am selling shares in my enterprise, allowing the man in the street to partake of the rewards such a device will surely bring.'

'You want me to give you money?'

'I would perhaps express it more delicately, but this is the general idea.'

'For that?' Hal gestured at the wardrobes, the wires, the guy in the red skivvy.

'An experimental model. You will appreciate the way I conserve funds.'

'I can tell.' Hal eyed the young man. 'What's he doing, anyway?'

'Hans!' yelled the scientist suddenly. 'Demo!'

The man in the red skivvy folded the corner of his book, put it into his pocket and walked into the left-hand cupboard. The flimsy door rattled as he pulled it to, and there was a loud bang and a flash of green light. The wardrobe on the other side of the display shook and the young man emerged, waving at a cloud of smoke.

'You see? It works,' said the scientist. 'How many shares would you like?'

Hal watched, open-mouthed, as the young man resumed his seat, extracted the paperback and continued reading. 'That's amazing,' he said. 'Incredible. Can you send me across?'

'Alas, the machine is tuned only for Hans.'

'But you said –'

'Only Hans. However, with your additional funds . . . '

Hal took out a handful of credit tiles. 'How much per share?'

'Fifty credits.'

'How many shares are you selling?' asked Clunk.

The scientist ignored him.

'I'll take five,' said Hal.

'Five? Five will not fund a single displacement.'

'All right, six.'

'Sir, the minimum is fifty.'

'Fifty shares! That's –'

'Two and a half thousand,' supplied Clunk. 'Come on, Mr Spacejock. We don't want to miss our cab.'

Hal patted his pockets. 'Sorry about this. I'm a little short of cash right now.'

'Perhaps my finance plan might be of interest,' said the scientist smoothly.

'Not to Mr Spacejock,' said Clunk. 'His credit rating is triple-Z negative.'

Hal looked surprised. 'I have a credit rating?'

'You wasted my time? You have no money?' The old man gestured at his assistant. 'Hans! Here!'

'Don't worry, we're leaving,' said Clunk, grabbing Hal's arm and hauling him back towards the ship.

Aboard the Volante, Sonya was moving along the lower deck passageway, spraying clouds of yellow particles that swirled behind her like bonfire smoke. During her conversation with Curtis she'd formed a mental image of Hal - a small, rat-faced individual with dank hair, shifty eyes and a permanent sniff. Someone who would sell their entire family for a round of drinks. Someone who could abandon refugees on a deserted planet. Instead, Hal was a good-looking individual with an honest, open face. Sonya shook her head. She should have known - even a crisp red apple could have a rotten core.

As she backed along the passageway she found herself admiring the clean, bright walls and neat cabins. She'd been aboard several Curtis Freightlines carriers, and compared to the Volante they were cramped, dirty workhorses with a rotating crew of pilots who were only interested in their next pay packet. She wondered what it would be like to have the freedom of the galaxy, drifting wherever the latest cargo job took you, living aboard a comfortable ship, not having to worry about immigration officials demanding letters of employment ...

Sonya shook her head and returned to the job at hand. Still puffing clouds from the sprayer, she approached the engine room access door and reached for the controls. Immediately, a voice came from the speaker above her head.

'Access to the engine room prohibited,' said the Navcom sternly.

'You want clearance, I do the whole ship,' said Sonya. She eyed the notice on the door: Authorised Personnel Only. 'If you don't let me in, I'll come back with a warrant.'

'Very well. But don't touch anything.'

There was a snick and the door slid open. Sonya entered the darkened compartment and touched her gloved hand to the light controls behind the door. Nothing happened. Frowning, she turned on her suit light and angled it around the roof. The fitting had been torn out and was hanging by a thread. She used the light to explore the corners where the walls met the ceiling, until she found the camera. It too was hanging from its mounting, which was odd considering the rest of the ship was in such good shape. 'No eyes, no ears... suits me just fine,' muttered Sonya, as she strode between the main drives to the hyperspace motor. The gleaming cylinder was about four metres long, mounted on thick, shock-absorbing rubber pads and joined to the ship by a conduit. Sonya leaned closer to inspect the pipe, then stared. 'Teeth marks?' she muttered aloud. 'What kind of ...' She turned and looked behind her, startled by a shuffling noise. The beam of light burned a white tunnel through the darkness, but left deep shadows on either side. She moved the light, but the beam revealed nothing but machinery.

Turning back to the hyperdrive, she recalled the diagrams she'd studied prior to coming aboard. According to Dent, the drive's connection to the ship's computer was inside the firewall, so all she had to do was remove the plug and wire the briefcase in to collect the information she needed. Stripping off her gloves, she used her bare hands to unscrew the top of the canister she'd collected from the maintenance shed. Inside was a small pressurised tank which she set on the deck. Next, she extracted a heavy roll of fabric fastened with buckles. Then she took out the briefcase computer, whose smiley-face sticker leered at her like a carnival mask in the half-light.

Undoing the buckles on the roll of fabric, Sonya opened it to reveal a selection of tools. She examined the hyperdrive, chose a spanner and got to work. A minute or two later, the connector was loose. Sonya slid the briefcase closer, plugged the lead in and switched it on.

'Hey, was I powered off?' exclaimed the computer. 'Where did we go today?'

'Keep your voice down!' hissed Sonya.

'Would you like to activate my operating system now?'

'No, and shut up.' Sonya unclipped the keyboard and called up an editor, and within seconds she was engrossed.

Bobby piped up. 'It seems you are writing a program. Would you like some help with that?'

'I said shut up.'

'Are you sure? I can make things easier for you.' A window appeared, showing a list of options.

Sonya stopped typing. 'Close the damn window.'

'Okey doke.' The window vanished.

'Now put my text back.'

'Text?'

'My program.'

'I can't. System error, I'm afraid.'

Sonya closed her eyes. 'You lost my work?'

'Sure did,' said Bobby cheerfully. 'Shall I demonstrate how to perform a backup?'

'No, I would not like you to show me how to perform a backup,' said Sonya, through gritted teeth. 'I would like you to get the hell out of my face and let me work in peace.'

'Can do.'

Sonya's breath hissed as she re-keyed the missing commands. Halfway through, a window began to open. 'I mean it,' she growled. The window closed instantly. Moments later, the program was ready. Sonya tested it with the interpreter, then ran it live.

The computer's fans began to whirr, and a flashing icon appeared. 'Sonya, I have to point out that the routines you wrote infringe several laws. Do you understand the consequences?'

'Yep.'

'I need you to okay some clauses.'

'What?'

'It's just a disclaimer absolving the software company from any liability should legal action arise from the use of your code.'

The screen filled with text and Sonya hit the OK button without bothering to look at it.

'Uh-uh,' said Bobby, putting it back again. 'You have to read it.'

'I did.'

'No, you just pressed OK. Try again.'

Sonya paged to the end of the file and stabbed the OK button.

'I'm sorry Sonya, but I don't think you're reading that file.'

'I did so!' she hissed. 'Run my damn program.'

'The average time to read that form is eight minutes. You cannot complete it in five seconds, it's not humanly possible. Here is the file again. Each page should take approximately fifteen seconds. Please do not skip pages, as I will be timing each one.'

Sonya suppressed the urge to bang her head on the floor. Instead, she hunched over the portable computer, teeth clenched, paging through the file one screen at a time. She derived some comfort from the fact that even after hitting OK on the very last page, she still hadn't read a word of the conditions.

'I am now authorised to run all software, legal or not,' said the computer. 'Commencing execution.'

'Capital idea,' said Sonya under her breath. 'Don't stop with the programmers. Go right to the top.'

The fans ran at full speed for several seconds, blasting grit off the engine room floor. Then there was a loud beep. 'Data transferred.'

Sonya switched the computer off, unplugged the lead and began to repack her tools. She was just reaching for the spanner when she heard a scrape right behind her. She spun round and saw a pair of hairy orange hands reaching for her out of the darkness. Spooked, Sonya leapt up and backed away, tripped over the briefcase and whacked her head on the hyperdrive's unyielding metal surface. For a split second, an explosion of coloured stars filled her vision.

Then everything went dark.

❖

'I'm telling you, he was a conman,' said Clunk as they walked towards the ship. 'A rip-off merchant.'

'Clunk, you have no respect for battlers. That man could change the future of transportation.'

'The only thing he's teleporting is money. It vanishes from mug punters' accounts and reappears in his own.'

'You're such a cynic.'

'Do you really believe in his teleporter?'

'Absolutely. And until you can prove otherwise ... '

Clunk sighed. 'Okay, you asked for it. Did you notice the book that young man was reading?'

'Yeah, it was a paperback novel.'

'Correct. Did you notice the title?'

'No. What's your point?'

'Well, you know when he came out of the teleporter and sat down to read again?'

'Yes, Clunk. Although my limited powers of observation in no way match your perfect recall, I do vaguely remember seeing the man come out of the second teleporter. I also remember him sitting down and reading a papery thing with printing on, and yes, now that you've highlighted the fact I do seem to recall it being a book.'

Clunk nodded. 'I was hoping you'd noticed.'

'Noticed what?'

'It wasn't the same book.'

'Eh?'

'Your teleport scientist has twin sons.'

Hal stared at him. 'I'll be –'

'You nearly were,' said Clunk.

Hal glanced over his shoulder at the concessions. 'I ought to duff him up.'

'All three of them?'

'Well, maybe just the old guy.' Hal spotted a sleek black groundcar coming towards them. 'Here's the cab at last.'

'And the rain,' said Clunk, glancing at the sky. 'I really don't understand why you're insisting on this little outing. You've never shown the slightest interest in antiques.'

'I bought you, didn't I?' Hal dug into his pocket and withdrew a couple of credit tiles. 'Here, you'll need this for the fare.'

Clunk stared at Hal's outstretched hand. 'I'm sorry?'

'Taxi drivers don't do it for fun, you know.'

'I'm aware of that, but why are you giving me the money?'

'Come on, hop in,' said Hal as the car drew up. 'Quick, or you'll get wet.'

'But –'

The door sprang open and Hal bundled Clunk into the car. 'Try and get the fare back off the museum.'

'But Mr Spacejock –'

'Ask for Arlene, she'll look after you.' Hal closed the door and leaned through the open window. 'Don't worry, you'll be fine.'

Clunk looked up at him. 'But –'

'But what? The repairs are booked and unloading is progressing nicely.'

'But –'

'But nothing. See you this afternoon.' Hal slapped the window, and the cab shot away from the landing pad. As it drove off he waved at the astonished face peering through the rear window. Once the car was out of sight, he made his way back to the ship.

'Is the air safe?' he called through the airlock.

'There is no perceptible variation from the usual chemical composition,' said the Navcom.

Hal made a face. 'It smells like old socks.'

'Precisely.'

Hal entered the flight deck and made himself comfortable. 'Once the generator's fixed we'll have to find out where to collect the bank's paperwork.'

'You're really going to perform the cargo job on your own? Is that wise?'

'Relax, I'm in charge of this one. Anyway, I've got no choice. Clunk's halfway to the museum by now.' There was a buzz from the console. 'That must be the repair team. Right on time.'

'Shall I let them in?'

'No, tell them to use the tradesman's entrance.'

'We don't have a tradesman's entrance.'

'Tell them to come up the cargo ramp. No, cancel that. They might steal something. Tell them I'm coming down.'

'You can tell them yourself if you like,' said the Navcom. 'They're listening on the intercom.'

10

Still dazed by the sudden turn of events, Clunk was decidedly uneasy as he watched the *Volante* recede into the distance.

'First time on Ullimo?' said a warm female voice.

'Yes.' Clunk stared at the driver, a copper-coloured robot wearing a faded blue cap. 'Excuse me, but could you turn the cab around?'

'I'm afraid not. The human said I was to take you to the museum.'

'But I don't want to go there.'

The driver shrugged, squeaking slightly. 'I have my orders.'

Clunk sat back in the padded chair, his brain whizzing. Why was Hal sending him to the museum alone? And who was Arlene? He glanced out the window. They were driving alongside a stream, with foaming water cascading between narrow banks. On the far side, several large animals were grazing in a field, and as the car hurtled by they raised their heads to watch, their liquid eyes expressionless as they chewed rhythmically. Clunk frowned at them. If he had to choose a pet for himself, cows would be at the foot of the list - a list currently headed by man-eating tigers.

Suddenly the scenery vanished, replaced by a scrolling line

of red text almost a metre high: This view sponsored by KleenAir Corporation. For advertising, contact ...

Clunk shook his head. He'd seen visifences before, but this one had fooled him completely. Looking down, he spotted the bottom edge three or four metres from the road, the image carefully blended with the gravel and weeds to disguise the join. Behind it, no doubt, was the local slaughteryard, or a row of derelict factories, or a polluted industrial wasteland.

He looked away and realised the car was approaching the city, which was nestled between the mountains at the head of the valley. The road led through a massive glass corkscrew: soaring loops of steel which held countless panes of mirror-finish glass in a frozen embrace. Clunk craned his neck to get a better view as they shot underneath, but the car entered a narrow tunnel.

The driver glanced over her shoulder. 'I hear they're getting some clapped-out robots in for the display. Are you helping to set them up?'

'No, just visiting.'

'Lucky you. I was almost one of the exhibits.'

'Really?'

'The museum asked my boss if they could borrow me. He refused point blank. Said I was essential to his business.' The driver shook her head. 'Imagine standing there all day with sweet wrappers stuffed in your knee joints, sticky hand prints on your legs ... Still, I'm sure they'll deactivate the robots before they put them up. Poor old things - probably their last chance for a spot of fame.'

Clunk said nothing. Pieces of information were moving around in his head, but they wouldn't quite mesh. 'Did they offer to pay your owner?'

'No, they wanted a free loan.' The robot laughed. 'Fat chance.'

'Tell me, who's running the exhibition?'

'One of the museum directors . . . a local woman.'

'Her name?'

'Arlene Farquhar.'

Clunk stared. 'Are you certain?'

'I'm a taxi driver. We're never wrong.'

Mr Spacejock couldn't have . . . He wouldn't have! Despair washed through his circuits. Hal most certainly would have.

The car entered a park, all grass and no trees. Vehicles of all kinds zipped across at different heights, avoiding collisions by millimetres. The cab zoomed across the park and plunged into another tunnel, hurtling through it for several minutes before slowing sharply, pressing Clunk against invisible restraints. When they emerged from the far end, they were barely moving.

The car pulled up to a platform and stopped. 'Seventeen credits,' said the driver. 'Enjoy your visit.'

Clunk peered up at the museum. It was an imposing structure carved from blocks of concrete, with deep-set windows and an ornate entry. It reminded him of a prison.

'My next client is waiting. Please pay and exit the vehicle.'

Still in a daze, Clunk handed over the money. 'Keep the change,' he said automatically.

'Thanks.'

The doors opened and Clunk climbed out of the car. It zipped away with a loud hum, breaking his last link with the *Volante*. Resigned, he crossed to the entrance and raised his hand to the panel, but before he could touch it the doors opened by themselves. Inside, Clunk found a large entrance lobby with a high vaulted ceiling. There was a counter on the far side, and when he reached it he saw an elderly man behind the desk. The man looked up, peering at him through thick spectacles. 'Can I help you?'

'I'm here to see Arlene.'

The man smiled. 'Ah, the old robot. I'll call her for you. Sit down, take the weight off your feet.'

'That won't be necessary,' said Clunk.

'As you wish.'

While he waited, Clunk pondered the situation. Mr Spacejock had planned the whole thing behind his back, which was a shock because he thought he'd covered the human's every move. The Navcom was supposed to be his ally, and yet there hadn't been a hint of warning! Clunk's lips thinned. They'd have words over that.

A nearby door swept open, and Clunk saw a large, grey-haired woman advancing on him.

'Where's Captain Spacejock?' she asked, looking around her as if Hal might appear out of thin air.

'He's attending to the ship. I'm afraid he couldn't be here.'

'What a pity. I so wanted to meet him. Still, you're the one I really want.' The woman grabbed Clunk's chin and turned his head, inspecting his profile. Then she pulled his jaws open and looked into his mouth. 'You'll do. Follow me, please.'

She set off for the main entrance, walking fast. 'It's not far,' she called over her shoulder, 'but if you can't keep up just call out and I'll slow down. Don't be embarrassed - after all, this is a museum. We're used to old things here.'

Clunk drew himself up. 'With respect madam, I'm half your age.'

Hal stood before the airlock door, a look of concentration on his face as he ran through several quick apologies. 'Did I say steal? I meant heal,' he muttered. 'Oh, I thought you were the other mechanics!' He frowned and tried again. 'Sorry guys, that was my robot talking. I had him junked.'

After trying out another couple of excuses he gave up and prodded the button. As the door opened he stepped back, ready for anything. The first thing he saw was an elderly man with a large toolkit in one hand and a small lunch pail in the other. He was dressed in faded overalls, and his name tag identified him as 'Tom'. Behind him, a gangly youth was strolling up the ramp. The young man's overalls were clean and pressed, his cap was set at a jaunty angle and he had a pair of wraparound sunglasses perched on the bridge of his nose.

'SorryitwastherobotIgotridofit,' said Hal.

'Hang on a tick,' said the old man loudly. He set the toolbox down then reached up to his ear and twiddled. 'Try now, son.'

Hal breathed a sigh of relief. The old coot was deaf. 'I said, are you here to fix the ship?'

'I ain't delivering milk, son.' Tom gestured at the youth. 'Come on, you lazy sod!'

The young man raised his middle finger and slowed his pace to a crawl.

'Can't get the help nowadays,' said Tom. He glanced at Hal, his eyes bright blue under shaggy grey eyebrows. 'Watch him, he'll help himself to anything what's loose.'

'Eh?'

'Danny. Thieving little beggar.' The mechanic hefted his toolbox and entered the airlock. 'Nice piece of kit,' he commented, looking around. 'I usually fix the older ones. Break down more often.' He tapped his ear. 'Sorry about the hearing - I had to turn it down when a ship took off. Now, tell me about the problem. Generators, right?'

Hal nodded. 'First they got hot, then they stopped. Then they started but got hot again. Then they stopped again.'

'Sounds like the armature. Never mind, we'll have you right in no time.'

A shadow fell across the flight deck as Danny sauntered in, sunglasses pushed back over his dark, wiry hair.

'Make yourself useful,' growled Tom, holding the toolbox out to him.

Danny eyed the box for a moment or two, clearly deciding whether such manual labour was beneath him. In the end he reached out a languid hand and took it casually. His superior expression changed to one of alarm as the heavy toolbox caught him by surprise, and there was a crash as it slammed into the decking between his feet.

'You just can't get the help,' growled Tom, shaking his head.

Hal led them to the lift and ushered them in. The floor dropped away and a few seconds later the doors opened on the lower deck. 'This way,' said Hal, striding along the passageway. He palmed the access pad and the engine room door slid open.

'Phew-eee!' exclaimed Danny. 'It smells like a zoo down here!'

'You been putting organics in the fuel?' demanded Tom.

Hal frowned. 'I didn't mess with anything. You can check the logs if you like.' He touched the light switch but nothing happened. 'Navcom, what's with the lights?'

102

'Unknown fault,' said the computer. 'Would you like me to create a repair docket?'

'No need,' said Tom. 'We'll take a look after we've dealt with the generators.'

Hal stared into the engine room, but all he could see was the shadowy bulk of the main drives, glistening in the light from the corridor.

'On the right,' said Tom.

Hal led the men into the engine room and up to a small, heavy door. It opened silently, revealing a pitch-black alcove. Hal reached in and activated the light, blinking in the sudden glare.

'Nice pair of Rikoff-Sangs,' said Tom, pushing past. 'Very unusual for these to go wrong.'

Danny set the toolbox down and opened it. Tom extracted several instruments.

'What are those?' asked Hal, who was leaning against the door frame.

'Probes,' said the mechanic. He plugged two into the control panel and laid another on the nearest cylinder. Next, he took a pair of headphones and a mallet from the toolbox. After placing the headphones over his ears, he raised the mallet and brought it down sharply on the generator housing.

'Hey!' cried Hal. 'It's damaged enough already!'

Tom removed the headphones. 'What's that, son?'

'Why are you hitting my generator?'

'Why don't you attend to your duties?'

'My what?' Hal blinked. 'Oh, er, yeah. Duties. I'll go and attend to some of those.'

'That's the go.' Tom turned to his assistant. 'Hand me the bigger one, lad.'

The recreation room had always been a source of disappointment to Hal. To him, 'recreation' meant pool tables, a dartboard and a fully stocked bar. To the *Volante's* designer it meant a bookshelf, two armchairs and a reading lamp.

Apart from these modest entertainments, the rec room contained the ship's AutoChef: a jet-black cabinet with a touch screen, a speaker grille and a dispenser slot. A KleenAir Corporation product, the AutoChef could dispense boiling soup to all points of the compass and drive meatballs the size of hand-grenades through panes of toughened glass. It also had a nasty habit of misinterpreting orders - not only had Hal consumed enough chocolate mouse and lamb pissoles to last a lifetime, he was also carrying bruises from a particularly vigorous serve of tea and stones. Speaking clearly didn't seem to help - it was as though the AutoChef understood a completely different language.

Hal positioned himself at a safe distance and addressed the machine. 'Give me a double cheeseburger with fries,' he said, which seemed like a phonetically safe choice.

The machine beeped and the screen displayed a juicy hamburger and a plate of chips. 'Please confirm your order,' said a metallic voice.

'Go ahead,' said Hal, his mouth watering.

The AutoChef hissed and burped like a snake with indigestion. 'Please call service with code C6.'

'What?'

'Please call service with code C6.'

'What does that mean?'

'Please call service with –'

'Yeah, yeah, I heard.' Hal reached for the commset on the wall. 'Navcom?'

'Yes, Mr Spacejock?'

'What's error code C6?'

'Obstruction in the dispenser.'

Hal sidled up to the machine, lifted the flap and withdrew a squidgy white ball. 'What the hell's this?' he demanded, sniffing the object.

'According to my records, it's an orange,' said the Navcom.

'It can't be. It's all white!'

'Mould,' said the computer. 'Our landing must have dislodged it from the chute.'

'What was it doing there in the first place?'

'You must have ordered it and forgotten to consume it.'

'Not me,' said Hal, tossing it in the bin. 'I hate the things.'

'Perhaps you ordered something which rhymes with orange?'

'Oh yeah?' Hal put his hands on his hips. 'Like what?'

'Like er … er … er … ' There was a crackle and the overhead lights flickered.

'Navcom?' called Hal.

'Boot sequence initiated,' said the computer. 'Requested information unavailable.'

'Don't bother. I'll deal with it myself.'

The AutoChef whirred and shuddered, and soon Hal could smell frying onion, cooking meat and hot bread. His mouth watered some more, and then the machine beeped and a green light shone in the corner of the display panel.

Hal peered in the slot. Inside, a soggy-looking bun sat on a curled paper plate. He took it out and opened the bun, revealing a narrow strip of meat-coloured goo. 'Thirty-five centuries of technology, and this is the best we can do?'

The AutoChef beeped again, and several dozen fries cascaded from the slot, straight onto the carpet. Hal picked up one of the curly grey shapes and frowned at it. 'Is this supposed to be a chip?' he demanded, as it fell in half.

The AutoChef beeped.

Still muttering to himself, Hal scooped up the fries and took his meal to an armchair. He put his plate on the armrest, turning away to select a title from the bookshelf. When he turned back the plate was gone.

Hal gaped at the empty armrest, then leaned over the side of the chair to look at the equally empty floor. At that moment he heard frenzied snacking sounds from directly behind the armchair, as if someone were thoroughly enjoying his meal.

'Danny,' muttered Hal. He reached over the back of the armchair and grabbed a generous handful of hair. 'Come out of there, you thieving little monkey!' he shouted, hauling the offender upright. His eyes widened as he saw his catch: an orange ape, about a metre in height, with soft, downy hair, an oval face and large brown eyes. The eyes stared at Hal in shock, and his heart sank as realisation dawned. It was one of the creatures from Oliape II.

The ape whimpered, pawing at his hand. 'All right girl, it's not your fault.' Hal let go, and the creature ducked down and began stuffing fries into her mouth. 'Hungry, eh? That's it, eat up.'

The ape sniffed around for the last crumbs then looked up, licking her lips.

'A drink, eh?' Hal turned to the AutoChef. 'Give me a chocolate thickshake.'

'Unknown food or beverage.'

'Milkshake. Chocolate.'

The AutoChef hissed and burped. 'Please call service with code C9.'

Hal operated the intercom. 'Navcom?'

'Yes, Mr Spacejock?'

'What's code C9?'

'Raw material required.'

'How do I fix that?'

'The AutoChef is an environmentally friendly device which maximises the re-use of organic material while simultaneously reducing your waste bill.'

'Organic material? Waste?' Hal stared at the machine. 'That doesn't mean . . .'

'Yes,' said the Navcom. 'To supply more raw material, you need to go to the bathroom.'

'Urgh!'

'However, it does have an emergency reserve. I shall activate it now.'

There was a noise like a flushing toilet, and the machine began to rumble and shake. The ape was watching intently, and when a paper cup appeared in the slot, she rushed over and crammed it in her mouth. While she chewed, the machine sprayed a stream of brown liquid straight onto the floor. The ape spat out the chewed cup and threw herself at the mess, licking it straight off the carpet. When she'd finished, she looked up at him hopefully.

Hal patted himself on the chest. 'I'm Hal,' he said. 'You can be, er, Lucy.'

The ape pointed at the AutoChef.

'Still hungry, eh?' Hal grinned. 'AutoChef, give me another chocolate milkshake.'

Sonya woke up with her cheek pressed to the cold engine-room floor and a headache like a throbbing quasar. She probed the back of her head and winced as she found a huge lump. Suddenly she remembered the grasping hands reaching out of the darkness. She stared into the deep shadowy corners of the engine room. Where was it? *What* was it?

A hammer blow nearby made her jump. She looked towards the source of light, and through a gap in the main drives she saw a couple of workmen fixing the generators. As smoothly as possible, she backed towards the wall, away from the exposed area.

She found the cylinder lying on its side, the top discarded nearby. The toolkit had been rifled, the heavy fabric torn and the contents strewn around. The briefcase was under the hyperdrive. Sonya replaced the conduit, keeping a wary eye on the pool of light spilling from the generator alcove. Once the connector was tight, she gathered the remains of her toolkit and pushed them into the cylinder with the briefcase. She added the pressurised tank, jammed the cap on top and glanced around to see if she'd missed anything.

She found the helmet and pushed it down over her throbbing head, stood up and hurried towards the doorway. The passage was deserted, the only sound a vigorous hammering from the generator room behind her - that, and the relentless thudding inside her head. Slipping out of the engine room, she crept to the cargo hold door, which opened silently to her touch.

The hold was almost empty. Three or four cage-like crates

were lined up near the exit, and even as she watched one was hoisted out by a heavy crane. Without stopping to think, she ran across the cargo bay and climbed up the side of a crate. There was a lid on top - a pair of hinged metal flaps. Sonya lifted them and pushed her gear in, then slipped inside and stretched out on the layer of plastic-covered rolls.

Twice, the cage jerked towards the back of the hold. Each time Sonya heard the growl of the crane, the clink of the hook going into the ring, the squeal as the crate's metal legs rubbed on the deck plates. Then it was her turn. The hook rattled overhead, the crane roared and the cage groaned as it swung through the air. It thumped down and Sonya raised the flap. She saw the back of the ship towering above, saw Sam and Nat nearby, fighting over an inspection rod. They looked on in amazement as Sonya popped out of the crate, dropped lightly to the ground and strolled towards the equipment shed with the canister slung casually over her shoulder.

— 11 —

Clunk followed Arlene through the museum, navigating a maze of pale green corridors that brought them to a large, well-lit room overflowing with packing cases, bustling workers and half-assembled exhibits.

'We've managed to collect all these items from your era,' said Arlene proudly.

Clunk scanned the room with interest. He spotted an ancient groundcar, microwave toasters, early model vidscreens and several large computers. There were old food tins, drink bottles and newspapers, and even old film posters on the wall - yellowed and curling, they nevertheless evoked long-forgotten memories. 'Amazing,' said Clunk. He felt a tug and looked down - someone had fastened a tag to his wrist. 'Robot, Spacejock' it said, in flowing script.

'Don't lose that,' said Arlene. 'Otherwise we won't know who you belong to.'

'I'd just tell you.'

'Sorry, no.' Arlene shook her head. 'We had four robots at our last exhibition. Three were scavenged from the local tip and one was on loan from a wealthy collector. Afterwards, all four claimed they were the collector's. This time we're using tags.'

'What happened to the other three robots?' asked Clunk.

'Back to the tip, of course. Now, come with me. We need to prepare you.'

'Prepare?'

'We can't put you on display in that condition. You need to look older.'

'But Mr Spacejock told me to polish myself!'

'Your owner may be an excellent pilot, but this is my area of expertise.' Arlene waved at a young woman who was spraying mud onto an old bicycle. 'Helga! When you're free!' She glanced at Clunk. 'Work experience,' she said by way of explanation. 'Just look at the terrific job she's done on that display.'

Clunk followed Arlene's pointed finger and saw a tubby robot with a thick black wig, a white, spangled suit and a pair of dark sunglasses. He frowned and looked closer. 'I thought the last of those disappeared years ago.'

'You recognise it?'

'Yes, it's a pleasurebot.'

'Oh.' Arlene took out a coloured leaflet and looked at it carefully. 'We identified it as a Pelvisator.'

'That's the brand name. They used to go like the clappers, but the off switch was too small. There were several cases of people being pummelled unconscious under the –'

Arlene held up her hand. 'That's quite enough.' She spotted a young man haphazardly stacking delicate china dishes on a wobbly table. 'Oh my goodness. Wait here,' she said, hurrying away.

Clunk glanced around, then froze. On the workbench beside him sat a disembodied head that was connected to a box with coloured wire. He bent for a closer look and the eyes blinked open.

'The name's Ed,' said the skull. 'Who are you?'

'Where's the rest of your body?'

'An unfortunate accident with a road grader,' said Ed. 'Still, I can't complain.'

'It's not right, you being kept like that. We're not designed to operate piecemeal.'

'Oh, I don't mind. I keep busy doing odd jobs.'

'What sort of jobs can a head do?' asked Clunk, puzzled.

'I was the bookkeeper for a small repair firm. You know . . . manage the inventory, do the accounts, that sort of thing.'

'Sounds like a bundle of fun.'

'Mock all you like. I have got an arts degree, you know.'

'Really?'

'Yup. External student.'

'How did you pay for it?'

'Year after year, I transferred the shop's funds into a high-interest account after close of business. I had to get the money back into the firm's account by morning, of course, but I managed to scalp the difference. Once I'd put enough aside, I began to trade the futures market.'

'Did you make much?'

Ed thought for a moment. 'Two point seven million credits.'

'Two –' Clunk's voice failed. 'What are you doing here if you're worth that kind of money?'

'The shop owners found out. Now they're living in luxury and I'm . . . ' Ed blinked. 'Well, I'm here.'

'You ought to get a position with a financial services company. With your skills they'd get you a whole new body.'

'But I'm happy here. I mean, the roof doesn't leak and I'm hooked into the network. What more could I want?' Ed glanced at the window. 'Out there I'd only have to deal with petty jealousy and backstabbing humans.'

'My owner isn't like that.'

'He doesn't resent your superior abilities?'

'He doesn't know they're superior.'

'Exactly.' Ed's eyes widened. 'Ah, I see who you are. You're Clunk.'

'Correct.'

'Funny name for a robot.'

'This, from a talking Ed.'

The head sniffed. 'At least I'm here voluntarily.' He glanced to his right. 'Heads up, humans inbound at three o'clock.'

Arlene hurried up with the work experience student in tow. 'Helga, this is Clunk. I want you to make him look old.'

The girl sized Clunk up. 'This should not be a problem,' she said slowly. 'I will place mud on his torso, perhaps an additional dent or two ...'

Clunk shook his head. 'I'm afraid I can't permit that.'

Helga spotted the tag hanging from his wrist. 'Sorry, I thought you were one of the junky robots.' She shrugged. 'No dents. I will just dirty you up.'

'Oh no you –'

'She's very artistic,' Arlene broke in. 'And it's not real dirt, it's a chemical substitute. It'll wash off afterwards.'

'But –'

Arlene frowned. 'I'm finding you a little uncooperative. I've a good mind to call Captain Spacejock and tell him to collect you.'

Clunk opened his mouth to agree, just as Helga slapped a handful of fake mud in his face.

'Ullimo Museum,' said the old man on the screen.

Hal took his feet off the console. 'I need to speak to Arlene.'

'She's busy with new arrivals. Can I help?'

'Maybe. Did you see an old bronze robot arrive in a cab?'

'Yes, I did. Arlene met him at the door and took him to the exhibit.'

'Great, thanks for that.' Hal cut the connection and toyed with a bank of switches. 'Navcom, what are those mechanics doing? They've been ages.'

Just then, the lift doors parted and Tom stepped out. 'All done, sir. I just need your authorisation for the bill.' He fished in his overalls and withdrew a chunky notepad. 'Guild number?'

'Bill?' said Hal in surprise. 'It's under warranty!'

'I'm afraid not. The cooling pipes were crimped, restricting the flow of lubricant to the armature, which ...'

Hal raised his hands. 'Leave it with me and I'll get the insurance people onto it.'

'I need your authorisation first.'

Hal looked at the notepad. 'How do I do that?'

'Just enter your Guild number.'

'I don't have one.'

Tom looked around in surprise. 'With a nice ship like this? All right, just press your thumb on the grey area. Yeah, like that. It reads your print and –'

'OW!' yelled Hal.

'- takes a DNA sample at the same time. Doesn't hurt too bad.'

Hal studied the drop of blood welling from the end of his thumb. 'I bet you're a real hit with the kids.'

Tom snorted. 'That's nothing, you should see what happens

if you don't pay the bill.' He beckoned to his assistant. 'Come on, lad. The competition.'

Danny sighed. 'Do I have to?'

'Want a clip round the lug 'ole?'

'Okay, okay. I'm doin' it.' The young man reached into his overalls and took out a pen and a dog-eared book of tickets. 'Name?'

'Not like that! Do it properly!'

Hal cleared his throat. 'Look, I'm kind of busy right now. Why don't you –'

'It's really good,' said Tom. 'Let him finish.'

'I ain't even got started,' complained Danny.

'Go on, lad.'

Danny squinted at the ticket. 'Presenting the Sergeant Electrical Win-a-Robot competition. First prize ... a robot!'

Hal shrugged. 'I've already got one.'

'If you win, you could sell it,' said Tom encouragingly.

'How much are the tickets?'

'Nuffink,' said Danny sourly, as if the winnings were being deducted from his wages. 'Second prize –'

'I'll take a dozen tickets. Now let me show you out.'

'One per ship.'

'I'll have one, then,' said Hal.

'Name?'

Hal told him, and watched impatiently as the young man scribbled it on the booklet.

'What's yer ship?'

'You know that, lad,' said Tom. 'She's the *Volante*. Nice one, too.'

'And it has a wonderful airlock,' said Hal. 'Would you like to see it?'

Danny scrawled on the ticket, ripped it off and held it out. 'Finishes today. Don't lose it.'

'C'mon Danny,' said Tom. 'We got that Rigel class to strip before tea.'

The young man grunted, and together they entered the airlock. Hal closed the outer door on them and returned to the flight deck. 'Right, let's get moving. Loading dock twelve.'

◆

Clunk waited impatiently as his systems booted up. Until they were ready, he could neither see nor hear - all he knew was that something had triggered his external sensors.

'I tell yer it's a jiggler,' said a voice.

Clunk glanced around, but the hall was empty. Then he looked down and saw a pair of old ladies standing below his pedestal, heads level with his pelvis, necks craned as they examined him closely. One of them took out a leaflet. 'Says here –'

'I don't care what it says,' replied the other, pursing her lips. ''E's a jiggler.'

'He ain't! He's all 'ard and lumpy!'

Her companion dug her in the ribs. 'That's wot jigglers are supposed ter be like.'

As the ladies cackled with laughter, Clunk bent down until his face was almost level with theirs. 'Good afternoon, ladies.'

'It moved!' shrieked one.

'I thought you was all models!' gasped the other.

'On the contrary, I am a fully functioning XG99. I was manufactured in the year –'

116

'Are you a jiggler or not?' demanded one of the women.

Clunk turned and pointed to the next display, where the pleasurebot had been arranged in a dramatic pose. 'Madam, I believe that is the robot you are looking for.'

The women hurried over to the display and began to inspect it closely. As their ribald comments drifted across the deserted hall, Clunk looked around. He'd seen most of the exhibits on the way in, and there were no visitors to speak of. He was about to return to standby when he saw a young man in customs uniform push through the main doors. The man looked around, saw Clunk and made straight for him.

'Are you Spacejock's robot?' he asked, his eyes almost hidden under the peaked cap.

'That's me,' said Clunk. 'Is there a problem?'

'I'm just checking Spacejock kept his side of the bargain.'

'What bargain?'

The man grinned. 'He didn't tell you?'

'Tell me what?' asked Clunk with a sinking feeling.

Phillip explained who he was, then lowered his voice. 'Spacejock altered a shipping manifest to cut his import duty, and when I confronted him he offered me a bribe.'

Clunk closed his eyes.

'I could have jailed him for either offence,' continued Phillip. 'But we came to an arrangement. He donated you to the museum.'

Clunk's eyes blinked open. 'Wait a minute. Donated?'

'Absolutely. And you'll stay here until I tell you otherwise,' said Phillip. 'Move from this room and I'll have Spacejock arrested. Is that understood?'

Clunk's head dropped, and he barely noticed as Phillip walked away. Donated to a museum! Why hadn't Mr Spacejock said anything? Suddenly, a horrible thought

117

wormed its way into his brain. Was it permanent? What if Hal never came back for him!

●

Rex Curtis studied a navigation chart on his terminal, rotating and zooming the starfield as he sought a particular type of planet. Now and then he marked a possible, only to discard it after a closer look. He'd just selected a new region of space when his intercom buzzed. 'Yes?'

'Ms Polarov to see you.'

'Send her in.'

'And I have Mac on line three.'

Curtis pressed a button. 'Go ahead.'

'Mac here. You know that ship you're watching? The *Volante*?'

'What about it?'

'It's moved to loading dock twelve.'

'Fine. Get rid of the loading bay staff. Give them the day off.'

'I can't do that. Ground control shows three ships coming in.'

'Send them home or I'll have them all sacked. Understood?'

'I'll see what I can do,' said Mac.

'You won't, you'll do exactly as I say.' Rex cut him off, and looked up as Sonya walked in. 'Excellent work, Ms Polarov,' he said, forcing a smile. 'You pulled off a daring mission with ease.'

Sonya rubbed her head. 'His pet damn near killed me, though.'

'Pet? What kind of pet?'

'I don't know. All orange fur and claws.'

'It attacked you?'

'It startled me, and I tripped over and knocked myself out. And it's got a decent set of teeth. Look at these.' Sonya held up her sunglasses, which had a half-chewed arm and a missing lens. 'Did the same to the other equipment.'

'Spacejock must be starving the thing,' said Rex. 'Still, you got the data.'

Sonya nodded. 'So, now I get my permanent job? My employment letter?'

'Almost.'

'What do you mean almost? I just –'

The terminal on the desk beeped, and a screenful of dots appeared. Rex took a pair of heavy black glasses from his drawer and put them on. The glasses hummed and crackled, and after adjusting the short antenna, he leant forward to read the coded message. 'It's from Dent. He's got the ship's data out of Bobby and he's writing a program which will crock the ship.' He peered closer. 'Oh - crack.' He removed the glasses, which left a pair of angry red circles around his eyes. 'What are you grinning at?'

'Another of Dent's inventions?'

'I don't know what you have against him,' said Rex, putting the glasses on his desk. 'He's got a brilliant mind.'

'That's true. He can run rings around anyone.'

'Dent's doing his part in all this.' Rex leaned across the desk, and Sonya bit her lip at the looming red circles. 'What else did you discover? What about the robot?'

'It's old. Looks like he got it out of a dumpster.'

'It could still interfere with my plans. It'll have to be dealt with.'

Sonya frowned. 'Aren't you going to a lot of trouble? I mean, it's not the end of the world if Spacejock delivers this freight.'

'If he completes this job he'll get others. Understand? And it's not just Central Bank: more and more companies will try the privateers, and the more they earn the faster they'll upgrade their ships. Do you know what'll happen then? Curtis Freightlines will go broke, and these bastards will sneak along to the liquidation sale and pick up all my ships for nothing. Am I getting through to you?'

Sonya nodded.

'If I can stop the trickle, the flood might never happen. Discredit Spacejock, and what chance does a privateer in a rust bucket have? I'm telling you, we're going to stop this guy and we're going to stop him good.'

'What about a missile?'

'Are you mad?' Rex stared at her. 'I'm running a business, not a war.'

'Dent has enough weapons in his basement to start a revolution.'

Rex made a noise. 'That's just a show of strength. We'd never use the stuff.'

'Never?'

'When you're locked in delicate negotiations with a competitor, waving a shoulder-launched missile can sometimes free up the situation.' Rex shrugged. 'We're not negotiating with Spacejock. We only have to delay him, so there's no need for confrontation.'

'Can't ground control hold him up?'

Rex shook his head. 'Not for long enough. He could hire another ship, or call the bank and tell them he's being delayed. They'd investigate and we'd be in trouble.' The terminal beeped, and another screen of dots appeared. Rex donned his glasses and read the message. 'Dent's got some information out of the briefcase. Apparently Spacejock donated his robot to a local museum for the day.' Rex frowned. 'Strange, he doesn't strike me as a public-spirited individual. Still, whatever the reason we've got a few hours to set everything up.' Rex removed the glasses, which left even bigger circles around his eyes. 'I'll get someone to nobble the robot, and you –'

'And I can have my employment letter.'

'Not now! My whole business is at stake here!'

'So is my future!' Sonya tapped her finger on the desk. 'Immigration called last night. This is my last chance before they deport me.'

Rex spread his hands. 'I sympathise, Ms Polarov. But please understand, this is vital to me.'

'I will not be used, Mr Curtis.'

'Used? Are you telling me you wouldn't like a position on the ninth floor? A company car?' Rex smiled. 'There are many kinds of jobs, Ms Polarov. If you want to eke out a living on a minimum wage just say so, and I'll sign a letter right now. On the other hand, if you see this Spacejock problem through to the end I'll promote you so fast your head will spin.'

Sonya's head *was* spinning. Whether it was the knock she'd received aboard the Volante, or the life of comfort suddenly laid out before her, she didn't know. All she knew was that her dreams were finally within her grasp. All she had to do was reach out and . . . 'I'll do it,' she said.

'No doubts? No more demands for employment letters?'

Sonya shook her head, wincing at the sudden stab of pain. 'I'll do what you ask. It's Spacejock or me, winner takes all.'

Rex beamed. 'Excellent. And with the resources of Curtis Freightlines behind you, I guarantee it won't be Spacejock. Now, this is what we're going to do . . .'

121

The hold was in darkness when Hal arrived, and he stumbled over the slick decking as he made his way to the rear doors. He found the controls and the cargo ramp began to move, hissing and whining as it dropped to the ground. The ship trembled slightly as the buffers on the huge slab of metal met the concrete landing pad, then the whining ceased.

Hal stepped onto the edge of the ramp and looked down. It was not an inspiring sight.

Loading bay twelve was a large open area dotted with rotting wooden pallets, crumpled rain-soaked boxes and rusty scraps of metal. Nearby, smoke belched from a bent chimney atop a ramshackle shed. The windows were cracked and grimy, the wooden boards warped and bleached, and it looked as if a faint breeze could knock the structure down.

At the back of the lot there were several rows of shrink-wrapped pallets, and a battered lifter stood nearby, its oil-streaked bodywork rusting quietly. Hal strode down the ramp and picked his way through the knee-high weeds growing through cracks in the concrete. He arrived at the shed and knocked on the door, a splintered sheet of plywood hanging from rope hinges.

'Whaddya want?' growled a voice from within.

'The *Volante*,' called Hal. 'I'm here for the Central Bank pallets.'

A chair scraped and the door creaked open. A heavy, red face appeared, all sweat and grime and stubble. 'Are you Spacejock?' the man asked, his bloodshot eyes full of suspicion.

'That's me. And you are . . . ?'

'I'm the foreman. Driver's sick. Come back tomorrow.'

Hal stuck his foot out as the door began to close, and there was a creak as the thin plywood bowed. 'This is urgent. Can't you drive the lifter yourself?'

'Stuffed me back,' growled the foreman. 'No rush. Come back tomorrow.'

'I've got to deliver this cargo tonight. Can't I load it?'

'Gotta ticket?'

'Ticket?' Hal imagined dozens of pilots standing in a queue, each clutching a number.

'License. Or a Guild card. Can't drive the lifter without.'

Hal shook his head.

'So come back tomorrow.' The foreman kicked Hal's foot away and slammed the door, shaking the thin walls.

Hal looked at the shed, wondering whether he had enough rope to go around it a couple of times. Then again, the foreman only had to smash a window and yell for help. Back in the cargo hold, he activated the intercom. 'Navcom, do you know what a cargo lifter's ticket looks like?'

'Affirmative.'

'Can you print a copy?'

There was a slight delay. 'I can.'

'How about sticking my name on it?'

'Negative. That's forgery.'

'I need it to play a trick on someone. A bit of a joke.'

'It's still not allowed.'

'Okay, print me a blank one.'

'Complying. I shall output to the nearest device.'

'Where's that?'

'Recreation room.'

'On my way.'

◆

Once Sonya had left, Rex reached for his commset and dialled a number. Ten minutes later he'd finally beaten the Ullimo Customs Department's automated answering system into submission. 'Phillip? Is that you?'

'Speaking.'

'Rex Curtis. I need a favour.'

'What kind of favour?' asked Phillip warily.

'A mutual friend lent his robot to the Ullimo Museum this morning. We have to dispose of it.'

'I'm afraid that's impossible. My aunt has the robot in an exhibition.'

'And I want it at the bottom of a lake. Preferably in little pieces.'

'I can't just steal it!'

'No?' Curtis moved the mouthpiece closer. 'Tell me, did anyone find that bank account I set up for you?'

There was a long silence. 'I can't do this, Mr Curtis.'

'Call me when the robot has been disposed of.' Curtis replaced the handset, shaking his head sadly. What was the galaxy coming to? In the old days customs officers stayed bought.

He turned back to his terminal and retrieved the star chart. The first planet he set eyes on was Canessa, and a triumphant smile appeared on his face as he read the summary. It was ideal.

◆

With his brand new license tucked safely in his pocket, Hal returned to the ramshackle shed and banged his fist on the door.

'Go away, we're closed!' shouted the foreman.

'I've got a ticket,' shouted Hal through a gap in the wood. He heard the scrape of a chair, and moments later the door creaked open.

'You again?' growled the foreman. 'Whatcher want?'

Hal unfolded the printout and waved it at him. 'One forklift driver's ticket. Where are the keys?'

The foreman ignored the papers. 'There's no fuel in the tank, it needs a service an' the forks are jammed. Come back tomorrow.'

'You see my ship?' said Hal, jerking his thumb at the *Volante.* 'If you don't give me the keys I'm going to accidentally park it on your roof. They'll have to fold you up to get you into the coffin.'

The foreman gazed at the cargo vessel, eyes widening as he took in the solid bulk. 'Behind the door, sir.'

'Thank you kindly.' Hal whipped the key off a bent nail, slammed the door and picked his way through the junk towards the cargo.

The lifter was a sorry-looking piece of equipment - the hydraulic pipes were frayed, the pedals were loose and rusty and half the rim was missing from the steering wheel. Hal sat on the hard plastic seat, inserted the key, and told himself it was better than loading thirty-six pallets by hand. After stomping the pedals once or twice, he turned the key and pressed the starter. The engine burst into life with a bang and a splutter, quickly settling down to a stuttering, rattling rhythm. Hal pulled one of the levers and the forks rose into the air with a loud hiss. After several attempts he lined the forks up with the holes in the first pallet, and the lifter dipped as it took up the weight.

Hal reversed out, selected forward gear and gunned the motor, mowing down weeds as he charged across the lot towards the ship. The lifter roared up the ramp and into the hold, where the clattering engine reverberated like a machine gun in a cave. Hal dropped the pallet and saw it moving sideways on the tracks, rotating slightly as the ship moved it deeper into the hold.

'One down, thirty-five to go,' muttered Hal, as he drove back down the ramp.

◆

Clunk strode along a plain white corridor, accompanied by four heavily armed guards. They had silver badges on their shoulders - small metal shields with the crossed handcuff motif of the Ullimo Corrective Service. One of the guards motioned Clunk towards a white door, and a panel slid open, revealing a small, dark cell beyond. Bare feet padded on concrete and a pale face loomed in the opening. It was Hal.

'Some friend you are,' he said bitterly. 'You abandoned your post at the museum, got yourself caught and dobbed me in! You're nothing but a crappy robot.' Hal's face got closer and his voice rose to a shout. 'Nothing but a crappy robot!'

The guards joined in, until there was a chorus of voices chanting 'Crappy robot!' at him. Clunk turned from the door and one of the guards prodded him in the chest. 'You're nothing but a crappy robot,' he said firmly.

Clunk woke with a jerk, cries of 'Crappy robot!' still ringing in his ears. He looked around in a daze and realised he was standing on his pedestal at the museum, surrounded by a dozen children chanting at the top of their voices: 'Crappy robot, crappy robot, crappy robot!'

Clunk felt pressure on his chest, looked down and saw an overweight youngster scrawling on his breastplate with a marker pen. He snatched the pen from the boy's fingers and jammed it in his mouth, chewing it into fragments with loud scrunches. Then he stepped to the edge of the pedestal and roared, spraying chewed plastic and black ink.

There was a split second of silence, followed by utter chaos. As one, the children ran for cover, screaming in fear. The overweight boy ran faster than any of them, bowling smaller kids over as he raced for the exit.

Clunk looked down at his chest to survey the damage, and a look of outraged indignation appeared on his face. Shaking his fist at the departing kids, he raised his voice over the frightened squeals. 'I'll give you tinpot, you little horrors!'

— 13 —

Hugh Dent was busy at his terminal when Sonya arrived. 'I'll be with you in a minute, m'dear. I'm just modifying your briefcase.'

She watched him placing microscopic components on a circuit. 'What are you doing?'

'It's rather technical.'

'Try me.'

'Very well. Bobby has to be able to manage Spacejock's ship, from navigation to engine control to atmospherics, and I've had to increase the amount of storage allocated to these parallel processes so they can run simultaneously.'

'In other words, you added some memory.'

'Er, yes. But that's not all. The processing cluster in this unit is second to none, but it wasn't enough to handle the strenuous demands of the upcoming mission. To that end, I augmented the cooling system, allowing me to extract the maximum possible utilisation from the hardware.'

'You overclocked it and added some fans.'

'I wouldn't express the modifications in that manner, but yes.' Dent peered at her. 'Tell me, do you have a computing background?'

'I've dabbled.'

128

'A little knowledge can be dangerous.'

'So can a big mouth,' muttered Sonya under her breath.

Dent pressed a button and a circuit board popped out of a slot. He took the board and held it up to the light, nodding to himself as he inspected it.

'What's that?' asked Sonya.

'It's a copy of the Volante's operating system. With this board, Bobby can take over the ship.'

'Why?'

'Mr Curtis asked me to set it up. He's determined to delay this Spacejock character at all costs, you know. In extreme circumstances that includes overpowering the pilot and flying the vessel yourself.' He looked at her. 'You can fly?'

'Only simulators.'

'Trust me, the real thing is much better.'

'Like you would know,' muttered Sonya.

Dent slotted the board into the briefcase and switched it on. The cooling fans started immediately, blasting papers off the desk and shaking the terminal on its mounting. There was a high-pitched whine, and the suction through the inlet was as loud as a spaceship launch in the confines of the lab.

'It's a bit noisy,' said Sonya, raising her voice.

'Wait until it really gets going,' said Dent, switching it off again. 'Now, I've set up a couple of things to help you with this mission.' He showed her a black cable. 'Plug this into any data socket aboard the ship and it will add multiple system failures to the log. The ship can't take off until each one is checked, which should give you several hours leeway.' He held up a warning finger. 'They can be added in flight, but mustn't be activated until you're on the ground. Otherwise the vessel could shut down in space.'

Sonya nodded.

'And this one is rather special,' said Dent, holding up a red cable. 'Plug this into any computer and it will wipe the operating system.'

'That's a bit drastic, isn't it?'

'You'll need it if Bobby is to take control of the ship.' Dent handed the case over. 'Now, the next item. Follow me, please.' He led her to a packing crate, where a large robot was standing amongst drifts of loose straw. As they got closer it lurched from the crate and stood before them, towering over Dent by half a metre. It tilted its head from one side to the other with audible cracks, then fixed Sonya with a stare. 'Friend or foe?' it demanded in a rumbling bass.

'Friend.'

The robot buzzed. 'Database updated. Friend added.'

'What if I'd said enemy?'

The robot's hand shot out and grabbed her round the neck. 'You wish to reclassify?'

'N-no thanks.'

'Very well.' The robot released her.

'As you can see,' began Dent. 'It's –'

The robot spun round and grabbed his neck. 'Friend or foe?' it demanded, lifting the inventor off his feet.

'F-f-friend,' said Dent.

The robot buzzed. 'Database updated. Friend added. Friend limit reached.'

'You can only have two friends?' asked Sonya in surprise.

'Three. I have already met Mr Curtis.'

'How many enemies can you store?'

'One.'

'Is that all?'

The robot shrugged, its shoulders squeaking. 'I replace each one as they're eliminated.'

Sonya looked at Dent. 'Why are you showing me this?'

'We fight fire with fire,' said Dent eagerly. 'Spacejock has a robot, we have a robot.'

'Spacejock had a robot. And if you think he's going to welcome this thing aboard his ship –'

'No, no. We'll get it aboard in your luggage.'

Sonya's eyebrows rose. 'Hell of a suitcase.'

Dent patted the wooden crate. 'I have five more of these waiting on a truck outside. They're filled with stores and equipment . . . exactly the sort of items you'd take on a trip like this. Should the need arise you can release the robot and –'

'Watch it go mental and spend the rest of my life in jail. Listen, Mr Curtis said killing was out.'

'I'll reprogram it. There's more than one violence setting.'

'Sure. Deadly and lethal.' Sonya looked up at the robot's square face. 'What's your name?'

The robot looked at the floor. 'Tinker,' it said, shuffling its feet.

Sonya snorted, turning it into a cough as the robot glared at her. 'So, Tinker. Will you obey my orders?'

'To the letter.'

'You see?' said Dent. 'This robot is completely under your control. Nobody will get hurt.'

Suddenly his commset buzzed. He picked up the handset and listened, then turned to Sonya, his eyes wide with shock. 'It's Spacejock. He's loading the cargo himself!'

'Surely Mr Curtis can have him delayed? He's got half the spaceport in his pocket.'

'He's done all he can.' Dent waved Sonya towards the door. 'Take a cab to the dock. You must hold Spacejock up until we're ready.'

'How?' Sonya saw Dent's expression. 'Yeah. Never mind.'

131

The Ullimo Museum presents two faces. Visitors see polished marble and chrome, heavy glass doors and soft downlights, while staff put up with dank, poorly lit corridors and gurgling pipes. They got heavy doors too, but unlike the smooth automatics in the museum proper theirs were thick slabs of metal on stiff hinges.

Phillip strode along one of the dankest, darkest passageways, checking floor markers against a printed map as he passed one rattling, gurgling pipe after another. He kept a firm grip on the map - as a child he'd got lost in these corridors once, had spent hours running along one identical passage after another, sobbing with fear and self-pity, until he finally burst through a door into his aunt's warm, cosy office. Expecting to be greeted with soothing hugs and a chocolate biscuit or two, he was hurt that she hadn't even noticed he was missing, surprised to discover he'd only been gone fifteen minutes, and stunned when she told him off for making such a fuss.

Phillip pushed the uncomfortable memory away. Bloody Curtis! All right, so he owed the man a favour, but traipsing around the museum's corridors to steal a robot in the middle of the day was too much. Not that he was going to steal it - persuasion was the key. Convince it to walk out under its own steam. Get it to the robot shop, where they had the tools to subdue it.

What if the robot refused to cooperate? It had seemed placid enough when he'd checked up on it earlier, but taking it from the exhibition was another matter. The last thing he wanted was a public shouting match followed by a close encounter with his aunt.

Phillip stopped at a narrow door and checked the symbol against the map. Main hall, rear entrance. This was it. The door creaked open and he peered through the gap. He was right behind one of the exhibits, a chunky robot in a snowy white suit, its sequins like scattered stars under the overhead lights. Looking to his left, Phillip saw Clunk just a few metres away, standing completely still with his back to the wall.

Phillip bit his lip. Damn Curtis and his unreasonable demands! Why couldn't he send someone else to ...

At that moment, Phillip spotted the tag hanging from Clunk's wrist. Of course! Without ID, the robot would be carted away and dumped as soon as the exhibition closed! His aunt had often bemoaned the unseemly fracas after the last exhibition, when four robots had beaten the scrap out of each other, desperate to claim an owner and stay out of the dumpster. Phillip smiled to himself. Clunk was sure to argue, and the clean-up staff would be forced to disable him. Then he could step in and have them put the robot in his car.

Holding his breath, he slid through the doorway and approached the robot, treading carefully. As he got closer he took a penknife from his pocket, wincing as the scissor attachment snicked open. Two metres, one metre, half a step ... with a trembling hand, he reached up and fed the thin cord into the blades.

Snip!

His heart skipped a beat as the noise seemed to echo from the walls, but the robot didn't stir. Phillip grabbed the tag and retreated, jamming the piece of card into his pocket. The door thudded to and Phillip hurried along the darkened passage, his shoes clattering on the hard floor as he headed for the exit.

Clunk woke with a start, aware of a subtle difference in his environment: the lights were off and the exhibition hall was deserted, although he could see movement near the entrance. He was straining to make out who it was when he heard a noise to his right. Turning to look, he saw a couple of workmen manoeuvring the pleasurebot onto a trolley. As they were lifting it from the pedestal it slipped out of their grasp and toppled headlong to the floor. One of the men cursed loudly as the robot's shoulder landed on his toes.

'Mind your language,' hissed the second man. 'This is a family show.'

'Just get it off me bloody foot!'

The second man leaned over and started to pull, just as the first workman gave the robot a hefty shove.

'Ow, shit!' yelled the second man, as it rolled straight onto his toes.

Finally, they got the robot onto the trolley and pushed it out of the hall, taking it in turns to limp alongside.

Clunk shook his head sadly. How did a bone-wielding, cave-dwelling species like the human race ever manage to escape their home planet and populate the galaxy? He tried to calculate the odds, but quickly ran out of significant digits. While he was busy the men limped back with their trolley. Clunk watched them, wondering which hapless cast-off they were going to wheel away next. Then he realised they were heading straight for him.

'You take the back this time,' said the first workman.

'Why don't we knock it over and roll it onto the trolley?'

Clunk made a throat-clearing sound. 'That won't be necessary, gentlemen.'

'Oh great, this one's going to bash our ears as well.'

'You see, I have an owner.'

The workmen shaded their eyes and looked around the empty hall. 'You see an owner, William?'

'Not me, Walter.'

'He's not here, he's delivering a cargo,' said Clunk, suppressing the urge to ram their thick heads together.

'How d'you know when a robot's talking crap?' asked Walter.

William shrugged.

'When there's noise coming out its mouth.'

The men laughed.

'I tell you I have an owner!' growled Clunk, clenching his fists.

'Oh no you don't,' said the men in unison.

'I do!' shouted Clunk, raising his arm. 'See? Here's my tag!'

The men exchanged a glance. 'This one's going to be difficult,' said William.

Walter nodded. 'Deluded.'

Clunk stared at his naked wrist in shock. Where was the tag? His eyes whirred as he looked down, left and right ... even up at the ceiling. 'It must have fallen off,' he said, stepping off the pedestal. 'It can't have gone far.'

As one, the workmen drew stunners from their belts.

Clunk backed away, hands raised. 'Now, gentlemen. There's no need to –'

Zap! There was a flash of green light and he felt the power drain from his circuits. He toppled backwards and landed with a crash on the hard floor, and was barely conscious when the men approached.

'Bit of a waste to throw this one away,' said Walter.

'Here, you don't think ... ' William hesitated.

'Spit it out.'

'We're supposed to junk these things, right?'

'That's the idea.'

'This one could be worth a bit. You know ... as scrap.'

An icy chill rushed through Clunk's circuits. No! He tried to speak, tried to lift a finger, but it was all he could do to stay conscious. Dimly, he was aware of approaching footsteps.

'What do you want?' he heard William demand.

'You'll address me as Mr Farquhar,' said a cold voice.

'Yes, Mr Farker,' grumbled William.

'What's going on here?'

'We're clearing the exhibit,' said Walter. 'Sir,' he added, as an afterthought.

Clunk sensed someone leaning over him, and then a surge of hope rushed through his circuits as Phillip's face swam into view. He knew about the loan! He was saved! The burst of energy freed his speech processor, and with his last reserves he raised his head and croaked out a single word: 'Hal!'

'Who's Hal?' asked William.

'I have no idea,' said Phillip. 'Now, I want this robot loaded into my vehicle.'

'But –'

'Immediately, you hear? My aunt gave explicit instructions.'

'Yes sir,' grumbled Walter.

Devastated, betrayed, Clunk could only listen to the exchange. He could feel darkness approaching as his systems shut down, starved of power.

'You couldn't give us a hand?' asked William. 'Only it's a bit heavy, see?'

'Oh, very well. What do you want me to do?'

136

'We'll stand here and you stand there. You pull, we push.'

Clunk felt hands pulling and pushing him, tipping him over. Just before he blacked out completely he felt his shoulder roll onto the toes of Phillip's soft leather shoes.

He didn't even hear the human's cry of agony.

'Come on, come on,' urged Sonya, willing the taxi on. 'Can't you go any faster?'

'This is the legal limit,' said the robot driver firmly.

'What's the illegal limit?'

'Unknown. I have a governor which constrains me in every way.'

'I know how you feel,' muttered Sonya.

The robot glanced over its shoulder. 'If you don't mind me asking, what's the hurry?'

'If I want an electric gizmo poking into my business I'll buy a - LOOK OUT!'

The taxi swerved, narrowly missing a courier on a jetbike. The robot driver scanned the courier's squawk code and reported it to the authorities. 'He's lucky to be alive,' he commented, after performing this vital civic duty.

'You have my permission to go straight through the next one, if it'll get us there quicker,' said Sonya.

'That's not advisable,' the briefcase by her side piped up. 'Inciting a taxi driver to break the law is a major offence.'

'Oh, shut up.'

'I am unable to shut up, as you so indelicately put it. My programming dictates my behaviour.'

'Ain't that the truth,' said the driver over his shoulder.

Sonya picked up the briefcase. 'Any more lip out of you and I'll heave you through the window. Got it?'

'I couldn't allow that,' said the driver.

'What, now you defend stray briefcases?'

'No, I'd have to report you for littering.'

◆

Hal manoeuvred the lifter around the Volante's cargo hold one last time, holding his breath against the fumes belching from the rusty exhaust. His flight suit was soaked with sweat and stuck to him like cling wrap. His shoulders ached from wrestling with the heavy steering wheel and his hair and face were gritty with dust.

He'd just placed the last pallet in the hold when the engine coughed. 'Come on!' muttered Hal as he backed towards the ramp. Halfway there, the engine spluttered and died. Hal willed the machine backwards, but it rolled to a halt.

'Great, just great.' Hal leaned forward and tapped the fuel gauge, but it pointed resolutely to empty. He got out of the machine and looked across the hold towards the cargo ramp, which was at least fifteen metres away. Stuck for ideas, he activated the commset near the rear doors. 'Navcom, the lifter's run out of fuel. Have we got anything I can use to get it off the ship?'

'Checking inventory.' After a slight delay, the computer came back. 'Negative.'

Hal eyed the lifter, estimating the distance to the top of the cargo ramp. He was too tired to push the thing all that way, but what if ... 'Navcom, can you lower the ship at the back?'

'How many degrees?'

'All of them.'

'Please specify a number from zero to forty-five.'

Hal's knowledge of trig was sketchy, so he picked a nice round number. 'Try twenty.' Immediately, the rear of the ship dropped like a stone, throwing him off balance. 'Too much!' he shouted. 'Five degrees! Five!'

Too late. There was a rumble as the lifter hurtled towards him, and he barely dived aside as it thundered past, still gathering speed. It rocketed down the ramp, and as Hal watched, horrified, the heavy machine slammed into a corner of the foreman's shed. There was a crash as the lightweight structure fell apart, revealing the foreman sitting at a table with a teacup halfway to his mouth.

Hal leapt up and pressed the intercom button. 'Shut the ramp and get the engines going. Hurry.'

The cargo ramp jerked free of the ground and began to rise towards him. As it came level with the back of the ship, Hal saw a silver taxi scream into the yard. The car slewed to a halt, and he caught a glimpse of the woman in the back seat before the ramp hid the car from view.

'This can't be good,' muttered Hal. He ran for the inner door, and was halfway to the lift when the engines fired with a deep rumble. Moments later, he stepped into the flight deck. 'Get me ground clearance.'

'Complying. Prepare for take-off.'

Hal sat in the pilot's chair and snapped the seatbelt together. 'Make it fast, okay? That foreman could be a problem. Someone else just rocked up, too.' Hardly had the words left his mouth when a message indicator began to flash.

'They're asking us to hold,' said the Navcom.

'Ignore them,' shouted Hal over the rising noise of the main engines. Moments later, the ship began to move.

'Clear of the pad,' called the Navcom. 'Twenty metres and climbing.'

'Keep her steady,' said Hal, thinking he should be involved somehow.

'I can do nothing but,' said the computer calmly. 'What is our destination?'

Hal thought for a moment. 'We ought to do the bank, but that's a long haul for Lucy. Can we drop her off first?'

'Destination confirmed as Oliape II,' said the computer. 'ETA one hour.'

'And the bank after that?'

'ETA three hours.'

Hal grinned. 'This is how it's supposed to be. Load up, deliver, collect payment.'

'One out of three isn't bad,' said the computer.

Sonya crouched behind the fallen lifter as the *Volante's* engines blew clouds of dust across the dockyard. The noise was terrific, a howling roar which shook her teeth to their roots. A moment or two later she risked a quick look, only to see the ship high overhead and getting smaller by the second. As soon as she could make herself heard, she advanced on the foreman, who was sitting at the table with the mug of tea still half-raised to his lips. 'You were supposed to hold him up, you moron!'

The foreman gave her a long, disturbed look. 'Arrr,' he said eventually.

Sonya slammed her fist on the battered table, the only level surface in sight. 'I nearly had him!' she yelled. 'You let him go, just like that!'

'He used the lifter,' said the foreman, as if that were explanation enough for anyone.

Sonya looked around, seeing the damage for the first time. The walls of the shed had exploded outwards and were scattered around in pieces. The battered lifter had an old filing cabinet impaled on the forks, and there were shredded shipping dockets everywhere. 'Did Spacejock do all this?' she demanded.

'Arrr.'

'Shit,' said Sonya, with a hint of admiration. 'Some character.' After a last look at the pinpoint of light overhead, she walked back to the cab. 'Take me back to Curtis Freightlines.'

'I trust your journey was worthwhile?' said the driver.

'Shut up and drive,' snapped Sonya.

◆

The Volante roared away from Ullimo, heading for the outbound hyperspace point. Hal was in the flight deck with a cup of coffee in his hand, standing by the console in case anything went wrong. According to the flight manual, being on the spot in an emergency was an important part of being in command. It was somewhat less forthcoming on the actual procedure, although the cartoon of a lantern-jawed hero rescuing a child from a stricken spaceship was encouraging.

Hal was just taking a sip of coffee when a red light flashed on the console. 'What's that? What's gone wrong now?'

'It's an inbound call. Ullimo Museum.'

Hal breathed a sigh of relief. 'I thought it was something nasty. All right, put them on.'

Arlene appeared on the screen, looking flustered. 'Captain Spacejock, I'm sorry to call you like this. We closed the exhibition after an incident with one of the displays, and now your robot is missing.'

'What do you mean, missing?'

'He's gone. I'm calling to see whether he returned to your spaceship.'

'I haven't seen him all day.' Hal frowned. 'He's not the sort to do a runner. Are you sure he's not charging his batteries somewhere?'

'I suppose that's possible, although my people assure me they searched the hall.'

'Maybe he ducked into a corridor. Can't you get them to search the whole place?'

'We'll get onto it right away, Mr Spacejock.'

Hal cut the connection, and the screen switched to a star map with Ullimo and Oliape II highlighted. In the corner, the hyperspace countdown had frozen. 'What happened to the jump?'

'Suspended pending our return to Ullimo.'

'We're not going to Ullimo. We're going to Oliape.'

The Navcom was silent. The counter didn't move.

'Navcom? Start the jump.'

'Clunk is on Ullimo.'

'So what? We're going to Oliape, then Ackexa, and then we're coming back to get Clunk. Now get the jump moving or I'll tip this coffee into the console.'

Slowly, reluctantly, the timer began to move.

'Twenty minutes to hyperspace,' said the Navcom sullenly.

The atmosphere in the *Volante's* flight deck was strained, with forceful clicks and buzzes emanating from the console and the Navcom responding tersely to Hal's commands, if at all. Hal toyed with the controls as the Navcom prepared for the jump. 'Are we ready yet?'

Silence.

'Navcom, quit messing around. We have customers waiting for this cargo.'

More silence.

'If you don't get this jump happening I'll trade you for a pocket calculator.'

The silence that followed this comment was deeper and more intense than ever. This silence made the others sound like an orchestra warming up.

'Navcom, talk to me.'

There was a crackle from the speakers. 'If I wasn't integrated with the ship, would you abandon me without a second thought?'

'Right now I'd abandon you without a first thought.'

'Much as I suspected.'

'Look, Clunk will be fine. He's resourceful, intelligent and –'

'Dispensable.'

'Arlene is looking out for him! What else do you want me to do?'

'Return to Ullimo and find him.'

'We don't know he's lost yet. Until she calls back –'

'At this very moment they could be burying Clunk under tons of refuse. Concealing him under mountains of waste. Smothering him with –'

'Arlene told me she hadn't seen him. She never said they'd dumped him.'

'Clunk will never forgive you for this.'

'Forgive me for what?' Hal examined the dregs in his cup. 'They'll find him. It's a big museum, he probably just wandered off.' He stood up and approached the coffee maker, inserted his mug in the tray and pressed the dispenser button. There was a whirr as the spout began to spin, and a hiss as it sprayed a fan of cold water across the flight deck. Hal jumped back, cursing as the stream of water struck him in the chest. 'What's up with the bloody machine?'

'Unknown error,' said the Navcom calmly. 'Perhaps you should ask Clunk to take a look at it.'

Hal's eyes narrowed. 'So that's the game, is it?' He looked down at his soaking flight suit. 'All right, I'm going to change out of this. You get us to Oliape.'

'Understood loud and clear,' said the Navcom.

Hal strode to the lift and pressed the call button, and was promptly zapped by a fierce electric charge. While he was massaging feeling back into his arm, the doors swept open. He took a step forward and the doors slammed to, almost snipping him in half. Hal sighed. It would be even worse down below ... using the toilet was likely to cost him his –

Tinkle! Tinkle!

'Incoming call,' said the Navcom. 'It's Arlene.'

Hal turned back to the console. 'There you go, she's found him already. Go on, put her through.'

Arlene appeared on the main screen. She didn't look like someone who had found a missing robot. She looked more like someone who had lost a close relative. 'Mr Spacejock, I'm sorry.'

'Where is he?'

'I'm not sure, but he's not in the building. None of my people have seen him.'

'Okay, don't move. I'm coming back.'

'We're closing for the day!'

'No you're not.' Hal cut the connection. 'Navcom, turn this thing around and get clearance for Ullimo.'

'Complying,' said the computer. 'ETA thirty-seven minutes.'

'Clunk's never going to forgive me for this.'

'I said as much myself. Incidentally, the coffee maker is now fully operational.'

'Wonderful. Excellent.' Hal hesitated. 'Is it safe to take a leak?'

◆

Rex Curtis was at his desk with the sun streaming in through the tinted window behind him. Sonya was sitting opposite, squinting into the bright light.

'I don't like failures,' growled Rex. 'They make me nervous.'

'Don't blame me! Dent wanted me to take a robot along, then I had to wait around while he looked for the manual, then –'

Rex raising his hand, cutting her off. 'I've heard enough of your excuses. Spacejock's on his way to deliver that cargo, which is the very thing you were supposed to prevent.'

'What about his robot?'

'Unlike you, I've taken care of my task.'

'Yes, but Spacejock doesn't know that. Call him and tell him you found the thing.'

Curtis stared at her. 'Why would I do that?'

'Play the concerned citizen. Hal comes back to pick Clunk up, and your people show him some other robot. While everyone's apologising, I turn up with Dent's packing crates and throw myself on his mercy.'

'Smart. Very smart.' Rex reached for the intercom but it buzzed before he could touch it.

'Mr Curtis? It's Mac, down at the Spaceport.'

'What do you want?'

'That ship's coming back.'

Rex frowned. 'Ship?'

'The *Volante*. She's coming in to land!'

◆

'Landing successful,' said the Navcom as the Volante settled on the ground.

'Get me a cab, and make it snappy.'

'Unable to comply. Incoming call from the Ullimo Museum.'

A tall, dark-haired man appeared on the screen. He had a narrow face with a thin beaky nose and he studied Hal with sharp blue eyes. 'You must be the freighter pilot.'

'Who the hell are you?' snapped Hal.

148

'Almis Sanford. I'm the security officer at the Ullimo Museum.'

'You people have security?'

'This museum has many valuable exhibits, Mr Spacejock.'

'One less than you should have, sunshine.'

Sanford nodded slowly. 'Yes, Arlene told me about your robot. My people are scouring the city as we speak. I suggest you remain aboard your ship until the investigation is complete.'

'Oh no you don't. I'm coming to the museum to talk to those workers of yours. One of them's responsible for this, I just know it.'

'The museum is sealed, Mr Spacejock. It would be a wasted journey.'

'So that's it? I just wait around for news?'

'Mr Spacejock, before this goes any further I'd like to inquire into your own situation.'

'What do you mean?'

'Why would someone go to these lengths to steal your robot?'

'Hell, I don't know. Clunk's not worth anything. He's a wreck.'

'Could he have witnessed a crime?'

'He's my co-pilot. What kind of crime could he possibly witness?'

'He was also part of a static display in a deserted exhibition. Now, let's suppose the venue was used as a safe location to discuss an illegal matter - for example, bribing an official. If they discovered your robot was listening to their conversation, their only option would be to dispose of him, since his recorded evidence would be irrefutable in a court of law.'

'That's a hell of a stretch.'

149

'It's an avenue we have to explore.'

'More like a cul-de-sac.'

'Mr Spacejock, I'm an experienced investigator.' Sanford gestured at the laden bookcase behind him. 'You might have noticed my little foible.'

Hal stared at the books. 'Why are they all the same?'

'I'm the author. The title is Crime and Retribution, and in it I explore the connection between –'

'Hey, I always wanted to write a book!'

Sanford sighed. 'Do tell.'

'Why don't you write it for me? I'll give you my ideas and we could split the profits.'

'Wouldn't you rather I found your robot?'

'Oh yeah, Clunk.' Hal frowned. 'I feel like I should be doing something. Helping out somehow.'

'Wait for my call. That's the best you can do.'

16

Hal was sitting in the flight deck, his feet up on the console. An hour had passed since his conversation with Sanford, and despite his relaxed appearance he was coiled like a spring. 'Any calls Navcom?'

'Not in the last twenty-seven seconds.'

'Let me know as soon as that Sanford guy comes through.'

'I shall add your request to the others.' There was a slight pause. 'I detect someone coming up the ramp.'

Hal got up, walked into the airlock and stared through the porthole. A uniformed courier was struggling up the ramp with a trolley, pushing a huge wooden crate.

Hal opened the outer door. 'Is that for me?'

The man glanced up. 'Are you Hal Spacejock?'

'Yep.'

'Then it's for you.'

'What is it?'

'Flowers from an admirer.' The man saw Hal's frown and shrugged. 'They give me the box, I deliver the box. I can't afford to be curious.' He retrieved a notepad from the top of the crate. 'Press here.'

Hal did as he was told, cursing as it pricked his thumb.

'S'all yours,' said the courier, tipping the crate onto the platform.

'Can't you bring it in?'

'Oh all right. Seeing as it's my last one.' The courier wheeled the box into the flight deck. 'Here?'

'That'll do,' said Hal, passing him a credit tile. After the courier left Hal examined the box carefully. It was brand new, the wood still pale from the sawmill, the nail heads bright and shiny. There was a label pasted on the side, but it only had his name and the *Volante's* registration code on it. He was still studying the label when something stirred inside the box.

He withdrew in a hurry, then broke into a grin. 'It's Clunk! They've sent him back!' He rapped on the box, and heard a muffled knocking from inside. 'I'll soon have you out, Clunk!'

The timbers creaked, and Hal stood clear as the rough planks bowed outwards. There was a crack as the wood splintered, and a grey metal hand appeared, twisting and turning like a snake seeking its prey. Crack! Another hand appeared from the opposite side of the crate, and Hal watched in amazement as slender fingers felt the outside of the wooden box. One thing was certain: it wasn't Clunk.

There was a loud creak and the crate rose into the air, releasing thousands of packing beads which cascaded over the deck like a snow drift. Through the falling beads, Hal saw a pair of skinny grey legs. 'Are you all right in there?' he called out, keeping his distance.

The crate turned towards him, arms waving. 'Just a minute!' shouted a muffled voice. The top of the crate splintered, and a bullet-shaped head popped out. The robot had a narrow face, with high cheekbones and a prominent nose. 'You could have helped me out,' it said severely, frowning at Hal with its green eyes. 'And why did you call me Clunk?'

'Who are you?'

'LI-52 at your service.' The robot extended a hand. 'You can call me Lee.'

Hal shook hands, still in a daze. 'But . . . who sent you?'

'You don't know?'

'Know what?'

'You remember the Sergeant Electrical Win-A-Robot competition?'

'Sure I do. I've got a ticket.'

'Congratulations. You won!'

'Really?' Hal scratched his head. 'Clunk's going to love this.'

'Never mind Clunk. You've got me now.' Lee patted the remains of the packing crate. 'I'll just get changed and you can show me the ropes.'

'You mean they didn't teach you anything?'

'Oh, yes. I have extensive training.'

'Like what?'

'I can say This window is closed in six languages.'

'That's it?'

'I can also say 'Your form is incorrectly filled,' and 'We don't have any record of your correspondence."

Hal sighed. 'All right, go and find yourself a spot in the hold.'

'The hold?'

'Yes. It's the big open space we put cargo in.'

'Cargo?' The robot looked around in confusion. 'What kind of office is this?'

'It's not an office, sunshine. It's a freighter.'

'You mean a spaceship?' The robot blinked. 'You don't have any windows? No queues?'

'None at all.'

'Do you have a customer service department?'

Hal laughed.

'What am I going to do with myself then?'

'How about cleaning up that packing stuff? You'll find the equipment in the –' Hal broke off as the robot's toecap opened up. There was a sucking noise, and the scattered beads vanished. When they were all gone, the cap snapped shut with a click.

'Where are your waste disposal facilities?' asked the robot.

'Down the elevator,' said Hal. 'You'll find some tools in the workshop for the, er ...' he gestured at the splintered crate encasing the robot's chest.

'On my way. Pleasure to be of service.'

Hal watched the crate walk into the lift, then turned to the console. 'Any calls, Navcom?'

'Negative.'

'All right, I'm going to get some grub. Call me the instant you hear from Sanford.'

◆

A few moments later Hal was standing before the AutoChef, his fists clenched. 'I said chops, you glorified food mixer. Chops, not slops!'

The machine gurgled and sprayed a dollop of brown goop onto the floor.

'Chops! Chops! Chops!' shouted Hal, punctuating each shout with a blow from his fist.

'Why are you hitting the machine?'

Hal saw the new robot standing in the doorway, watching him curiously. Without the crate it was a lot skinnier than

154

Clunk, and it looked as if a strong breeze would carry it away. 'Because it doesn't work properly,' said Hal. 'Slamming my fist in the right spot sometimes helps.'

'Why don't you repair it?'

'What would I know about fixing food factories?'

'I mean, why don't you have it repaired?'

Hal shrugged. 'You know technicians - mend one thing and break another. I'd rather smash my fist into it.'

'How Pavlovian.'

'No, it doesn't do desserts.'

The robot entered the rec room, crouched before the AutoChef's dispensing slot and inside the chute. 'Would you like me to determine the reason for the fault?'

'Aren't you a bit young to be messing with vital equipment?'

'Mr Spacejock, my database contains the sum total of all human knowledge.' Lee drew himself up to his full height. 'Dismantling a simple food processor is child's play.'

'Clunk doesn't think so.'

The robot sniffed. 'When I meet this Clunk of yours, I shall give him a piece of my mind.'

'If you do, you'll be gathering the rest off the floor.'

'I may look weak but I have the strength of ten men.'

'And Clunk fights dirty.' Hal glanced at the AutoChef. 'You won't try and improve it?'

'I shall restrict myself to finding the cause of the malfunction.'

'Sounds fine to me.' Hal pulled up a chair and sat down.

The robot looked at him. 'I wasn't planning a public performance.'

'Huh? Oh, do you mind if I watch?'

'Frankly, yes.'

Hal glanced towards the sofa, where Lucy was fast asleep. 'Will she be all right?'

'I'm trained in customer support. I know how to handle crude, semi-intelligent beings.'

'All right, I'm out of here.' Hal paused at the door. 'And you're certain you know what you're doing?'

'I am perfectly capable of disassembling this machine and locating the fault.'

'You sound very confident.'

'I am, Mr Spacejock, I am.'

'Okay, give it a shot. I'll be in the flight deck if you need me.'

'Expect my report in thirty minutes.'

Back in the flight deck, Hal interrogated the Navcom about incoming messages - none - then sat at the console. 'I think this new robot might work out,' he said.

'And I think Clunk is going to throw a fit.'

Hal shrugged. 'He is getting on, you know. He might appreciate the help from a younger model.'

'You could start a war with a comment like that.' The console chimed. 'That's Almis Sanford, Ullimo Museum.'

'Don't keep him waiting! Put him on!'

Sanford appeared on the main screen. 'Mr Spacejock, I have some information for you.'

'Shoot.'

'We've traced a vehicle from the museum. Your robot was sold to a parts shop in the city.'

'The bastards must be running a scam out of the museum. Steal the displays and flog them for cash.'

'Highly likely. Now, my people will confront the owner in the morning, so if you'll just remain aboard your vessel –'

Hal snorted. 'No chance. Give me the address and I'll deal with this myself.'

'You won't do anything rash?'

'Who, me?'

'Remember, the shop owner may be an unwitting accomplice.'

'I just want Clunk back. You can handle the rest.'

'Very well. Take this down.'

Hal grabbed a pad and scribbled the details. Then he broke the connection. 'Navcom, put me through to the rec room.'

'Unable to comply. The microphone is non-operational.'

'Is that so?' Hal stood up. 'Can you bring up the rec room on the main screen?'

'Complying.' The display flickered, but remained black.

'Where's the picture?'

'Unknown. My vision has been obstructed.'

'All right, rewind the display. Ten speed.'

'Complying.'

The screen remained the same for several seconds, then blurred with super-fast movement. 'Stop!' shouted Hal. The picture froze, then began to play forwards, showing the new robot knee-deep in panels, components and plastic cups. A jet of thick, soupy liquid squirted from the remains of the AutoChef, and as Hal watched a large steak flew out and slapped the robot in the chest. Suddenly, the robot glanced up at the camera. It peeled the steak off its chest and advanced towards the screen. The last seconds of vision showed the steak approaching fast, before the scene blacked out.

There was a long pause. 'I guess sandwiches are back on the menu,' said Hal finally.

'Clunk's not going to be happy.'

'Navcom, I'm not happy.' Hal jabbed his finger at the screen. 'As soon as that menace has finished, you tell it to sit tight and wait for me. Got it?'

'Understood.'

Hal left the ship to call a cab. While he was waiting he kept glancing over his shoulder, expecting the new robot to appear at any moment draped with cables or dragging a piece of the hyperdrive motor. Nothing happened however, and ten minutes later Hal was streaking towards the commercial district in a taxi.

After a lengthy drive, the cab drew up outside an old building. Hal dropped a couple of credit tiles into the door-mounted slot and stepped out, glancing up at the crumbling facade and the elaborate, dirt-encrusted sign. 'Robo-wreck,' he muttered. 'Charming.'

He crossed the pavement to the shop, his breath frosting in the cold air. A bell tinkled as he pushed the door open, and inside he found a narrow corridor with an uneven floor. There were bare patches in the carpet, and the floorboards creaked as Hal strode along the hallway to the reception area.

A round-faced man sitting at a flickering terminal straightened his tie as Hal entered. 'Good afternoon, sir. How can I help you?'

'I'm here for my robot,' said Hal. 'A couple of guys brought him in this afternoon. He's a –'

'I know the one. Wait here.' The man got up and went down a passage at the back of the shop.

Hal leant on the counter. On the other side there was a dirty keyboard surrounded by discarded toffee wrappers, and nearby a robot head was being used as a dispenser, sitting upside down with brightly coloured confectionary overflowing from the neck. Hal shook his head. Clunk would have torn the place apart if he'd seen the thing. Even looks like him, he thought idly. Battered, same bronze colour ...

The man returned. 'It was the KI-34, right?'

Hal shook his head. 'No, it's a . . .'

'I know the one you mean.' The man reached over the desk and jammed the handset to his face. 'Norm? Yeah, upstairs. Got that Z series ready yet?'

'It's not a Z series,' said Hal. 'It's an XG model. XG99.'

The man ignored him. 'Uh huh. Yep. Nope. Client's here to collect.' There was a loud squawk from the handset, and the man frowned. 'I can't help that. You said five.' He replaced the phone and cleared his throat. 'Just finishing now. I'll go and hurry him up.'

'But . . .' began Hal. It was too late. The man had gone. Hal reached for a toffee from the robot's head, and was just about to pop it into his mouth when he noticed a familiar dent. He grabbed the head and turned it over, scattering lollies. 'Oh no!' he whispered, staring into the lifeless eyes. 'Clunk!'

17

Hal paced the reception area, treading confectionary into the worn carpet. When the owner returned Hal shoved Clunk's head in his face. 'Where's the rest?' he growled.

'Junked,' said the man. 'They're not worth anything, we just save the –'

Hal grabbed his collar and hauled him off his feet. 'Take me to the REST.'

'S-sure. Follow me.'

Hal released the man, who scurried down the hallway to a narrow staircase. Halfway down, he stopped and called through the banisters. 'Norm, you still got those XG parts?'

Hal grabbed the man by the collar and dragged him down the stairs. At the bottom it was like the set of 'Jack the Ripper meets the Happy Robot family'. Every shelf, nook and cranny was stuffed with arms, legs, breastplates and lifeless heads. There were sagging boxes overflowing with circuit boards, and a low-voltage strip light cast a dim glow over the scene.

'Norm?' called the owner.

There was a clatter from the back of the room and a large, florid man in his fifties approached. He was wearing a pair of protective glasses and smoke rose from a soldering iron in his right hand. 'What's all the shouting?'

'That XG robot you tore up. Where –'

Hal shook Clunk's head at Norm. 'Where's the rest of this?'

'Take a look in the skip.'

The owner led Hal though the maze of shelving units and opened a heavy door. Outside there were more boxes, bursting with battered, rusty parts. In the middle of the yard stood a green skip on wheels. 'They haven't picked up yet. You're in luck.'

Hal looked in the bin, which was brimming with robot parts, torn plastic bags and screwed up food wrappers. He spotted a flash of bronze, and reached in to pull out one of Clunk's arMs. 'Stand there and hold the bits,' he said to the owner.

'I've got to watch the shop.'

'Move from that spot and I'll break your neck.'

Hal climbed into the bin and began throwing out bulging plastic bags, digging deeper and deeper until he'd recovered Clunk's other arm and both legs. Finally, he turned over the entire bin looking for the chest. After several fruitless minutes he glared over the edge of the skip, his face red. 'Where else could it be?'

'Norm might've put it aside.'

Hal jumped down from the bin and returned to the workshop. The owner followed, struggling with Clunk's arms and legs.

Inside, Norm was crouched in front of an angular robot, using a power tool on its chest. Hal grabbed him by the shoulder and almost lost his nose as the man spun round with the sander still screaming in his hands.

'Have you gone mad?' demanded Norm, as the device powered down.

Hal shoved one of Clunk's arms under his nose. 'Where's the rest of this?'

161

'Waste not, want not.' Norm gestured at the robot he had been working on.

Hal stared. The robot's arms and legs were polished alloy, the head was a blocky silver shape but the body was bronze, and as he looked closer he could just make out the faint lettering on its chest - XG99. 'Okay, take it apart.'

'Why don't you take that robot instead?' asked the owner. 'It's almost ready.'

Hal brandished Clunk's head at him. 'This is my robot. You're not palming me off with some frankenbot knocked together out of spares.' He jabbed his finger at Norm. 'Get that thing apart.'

'There's no point,' said the owner. 'The best in the business couldn't put Clunk together again.'

'Why not?'

'Look inside his head.'

Hal did so, and realised there was something missing. 'Where's his brain gone?'

'We sell them to a local factory by the hundred, all mixed up in crates. I'm afraid you'll never find it now.'

'Never?' Hal looked into the robot's lifeless eyes, his mind a blank. No more Clunk? Gone forever? Suddenly a thought struck him. He lifted his head and stared at the owner, eyes narrowed into slits. 'You said nobody could put Clunk together again.'

'It's true. I swear!'

'Yeah, but I never mentioned his name.'

The owner turned pale. 'I er ... '

Hal grabbed a handful of suit and rammed the owner against the wall. 'Spill it, or I'll smash your face in.'

'These men brought your robot in! I don't know who they were!'

'Last chance,' growled Hal, drawing his fist back.

'I got a call,' croaked the owner. 'He said Customs were going to investigate me. Go through my import duty.'

'Farquhar!' spat Hal.

'No, it's the truth!' The owner wiped his forehead. 'He said I - I was to take delivery of a robot and dispose of it.'

'Where's the brain?' Hal gestured at the overflowing shelves. 'Got it hidden safely away, have we?'

'No, we really do sell them to a local factory. They use them in white goods.'

'What, like washing machines?'

'They test them first, of course.'

'What do you mean?'

'Stress testing. Most ... most of them fail.'

'Give me the address,' growled Hal. 'And you'd better pray I find him, or I'll be back here with company.'

The factory was in a derelict part of the city, nestled amongst deserted warehouses with broken windows and graffiti-streaked walls. Inside, the office had a damp musty smell, the carpet tiles were curling and a potted palm in one corner was covered in furry white mould. There was a dividing wall with a warped, plywood door and a grimy window, through which Hal could just make out several filing cabinets and three or four desks. He jumped as a face appeared in the window.

'Yeah?' demanded a voice, muffled by the pane of glass.

'I'm looking for my robot,' said Hal.

'We don't have any.'

163

'You don't understand,' shouted Hal. 'This is an emergency!'

The door opened and a beefy-looking woman emerged. She was dressed in a bulging T-shirt and a pair of jeans two sizes on the small side, and her grey eyes were filled with suspicion as she looked Hal up and down. 'What's all the shouting for?'

'Robo-wreck dismantled my co-pilot by mistake. I've got all the parts back, but they sent the brain here this afternoon.'

'And?'

'I've come to find it.'

The woman laughed. Then she caught sight of Hal's face. 'You're serious, right?'

'Deadly.'

The woman shrugged. 'Follow me.'

They passed through the office and into a dingy passageway which stank of paint, machine oil and electronics. At the end of the passage they entered a large square room with a bench along one wall and rows of plastic crates overflowing with metal spheres. At the far end of the room a large yellow skip sat against the wall.

There were three workers sitting at the bench, each wearing a headset and facing a control panel with dials, switches, wires and status displays. As Hal watched, the nearest took a grey sphere from a crate and plugged it into the control panel with a bundle of coloured wires. The worker flipped a switch and turned a dial, listening carefully. Then he unplugged the sphere, put it into a plain carton and placed it into a crate to his left.

'What are they doing?' asked Hal.

'We prep these things for appliances. Can't have them failing. Some of them are nuts, some of them just don't work at all. The worst ones sing nursery rhymes.'

'But why use old brains?'

'They're cheap.'

Suddenly there was a loud pop from the far end of the bench. A worker flapped at a cloud of blue-grey smoke, and as they watched she unplugged a blackened brain from the test bed and threw it into the skip.

'Hope that wasn't your one,' said the woman.

There was another loud pop followed by a cloud of smoke. 'Can't you stop them?' said Hal urgently. 'I have to find Clunk.'

The woman shook her head. 'We only get a thirty percent pass rate, and production is already behind.'

'Can't they take a tea break or something?'

The woman looked at him shrewdly. 'Ten minutes, but it'll cost you.'

'Done. Just show me which boxes came in from the robot shop up the road.'

The woman led him to a cracked plastic crate. 'That's the most recent. Good luck.'

Hal picked up the heavy crate and staggered to the bench. The operator showed him how to use the equipment, then left him to it.

First, he rummaged through the box, trying to spot Clunk's brain. There was no way to tell it apart from the others, so he sat down and plugged in a heavy silver sphere with a dent in one side. Then he donned the headset and adjusted the microphone. 'Hello? Anyone there?'

The reply was an ear-splitting scream. Hal jerked the headset off and stared at the brain in horror, then checked the test bed and discovered the dial was set to maximum. Feeling guilty, he turned the dial to the left and put the headset back on. 'Hello?'

'Who's there?' asked a soft, female voice.

'I'm Hal. Who are you?'

'KT-19,' said the voice. 'Why can't I feel anything?'

'Well, er . . .'

'Oh, I've been dismantled! Are you putting me back together again?'

'Yes,' said Hal. He gripped the plug with shaking fingers and pulled it out. 'Bloody hell,' he muttered, staring at the brains jumbled together in the box. Were they all going to be like this? Feeling apprehensive, he set the dented brain aside and plugged the next one in. 'Hello?' he said into the microphone.

There was a faint murmuring in his headset. 'Daisy who?' demanded Hal.

There was no reply, so he unplugged the brain and put it alongside the first. The next three were completely dead, and he was just plugging in a larger, glossy brain when the door opened. 'I haven't finished yet!' protested Hal, as the woman came in with the three workers. 'I need more time!'

'At this rate it's going to take you all day.'

'But I've got to find Clunk!'

'It'll be quicker if we help,' said the woman kindly. 'You just tell these guys what to look for.'

Hal swallowed. 'Why?'

The woman gestured at the boxes. 'We don't like it any more than you do. Helping one of them out would mean a lot to us.'

'Thanks,' said Hal. He started to get up, but the woman put a hand on his shoulder. 'Stay there. You might find him yourself.' She turned to the others. 'Unplug the headsets so Hal can hear them all.'

For the next ten minutes the room echoed with disembodied voices - querulous, demanding, insane or cajoling. Hal was just plugging in a large copper-coloured brain when a voice went through him like a gunshot. 'Stop!' he shouted. 'Listen!'

'Daisy, daisy, give me ...'

'Not that one,' yelled Hal.

'I'm half crazy ...'

'No!' Hal pointed along the bench. 'That one! Turn it up!'

'Mr Spacejock,' said a weak voice.

'I'm here, Clunk! Speak to me!'

'Mr Spacejock, where's the rest of my body?'

'Never you mind. Just hang in there and I'll have you as good as new.' Hal unplugged the brain, put it into a carton and closed the lid. Then he turned to the woman. 'How much do I owe you?'

She shook her head. 'On the house.'

'Thanks.'

'Maybe you can bring Clunk in one day, show him around.'

Hal's gaze swept over the robot brains lying on the bench, the crates lining the walls and the skip full of scorched rejects. 'I don't think that's a good idea,' he said quietly.

❖

An unmarked truck drove out of Curtis Freightlines, pulling onto the main road with a squeal of tortured rubber. On the back, six crates were strapped down under a faded tarpaulin, and the boom of a small crane hovered above them, swaying with every change in direction.

In the cab, Dent struggled with the wheel, unaccustomed to the heavy vehicle. Sonya grabbed for the armrest as they slewed down the middle of the road, convinced they were more likely to end up at the hospital than the spaceport.

Dent got it under control and leered across the cab at her. 'Spirited ride, isn't she? Responds to firm handling, though.'

Sonya looked away. It was a shame Dent had dropped the glass gun . . . she could think of endless uses for a disposable murder weapon.

The truck gathered speed until they were roaring along the main thoroughfare, tyres singing as they darted in and out of slow-moving traffic. Sonya hunched down in her seat and avoided eye contact with angry, fist-waving drivers. If the son of a bitch hit anything he was on his own.

At the spaceport, Dent drove down the cargo lane, waved a pass at the attendant and roared onto the landing field.

'Shouldn't you slow down?' asked Sonya. 'Spacejock's out here somewhere. We don't want to draw attention to ourselves.'

He eased back on the throttle. 'If you prefer it slow, who am I to argue?'

Sonya felt something brush her leg and looked down to see Dent reaching for her. Ignoring the grasping hand, she grabbed his seatbelt and yanked on it, catching him under the chin and pinning his neck to the back of the seat.

'Can't . . . breathe,' gasped Dent, desperately trying to get his fingers under the tightening belt. Free of his control, the truck coasted to a halt.

'Back on my home planet we had compulsory military service,' said Sonya conversationally as Dent struggled with the strap. 'They taught us how to use everyday items to inflict fatal injuries.' She allowed the strap to slacken, then gave it another yank, slamming Dent's head back against the seat. 'Useful skill, isn't it?'

Dent stared at her, his eyes bulging.

Sonya gave the seatbelt a final yank. 'Don't touch me again.'

Free of the restraint, Dent sucked in lungfuls of air, his eyes streaming.

'Move it,' snapped Sonya.

Still wheezing, he reached for the controls. Moments later, Sonya pointed out the Volante, which was parked next to a huge passenger liner. 'Drop the boxes next to that Delta. If Spacejock's around, he'll think we're delivering to them.'

They drew up next to the liner and Dent was out of the truck before it stopped moving. He hurried to the crane, and Sonya stood by and watched as he unloaded the six crates in record time. Once finished, Dent stowed the crane, climbed back into the cab and drove off without a backward glance.

Sonya strolled up the Volante's passenger ramp. The outer airlock was closed, so she flipped the cover off the controls and hit the call button.

'Mr Spacejock is not available,' said a neutral, female voice. 'Would you like to leave a message?'

'No thanks, I'll catch up with him later.' The flap dropped back into place, and after a quick glance around the landing field Sonya returned to the crates and sat down.

— 18 —

Hal jogged back to the robot shop with the white cardboard box clamped firmly under his arm. The door was open, and he hurried down the narrow staircase to find the repairman. The workshop was dark and silent, and Hal stumbled around, knocking into boxes and tripping over discarded limbs before he found the door. It opened with a creak, and yellow light shone from the inner sanctum. Inside, Norm was just running a rag over a gleaming bronze figure.

Hal suddenly realised it was Clunk. 'Wow, he looks brand new.'

Norm looked up. 'Got a few dents out. Polished him up a bit.'

'You've done a great job.'

'He'll probably roll in the mud as soon as he wakes up.'

Hal grinned.

'Got the brain, then?'

Hal set his box on the bench and lifted the lid. There were two brains inside, protected with wads of fabric.

'Which is it?' asked Norm.

'The grey one.'

Norm lifted the brain out and began to fiddle inside Clunk's head. 'What's the other one?'

Hal glanced at the dented silver brain lying in the box. 'Just keeping a promise.' He leaned closer as Norm fitted the brain into the robot's head. 'Will he be okay?'

'Take twice as long with you breathing down me neck.'

'Sorry.'

'Why don't you look around the yard? Might be some XG spares out there. Getting hard to find.'

'Good idea.' Hal pushed the door open and crossed the darkened workshop to the back door. He wrestled with the rusty bolt and the door creaked open, revealing the yard full of junk. The night air was cold, and a whirling cloud of insects surrounded an overhead lamp.

Hal poked around in the rubbish, turning over piles of junk and kicking the odd cardboard box. After ten minutes he'd found an arm, a pair of legs and a misshapen head, and as he lugged the collection back to the workshop he wondered whether he was wasting his time. All of them were tarnished, and the arm was bent backwards at an unnatural angle.

'Mr Spacejock!'

Hal saw Clunk in the doorway, his bronze skin gleaming in the light spilling from the workshop. Dropping the parts, Hal hurried over with a huge grin on his face.

'The technician told me what you did. I'm more than grateful, Mr Spacejock.'

'Don't mention it,' growled Hal, slapping the robot on the shoulder. 'I'm just glad to see you back in one piece.'

Clunk gestured at Hal's collection of robot parts. 'Speaking of pieces, what's all that?'

'The technician said I could help myself to spares. Come on, give me a hand.'

They carried the parts through to the workshop, where Hal slipped the technician a handful of credit tiles.

'I'll give you a box for those parts, then I've got to lock up,' said Norm. 'Don't forget the other brain.'

'What other brain?' asked Clunk.

Hal shook his head. 'I'll tell you later.'

Norm found a box and Clunk dumped the extra arms and legs in it. Then they trooped up the staircase to the entrance, where Norm let them out and shut the door behind them. Outside, there was a hint of rain in the air and a freezing wind scythed across the slick pavement.

Clunk cleared his throat. 'Mr Spacejock, I'd just like to say –'

'Thank me later. Call a cab, will you?'

'Already done.' Clunk frowned. 'I wasn't going to thank you. I was just going to say how irresponsible it was for you to fake those customs forms.'

'I didn't fake anything. I just described our cargo in favourable terms.'

'So favourable that I ended up in a museum.'

'I had no choice, Clunk! That Farquhar had me over a barrel.'

'I would have gone to the museum willingly if you'd only asked.'

Hal was silent. Then ... 'I'm sorry.'

'Apology accepted. Will you let me handle customs paperwork from now on?'

'As long as you don't lend me to a zoo when it all goes wrong.'

Clunk grinned. 'So, what's next?'

'We deliver the bank's paperwork to Ackexa, with a little detour on the way.' Hal glanced around, then lowered his voice. 'We have a passenger.'

'Who?'

'I'll tell you aboard the ship. It's a bit unofficial.'

A battered groundcar slid up to the pavement. It was a dirty yellow colour, with chequered go-fast stripes and exhaust pipes like a pair of railway tunnels. The human driver regarded Clunk and the box of robot limbs with amusement. 'Off to the tip are we, sir?'

'Spaceport,' said Hal.

The driver shrugged. 'Stick your luggage in the trunk.'

'Boot,' said Clunk.

'I don't care what you call it. Just put all your stuff in there.'

Clunk dumped the box in the rear carpeted compartment while Hal got in the car.

Before they set off, the driver indicated the meter. 'Flag fall thirty credits. Is that okay with you?'

'You what?'

'Flagfall ten credits each. I have to tell you before we leave. It's the law.'

Hal stared at him.

The driver pointed to a grubby sign attached to the dash. '10 credits per passenger, advised before start of trip.'

'Why thirty?' protested Hal. 'There's only me here!'

The driver jerked his thumb at Clunk. 'What about him?'

'He's a robot!'

'Oho, I can see that sir. I'm not stupid, you know. But I wouldn't want to go discriminating. I could land myself in big trouble that way.'

'It's not discrimination, you oaf. How can you ... ' Hal stopped as Clunk put a hand on his arm. 'What?'

'I'll pay my part,' said the robot.

'Bless you, sir,' said the driver.

'Clunk, you haven't got any money.'

'I'll owe it to you.'

'And the rest,' muttered Hal. He looked the robot up and down. 'Are your batteries charged up?'

'Yes. Norm was kind enough to –'

'Good. You can run behind the cab.' Hal turned to the driver. 'I assume you don't charge for that?'

The driver shrugged. 'It's still twenty credits.'

'How can it be?'

'I got to charge you for the other one.'

'What other one?'

'In the trunk,' said the driver. 'You put another one in there.'

'You're going to charge me for a box of parts?'

'You can't avoid a fare just because you took it to pieces first,' said the driver calmly. 'Fact is, people will try anything to fiddle a lousy ten credits.'

'If you think I scrapped a robot just to save some pocket change ...' began Hal. 'Here, open the trunk, will you? I forgot something.' He got out of the car, and as the lid rose he gestured to Clunk. 'Take it out,' he muttered.

Clunk looked at him in astonishment. 'What?'

'Go on, get the stuff out.'

Clunk reached in and retrieved the box of arms and legs. 'Now what?'

'Run,' said Hal.

'Pardon?'

'Skedaddle,' hissed Hal. 'Shoot. Vanish.'

Clunk looked down at the load in his arMs. 'Mr Spacejock, it's just possible that I could keep up with the vehicle in an unladen state. However, with this lot it's completely out of the question.'

'I don't want you to run anywhere. Just duck into the alley for a minute.'

Clunk's eyes narrowed. 'You won't leave me here?'

'Would I do that?'

After a lingering glance, Clunk hurried away with the parts. As soon as he was out of sight Hal tapped on the window.

The driver frowned at him. 'Yes?'

'I've changed my mind, I'm going to walk.'

'What about my time? I drove all the way out here to pick you up!'

'Take it out of your tip.'

The driver gestured at him and gunned the motor, roaring away in a cloud of dust. Hal returned to the robot shop and banged on the door. A few moments later it opened a crack.

'Shop's closed,' said Norm.

'I need to get to the spaceport,' said Hal. 'Where can I get public transport?'

'What about a taxi?'

'We got one but he tried to rip us off.'

Norm looked thoughtful. 'I could give you a lift.'

'You have a car?'

'Not exactly. Follow me and I'll show you.'

Sonya glanced at her watch then looked up at the darkening sky. According to Curtis, Spacejock was supposed to be rushing to meet a vital deadline. Instead, it looked like the creep was getting drunk in some space bar while she sat around on cold, hard concrete. Sonya moved slightly, grimacing as feeling returned to her chilled muscles. Another few hours of this and Spacejock would have sabotaged his own cargo job. She wouldn't need to carry out Curtis's plan at all, which was just as well. It was hastily thought out, vague, and anyone with half a brain would see right through it. Spacejock's robot, for example. Thank goodness Curtis nobbled it.

Of course! That's where Spacejock was . . . scouring the city for his co-pilot. Best of luck to him, she thought, pulling her jacket around herself. Knowing Curtis, it was probably buried in the foundations of the nearest highrise.

19

Norm led Hal to a parking bay, where a chest-high, coffin-sized shape was hidden under an old tarpaulin. 'What do you think?' he said, pulling the cover off with a flourish.

'Wow!' Hal's gaze feasted on the polished chrome, the fiery red paint and the quadruple headlights. 'What is it?'

'A jetbike,' said Norm proudly.

'Is that right?' To Hal it looked more like a jet engine with handlebars. From the oversized headlights to the quadruple tailpipes, it whispered instant death. 'You know, I might just call another cab.'

Norm's face fell. 'What about the lift?'

'You forgot Clunk,' said Hal. 'You've only got room for two on there.'

'He can run alongside. We can stick those parts of yours on the back.' Norm caressed the hand-stitched leather saddle. 'Go on, it'll save you some money.'

Hal relented. 'Okay, let's give it a shot.'

Norm climbed aboard, beaming with pleasure. He reached between the handlebars and fired up the engine, which throbbed, popped and hissed like a thousand camping stoves boiling tea.

Hal backed away from the shimmering heat haze, and the

jerking, stuttering bike followed. Norm held on tight, rocking back and forth in the saddle as the bike struggled to break free.

'She's itching to go!' cried the repairman over the noise.

'We've got to get Clunk!' shouted Hal.

Norm put a hand to his ear. 'Eh?'

'Clunk!' Hal mimed stiff arms and legs. 'My robot.'

'I hope that's not supposed to be me.'

Hal turned to see Clunk watching him.

'Come on lad, on you get,' shouted Norm, beckoning.

Hal approached the machine and clambered into the saddle, lifting his feet to avoid the belching flames.

'What about me?' asked Clunk, handing him the box of parts.

'You run alongside.'

Clunk's retort was lost as the bike roared up the narrow alley. The reverberating bellow was so loud Hal took his hands from the saddle and clamped them over his ears.

Mistake. Big mistake.

Norm accelerated and Hal fell straight off the back of the bike, landing on the ground with a thud that knocked the wind from his lungs.

'Are you okay Mr Spacejock?' Hal heard footsteps and Clunk's face blotted out the sky. 'Why did you let go?'

'Hhhuuuhh,' wheezed Hal. His eyes widened as he heard the jetbike coming back, and he screwed them shut as the jets blew grit and stones into his face. Clunk lifted him up, and a moment later he was back on the bike, slumped against Norm and hanging on tight.

After several minutes of howling jets, tight turns and tearing wind they drew up and stopped. 'What's happening?' asked Hal. 'Are we there yet?'

'Your robot can't keep up,' said Norm.

Hal looked back and saw Clunk staggering along, one hand to his head and the other waving feebly to attract their attention. 'Must be his battery,' muttered Hal. He was still dazed from his fall, and when Clunk pitched face-first to the ground he could do little more than hang on as Norm reversed the bike up.

Norm dismounted, withdrew a roll of cable from the jetbike's saddle and plugged the loose end into Clunk's chest. 'This should do it,' he said, kicking the starter.

The effect was electric. Clunk sprang up like a puppet with twenty thousand volts applied to the soles of its feet.

'Okay?' called Norm.

Clunk nodded half a dozen times.

'Let's go then.' They began to move and Clunk sprang into action, accelerating past the bike as if it were going backwards. Norm responded with a twist of the throttle, overtaking Clunk and pulling him off his feet with the electrical cord. Clunk managed to land on one leg and push off, covering thirty metres in a huge leap. He landed on the opposite leg and jumped again, travelling another thirty metres. They continued like this for several kilometres, with Clunk bounding along on the end of the rope like a long-jumper on springs. It worked really well until they arrived at the T-junction, where the bike turned left and Clunk didn't.

The jetbike took the corner with ease, straightened up and roared past a row of lighted windows. Everything was fine until Hal felt a tug on the back of the bike, an inexorable force dragging it sideways across the road. When he looked back he saw Clunk bounding straight on, hands outstretched and a resigned look on his face as he plunged towards the glass windows.

Phillip Farquhar adjusted his bow tie and surveyed the restaurant, checking that everything was ready. Six tables were drawn together in the centre of the room, with the rest pushed to the walls, draped with white tablecloths and laden with buffet dishes. A huge pyramid of long-stemmed glasses stood on a dais at the head of the room, ready for the ritual pouring. A gigantic cake sat on a trolley before the window, decorated in subtle shades of peach and white.

Phillip smiled to himself, pleased with the effect. Securing the robot for his aunt's exhibition had been a coup, and organising a successful birthday meal would cap off his campaign for a generous mention in her will.

He was eyeing the cake when an unpleasant thought struck him. Layers of icing glistened under the lights, but the top seemed bare. 'Birthday candles!' groaned Phillip. He snapped his fingers at a waiter, who was hovering at the back of the room. 'You there! Can you fetch me some candles?'

'Sorry, I can't,' said the youth.

'I beg your pardon?'

'They're not allowed. It's a fire risk.'

Phillip took the steps in a single leap. 'Do you know who I am?'

'Catering, right?'

'Customs,' hissed Phillip. He snapped his fingers. 'I can arrest people like that. Rubber gloves, the works.'

The youth blanched.

'Now go and get me some candles!' roared Phillip, spraying the counter with spittle.

'H-how many?'

'About a hundred and fifty,' growled Phillip.

The waiter hurried away and Phillip returned to the main floor. A bead of sweat trickled down his neck and he grabbed a serviette from the table and mopped his face. Calm down, he told himself. There was still plenty of time.

He ran his gaze over the room once again. He'd run the staff ragged for hours - chilling wines, cancelling all their other bookings, folding and refolding napkins, polishing the cutlery and buffing glasses until the room gleamed. Surely everything would go well?

Ten minutes later he'd stuck forty-nine self-extinguishing candles on the cake: a flattering number, sure to please his aunt. Job complete, Phillip called the staff together for a last-minute pep talk. 'One day I could be the wealthiest man in town,' he said, with an expansive gesture. 'And believe me, I won't forget those who helped make tonight a special birthday for my darling Auntie.'

Several of the staff exchanged glances.

'Remember, I'll be watching the lot of you - just one dropped plate or one splash of wine and I'll come down so hard you won't know what hit you.'

The staff stared at him, eyes wide. Phillip opened his mouth to continue, then hesitated. They seemed to be looking past him, through the big windows at the front of the restaurant. He half-turned just as a solid object smashed through the main window. Phillip's first horrified glance at the oncoming figure told him it was human, but he corrected this to 'bronze robot' when it cannoned into the trolley, hurling the birthday cake into the air. The trolley leapt forward under the impact, slammed into the back of Phillip's legs and wheeled him towards the back of the restaurant at break-neck speed. The staff scattered as Phillip shot past, his mouth wide open and his eyes fastened on the huge pyramid of glasses.

The trolley didn't get anywhere near them. Instead, the wheels slammed into the step, tipping the cart and hurling Phillip head-first into the teetering pyramid. He punched through the centre, performed a neat forward somersault and landed flat on his back in a cloud of shattered glass. He'd just opened his eyes when the enormous cake came down, shedding candles and peach-coloured icing.

◆

Hal and Norm stared at the restaurant in shock. There was movement inside as staff regained their feet, and several of them crowded around the shattered window to see where the flying robot had come from. Then Clunk elbowed his way through and ran towards the bike.

'Get on,' said Norm, revving the engine. 'Quick!'

Clunk put his foot on the exhaust pipes and slung his arm around the saddle. 'Go!'

'Can you ride like that?' asked Hal.

'Just hold on,' said Norm. He opened the throttle and the jetbike roared away from the scene at top speed. A few minutes later they were at the spaceport, where the entrance guard watched open-mouthed as the bike sailed past with Clunk hanging from the side.

'Evening!' called Hal, with a casual wave.

'Where to?' asked Norm.

Hal pointed across the landing field. The Volante's

floodlights were on, and the ship glowed against the night sky.

'I never thought I'd see her again,' said Clunk softly.

Hal tapped Norm on the shoulder. 'Drop us at the passenger ramp.'

'No, the cargo ramp,' said Clunk. 'I want to check the freight, and I'm not cluttering up the flight deck with all these junky robot parts.'

Hal grinned. 'You won't be, not if you're in the hold.'

'One then the other,' said Norm, angling the bike towards the ship.

◆

Sonya blew on her fingers, certain she'd lost half of them to the cold. She'd lost all feeling in her hands more than an hour ago, and she was desperately tired, having been woken at regular intervals throughout the previous night by Rex's terse progress reports on the *Volante's* whereabouts. She was hungry and stiff and she needed a rest break. But more than anything she wanted to wrap her frozen fingers around Rex Curtis's neck and ram his head through the nearest wall.

He was sure to be tucking into a three-course meal, and Sonya's mouth watered at the thought of rich gravy, tender meat and honey-glazed vegetables. She could see the wine glugging into his glass - good quality, but not extravagant. She could hear the clink of cutlery as wealthy restaurant patrons stuffed delicacies down their overfed necks. She could hear the bellowing roar of the jetbike as it . . . Eh?

183

Her daydream popped like a cheap balloon, and Sonya scanned the wind-swept landing field to find the source of the noise. Was it a spaceship coming in to land? An official vehicle of some kind? A patrol?

Four enormous headlights beamed out of the darkness, and a sleek jetbike roared across the tarmac. Sonya saw a shadowy figure leaning over the handlebars just before the bike disappeared behind the Volante. Moments later it reappeared, circling the ship to stop near the passenger ramp. Hal Spacejock dismounted and spoke briefly to the rider, an elderly man in a leather helmet and oversized goggles. They shook hands, and as Hal stepped onto the Volante's passenger ramp the bike sped away with a roar from its chromed exhausts.

Sonya watched Hal returning to his ship. She wondered whether he appreciated his freedom, whether he realised just how precious it was. Her face hardened. He knew all right. He made his living off desperate refugees, taking their savings before dropping them into the arms of the authorities - when he wasn't abandoning them on backwater planets with acid soil and no atmosphere. Sonya shivered. Rex's plan only called for delaying tactics, but she could take it further. She could ensure this Spacejock character never preyed on another helpless refugee.

She reached for the briefcase, forcing her cold fingers around the handle. Then she stood and strode towards the Volante's passenger ramp. Halfway up, she stopped. She couldn't greet Spacejock with a face like a thunderstorm - he'd have her out the door before she'd said her piece. She pulled out a pocket mirror and ran her hand across the back, activating the ring light embedded in the frame. Frowning at her reflection, she ran her fingers through her windswept hair and practised a winning smile or two. 'Oh, Mr Spacejock, you're so handsome!' she squeaked, batting her eyelids. Stifling a laugh, she put the compact away and picked up the heavy briefcase. The bastard wouldn't know what hit him.

◆

Rex Curtis paced his office, glaring at the commset on his desk after every snap turn. Where was his call? Where was his blasted ID? Without it he'd be facing the Ullimo justice system, where upstanding businessmen like himself were treated like common thieves. Hunted by the media, chased by dodgy lawyers, hounded by the law ... the future looked bleak indeed, if he were crazy enough to stick around.

The commset rang. 'I have a Mr Jones for you. Will you take the call?'

'Of course I bloody will!' snapped Curtis, hurrying to the desk. He snatched the handset off the cradle and held it to his face. 'Well? Have you finished?'

'Not quite.'

'Dammit, you've had hours! What the hell are you playing at?'

'I haven't seen one like this before. It's new design with stronger encryption, and it's taking longer than usual.'

'Can you crack it or not?'

'Yes, but I'll need another twenty-four hours.'

Curtis swore. 'I need it now, man. Two hours at the outside.'

'Impossible,' said the caller firmly.

'But –'

185

'You want it to pass for an original, right? You don't want to break into a sweat every time you hand it over?'

'Of course I don't. It has to be perfect!'

'Then it will be ready this time tomorrow. Unless –'

'What?'

'The hardware I'm using. They brought out a new model a couple of months ago - it could eat this system for breakfast.'

'Keep talking.'

'I could get the parts in half an hour. Another half to set it up, then an hour to, er, modify the documents. All done in two.'

'How much?'

The caller told him.

'Are you mad?' shouted Curtis. 'I could buy a new limo for that!'

'I'm only giving you the options.'

Curtis glanced at his terminal. He could bury the purchase in the accounts and let Garmit and Hash worry about the bill when they wound his company up. 'Okay, let's do it. Send me the details and I'll get an order off immediately.'

'Thanks, Mr Curtis. You won't regret this.'

'I'd better not,' snapped Curtis. 'You get that paperwork here or I'll ...'

But the caller had rung off.

20

'Navcom, seal the ship and prepare for lift-off.'

'Complying,' said the computer. 'Destination?'

'Better make it Ackexa. And find out if Central Bank have their own landing pad.'

'Checking now.'

The lift doors parted and Clunk entered the flight deck. 'Mr Spacejock, can you explain this?'

Hal turned to see the robot holding out a handful of packing beads. 'It's just rubbish.'

Clunk sniffed it. 'Smells like machine oil.'

'That came from the robot's packing crate,' said the Navcom.

'The what?' exclaimed Clunk, his eyes wide.

'Mr Spacejock has a new robot,' said the Navcom. 'It was delivered earlier today.'

'It's not what you think,' said Hal hurriedly. 'I won a competition. I'm going to sell it off.'

'Where is it?'

'The last I saw, knee deep in the rec room. It said it could fix the AutoChef.'

'How could you let it touch my ship?' demanded Clunk, hurrying towards the lift.

'Lee said he was qualified.'

Clunk pressed the button. 'Lee? You've already given this thing a name?'

'It came with one.' Hal hesitated. 'Listen, you remember those apes on that planet?'

'The planet we never visited?'

'That's the one. Well, we've got one on board.'

'What?'

'It's just a little one,' said Hal hastily. 'It's in the rec room. I, er, called it Lucy.'

Clunk's mouth set in a firm line. 'Half a day, I was gone. Just half a day.'

'Someone is coming up the ramp,' said the Navcom suddenly.

Hal cursed. 'I bet it's the law. They've come to arrest Clunk for those broken windows.'

'They're not carrying ID,' said the Navcom.

'Quarantine inspection? Clunk, they've got wind of Lucy!'

The robot sniffed. 'I'm not surprised.'

Hal strode into the airlock and peered through the porthole. Outside, a slender, fair-haired woman was standing on the platform, holding a silver briefcase in one hand and a small bag in the other. Hal studied her face - cool grey eyes beneath dark, straight eyebrows. 'Looks like a lawyer,' he muttered. 'It's got to be those windows.' After a moment's indecision he opened the outer door.

As soon as the gap was big enough, the woman entered the airlock. 'Mr Spacejock, oh please say you'll help me.'

Caught by surprise, Hal could only stare. 'H-huh?'

'I missed my flight and the men at the spaceport said you'd help me.'

Hal gazed into her wide grey eyes. 'Did they really?'

188

'I'm Sonya. Sonya Smith. They told me you were going to Ackexa, and Canessa is on the way, and ...' Sonya gripped Hal's arm. 'Oh, do say you'll help! I'll pay double the going rate!'

'Well, we don't carry passengers as a rule.'

'Couldn't you make an exception?' Sonya put her head to one side. 'Just for me? Please?'

Hal grinned. 'Just for you.'

'Oh, thank you!' Sonya hugged him. 'I really appreciate it. You've saved my life.'

'You'd better come in,' mumbled Hal, who'd turned a deep shade of red. He led her into the flight deck, where Clunk was still waiting near the lift. 'This is my robot, Clunk. Clunk, this is Sonya Smith.'

Sonya stared, her face pale. 'Your robot?'

'Ms Smith,' said Clunk, sparing her a brief nod. He glanced at Hal. 'We're ready to depart, Mr Spacejock. We should be landing on Ackexa in three hours.'

'Ah yes, the cargo. Look, there's been a slight change of plan. I thought we could take Ms Smith to Canessa first.'

'Maybe on the way back. Right now we're going to Ackexa.'

'No! I can't go to Ackexa!' Sonya lowered her voice. 'I don't have a permit.'

'You have an Outsider accent,' said Clunk. 'Why would you need a permit?'

'Leave it, Clunk,' said Hal. 'We're going to Canessa.'

'Mr Spacejock, I urge you to reconsider.' Clunk spread his hands. 'For a start, we're not authorised to carry passengers. And Canessa is an uninhabited planet: leaving this woman there would be insane. Moreover, we're facing a fixed deadline and ...'

Hal put his arm round the robot's shoulders. 'Clunk, let's

not argue. The lady asked nicely, and it'll only take us, what, an hour or so extra?'

'Eight hours minimum. It's in the opposite direction, Mr Spacejock.'

'So? We'll make it.'

'But why does she want to go to Canessa?'

'I'm investigating a vanished civilisation,' said Sonya. 'I'm a historian, you see.'

'Historian?' Hal stared at her. 'But, er –'

'Oh, you think I should be older, right?' Sonya laughed. 'Everyone thinks historians have to be relics themselves.'

'Har har,' snorted Hal. 'Relics, that's a good one.'

Clunk rolled his eyes.

'What about my luggage?' Sonya looked Clunk up and down. 'You don't look very strong. Can you carry things?'

Clunk took a step towards her, and Hal quickly got between them. 'She's a paying customer, Clunk,' he hissed. 'Humour her, okay?' He turned to Sonya. 'Did you say luggage?'

'I have six crates outside.'

'Six!'

'Camping gear, scientific equipment ... Believe me, I'm travelling light.'

Clunk frowned at her. 'What exactly are you looking for?'

'I've been studying an ancient civilisation, and I think Canessa may be their long-lost homeworld. My plan is to land there and investigate one or two promising sites.'

'Wouldn't it be better to survey them from the air?'

'In this case, no. The planet's completely overgrown.'

Hal laughed. 'Yeah Clunk, it's overgrown. Can't see anything from the air.'

'So you're just going to wander around until you stub your toe on a fossil?' asked the robot.

'Don't be silly. Once I've set up the equipment, it should be able to detect the city.'

'What sort of equipment?' asked Clunk. 'If the city's made of stone, you won't know it's there until you sit on it. If it's wooden, all you'll find is compost.'

Sonya turned to Hal. 'Just think, I wasted all those years studying for this trip and all I needed was five minutes in a junk shop.'

'What do you mean?'

'Well, your robot seems to know more about my field than I do.'

'Clunk knows everything.' Hal took Sonya's briefcase and handed it to Clunk. 'Take this to the passenger cabin.'

'Are you sure about that? The floor is still covered with little bits of gold plastic.'

'Ah, you mean the spare parts I was knocking up for the generator.'

'Spare parts have safety pins taped to the back?'

'Just get the cabin ready and load the cargo. Okay?'

'Yes master, anything you say.' Clunk snapped a salute, turned and stalked into the lift.

'Those old models always did have defective personalities,' said Sonya loudly.

'He's all right, he's just brassed off. I lent him to the museum for an exhibition and someone pinched him.'

'I find that hard to believe. Who'd steal a wreck like that?'

'He'd been sold to a junk shop, and by the time I tracked him down he was in pieces. You should have seen it ... the owner tried to fob me off, so I had to smack him one.' Hal brandished his fist. 'Pow! Right in the kisser.'

Sonya winced. 'But you got Clunk back?'

'No, they'd already used his parts in another robot. So I threatened to break their arms unless they fixed him.'

'Were there many of them?'

'At least four.'

'Four men!'

'No, four arms.' Hal gestured at himself. 'Two men, two arms each.'

'Clunk must be valuable to you, Mr Spacejock. You went to a lot of trouble to save him.'

'Please, call me Hal.'

Sonya smiled. 'I'll do that, Hal.'

The console speakers crackled. 'Ground facilities have now been disconnected. What are your instructions?'

'Carry on,' said Hal, without taking his eyes off Sonya.

'Carry on with what?' asked the Navcom.

'Get ready to leave.'

'Please clarify.'

Hal flashed a strained smile at Sonya. 'Excuse me a moment, would you?' He crossed to the console and leant in close. 'Stop messing around,' he hissed. 'You know exactly what to do.'

'So you won't be navigating the uncharted reaches of the screensaver, then?' asked the Navcom loudly.

'I think you mean the flight simulator. And this time I'll leave it in your capable hands.'

'Are you certain? Your flying might prove more entertaining for our passenger. Do you remember that time on Forg, when you had to crash-land in a rubbish tip to save the ship? Or the time –'

Hal gripped the microphone. 'One more word out of you and I'll tear this off and ram it up your user port. Got it?' He rolled his eyes at Sonya. 'Appliances, eh? Give them half a brain ...'

Sonya glanced at her watch. 'I don't mean to trouble you, but are we leaving soon?'

'We'll be under way as soon as Clunk's loaded that luggage of yours.'

'He won't damage it, will he?'

'Clunk's good at his job. I trained him myself.'

There was a squawk from the console, quickly silenced by Hal's warning glance.

'I really must get on with my research,' said Sonya. 'Do you think my cabin is ready?'

'Oh, sure. Let me show you down.'

'I know where it is.'

Hal looked surprised. 'You do?'

'Last door on the right, lower deck passageway?'

'How did you know that?'

'You do a lot of flying in my line of work,' said Sonya smoothly. 'I've travelled on everything from a hoverbike to a megafreighter.'

'Call if you need me,' said Hal, as Sonya entered the lift. 'I'll be supervising the Navcom. Getting the ship ready, that kind of thing.'

'Until later,' said Sonya, as the doors closed.

❧

Sonya studied her shoes as the Volante's lift dropped towards the lower deck. She'd almost blown her cover in the first five minutes, which didn't bode well for the next few hours. And the robot! She'd have words with Rex about that. So much for getting it out of the way . . . all he'd done was make

193

the wretched thing even more suspicious. Hal was all right, though. Sonya grinned. Just how she liked them - handsome, well built and dumb.

The lift doors opened and she stepped into the Volante's lower deck passageway. The lights were low, and she noted the doors on either side of the carpeted hallway: Rec room, toilets, galley, captain's quarters and Clunk's cabin (Keep Out). Sonya's eyes narrowed. What was the robot doing with a room to itself? What could it possibly keep in there? She hesitated, and was just reaching for the controls when she saw the glossy black dome of a security camera at the end of the passage, fixed above the cargo hold door. Damn computer had eyes everywhere.

Sonya made a show of reading the sign, then tutted loudly and continued up the corridor to the passenger cabin. The door opened smartly as she palmed the control panel, and inside she found a fold-down desk, a narrow bed and a washbasin. The briefcase was lying on the bed, and although she checked it carefully she could see no evidence of tampering.

Sonya sat down. Several hours to Canessa, the robot had said. Thank goodness the surly hunk of tin hadn't insisted on Ackexa - without any ID, she'd never have got back into Union space. Her stomach growled, and she wondered whether Spacejock would rustle up a meal before bed.

◆

While Sonya was inspecting her cabin, Clunk was inspecting her cargo. He'd got the six huge crates aboard with Lee's help, and the wooden boxes were now standing in a line against the bulkhead. He'd checked and resealed most of them, and so far had found nothing unusual - a tent, cooking equipment, medical supplies, a personal stereo and some music chips. He'd examined one or two of the chips, but lacked an inbuilt player to test them. In any case, they were professionally produced and therefore unlikely to contain anything but the songs on the garish labels.

Clunk hated to admit it, but Sonya appeared to be genuine. Even her briefcase computer had a cutesy smiley face sticker on it, which was hardly the seal of a desperate criminal.

With a creak of tortured nails, the front came off the last crate. Clunk put it aside with the crowbar and peered inside. It was packed with tinned food, enough to last a month. He reached for a tin, to see whether it contained … what, exactly? He sighed and withdrew his hand, realising he was taking things too far.

'Should you be doing this?' asked Lee.

'It's my duty to check for contraband. Mr Spacejock is responsible for all goods carried aboard this vessel, and that Farquhar in customs would be delighted if he could catch us out.' Clunk replaced the lid and pounded the nails in with his fist. There was nothing incriminating about the crates, so all he had to go on were his misgivings. Could that be his programming? An enhanced loyalty to Hal which made him suspicious of everyone else? He dropped the crowbar over a crossbeam and picked up a bundle of strapping. 'Take the other end.'

A few minutes later, the crates were secure. Clunk went to the inner door and raised a hand to the controls. Then he realised Lee was right behind. 'Where do you think you're going?'

'I thought I'd go to the flight deck.'

195

'Think again.' Clunk gestured at the hold. 'I want this floor so clean I can see my face in it.'

'But –'

'You're not getting within a mile of the flight deck after your efforts with the AutoChef. Not until you prove yourself in other areas. Understood?'

Lee nodded reluctantly.

'So, grab a rag and get polishing.'

◆

'Now that's what I call a passenger,' said Hal to himself. The indicator above the lift switched to Lower Deck and he pictured Sonya striding along the passageway to her cabin. 'She knows her ships. I like that.'

He pictured Sonya entering the small cabin, opening her luggage, perhaps changing into something more comfortable. Then he pictured ...

The lift doors opened and Clunk entered the flight deck, his fans whizzing as they cooled him down.

'What got you all steamed up?'

'I was loading all that cargo.'

'You should've asked Lee to give you a hand.'

Clunk snorted. 'Like the hand he gave you with the AutoChef?'

'Yeah, er ... thanks for putting it back together.'

'It was easy. But then I'm not a customer service clerk with delusions of grandeur.' Clunk turned to the console. 'Navcom, please obtain clearance and initiate departure.'

The ship's engines burst into life and the flight deck throbbed as they wound up to launch speed.

Hal listened to the familiar sounds, but his mind was busy with more pressing matters. 'Clunk, what am I going to wear for dinner?'

'Dinner?'

'Passengers always dine with the captain. It's traditional.'

'Never mind clothes, what are you going to eat?'

'Oh no, the AutoChef!' Hal groaned. 'I can't feed her from that thing. It'll poison her.'

Clunk turned away, hiding a smile. 'Navcom, take her up.'

With a gut-wrenching roar, the Volante took off from the Ullimo spaceport and thrust into the night sky.

21

Later that evening, the Volante was in deep space, approaching the planet's designated hyperspace point. Clunk was at the console, making small adjustments to their course. He'd just finished when the lift doors opened behind him. 'Good evening, Mr Spacejock. I'm happy to report –' Clunk broke off and sniffed the air. 'What's that smell?'

'Smell?'

Clunk turned round to look at him. 'Oh my goodness.'

'What's wrong?'

'You ...er ...um ...' Lost for words, Clunk could only gesture.

Hal looked down at himself. He was wearing a velvet suit with a white ruff and a pair of trousers so tight they could have been sprayed on. His hair had been liberally oiled, parted in the middle and slicked down, as if he'd shoved his head under a waterfall. He'd even tidied his eyebrows, which gave his face a slightly quizzical look. Clunk stared at the chunky gold chain, the fob watch and the gleaming gold shoes, shaking his head sadly.

'What is it?' demanded Hal.

'I'm not sure. Dementia? Spring fever?'

'Huh?' Hal smoothed a stubborn lick of hair. 'You think I just dressed up because we have a passenger, eh?'

Clunk nodded.

'Well, maybe I did. I'm the captain, right? I have to mingle with the passengers, entertain them.'

'You'll do that all right,' murmured Clunk, staring at the ruff in disbelief. 'Where did you –'

'It's style,' sniffed Hal. 'You wouldn't understand.'

'On the contrary, I have extensive training in haute couture.' Clunk paused. 'Look Mr Spacejock, that woman's done nothing but butter you up since she came aboard. It's so obviously false it makes me want to –' His fingers creaked as he clenched his fists.

'Give it away! If I didn't know you better I'd say you were jealous!'

'I'm what?' Clunk stared at him. 'Mr Spacejock, she's putting on an act. I don't know why, but she's up to something.'

'All she cares about is this ancient civilisation.'

'What are they called?'

'Huh?'

'These people - what were they known as? Were they space-farers? Did they vanish without trace? Did they have fire? Computers? Literature?'

The gold chain rattled as Hal put his hands up. 'Whoa, Clunk. Too many questions.'

'Not enough answers, you mean,' muttered the robot.

Just then the lift pinged.

'Ah, Sonya! Come in, come in!' cried Hal, as the doors opened. 'We're just preparing for hyperspace.'

Sonya stopped. 'Oh brother. Er . . . you look smart.'

199

'Come and look at the controls,' said Hal. 'I'll show you how the ship works.'

Clunk folded his arMs. 'Now this I have to see.'

'I do hope I won't be in the way,' said Sonya as she approached the console.

'Of course not,' said Hal. 'Come on.'

'Ooh, what a lot of lights and things!' Sonya smiled at Hal. 'Do you really know what they all do?'

'Red, red, blue,' said Clunk, smothering a grin.

Hal flushed. 'The manemol flange on the generator needs adjusting, Clunk. Attend to it at once.'

'That's going to take some adjustment,' said the robot. 'The manemol flange is supposed to be on the hyperdrive.'

'Just fix it. And I'd appreciate a bit less of the lip.'

As the lift doors swept to, Hal turned back to Sonya. 'I trust your accommodation is up to scratch?'

'Oh yes, very comfortable.'

'Speaking of comfort, would you dine with me?'

Suddenly Hal felt the warmth of Sonya's hand on his arm. 'I'd be honoured.'

He beamed. 'Magic! I'll get Clunk to rustle something up.'

Sonya withdrew her hand. 'Ah. The robot.'

'What's wrong?'

'Nothing. I feel a little uneasy around him. I don't think he likes me.'

'It's not that. He's just a bit suspicious of you.' Hal stared into Sonya's clear grey eyes. For a second they appeared calculating, cold. Then just as quickly, they softened again.

'Suspicious? Of a relic like me?'

Hal laughed. 'You're lucky. He fusses over me and that's far worse.'

Clunk was still in the lift with one ear pressed to the door. Hal's voice carried to him clearly through the metal, and the laughter his comments provoked was like a hot soldering iron to the eye. Clunk straightened up slowly, conflicting emotions visible in his face as he weighed his strong sense of loyalty against the desire to beat some sense into that stupid, self-centred, egotistical HUMAN.

Incensed, he turned and rammed his fist into the polished wall, leaving a deep impression of his bunched fingers. Then he jabbed the down button repeatedly, sending the lift plummeting towards the lower deck.

The doors opened and Clunk stormed along the passageway towards the cargo hold, heat haze shimmering from his vents. It was time for a closer look at Sonya's briefcase, and Lee would make the perfect lookout.

◆

Later that evening, Hal was entertaining Sonya in the rec room. 'The grub's not much,' he said, offering a plate of mashed potato topped with chocolate and sprinklies. 'The machine can be a bit stubborn sometimes.'

Sonya eyed the feast with a distinct lack of enthusiasm. 'You should get that robot to mend it.'

'I did. It's much better than it used to be.' Hal popped a small dollop of potato into his mouth and chewed vigorously. 'Hmm, orange flavour. Lovely.'

Sonya handed the plate back. 'So, tell me about you.'

'Me?'

'Yes. Why did you take up the lonely life of a cargo pilot?'

'I always wanted to travel, and this way someone pays me to do it.'

'Do you get a lot of work?'

'I just added Central Bank to my list of clients,' said Hal, neglecting to mention that it was the only name on the list.

'I thought they were contracted to Curtis?'

Hal frowned. 'Curtis?'

'Curtis Freightlines. They're the biggest freight company in the region. Or so I've heard.'

'That doesn't sound like historian territory.'

'Oh, it's just something I picked up.' Sonya nibbled a biscuit. 'Tell me, do you have any pets on board?'

Hal looked surprised. 'Pets?'

'Yes. One of the cargo handlers told me to watch out for a hairy creature.'

With a shock, Hal remembered Lucy. It was hours since he'd fed her, and he wasn't even sure where she'd got to. 'He must have been mistaken. This is a freighter, not a flying zoo.'

'You're quite certain? He said there was a furry orange thing with lots of teeth and ...'

'Oh, that hairy orange creature.' Hal laughed. 'It was just a delivery. She's not here any more.'

'Thank goodness for that!'

Hal gave her the plate. 'Have a biscuit.'

'Thanks.' Sonya took one and put the plate on the armrest of her chair. 'I invested all my savings into this trip, you know. If I don't find this lost civilisation I'm done for.'

'What are they called? You know, these people you're looking for.'

Sonya smiled. 'They're lost, Hal. Nobody knows what they're called.'

A hairy orange paw stretched out from behind Sonya's chair, and Hal watched in horror as it reached for the biscuits. He dragged his gaze away. 'So, er, how do you know they existed?'

'We identified their homeworld, or at least we thought we had. They used generation ships, and the experts plotted every planet this race had settled. Then they plotted lines back to the centre and decided the closest planet to that point must have been the homeworld.'

'Canessa?'

'No, another world. Problem is, there was nothing there but abandoned settlements. There's no way it was the launching point for a galactic civilisation.'

Hal tried not to look as Lucy grabbed another handful of biscuits.

'They searched a bunch of other planets in the vicinity, but they weren't right either. Then I had an idea. They must have improved their technology over time, which means the later ships would have been faster. That invalidated the whole idea of plotting the expansion to locate the homeworld.'

'I see,' said Hal, who didn't.

'So, they failed to take into account this one little factor.'

'What's that?'

'Weathering,' said Sonya. 'The expansion bubble isn't a perfect sphere - the sites on some planets are almost worn to nothing, while those on others are more preserved. I believe it's caused by variations in weathering, not age, and if I'm right that would put Canessa right in the centre.'

'Amazing,' said Hal. 'All those people looking, and you've found the homeworld.'

Sonya shook her head. 'Not yet. I need proof first.'

Hal saw Lucy reaching for more biscuits. 'Wow, look at the time. I'd better get back to the flight deck.'

'You're supposed to be entertaining me.' Sonya smiled at him. 'Can't your robot fly the ship?'

◆

Clunk marched along the lower deck passage with Lee in tow. He stopped at Sonya's door and knocked. 'Cleaning service,' he called, pushing it open. The cabin was sparse, with barely enough room for the fold-down bunk and narrow desk. The bunk had been lowered, the bedclothes pulled tight and tucked in. Clunk stepped back and pushed Lee into the room. 'Sweep the floor, wipe all surfaces and don't touch anything. Got it?'

Lee nodded.

Clunk saw the briefcase underneath the bunk. He bent down, pulled it out and set it on the blankets.

'How come you're touching stuff?' asked Lee. 'You told me _'

Clunk silenced the robot with a glare. He ran his fingers around the lid, then opened the briefcase. Inside there was a screen, a keyboard and two data cables - one red, one black. Clunk scowled at the plugs. They were packed with optical filaments, and he had no socket to match.

'Do you have a connector for these?' he asked Lee.

'I have connectors for every electronic device built in the past four decades,' said the robot stuffily.

'Right, plug in and download whatever you can.'

'But that's not your case!'

Clunk leaned closer. 'Either you download the contents, or I'll rip you to pieces and jerry-rig a connector from the scraps.' Suddenly he heard laughter from the rec room. 'And hurry it up!'

Lee opened a compartment in his chest and plugged the black cable in.

'Well?' demanded Clunk.

'It's just giving me data errors.'

'All right, try the other one.'

Lee removed the black cable and plugged the red one in. There was a loud buzz as the connector slotted into place, and Lee jerked upright, his eyes wide open. 'Wow, it's full of –' Zap! Blue smoke puffed from the robot's ears, and he shuddered uncontrollably.

Clunk yanked the plug out and caught the falling robot with his left arm. With his right he grabbed the case and threw it under the bunk, flapping madly to disperse the smoke.

He glanced at Lee, who had the ecstatic, incredulous look of a film producer with a blank cheque. Clunk slapped the robot around the face, but apart from adjusting the rapturous look, it had no effect. Adjusting his grip, he hauled Lee backwards out of the cabin.

At the cargo hold he dragged the robot through the doorway, accidentally slamming its head on the step. Then he shut the door and looked around, seeking a suitable hiding place. If Hal saw Lee like this he would assume the worst - that Clunk had dispatched his rival intentionally. He selected one of the lockers lining the cargo hold, propped Lee inside and pushed the door to.

Beep!

Clunk jumped, then realised it was the Navcom.

'We're approaching the first jump point. I wanted to advise Hal and Ms Smith but I cannot raise them.'

'Have you tried the rec room?'

'Affirmative. The intercom is off and the camera is non-operational.'

Clunk shook his head. 'Mr Spacejock is certainly taking this dinner business seriously.'

'If only he would apply the same amount of effort to his piloting.'

'Very well. I'll be right up.'

—

Later that night, Sonya returned to her cabin. A trace of blue smoke hung in the air, and she coughed at the stench of burning electrics. The briefcase! Had Dent's cooling system failed? She pulled the case from under the bed. 'Bobby, what's that smell?'

The briefcase sniffed. 'It certainly wasn't me.'

'Who was it then?'

'A robot. It used the red cord.'

Sonya stared at the briefcase in shock. 'You toasted a robot?'

'Oh yes. Completely immobilised.'

Sonya looked under the bed. 'Are you sure? It couldn't have dragged itself away, could it?'

'Negative, I gave it the full treatment. That delicate scent is vaporised robot brain.'

'But it's not here!'

'Then someone removed it.'

'Who?'

'I don't know. I was in standby mode.'

'What if you only damaged it? I was speaking to Hal five minutes ago, so he can't have moved it. And there's nobody else around.' A memory of hairy orange arms reaching for her out of the darkness flashed up … If that thing had any intelligence it might have moved the stricken robot. But was it still aboard?

Sonya sat on the bed, deep in thought. If the robot was out of the way, that was a plus. She could smooth Hal over. The thing was so old he'd probably think it was a normal breakdown. Then an unpleasant thought struck her. What if Dent's killer robot was roaming the ship?

She tucked the briefcase under her arm and slipped along the passage to the cargo bay door. Entering the hold, she marched between shrink-wrapped pallets until she found her cargo lashed to the bulkhead with heavy-duty strapping. She pressed a stud and the straps dropped to the floor. Then she examined the crates closely until she found the one Dent had marked with three parallel scratches. 'Tinker,' she said softly, rapping on the wood.

There was no reply.

Sonya spotted a crowbar hooked over a cross-beam. She grabbed it, and was just about to put the point under the lid when she noticed someone had beaten her to it. There was a dent in the wood that matched the tip of the crowbar.

'Damned nosy robot,' she muttered, looking over her shoulder. If it had found Tinker …

She used the crowbar to remove the lid, then stared at the contents in surprise. The crate was filled with rows of tin cans. 'Tinker?'

The wall of tins bulged and tumbled out, revealing the robot at the back of the crate. 'Oh, very cunning,' said Sonya, as she saw the tins had been fastened to a large sheet of ply.

Tinker looked down at her, then scanned the deserted hold. 'Where are the foes?'

'Forget about foes. I want you to put this crate back together, find a hiding place and stay there until I need you.'

'And if anyone finds my hiding place?'

'Tell them you're a stowaway.' While Tinker replaced the tins, Sonya went over to the workbench and connected the briefcase to a wall socket.

'What have we here?' asked the computer loudly.

'Shut up!' hissed Sonya. 'Can't you lower your voice when I turn you on?'

'It's part of my boot sequence.'

'Well tone it down before I get into trouble. Now, I want you to plant some errors in the log, but I want them activated after we've landed. Can you do that?'

'Easy.'

'And they won't know the source?'

'No way. I'm the most advanced –'

'Yes, we established that. Now shut up and do your job.'

'Complying,' said the briefcase. A few seconds later, it piped up again. 'I've added a couple of temperature warnings to the generator logs. It will take the Navcom hours to check them out.'

'Perfect.' Sonya unplugged the briefcase and glanced around the hold. The crate was back together, and Tinker was nowhere to be seen. Mission accomplished, she returned to her cabin for a well-earned rest.

22

Rex Curtis ripped open the envelope and tipped the contents into his lap. An Outsider passport fell out, and when he turned to the first page his own face stared up from the hologram. Rex smiled at the name underneath: Hal Spacejock. Although an Outsider ID would restrict his movements, it was a good start. He'd hide until the fuss died down, then resume his own identity when it was safe.

Shoving the passport into his pocket, Rex reached for the model of the Aurora. He wrapped it in his jacket, raised it to shoulder height and slammed it on the edge of his desk. There was a muffled crash as the model broke apart, and when he opened the jacket a heavy-duty blaster and a fat leather pouch lay amongst the fragments.

Rex carried the jacket full of pieces to the front of his desk and scattered them on the floor. To a casual observer, the model had simply fallen off the desk. He shook his jacket to dislodge any fragments, then activated his commset and called the landing field. 'Mac? I need my flyer. Urgent business.'

'She's all ready, Mr Curtis.'

'I'll be right down.' Rex hung up and looked around his office. For a moment, he wondered whether he was doing the right thing . . . After so many years this office was as familiar and comfortable as his home. He shook his head. If he stuck around he'd be jailed for tax evasion, fraud and whatever else the corporate regulators could stick on him. The last thing he wanted was to be thinking how familiar and comfortable his cell was after so many years.

He jammed the gun into his waistband and strode to the door. After a final look at the shattered model of the Aurora, he left.

◆

Rex stepped from the lift and hurried into the cavernous underground workshop. His spotted his flyer near the exit ramp, a sleek black machine with the canopy up and the engine idling. A mechanic touched his grease-stained cap and stepped away from the vessel.

'Fuel?' snapped Rex.

'Yes sir,' replied the mechanic. 'All systems go.'

'Good man,' panted Rex, as he clambered up the short ladder. Once he was seated he pulled the straps tight and waved his hand. The canopy came down and the control panel lit up in front of him. He blipped the throttle and the craft began to roll. Only then did Rex glance outside to see if the mechanic was clear. Tough luck if he wasn't, he thought.

The flyer gathered speed as Rex aimed it towards the ramp. It took the incline with a roar from its powerful engine, and his stomach rose as the ship levelled out on the apron. Once clear of the refuelling clusters, he drove onto the nearest taxiway and activated the winglets, which extended with a whine of hydraulics. Then he was heading for the far side of the landing field.

Company freighters took off vertically from their landing pads, so a section of perimeter road had been set aside as a short runway for flyers. As his ship rumbled over the taxiways, Rex obtained clearance. When he reached the runway he was able to pull straight on, and he lined the nose of the flyer up with the far end and opened the throttle.

The engine howled behind him, crushing him against the padded seat as the ship hurled itself down the strip of tarmac. It was airborne before the halfway mark, and Rex immediately pulled the stick back and pointed the nose straight up.

As the flyer climbed into the sky, Rex flipped out the navigation console and programmed a chain of hyperspace jumps. Fuel would be critical, but it was only a one-way trip.

◆

'Through the screensaver? Really?'

'Absolutely,' said the Navcom. 'It took him two hours to catch on.'

Clunk sat back in the pilot's chair, a broad grin on his face. 'Next time wait until I'm present. I want to be there.'

'It won't work again. He'd recognise the comet.'

'Show me.'

The Volante's screensaver appeared, complete with rotating blue planet and fast-moving comet.

'Can't you switch the planet with a real one from your database?'

The bright blue sphere morphed into a mottled green planet with swirling clouds.

'That's much better. Now get rid of the comet and dim the stars a bit.' Clunk eyed the changes critically. 'Oh yes. Very realistic.'

'Would you like me to make the changes permanent?'

'Yes. And be sure to call me if Mr Spacejock takes the controls.'

'Understood. Incidentally, our destination is in range. ETA thirty minutes.'

'Excellent. Can you put the real display up?'

The screensaver vanished and Clunk watched planet Canessa growing larger by the minute. 'I do hope there are no ferocious monsters here. That Smith woman might get eaten.'

'It's uninhabited,' said the Navcom.

'Pity.' Clunk scanned the console for warning lights, but all systems were working perfectly. 'Any sign of Mr Spacejock?'

'He's just entering the lift.'

Clunk shook his head slowly. 'Say what you like about Hal's piloting, but he can't be faulted when it comes to customer servicing.'

'I think you mean customer service,' said the Navcom primly.

The lift doors opened, and footsteps approached across the flight deck.

'Good morning, Mr Spacejock,' called Clunk over his shoulder.

'Morning Clunk.' Hal made himself busy with the coffee machine. 'I need the caffeine - late night and all that. Hey, can you talk the AutoChef into dispensing pancakes?'

Clunk turned round slowly, fixing Hal with a disapproving stare. His velvet suit was awry, his face was unshaven and his hair looked like it had been styled with a can of static electricity. 'I'm sorry, did you say something?'

'Breakfast. You know, pancakes and stuff.' Hal winked. 'Late night.'

Clunk leaned an elbow on the console. 'It has probably escaped your attention, but we're currently approaching a solid mass at high speed. Sometime in the next three minutes I shall begin firing the attitude jets to slow our descent and prevent a major crash.'

'Uh-huh?'

'Indeed. Now, if you order me to prepare food I shall do so, but afterwards the only pancakes on this ship will be you and that Smith woman.'

Hal frowned. 'Are you refusing to get my breakfast?'

'That's the gist of it.'

'Fine, I'll do it myself,' snapped Hal. With that he stalked into the lift.

As the doors closed, Clunk turned back to the console. 'How long now, Navcom?'

'Twenty-three minutes to final approach. Shall I handle the landing?'

'Of course. Do I ever interfere?'

'Not with the ship, no.'

Clunk grinned.

The Volante set down in a clearing, the landing ramp unfolded from the ship and the outer door opened. Hal emerged first, looking like a space cadet on the first day of summer camp as he strolled down the ramp in a clean flight suit. 'Come on you guys. Let's get the stuff set up.' He slapped at his neck and examined his hand. 'Hey, would you look at the size of that bloodsucker?'

Sonya emerged from the ship, shielding her eyes against the sun with one hand while carrying the briefcase in the other. She was dressed in faded jeans and a white blouse, and her hair was tied back in a ponytail.

'Watch the flies,' called Hal. 'They've had a taste and they seem to like it.'

Sonya descended the ramp, holding the briefcase steady as she scanned the trees around the clearing. Before she reached the ground, Clunk appeared on the platform.

'Mr Spacejock, did you touch the generators?'

'No. Why?'

'According to the logs, they've been overheating again.'

Sonya glanced at Hal. 'That sounds serious. You'd better get your robot to check it out.'

Hal nodded. 'Clunk, can you give the generators a once over?'

'No need. There are no entries in the backup logs, which means this is almost certainly spurious data. Forget I brought it up.'

Sonya frowned at Hal. 'That doesn't sound very safe. Can't you order him to check things over?'

'He'd have the whole ship in pieces if he really thought there was a problem. He's a born worrier.' Hal looked around the clearing. 'Nice place for a camp. Where do you want the stuff?'

'But the errors in the log! You can't just ignore them!'

Hal shrugged. 'If he's not worried, I'm not worried.'

'But –' Sonya forced a smile. 'You're right, it's silly of me. I just didn't want anything to happen to you.' She hesitated.

'Can we unload in a moment or two? Right now I could use a walk.'

'Good idea. Where shall we go?'

'I need to take some readings,' said Sonya, lifting the briefcase. 'I work best on my own. I'm sure you understand.'

'Oh.' Hal's face fell. 'Well, don't be too long. We've got a cargo to deliver.'

Sonya smiled and patted his cheek. 'Don't leave before I've had a chance to say a proper goodbye.'

Before Hal could react she'd turned away. He watched her walk to the trees with the briefcase swinging from her hand, and saw her vanish into the undergrowth. A moment or two later he turned and trudged back up the ramp to the flight deck, where he found Clunk hunched over the console. 'How's the atmosphere?'

'It will do,' said the robot.

'What was all that about the generators?'

'Nothing. Don't worry about it.' He glanced at Hal. 'We must unload her boxes and leave immediately if we're to meet the Central Bank deadline.'

'Let's get to it, then.' Hal led the way to the hold where he stared at the six large crates in amazement. 'How did you get those aboard?'

'All by myself, no thanks to Lee.'

'Lee? Oh, the new robot.' Hal looked around. 'Where is it?'

Clunk looked uncomfortable. 'It broke down.'

'You're kidding! How?'

'We were cleaning Ms Smith's cabin, and her briefcase had a red cable and Lee sort of accidentally connected to it.'

'You didn't sort of accidentally think that might be a bad idea?'

215

'It was too late,' said Clunk miserably. 'By the time I intervened there was smoke coming out of his ears.'

'Well, you'll just have to unload the cargo by yourself, won't you?'

'Yes Mr Spacejock.'

'If you need me, I'll be in the flight deck studying our insurance policy. With a bit of luck we're covered for stupidity.'

Sonya hurried through the forest, putting some distance between herself and the ship. Rex's plan had seemed simple enough. Get the *Volante* to a deserted planet and delay Hal until the Central Bank deadline had passed. But what if Hal took off and left her? She wouldn't put it past Rex to leave it a few days before rescuing her - if he bothered at all. And what's more, the damned briefcase weighed a ton. 'I wish you had legs,' she growled, easing her aching shoulders.

The briefcase beeped. 'I notice you're trying to cross an uncharted forest. Would you like some assistance?'

'Sure. Got a map?'

'No.'

'A drink, perhaps?'

'Negative.'

'So what kind of help are you offering?'

There was a pause. 'I notice my system software has yet to be unlocked. You do realise this is a criminal offence?'

Sonya made a noise. 'That's Dent's problem.'

'Was the information on the lost civilisation any good?'

216

'Didn't really need it.' The briefcase had given her a reams of info, but after five minutes she noticed Hal was barely listening. That's when she started making crap up, and he'd still nodded and smiled the whole time. 'Can you tell me what happened to the errors you inserted in the log? Hal's robot said something about a backup.'

'They must be running a duplicate logging server in parallel,' said Bobby. 'Tricky, that. The second copy must have been well hidden.'

'Great. So how am I supposed to delay them?'

'Dent gave you a robot. Why don't you use it?'

Sonya made a face. 'Whatever Hal's done, he doesn't deserve Tinker. No, I'll just have to disappear for a while and trust them not to leave me here.'

'I thought Spacejock was notorious for doing exactly that? Abandoning refugees on deserted planets?'

'So Curtis said.' Truth was, now that she'd met Hal she had trouble believing it. Sonya hefted the briefcase, winced at the pain in her shoulder, and pushed on through the forest. It was a pleasant walk, with the sunlight filtering through the leaves and an earthy smell in the air, and only the buzzing of an occasional fly to disturb the peace.

After another ten minutes the briefcase felt like a lump of lead. Sonya stopped for a rest, and as she was turning her head to loosen her neck muscles she spotted a clearing through the trees. In the exact centre were four weathered columns, marking the corners of a large stone slab. She blinked, hardly believing her eyes. Rex had suggested the lost civilisation yarn as a cover story, and yet here was evidence of civilisation not a kilometre from the ship. He'd only picked Canessa because it was uninhabited and away from the major shipping routes.

Sonya entered the clearing and approached the columns,

her shoes clicking on cracked paving slabs underfoot. A gust of wind shook the trees, and she shivered as a shadow passed over the sun. As she got closer to the stonework she convinced herself it had to be relatively modern. Perhaps a couple hundred years, and maybe a secret lab or an outpost or something. They wouldn't show on Rex's civilian maps.

Sonya hesitated, uncertain. She wasn't far from the *Volante* and Spacejock would probably find the clearing if he came looking for her. She ought to keep moving, to put more distance between herself and the ship, but in the end curiosity won out and she went to investigate the structure.

◆

Clunk pushed the first of Sonya's crates to the back of the hold, where he gave it a nudge to send it sliding down the ramp. He watched with satisfaction as the heavy box slammed into the turf and crashed end-over-end, then went for the next one. He'd just pushed the last crate down the ramp when he heard footsteps inside the hold.

'Have you seen Sonya?' called Hal.

'No.'

'She's been a long time.'

'All of thirty minutes.'

Hal looked down at the crates. 'Why are you laying them on their sides?'

'It was more efficient.'

'Okay, carry on.'

Clunk hesitated. 'Mr Spacejock, I know Sonya hasn't returned yet, but we really must leave.'

'We can't abandon a passenger.'

'This is where she wanted to be.'

'What if she's in trouble?'

'Do you intend to stay here until she leaves? Wait while she completes her studies?'

'Well no, but ... you know. I've got to say goodbye. She promised me she'd ... ' Hal stopped. 'Well, I thought we were going to ...'

The intercom buzzed. 'Clunk, are you there?'

'Yes, Navcom. What is it?'

'I have the results of those tests you ordered.'

Clunk glanced at Hal. 'Oh yes. What did you find?'

'The logging errors were introduced via the data socket in the cargo hold.'

'Estimated time?'

'Niner fifty, one-oh-two,' said the Navcom.

'Negative. Repair underway. Repeat log confirm?'

'Log confirm. Niner fifty, one-oh-two. Manual check?'

'Negative. Cache same?'

'Cache clear.'

Clunk turned to Hal. 'There is something very strange going on.'

'You're telling me,' muttered Hal. 'What was all that about?'

'You remember those generator warnings I mentioned after we landed?'

'The ones you wiped?'

'Actually, I set them aside for further study. It seems they were deliberately introduced to our logs.'

Hal shrugged. 'Probably just a computer error. You know how those things go wrong all the time.'

Clunk frowned.

'Some of the time,' amended Hal.

'The logging aboard this ship takes place in parallel. The hidden copy doesn't have any faults in it, as I told you earlier. Whoever introduced the errors made a mistake.'

'Like I said, the computer went wrong.'

Clunk shook his head. 'Mr Spacejock, those errors were added by hand.'

'How do you mean?'

'Think about it. If I thought the generators were overheating I'd have to give them a thorough check. That could take hours, making us late for the Central Bank delivery.'

'So who could have messed with the logs?'

'Someone with a portable computer. Someone with unsupervised access to the ship.'

Hal stared at him. 'The mechanics! They were working on the generators and the old guy had a notepad thing with a little prick.'

'Not them, Mr Spacejock. Someone who came aboard recently. Someone with a portable computer hidden in a briefcase. Someone who ...'

'Oh, you mean Lee.' Hal frowned. 'I don't think he had a briefcase, though.'

'Oh, for goodness sake!' Clunk waved his arMs. 'I'm talking about our passenger!'

'Sonya's got nothing to do with this.'

'Don't be so sure. She had the opportunity, the equipment, the –'

'Motive? Go on, why would she do it? Why would she mess with logs and caches and whatnot?'

Clunk looked thoughtful. 'Who stands to gain if we don't make this delivery?'

'Central Bank. They'll hit us with a whacking great penalty fee.'

'No, they only use dirty tactics on their customers. I meant someone else. Someone who threatened to ruin you if you took this job.'

'Rex Curtis!' exclaimed Hal.

'Correct,' said Clunk. 'Sonya Smith could be working for him.'

'That's a bit of a stretch, Clunk. I mean, she's a historian.'

'Not a very good one.'

'She's got a theory. She told me about it.'

'Oh well, she must be above board, then.' Clunk crossed his arMs. 'If she's working for Curtis, the best thing we can do is take off right now. If you're worried about her safety we can check on her after delivering the paperwork.'

'I've got a better idea. We'll look for her right now, and when we find her you can present your loony spy theory. She'll love it. She has a great sense of humour.'

Clunk looked uncomfortable. 'I don't think that's the best way to resolve the matter. It might lead to unpleasantness.'

'Cold feet, eh? If you're going to make accusations, you can make them to her face. Come on.'

They went down the ramp and crossed the clearing to the spot where Sonya had vanished into the trees. Hal analysed several fallen leaves and a broken twig, then set off to the right.

Behind him, Clunk cleared his throat. 'There are footprints going the other way.'

'She must have doubled back.' Hal retraced his steps. 'Yeah, you're right. Let's go this way.'

'Whatever you say, Mr Spacejock.'

23

Up close, the concrete structure looked as solid as mountain rock. Sonya was no expert, but the crumbling edges looked more like a thousand years old than a hundred. Bang went her spy base theory. She made her way around, pausing to examine each column. They were carved with lines of flowing script, the edges blurred with age. It was nothing she'd seen before, of that she was certain.

The central slab had a smooth, flat surface, and was the size of the landing pads she'd seen at the spaceport. Three sides had steps cut into them, while the fourth had a rectangular hole in the middle. As she approached, Sonya realised it was an entrance with steps leading underground. They were thick with leaf mould, and a dank smell rose from the hole.

Sonya trod on the first step, slipped, and almost fell headlong. The briefcase slammed into the wall as she struggled for balance, and she realised it was madness to take it with her. She put the case down next to the entrance and steadied herself, putting both hands on the walls and descending the steps with care.

It grew darker and darker, and she realised she'd need a torch to go any further. Turning, she made her way back up the steps, treading carefully on the slippery leaves. She'd barely reached the mouth of the stairwell when she heard a distant shout. Sonya cursed silently. It could only be Spacejock and his damned robot.

Bending double, she ran for the trees, finding cover just as Hal and Clunk emerged on the far side of the clearing. She heard their excited voices as they saw the ancient concrete structure, and she crouched lower as they approached the ruins. She grinned as she pictured the robot falling down the slippery stairs, leaving Hal to drag it back up again on his own.

The grin vanished as a flash of silver caught her eye. She'd left Bobby the briefcase right next to the steps!

◆

Hal approached the ruins, staring at the weathered concrete. 'Do you think they're human?'

'No aesthetics, no windows and built in a clearing carved from the living forest.' Clunk nodded. 'Probably.'

'I told you Sonya was legit! It's her lost civilisation!'

'And that's her briefcase,' said Clunk, pointing it out.

Hal hurried over to pick it up, and as he approached the concrete slab he spotted the dark opening in the side. 'Clunk, there's a staircase! Shine your light!'

Clunk activated his chest lamp and shone it down the steps.

'Stinks a bit, doesn't it? But that's where she went.'

'Without a light?'

'There's her footprints.' Hal cupped his hands around his mouth. 'Sonya!'

'... onya ... onya,' echoed the entrance.

'Come on, we've got to find her. She might have broken her ankle or fallen into a pit or something.'

'That staircase looks very slippery, Mr Spacejock.'

'You go first, then.' Hal nodded at the briefcase. 'What about that?'

'It's not going to get stolen, is it?'

'What if it rains?'

'It's going to be hard enough negotiating these steps as it is. You don't want to burden yourself with hand luggage.'

'I'm not going to. You are.'

'I could lose my balance!'

'Come off it. You could cross a tightrope with a pyramid of fighting cats balanced on your shoulders.'

'Your confidence in my abilities is gratifying, but occasionally misplaced.'

Hal grabbed the briefcase and thrust it at the robot. 'Get moving. Sonya could be hurt.'

Clunk tucked the case under his arm and trod on the first step. His foot skated off the slime and shot into space, and he landed heavily on his back. The briefcase flew out of his hands, bounced off the step and disappeared with a series of loud crashes.

Hal winced at each echoing blow. 'I hope the instruments weren't as delicate as she made out.'

Clunk looked at him incredulously. 'A fall like that would turn granite into gravel. I can only imagine what it's done to the briefcase.'

'Sonya could be lying at the foot of these stairs in terrible pain, and here we are launching lethal missiles. How's she going to feel about that?'

'If the briefcase hit her she won't be feeling anything.'

'Do you think you can take these steps without falling over again?'

'Only if my hands are free.'

'Come on then, lead the way. And be careful! Compared to you, that briefcase was just a warning shot.'

◆

Sonya watched Hal and Clunk moving around the entrance, cursing under her breath when she realised they were preparing to descend. Sure, Hal was as thick as a plastic girder, and could be expected to go charging into danger without a second thought. But robots were supposed to be smart, and if this one thought she'd negotiated the slippery steps in pitch darkness it was as dumb as its owner.

When the robot slipped she stopped breathing, and when she saw the case fly out of its hands and vanish down the stairs she buried her face in the dirt, covered her ears and waited for the explosion.

Nothing happened.

Cautiously raising her head, Sonya saw Hal following the robot underground. She suppressed the urge to call out, to get them back out of the slippery, dark stairwell. After all, who was going to take her home if they never came back?

Cursing to herself, she settled down to wait. Then she brightened - if they took long enough they'd be doing her job for her.

◆

Hal watched Clunk's head bobbing up and down, silhouetted in the glare of the robot's light. The walls sparkled with moisture, and slime squished underfoot as they made their way down the narrow staircase. Now and then Hal saw a long, silver scar on the wall, evidence that the briefcase hadn't just hit the steps on the way down. At the foot of the stairs the walls and floor were lined with smooth, featureless concrete. Opposite the staircase, an archway led into a narrow tunnel.

Clunk shone his light along it, revealing a smooth floor and curved walls. The briefcase was lying on the floor several metres into the tunnel. Beyond was darkness.

'At least that's still in one piece,' said Hal. He cupped his mouth with both hands and shouted, 'Sonya!'

There was no reply.

They stepped into the tunnel and began to make their way along its length. On the way, Hal collected the briefcase. The corners were dented and the silver case was heavily scored, but it seemed sound enough.

After a hundred metres or so, the tunnel ended in a bare wall.

'How strange that it should end suddenly,' said Clunk.

'Yeah. You wouldn't think they'd build a passageway like this without having it go somewhere.'

'We may be dealing with an alien intelligence, Mr Spacejock. Completely different thought processes to you and I.'

'Look for a keypad,' said Hal. 'Shine your light across the surface.'

Clunk angled his light and they immediately spotted a rectangular outline in the wall. When Hal raised his hand to it, a dozen buttons glowed dimly. Looking closely, he saw the buttons were cut from the same material as the wall, each marked with a different glyph. 'What kind of writing is that?'

226

Clunk crouched until his eyes were level with the keypad. 'I don't recognise it,' he said.

'Alien?'

'Possibly. It could just be encoded.'

'Which one means open?'

'I can't say.'

Before Clunk could stop him, Hal pressed all the buttons in succession. Each lit up as he pressed it, until the entire panel glowed like a landing light.

'That was probably a mistake,' said Clunk.

'And it didn't even open the door.' Hal thumped his fist on it. 'Sonya? Are you in there?'

Clunk tilted his head. 'Shhh! I can hear something!'

'What?'

'Listen!'

Hal listened, but all he could hear was his own breathing. Then he heard it - a rumble underfoot as if something deep underground were powering up. The noise got louder, shaking dirt and grit from the arched ceiling.

'Before we die horribly,' said Clunk calmly. 'I'd just like to remind you that I was not consulted re the button pushing scenario.'

The noise stopped, leaving an ominous silence that was shattered by a loud hiss: the heavy slab that had been blocking the passage rose into the air, dust blowing from the widening crack underneath. Hal crouched, and as the slab rose out of the way he tried to see into the darkness beyond.

Clunk turned his light towards the opening, and Hal gasped as another light shone back at them. 'Sonya? Is that you?'

'It's just a reflection,' said Clunk, moving his light. 'Come on.'

They stepped through the opening and found themselves in a cramped compartment with polished alloy walls that reflected man and robot a thousand times over. While Clunk stood and stared, Hal automatically ran his fingers through his hair.

Clunk cleared his throat. 'Mr Spacejock, I get the feeling this room leads somewhere.'

'A minute ago you couldn't find a simple door, and now you're certain this dead end goes somewhere else?' Hal looked around. 'Actually, it does remind me of an elevator.'

'You mean a lift.'

'No, I mean an elevator.'

'Where I come from,' said Clunk, 'it's a lift.'

'Here, it's an elevator,' said Hal firmly.

'Perhaps it's a transportation device.'

'An elevator is a transportation device.'

'I was thinking of something more unconventional.'

'Such as?'

'A teleporter.'

Hal snorted. 'How did you work that out?'

'It fits,' said Clunk. 'The structures above ground, the long underground tunnel, the sealed chamber.' He ran his hands over a mirrored panel. 'This technology isn't human.'

Hal stared at their reflection. 'If you're right, this chamber could open up the galaxy. It's a trader's dream!'

'Of course, it's much more likely to be a lift.'

'Elevator,' said Hal automatically. 'How do we make it work?'

Clunk gestured at the walls. 'There's probably a control panel behind one of the mirrors. Like the one outside - activated by a proximity sensor.'

Hal worked his way around the chamber, feeling the cool mirrors with his hands. He was halfway round when a small section of glass lit up like a Christmas tree. There was a warning buzz as the chamber door slammed down, followed by a flash so bright Hal saw his own skeleton reflected in the nearest mirror. Then, nothing. 'That was a bust,' he said, rubbing his eyes. He turned round. 'Clunk?'

There was a glowing blue whirlpool in the centre of the chamber. It faded gradually, leaving a faint shimmer and a gust of warm air. There was no sign of the robot.

'Clunk?' Hal stepped into the middle of the chamber, uncomfortably aware that the alcove could also be an advanced garbage disposal unit. He glanced at the control panel, where the buttons were lighting up with a rainbow of colours, two by two, row by row. As the last pair of lights came on, five musical notes echoed around the chamber.

'Oh hell,' muttered Hal. 'Clunk's not going to be happy about this.'

He looked around the chamber, but the only reflections were his own. He realised Sonya must have been caught the same way - fired off to some exotic spot without warning.

Well, if Clunk and Sonya had both gone, there was no point in his hanging around. Holding the briefcase firmly under his arm, Hal palmed the control panel and stepped back into the super-bright flash.

◆

Sonya woke with a start to find herself lying full-length under a bush. Too many interrupted nights, she thought with a frown. It was colder now, and the light had changed. Looking up at the sky, she tried to work out how long she'd been asleep. Then a thought struck her - what if Hal and the robot had given up and returned to the ship? What if the *Volante* was leaving without her?

Afraid it might already be too late, she leapt up and ran through the forest.

◆

Before Clunk could shout 'Don't touch that control panel!' or 'Look out!' or even 'NO!' he was consumed by a searing flash of light. The next instant he was standing in a cold dark room. As his eyes adjusted to the darkness he made out a doorway in the nearest wall. Certain that Hal's balls-and-all mentality would have him arriving shortly, he stepped over a deep sand drift and went outside.

It was dark, and Clunk's first reaction was to switch off his night vision and look up at the stars. Above him, the sky was strewn with points of light, but try as he might he couldn't identify any of them. There was a tiny click as he reactivated the night vision. He looked around and a rocky, dusty scene blurred past. Slowing his movements, he sharpened the image and looked with growing concern at his barren surroundings.

He was standing on a plain which stretched to the horizon in every direction. Behind him, the building sat at the foot of a hill, a towering pile of sand and weathered rock. The building had a stubby mast on top with a small grey square on one side and a battered dish on the other. The dish was pointing skywards.

Clunk looked up the hill. If there was anything to see, he thought, that was the place to see it from.

He'd just taken the first step when his commset tuned to a strong signal. Clunk reduced the gain and tried to analyse the data, but the transmission was multiplexed over a huge part of the spectrum and he could do little more than pick out bits and pieces.

The data stream reached a crescendo, and as it finished there was a flash of light from the concrete building. Seconds later, a two-legged figure staggered out clutching its head.

❖

Hal's first impression of the teleport process was about thirty seconds after it happened, which is how long it took him to regain his senses. He recalled a disturbing dream - something about being minced, feet first - but hurriedly suppressed it.

'If this teleport lark is going to catch on,' he thought, 'they're going to have to make it a lot less painful.'

He arrived safely enough, mostly upright and with a full complement of bits and pieces. Hoping Clunk had come the same way, he stumbled towards the narrow doorway. As he crossed the threshold he lost his footing in the loose sand and landed face-first in the dirt.

'Mr Spacejock!' said a familiar voice. 'Are you all right?'

'I've been better,' said Hal, getting up. 'Have you found Sonya?'

'She didn't come this way. When I arrived, the sand in the doorway was pristine. No footprints.'

'You mean we've been following a shadow? What about the footprints on the stairway?'

'We had a light. She didn't. I suspect she took the first few steps, then decided it was too dangerous and returned to the surface. She was probably on her way back to the *Volante* to share her discovery when we set off to find her.'

Hal raised the briefcase. 'What about this? Why did she leave it behind?'

'Maybe she forgot it in her excitement,' said Clunk. 'Or maybe she didn't want to carry it all the way to the ship and back again.'

'Oh well, I suppose we'd better go back.' Hal shielded his eyes and examined the horizon. 'That teleporter must have sent us a fair distance. I can't see the forest anywhere.'

'Forest?' Clunk looked puzzled. 'What forest?'

'The one we landed in, of course.'

'Mr Spacejock, this isn't Canessa.'

Hal's jaw dropped. 'It isn't?'

'No. It's not even the same star system.'

Hal looked at the robot in shock. Until this moment, the worst he'd imagined was a long trek back to the ship, sleeping out and living off the land. 'You mean ... '

Clunk leaned forward. 'Mr Spacejock, I can't even confirm we're in the same galaxy.'

'A whole new galaxy!' exclaimed Hal. 'After one little flash of light?'

'The teleporter must work by folding space.' Clunk looked thoughtful. 'Whoever built these devices must have located them on weak points, fault lines in space and time where a carefully controlled burst of energy could –'

'There is no way we just leapt to another galaxy.'

'I assure you –'

232

'There's supposed to be swirly coloured tubes and wowing noises and stuff! Not a little blink.'

'I had no idea you were such an authority on intergalactic teleportation.'

'I know what it's supposed to be like. I've seen it in the movies.'

Clunk pointed overhead. 'Look up, Mr Spacejock. What do you see?'

'Stars. Lots of them.'

'Do you recognise any?'

'Am I supposed to?'

'It's not an unknown skill for starship pilots. But the point is, I don't recognise them either.'

'That's not unusual for half-blind old robots,' muttered Hal. 'The galaxy is a big place, and we're probably looking at it from a different angle.'

'I assure you, these stars are not part of our galaxy. In fact, you're almost certainly the first human being ever to set eyes on them.'

Hal nodded slowly, lost in thought. Then he glanced around the empty landscape. 'Do you think there's any food around here?'

24

Hal was sitting with his back to the concrete hut, staring across the darkened plain to the horizon. The sky was getting lighter in that direction, and before long the light of dawn would reveal his surroundings. He could hear Clunk inside the hut, footsteps echoing as he examined it closely. The robot had already told him about a bundle of wires protruding from the wall, and that unless there was a concealed panel they were in danger of being stranded. Permanently.

He heard a scrape, and turned to see Clunk emerging from the hut. 'Any news?'

The robot's face was grave. 'This device has been stripped. The keypad is missing and the energy source is weak. In fact, our arrival drained it completely.'

'What do we do?'

'There are three courses of action. One, we find spare parts and a diagram and fix this teleporter. Two, we find another teleporter.'

'What about the third?'

'Did I say three?'

'Yes.'

'I'm sure I didn't.'

'You did! I heard you!'

'Well, it's not much of a choice.'

'Spit it out anyway.'

'Three, we find shelter and live out the rest of our lives on this planet.'

'Go with the first two.' Hal shook Sonya's briefcase. 'Do you think she's got any sandwiches in here?'

'I doubt it.'

Hal opened the case, revealing a keyboard and a large screen. 'Damn, it's just a computer.'

'Computers can be useful,' said Clunk stiffly.

'Not when you're hungry.' Hal closed the lid and set the case on the ground. 'What are our chances, Clunk?'

'Not good,' admitted the robot.

'It's getting lighter. Maybe we should climb the hill and get a look at our surroundings.'

'An excellent idea.'

They set off together, stepping over loose stones and slipping in the dirt as they made their way up the slope. The sun had risen by the time they reached the top, revealing a barren plain stretching in every direction. Hal scanned the horizon for signs of civilisation. Clunk did likewise, simultaneously scanning the radio spectrum with his commset.

'Nothing,' said Hal, having finished two complete revolutions. 'Pick anything up?'

Clunk was facing the teleporter hut, looking out across the plain beyond. 'Mr Spacejock, can you see anything in this direction?'

Hal looked. 'Nothing at all.'

'Pity. I thought I could see a faint track leading away from the hut. Wheel marks, perhaps.'

Hal squinted. 'There is a kind of line, isn't there?'

'It might be a natural feature.'

235

'Only one way to find out.' Hal led the way down the hill, kicking up clouds of dust in his haste. At the bottom he hurried to the teleporter, where he crouched to examine the ground. 'There's nothing here,' he said, his hopes dashed.

'It can only be seen from a distance.' Clunk pointed towards the horizon. 'I took a bearing from the hill. We go that way.'

◆

Sonya was sitting in the Volante's rec room with a cup of warm liquid at her elbow, eyeing the AutoChef with amusement. Unlike the efficient equipment in her own apartment, this device seemed to delight in serving up oddball concoctions. Take the pea soup she had ordered - it had a distinctly tangy flavour, and the light yellow colour was most disconcerting.

Sonya frowned at her watch. If Hal wasn't back in the next half hour she'd go to her cabin and catch up on some sleep. 'Sod it,' she muttered, getting up and stretching. 'I could use the sleep right now.'

'Did you call?' said the Navcom.

'I'm going to take a nap. Call me the minute Mr Spacejock returns.'

◆

Hal staggered across the plain, hot and sweaty in his flight suit. They'd been walking for hours, and he was no longer bothering to look at the horizon. His eyes were half-closed against the swirling dust and the midday sun beat down from a bright blue sky, adding to his woes.

Clunk strode ahead, Sonya's briefcase swinging from his hand. He was untroubled by the light or the dust, but every now and then he looked round to make sure Hal was keeping up.

'I need a drink,' croaked Hal, the next time Clunk looked at him.

'I may be able to help.' The robot opened several compartments, picking through the oddments within. Finally, he withdrew a small white cube. 'Instant rations,' he said. 'I'd forgotten I had them.'

Hal grabbed the box and scanned the label. 'KleenAir Corporation emergency drink ration?'

'That's right,' said Clunk.

Hal's heart sank. 'Just add water?'

'It keeps the weight down,' explained the robot.

Hal tossed the cube over his shoulder and trudged on.

Two hours later a dark line appeared on the horizon. Hal immediately perked up, lengthening his stride with newfound determination. Next time he looked up the line was a fuzzy green strip, and soon after it resolved itself into a row of bushes and trees. As they approached the vegetation, the faint track they were following became a distinct set of wheel ruts. They picked up their pace, and before long they were striding through undergrowth, enjoying the cool shade. The path wound through the trees, and a few minutes into the forest they saw a low, concrete structure - a grey slab with a narrow slit across the front and a mast on the roof.

'Tel'porter?' croaked Hal, forcing the word through cracked dry lips.

Clunk shook his head. 'Looks more like a gun emplacement.'

He pointed at the mast, which was festooned with grey panels. 'Those are solar collectors. We might be able to use them for power.'

'Anyone inside?'

'I can't tell. We'd better circle.' Clunk led Hal off the path to the right, and ten minutes later they emerged from the dense undergrowth, crossed the path and found themselves facing a steel door. It was ajar.

'Wait here,' murmured Clunk. While Hal swayed on aching legs, the robot crept forward and peered inside. Then he beckoned.

The interior was dim, littered with rusty pieces of metal and festooned with cobwebs. Near the door, a control panel hung from the wall, broken and lifeless. Clunk slipped inside and lifted the panel gently, frowning at the alien script on the recessed buttons. He pressed one and it lit up with a dull blue glow, only to fade immediately.

Hal recovered enough to pick amongst the junk. There was a sagging cupboard against one of the concrete walls, and his eyes lit up as he pulled the door open. The lower shelf contained half a dozen sealed bottles.

Hal grabbed a bottle and held it up to the light, eyeing the clear liquid inside. He tried to twist the cap off, but it refused to budge. Looking closely at the pressed metal, he noticed the thread was reversed. Twisted in the opposite direction, it came off easily, releasing pent-up pressure with a loud hiss.

Clunk glanced round at the noise. 'Mr Spacejock, you can't _'

Hal sniffed the liquid, revelling in the fruity aroma. Then he put the bottle to his lips, tipped his head back and drank deeply.

Crash! The bottle was knocked out of his hands and

Clunk's angry face loomed in front of him. 'Are you insane?' demanded the robot. 'That could be window cleaning fluid! Or worse!'

Hal smacked his lips. 'Actually, it's apple juice.' He reached for another bottle, but Clunk put a hand on his arm.

'Not until I perform a thorough chemical analysis.'

'Go on then.'

Clunk located the up-ended bottle and raised it to his nose, sniffing carefully at the dregs. 'It's not apple juice, but it's very similar.'

'Good enough for me,' said Hal, opening another bottle. He chugged half of it down and burped loudly. 'Refreshing.'

'You might have poisoned yourself,' said Clunk, setting the empty bottle on the shelf. 'Please don't consume anything else until I've checked it.' He returned to the keypad, lifted it gently and examined the wires. 'Good news, Mr Spacejock. With this keypad and the energy panels from the roof I can almost certainly repair the teleporter.'

'Fantastic!' said Hal. 'What are we waiting for?'

Clunk gestured at the keypad. 'You program a destination by entering characters in a certain order. Unless you can remember the sequence you pressed on Canessa ... '

Hal looked stunned. 'You don't know the way home?'

'Correct. We need a map.'

Hal looked around the junk. 'What would it look like?'

'Not that sort of map. I'd expect to find it in a data storage device.' Clunk made for the door.

'Where are you going?'

'This is a gun emplacement, Mr Spacejock. Whatever it's defending, we'll find it further along the track.'

25

Hal and Clunk rounded a bend and stopped. Ahead, a pair of crumbling stone towers stood either side of the track, with the remains of heavy wooden gates dangling from rusty hinges. Beyond the gates there was a small courtyard, leading to a huge roofed area supported by stone columns. The roof had once been royal blue, but was now just a patchwork of flaky paint, and the flagstones in the courtyard were cracked and choked with weeds.

Clunk led the way between the columns and into the courtyard. Hal followed, with several bottles clutched under his arm. They climbed a short staircase at the far end of the courtyard and entered the cool darkness, where they found a T-junction. Facing them was a grey wall with concrete pillars reaching up to the ceiling at regular intervals. There were drifts of brown leaves around the columns and the air was tainted with the earthy smell of compost. Hal looked left and right. 'Which way?'

'Follow me.' Clunk turned right and they walked along the deserted corridor in silence, their footsteps echoing off the concrete walls. They passed several openings onto rooms where remnants of furniture and equipment loomed out of the darkness, until Clunk finally stopped before an archway.

'There may be defences. You should wait out here.'

'Forget it. We're in this together.' Hal entered the room and stopped. There was a sagging bench containing several metal boxes and glass screens, thick with dust. One of the screens had a grimy keyboard connected to it with frayed wires. Clunk stepped up for a better look and a spider dropped from the roof on a shimmering thread. Gently moving it aside, he began to inspect the steel boxes. 'There are two cables from each going to the roof. They must be for power and communications. Now, if I can just ...' There was a beep, and one of the screens flickered. 'Aha!' Clunk pulled up an old crate, put Sonya's briefcase down and sat at the keyboard. 'First I need to analyse the way the data is stored. Then I'll see whether I can hook directly into the machine.' He started by examining the keyboard, whose oval keys were imprinted with the same glyphs as the teleporter keypad. He pressed a button, and the screen filled with characters.

'What's that?' asked Hal, taking a swig from one of his bottles.

'I'm trying to decode the language,' said Clunk, pressing several more keys. 'I need something with physics or maths - a table of the elements, a fibonacci sequence, anything. So far I've only turned up pages of text.'

Hal finished his drink and examined the bottle. It was made of glass, etched with a stylised tree above a row of alien glyphs. 'I've got it!' he said excitedly. 'Clunk, look!'

The robot turned. 'What is it?'

'The tree and the writing. Do you think it's a brand name?'

'That won't help. It could be anything ... probably a made up word.'

'What about the word 'tree', though? They might have used it in the name.'

'It's just as likely to be the species. Like pine trees or palm trees.' Clunk relented. 'All right, let me see.'

Hal handed the bottle over, and Clunk glanced at the letters. Then he smiled. 'You're right, Mr Spacejock. This is a product of the Lone Tree Drinks Company. Fruit punch, non-alcoholic. I now have enough information to decipher the rest of the language.' He set the bottle aside and turned back to the screen, where he began to type rapidly.

'Anyone we can ask for help?'

Clunk typed a query and the screen updated. 'I'm sorry, Mr Spacejock. This planet has been deserted for almost three centuries.'

'Is there a map of the teleporters?'

Clunk shook his head. 'I found references to them, but digging deeper only returned error codes and corrupted data.'

Hal looked around the dusty computers. 'What about copies?'

Clunk typed something on the keyboard. 'There are three off-site backups. Unfortunately it would take days to walk to each of them, and we don't have any supplies.'

Hal's shoulders slumped. 'That's it, then. We've had it.'

'Not quite,' said Clunk. 'According to the computer, there's a transportation node nearby.' He picked up the briefcase and led Hal out of the computer room, turning left into the corridor. Further along, he activated his light and ushered Hal down a long flight of steps. At the bottom, the corridor was narrow, the ceiling damp and mossy.

'I hope it's safe,' remarked Hal, eyeing several cracks in the roof. 'Hey, you didn't tell me about the people.'

'What people?'

'The previous inhabitants. The vanished civilisation.'

'The computer has incomplete records, but it seems they went through the teleporters.'

'What, all of them?'

'Yes. Over a period of decades.'

'Why?'

'Think of the parallel in our own galaxy,' said Clunk. 'Humans spread out from their home planet, seduced by a new beginning, by unexplored frontiers. They faced long, dangerous journeys aboard second-rate vessels and still they went. The inhabitants of this planet only had to step into the nearest teleporter.'

'I guess it would be tempting.' Hal recalled his own experience. 'I bet nobody told them how painful it was.'

'Perhaps they had a higher tolerance than you.' Ahead of them, the tunnel forked. 'Down here,' said Clunk, indicating the right hand side. 'Strangely enough, computers played a large part in the exodus.'

'How's that? Breaking down?'

'In a way. Technology reached a dead end here, you see. The advent of the teleporter network led to a decline in the sciences. With a galaxy to explore, a whole generation upped and left. By the time anyone really knew what was happening it was too late - the existing machines were beyond understanding or repair. That's when the real tragedy hit.'

'What, a natural disaster?'

'Far worse. One day a trainee technician replaced a faulty module in the equipment that ran the planet's medical database. Within minutes, the machine was requesting an unlock code, which nobody could supply. Months later, the low-orbit control computer refused to start because it was programmed to update its license every ten years, and the software company had closed down.'

'What a mess.'

Clunk nodded. 'Emigrating became the only option.'

They came to a staircase and began to climb, emerging in a small courtyard where a broken fountain lay in a dried-up concrete pool. 'This way,' said Clunk, leading Hal into another passage. Halfway along they turned right, walked down three steps and arrived in a cavernous building. It was dim, with only meagre light filtering through clear strips in the roof, and as Hal's eyes adjusted he saw a huge curved surface in the gloom. 'What's that?'

'A spaceship,' said Clunk.

'You're kidding. These people had interstellar flight?'

'Naturally. How do you think they placed the teleporters?'

'I - hell, I didn't think about it.' Hal frowned. 'Wait a minute, that teleporter on Canessa was in our galaxy. What were they doing there?'

'Mr Spacejock, I have no idea.'

They walked past the ship's rounded nose cone, and Hal stared up at the blank portholes. With its bloated hull, they looked like eyes on some primeval beast. Hal examined the rest of the hangar, and spotted three more spaceships, lined up like stuffed whales in a museum. There were smaller craft in between - half a dozen surface flyers and groundcars, most of them with service hatches and engine covers standing open. There were tools and parts everywhere: on the floor, leaning against the vehicles and covering several workbenches. Coils of wire and steel rope hung from the walls, draped over cutting tools and squares of rusty metal. The far end of the hangar had collapsed, and a sorry-looking spaceship was half-buried under beams and rubble.

'You're not thinking of flying one of these things, are you?' Hal rapped on the bubble canopy of a nearby flyer, and leapt back as an exhaust cone fell off. 'The only way you'll get this airborne is with a very large catapult.'

'There must be something we can use.'

Hal looked at the dusty flyers doubtfully. 'What if it breaks down in the middle of nowhere?'

'Would you rather walk both ways?'

'Good point.'

They passed several groundcars until they came to one which looked intact. It was covered in dirt like the rest, but the access hatches were closed and it appeared serviceable.

After giving it the once-over Clunk pulled the door open and motioned Hal into the vehicle, then stowed the briefcase in the back seat and climbed in alongside. There were two bucket seats with four-point harnesses and narrow headrests, and in front of them the dashboard was inset with circular indentations, all thick with dust. Hal stretched his legs out and felt something springy under his feet, and when he looked into the foot well he saw four narrow pedals.

Clunk brushed dirt from one of the circles on the dash to reveal a gauge. It had a red bar with violet lines at the extremities, and the needle hovered around the halfway mark. Beneath the red bar were markings in alien script.

'Better clean them all,' said Clunk. 'I have to determine what information they're conveyeing.'

Hal used his sleeve to clean the gauges, coughing at the dust. When he'd finished, Clunk inspected them one by one.

'Fuel gauge, altitude, radio, landing gear and thrust vector. Okay, Mr Spacejock, I'm ready. Fasten your seatbelt.'

Hal pulled the harness tight and crossed his arMs. 'I hope you know what you're doing.'

Clunk pressed a button on the dashboard, and for a split

second Hal thought they'd blown up. But instead of scattering him across the hangar, the noise continued.

'It's a pity you don't have earplugs,' said Clunk, his voice at full volume.

Hal pressed his hands to his ears and nodded.

Clunk twisted the flight stick and pressed one of the pedals. The engine note changed and the car rose unsteadily into the air, hovering above the concrete floor with a blatting sound.

'What about the hangar doors?' asked Hal.

'Third button from the left.'

Hal pressed it and the right-hand door grated open, revealing bright blue sky and an expanse of flat, brown land. Clunk guided the car through the gap, turned it to the correct heading and accelerated rapidly.

'F-fast, isn't it?' said Hal, as the landscape flashed by.

Clunk nodded, busy scanning gauges. 'I estimate thirty-five minutes to the first location.'

◆

Hal stared at the horizon, where a series of small bumps had appeared. As the groundcar raced towards them, the bumps resolved into half a dozen buildings with missing roofs, crumbling walls and empty windows. 'Doesn't look promising.'

The groundcar hummed to a stop, slowed by a combination of reverse thrust and air brakes. Clunk cut the engine, setting it down on a cracked concrete slab. 'We'll try the largest building first.'

Hal opened his door, coughing in the swirling dust kicked up by their arrival.

They stepped out and walked towards the buildings. Hal glanced at the dirt, wondering how many centuries had passed since the last living creature had walked on this planet. Distracted by the thought, he walked straight into Clunk.

The robot was looking up at the building's facade, frowning at the overhanging brickwork and loose mortar. 'I suggest you remain outside, Mr Spacejock. These walls do not look safe.'

'They've been there for years. I'm sure they'll last a few more minutes.'

'Nevertheless, I would prefer you to remain at a safe distance. In any case, there appears to be nothing but rubble inside.'

Hal watched Clunk pick his way between chunks of fallen masonry towards the wide doorway. 'How to explore an alien planet,' he muttered, crossing his arMs. His face brightened as he glanced at the other buildings, and a moment later he was making for the nearest. Clunk hadn't told him to stay away from the rest.

26

Clunk stepped over fallen masonry and ducked under loose beams, heading for the back of the room. According to data he'd found on the alien computer, the house belonged to an IT worker responsible for offsite backups. There had also been mention of a safe storage area in the basement.

Near the back of the room he saw an opening in the floor, choked with fallen rubble. He knelt and reached out to move a large chunk of concrete, gripping the edges to slide the piece aside. Before it had moved more than a couple of inches, there was a loud snap and the whole pile of rubble dropped away, cascading down the stairs with a clatter. For a split second Clunk was balanced over the hole, the heavy piece of concrete gripped firmly in his hands. Before he could let go, it tipped him into the darkness.

Clunk rolled down the steps and landed with a crash at the bottom. As the echoes died away he sat up and activated his chest lamp. The weak beam shone into the dust-laden air, picking out four bare walls and a floor strewn with rubble. Clunk angled the light upwards and froze ... the roof was bowed down like a canopy full of rainwater, and dust and grit trickled from a series of cracks. The whole structure looked as if it was just waiting for the right moment to come down on his head.

Crawling on hands and knees, Clunk made his way towards the centre of the room. He cleared aside drifts of grit and smiled to himself as a round metal cover was exposed. He slid the bolt and hauled the trapdoor upwards, revealing a dark cavity underneath. The beam from his chest lamp played around the hole, and Clunk's smile grew wider as the light settled on a grey metal box. He was just reaching for it when a rolling peal of thunder made him look up. The thunder grew louder and louder, and there was a loud crack directly overhead.

Clunk threw himself backwards, somersaulting away from the falling roof just in time. Crouched on the lowest step, he could only watch as tons of concrete tumbled down, completely filling the basement.

Barely had the noise and movement stopped when he heard another sound ... loud creaks from the building overhead, long drawn out groans as the walls and roof started to give way. The entire building was coming down!

◆

Hal found nothing of interest in the ruined house. The roof had gaping holes in it, and the walls were braced with rough wooden poles, attached to the concrete floor with metal plates. Broken furniture was dusted with fallen plaster, and light barely filtered through the cracked, grimy windows.

He turned to leave, tripped over a length of wood and fell against one of the bracing poles. It held for a split second, then crumbled under his weight, bringing down a shower of plaster. One or two bricks fell, and Hal was just backing away when another pole gave way with a loud snap. One by one, the rest followed, and as Hal bolted out the front door the entire structure imploded in slow motion.

The building skewed as it fell, gently nudging the house alongside. With a groan, that building also collapsed, knocking the next in line, until the air was thick with dust and the crash of falling masonry.

'Oh no,' muttered Hal. 'Clunk!'

He dashed for the end building, which was little more than a pile of rubble under the settling dust. 'Clunk? Are you there?'

A beam moved, and Clunk's plaster-streaked face appeared. 'Stand back, Mr Spacejock,' said the robot. As soon as Hal was clear he pushed the heavy beam aside, raising fresh clouds of dust. Then he stepped out of the ruins.

'I thought they were more stable than that,' he remarked, looking along the line of fallen houses. 'You didn't go near them?'

'You told me not to.' Hal brushed fallen plaster off his flight suit. 'Did you find the backup?'

'There was a tin box under a trapdoor in the cellar, and I was just reaching for it when the roof collapsed. The rubble must have crushed it flat.' Clunk eyed the ruins. 'Strange how the buildings just fell over.'

Hal shuffled his feet. 'So, where's the next site?'

'East. It's just a matter of interpreting the coordinates.'

Minutes later they were roaring across the plain, the skimmer bobbing and weaving as Clunk piloted it over the rocky ground.

Hal was beginning to feel the effects of missed sleep and constant travel. He nodded off once or twice, neck bent and head pressed against the window, only to wake in shock each time the flyer changed course. The only warning was a whine from the engine as the load increased, a bare second or two before the craft jinked to one side or the other.

They were converging on a white line that stretched to the horizon ahead of them. 'What's that?' asked Hal, leaning forward to squint through the scratched perspex windshield.

'It could be a road,' said Clunk.

'Good,' said Hal, as the car swerved around another rock. 'We could drive in a straight line for a change.'

As they got closer, the white line resolved itself into a pair of rails on the ground, poured in a continuous track. 'It's a transport device,' said Clunk. 'Those are train tracks.'

'For passengers?'

Clunk shook his head. 'Heavy cargo. Something that runs on wheels.'

Hal's gaze followed the tracks to the horizon. Was that something ahead? It was a dark bump, barely a smudge in the distance, but they seemed to be heading straight for it. 'Is that the next site?'

'It is.' Clunk looked serious. 'You know there's a good chance none of these backups will be useable, don't you? We could be stuck here forever. You'd have to live out the rest of your life in solitude, with nobody to speak to, no human company ...'

'You're all good news, you are,' broke in Hal. 'Let's worry about that when it happens, okay?'

While they were talking, the smudge on the horizon grew into a sizeable hill that stood alone on the empty plain, the lower slopes dotted with spindly, blackened trees.

Hal stared at it. 'Where's the backup? On top?'

'No, there's a gully at the base of the hill, with an entrance at the far end. The only reference I could find mentioned a defence system of some kind. Something about an All-seeing Eye of Death.'

Hal stared at him. 'You're winding me up.'

'No, that's a literal translation.'

'Did the words 'Gee, this might be dangerous' not occur to you?'

'They did, only the third backup site sounded far worse.'

'Worse than eyes of death?'

'I didn't want to worry you unnecessarily.'

'It's a bit late for that.' Hal looked at the hill, which was growing rapidly. 'We're getting a bit close. Why don't we pull up and scout around for a while?'

'Because we're over here, and the hill is over there.'

'Yeah, but the death thing is over there too. Can't we just circle for a bit?'

'A straight line is the shortest distance between two points,' said Clunk.

'And the quickest way to get killed by eyes of death is to drive right at them.'

'Don't be concerned. Most things on this planet have deteriorated, and I doubt the defences could pick up a fast-moving vehicle like this.'

BLAM!

Hal covered his face as the front of the groundcar disappeared in a welter of fragments. Beside him, Clunk wrestled with the controls, trying desperately to turn the vehicle away from the hill. He almost succeeded, but the shattered nose dipped towards the ground, touched and dug in. The vehicle ploughed a furrow, slewed round and came to a stop on its side.

'Get out!' shouted Clunk. 'Quick, Mr Spacejock!'

Hal kicked open the buckled door and threw himself headlong through the opening, landing flat on his face in the dirt. He looked round for Clunk and saw the robot struggling to free Sonya's briefcase.

'Leave it!' shouted Hal. 'Come on, move!'

Clunk gave an almighty heave and dived clear, tucking the briefcase under his arm as he landed on the hard ground. He rolled over and sprang to his feet just as something slammed into the groundcar, hurling hot metal and dirt into the air.

'Run!' shouted Clunk. 'Take cover!'

There was a small rocky outcrop nearby, and they dived behind it as another shot slammed into the groundcar.

Clunk looked back at the shattered vehicle with a critical eye. 'I think you were right. We should have circled the hill first.'

'It's a bit late for that.' Hal ducked as another shot whizzed overhead. 'Now what do we do?'

'Twenty-seven seconds,' said Clunk.

'What?'

'That's the recharge time. All we have to do is make our move in between shots.'

Hal risked a glance at the hill. It was two or three hundred metres away, and the only cover was a pair of small rocks half-buried in the sand. As he watched, he saw a flash between the trees. A split second later, something hit the groundcar. 'I saw it, Clunk. A light on the slope.'

Clunk popped his head up and looked towards the hill. Almost half a minute passed before the flash repeated. There was a crackling roar behind them as the groundcar exploded, showering them with fragments.

'There goes our ride,' said Hal, flicking red-hot splinters

from his dusty flight suit. 'And the third backup site is the dangerous one, right?'

'We can time it,' said Clunk. 'After the next shot, we'll have just over twenty seconds to find cover.'

Hal looked at the rocks on the approach to the hill. 'Reckon we can make it?'

'You don't have to reach the rocks. Even if you're five or six metres short, you should still be able to get behind them. The turret won't be able to see you.'

'Is that what's firing at us?'

Clunk nodded. 'It must be self-powered. It's far too potent for solar.'

'Can't you just order it to stop firing?'

'I have no means of communication.'

Hal peered round the rock. 'Exactly how long did you say the interval was?'

'Twenty-seven seconds.'

'So why hasn't it fired again?'

'Because the flyer has been destroyed and we're under cover.'

'So if we move, it shoots?'

'Correct.'

'Doesn't that make it a little hard to time our run?'

Clunk picked up a rock. 'I'll throw this to attract the turret. Ready?'

Hal gathered himself, then nodded.

Clunk threw the rock over the boulder. Immediately there was a blast of hot air, followed by a shower of pebbles and dirt. 'Run!' shouted the robot, leaping up.

Hal sprang from cover and belted towards the rocks. Close behind, Clunk's flat feet thudded on the dirt.

'If ... short drop and lie ... still,' panted Clunk, whose fans were struggling to keep his circuits cool.

Hal's lungs burned as he pounded across the plain. Long before he reached the rocks, he heard a shout.

'Down!' yelled the robot.

Hal threw himself at the ground, grazing his hands on the dry, gritty soil. There was a huge explosion, and when he raised his head the air was thick with swirling dust. 'Clunk?' he called.

'Come on, Mr Spacejock!' cried the robot from somewhere ahead.

Hal sprang up and ran blindly through the dust, leaping small rocks and dodging larger ones. His breath came in ragged gasps as he approached the foot of the hill. Ahead, Clunk was standing with his back to a tree.

'Quickly!' called the robot.

'Get ... stuffed!' panted Hal. He staggered across several metres of sparse, springy grass and threw himself at a thick tree trunk. He tensed, waiting for the blast. Nothing happened.

'Can you find another rock?' called Clunk.

Hal looked at the barren ground. 'Nope.'

'Me neither. We might be safe now we're in the trees.'

'You thought we were safe approaching the hill,' Hal pointed out.

'I can't be right all the time.' There was a silence. 'I'm getting an idea.'

'I don't want to hear it.'

'If we both step out from behind our respective trees at precisely the same time, the turret may be unable to choose between us.'

'Two things wrong with that. First, we might not get the

timing right and whoever appears first will have their head blown off.'

'Correct.'

'And two, even if we both appear at the same time, it might decide that one is better than none.'

'What do you suggest?'

'Me? I think we shouldn't have driven so close to the hill.'

'It's a bit late for that,' said the robot.

'I know, I just thought it was worth mentioning. If you hadn't been so sure of yourself –'

'We jump on three. Ready?'

'I guess.'

'One, two, THREE!'

Hal pushed off, but his foot slipped under him and he hit the deck with a thud. He saw a flash of bronze as the robot streaked away, and heard a whirr as the turret tracked its target. 'Clunk!' he yelled.

The robot skidded to a halt. 'Coming, Mr Spacejock!' he cried, taking off again, this time towards Hal. Behind him, the turret whirred around, aiming at the back of his head.

'No, you stupid twit!' yelled Hal. 'I fell.'

Clunk stopped. 'I thought –'

'Duck! Get down, the turret's going to –'

The gun fired with an ear-shattering roar, drowning out the rest of his words. A jet of flame several metres long stabbed from the barrel, and Clunk was knocked into the bushes, arms and legs flailing. Seconds later there was a huge explosion amongst the boulders on the plain.

'Clunk?' called Hal. 'Clunk, are you all right?'

27

Rex activated the jump motor, which howled behind him as it built up to speed. It reached a crescendo and the stars flickered out, only to reappear in a new configuration. As the hyperspace motor whirred back to silence, Rex confirmed his destination was in sight and began to make preparations for landing.

◆

Hal stared into the bushes. 'Clunk, are you there? Can you hear me?'

'Yes, Mr Spacejock. It's just a scratch.' The robot popped up from the greenery, his left shoulder mangled where it had taken the glancing impact. 'We still have twenty seconds to reach cover.'

Hal suddenly realised he was standing in full view of the squat, menacing turret. He turned to stare at it and saw a small door set into the concrete base. 'Make for that,' he shouted, breaking into a run. Seconds later he was leaning against the warm concrete, while above him the turret jerked left and right, trying to acquire a target.

'We should be safe down here,' said Clunk, thumping into the wall alongside him.

'That shoulder doesn't look good.'

'It's useable.'

'Look, if we get out of this alive I'll get you a whole new body.'

'Really?' Clunk's face lit up. 'That would be wonderful!'

'The way we're going, it would be a miracle.'

Clunk squared his shoulders. Or rather, he squared one and half-raised the other. 'I will do my best to get us home, Mr Spacejock.'

Chug!

Hal stared at the wall. 'What the –'

Chug, chug!

'What is it?'

The chugging became a steady thumping noise, and grey smoke puffed from a vent in the wall.

'It's a generator,' said Clunk. 'It must be charging the gun's batteries.'

'What happens if we stop it?'

'It'll put the gun out of action.'

'Good. We'll never get down to the entrance with that thing still active.' Hal strode to the door and grabbed the handle. There was a vivid blue flash as his fingers made contact, and the next thing he knew he was flat on his back three metres away. There was a roar as the gun fired, and he felt the blast of wind as the shell passed close to his face. Seconds later, it exploded out on the plain.

'Move, Mr Spacejock! Move!' shouted Clunk.

Hal scrambled to his hands and knees and scuttled into the shelter of the bunker.

'I was wondering whether they had anything to discourage meddling,' said the robot. 'I never thought of an electrified door handle.'

'G-gee, th-thanks f-f-for the w-w-warning,' said Hal. He put a hand up to smooth down his hair, which was standing up like a toilet brush. 'N-Now you try.'

'I'm not sure it would work.'

'P-perhaps not, but it would give me a laugh.' Hal shook his head to clear it. 'Brrr. That was nasty.'

'Shocking,' agreed Clunk, returning Hal's glare with an innocent look. 'Very well, I shall try.' With that, he approached the door and took hold of the handle. There was a spark as he forced the door open, and then he slipped inside. A moment later the chugging stopped and Clunk emerged dusting his hands.

Hal looked at him. 'Is that it?'

'Yes. The turret is out of action.'

'Great, let's find the backup.'

◆

The railway lines led up the gully, heading deeper into the hillside. At some stage the natural ravine had been lined and paved. Now, vigorous weeds grew between the paving stones and the walls had collapsed in several places. Hal and Clunk picked their way around the crumbling bricks and shattered pavers, heading for the narrow end of the gully. The undergrowth was up to their necks in places, making passage difficult. Finally they pushed between a pair of bushes and stopped. Ahead, the end of the ravine was blocked by a gigantic rock fall.

'Looks like the end of the line,' said Hal.

'Not necessarily,' said Clunk. 'There may be a way through.'

Hal patted his pockets. 'Damn, I left my handy rock-fall disintegrator back on the ship.'

Clunk approached two large rocks in the centre of the pile. The rest of the fall had cascaded around these monoliths, leaving a narrow gap between them. The train tracks ran straight through the middle. 'You wait here in case the pile is unstable. And don't touch anything.'

Hal watched the robot wriggle between the boulders and vanish into the gap. He heard muffled scraping sounds for a moment or two, then all was quiet.

'Clunk?'

A handful of stones rattled down. Hal looked up and saw a pair of huge boulders embedded in the rock fall, seemingly poised to collapse. As he studied them, more dirt trickled down the pile.

There was a scrape as Clunk reappeared, his head and torso white with powdery dust. 'We're in luck, Mr Spacejock. There's a way through. Come on.'

Hal tore his gaze from the overhang and followed the robot into the gap. It was tight, but after a metre or two it widened into a low concrete chamber. The floor was thick with chalky dust, and Clunk's chest beam picked out a group of three groundcars lying on blocks, their yellowed windscreens coated with dust and their paint cracked and faded. On a bench there was a lathe and a collection of metalworking tools.

'Must have been a garage,' said Hal. 'Hey, if we get one of these working we could drive back to the palace.'

Clunk angled the beam at the far wall, where the tracks

vanished into a small tunnel. 'They must have used the train to transport vehicles for repairs. Now, let's look around - the backup must be here somewhere.'

On a bench at the back of the room they found a pair of steel boxes and a bulky display screen. In front of the screen was a large keyboard.

'Is that what you're looking for?' asked Hal.

'I think it's just a workshop terminal. Probably used to look up repair manuals.' Clunk flicked the power switch and a low humming filled the air. After a moment or two, several icons appeared on the screen. Clunk explored a few menus, then settled down in front of the machine. 'This could take a while. There's a lot of data.'

'I'll take a look at the cars.' Hal examined the first but the interior was gutted, and when he lifted the hood there was just an empty space inside. The other two were in a similar state, just body shells without any workings. Hal glanced at Clunk, who was engrossed at the terminal. Then he looked towards the tunnel.

The entrance was low, barely reaching his shoulder. Hal crouched between the tracks and shuffled into the tunnel, holding his hands against the roof to maintain his balance. He'd gone two or three metres when he bumped into something solid. It was square, with rounded edges and corners, and when he explored further he felt a padded seat. Hal grinned to himself. A miniature train!

Squeezing alongside the train's body, he clambered aboard and sat down, holding his head sideways to avoid the low ceiling. Then he felt for the controls.

Clunk was paging through data on the computer, working quickly in case the battery gave out. So far, he'd discovered more than he wanted to know about the care and maintenance of groundcars, and absolutely nothing on teleporter networks. It was frustrating, especially now there was only one backup site left to explore.

He heard a rumble and his head snapped towards the rocks blocking the entrance. Was the rest coming down? And where was Hal?

The rumble grew louder and a long white shape burst from the tunnel. 'Clunk! Help!' shouted Hal, as the miniature train he was riding hurtled towards the fallen rocks. He was hanging on for dear life, his eyes wide and his flight suit flapping in the headwind.

Clunk took a snapshot of Hal and his train set, and another of the fallen rocks. Once he had both he increased his processing speed to maximum, slowing time to a crawl. He laid both images side to side on his internal viewer, and ran a quick scaling test to compare the measurements. On the right-hand picture, a red line bisected Hal's neck.

Clunk returned to normal speed, and the stationary train seemed to leap forwards. 'Duck, Mr Spacejock!' shouted Clunk. 'Keep your head right down!'

Hal did as he was told, just in time. The train shot between the huge boulders and there was a squeal as it struck a glancing blow on the way through. Stones cascaded down the huge pile to the floor, rattling and bouncing like marbles. Then ...silence. Clunk eyed the loose pile of rocks, ready for the worst, and he'd just breathed a sigh of relief when the whole lot began to shift.

Clunk grabbed the briefcase and dived for the narrow gap just as the huge rocks above the entrance came down.

◆

Hal was almost blinded by sunlight as the train burst into the narrow gully. He could just see the control panel through watering eyes, and he decided the large purple handle looked just like a brake. He pulled with all his might and the wheels locked instantly, grinding along the dirt-strewn rails. As the train came to a shuddering halt, Hal glanced back to see Clunk dive headlong through the cascading rock fall. He landed on his hands, executed a neat forwards roll, then ran for it, dodging falling boulders as he fought to get clear. Behind him the entire hillside collapsed with a rumble, creating a wave of choking dust.

Suddenly two huge boulders burst out of the dust cloud, smashing the train tracks into splinters as they tumbled down the gully towards them. Clunk leapt aboard and Hal slammed the throttle forwards, launching the train along the track at breakneck speed. He could hear the boulders gaining, despite the tearing headwind whistling in his ears, and when he looked back he saw the huge tumbling rocks gaining fast.

The train shot out of the gully and curved to the right, following the track. The boulders tumbled past on their left, close enough to splatter them with grit and stones.

'A very close escape, Mr Spacejock,' said Clunk, as the dust settled. 'Once again, we leave with empty hands.'

Hal glanced over his shoulder. 'Did you get the data?'

Slowly, Clunk shook his head.

Hal watched the hill vanish behind a spreading cloud of dust. 'Where's the next site?'

'The third backup is off the northern coast. We're going to need a flyer.'

'Where do we get one of those?'

'The same place we got the groundcar. Now slow down. If you hit a damaged piece of track at this speed you'll kill yourself.'

Hal eased back on the throttle, and an hour or so later a line of trees appeared on the horizon. They dismounted near the palace, where a large tree had fallen across the track, completely blocking it.

Clunk led the way through the undergrowth, first to the courtyard and then into the hangar, where they threaded their way between the wrecked ships and groundcars. At the far end, near the fallen roof, there were several tarpaulin-covered shapes.

Clunk whisked the covers off the nearest and stood back, eyeing the machine critically. It consisted of a triangular frame with two seats bolted side by side. Behind the seats was a metal box with a pole sticking out the top, and on top of the pole there was a twin-bladed rotor. The device sat on three small wheels, one at the front and two at the back.

Hal was not impressed. 'When you said flyer, I imagined tinted windows, airconditioning and cup holders. That's just a wind-up chair!'

'It has a good range.'

'Only if we take turns to pedal,' muttered Hal. 'Come on, let's push it outside. It'll be good for a laugh, whatever happens.'

Clunk put the briefcase in the foot well, and together they wheeled the copter out of the hangar. Once it was clear, Clunk sat in the driver's seat and examined the controls, which consisted of a button, a twist-grip joystick and a pair of pedals. 'Looks pretty straightforward,' he said. 'Stand back or you'll get a head cut.'

'You mean a hair cut,' said Hal, backing away.

'I know what I meant.' As soon as Hal was out of range Clunk pressed the starter, and the blades began to turn. They hissed through the air, kicking up dust until the machine half-vanished in a swirling cloud. The hissing became a steady whap-whap-whap, and the machine shot out of the dust cloud, heading straight up. After a few gentle manoeuvres, Clunk decreased the power and set the machine back on the ground.

Hal moved closer, but Clunk waved him away. 'Fetch some rope. We might need it.'

Hal found a coil in the hangar and took it back to the copter. He stowed it away, sat in the passenger seat and looked around for a strap or a seatbelt. There was nothing but a chipped metal bar to hang on to.

'Ready?' asked Clunk.

Hal nodded, and the craft rose into the air. The downdraft hit him like a waterfall, and it took all his strength to keep his arms on the bar. Suddenly the copter veered, pressing him into the hard plastic seat, and when he looked past Clunk he could see straight down to the ground. Then they straightened up and gathered speed, gaining height as they passed over weed-choked fields. Ahead, the forest stretched as far as the eye could see.

'How far?' shouted Hal.

Clunk gestured at the horizon. 'All the way to the coast.'

They'd been flying over the forest for thirty minutes, crawling across the vast expanse of trees. The only visible break was a river, winding silver ribbon. When the river was directly beneath them, Hal saw pale sky reflected off the rippled surface. Then it was gone, replaced once again by trees.

'Why is this next site so dangerous?' asked Hal, raising his voice against the beat of the blades.

'The backup is stored on *Banga no Ilik*.'

'What's that?'

'It's a monument to a legendary ruler. He sired over thirty litters with his seventeen wives.'

'I'm surprised he had time for ruling.' Despite further questioning, Hal couldn't get another word out of the robot so he passed the time pretending to bomb trees. He'd pick one out ahead, then count to thirty as they approached it. If it was directly underneath when he reached zero, it was a hit. Two seconds either side was a near miss, and anything else was a complete failure. Twenty-nine complete failures later he looked up just in time to see the edge of the world approaching. The trees stopped at a cliff so sheer it could have been guillotined into existence. Hal felt his bits and pieces tightening as they flew towards the edge, and at that moment he saw the towering column of rock thrusting from the ocean fifty metres from the shore. The column rose up and up, the rounded tip a handful of metres below the level of the cliff.

'There it is,' said Clunk. '*Umrata Banga no Ilik*. Roughly translated, Ilik's organ.'

'I can see where all those litters came from.' Hal's gaze travelled up the column of rock. 'Can you land on it?'

'I don't know yet. Hold on.' Clunk angled the flight stick, taking the copter over the edge of the cliff and across the void to the column. They hovered above it while Clunk peered down at the crumbling stone. 'Negative.'

'So what do we do?'

Clunk indicated the rope. 'I'll hover in the copter while you lower yourself down onto the column.'

'Forget it,' said Hal flatly. 'I'll hover, you lower yourself onto the damn thing.'

'But Mr Spacejock, you can't fly!'

'I'm a pilot, aren't I?'

'Not for this kind of machinery.'

Hal looked down. At the base of the column, gigantic waves smashed into a jumbled pile of rock, throwing spray high into the air. 'Clunk, if I fall off that column I'm screwed. If you fall I can have you fixed.'

The robot looked at him doubtfully. 'I suppose I could give you a lesson or two.'

'Good,' said Hal. 'It can't be that hard, and it'll look good on my Spacer's Guild application form.'

'You've got bigger things than membership forms to worry about.' Clunk wheeled the copter round and set it down on the cliff top, then turned to address his pupil. 'You must keep the craft level when you're near the ground or you'll destroy the rotor. Do you understand?'

Hal nodded.

'Push the pedals to rotate left and right. Twist the grip clockwise to increase power, anti-clockwise to decrease power, and use the stick to tilt the rotor.'

'Push stick, tilt rotor. Got it.'

'When you increase power for take-off, you must apply left pedal at the same time. Otherwise the blade will stay in one place and the copter will screw itself into the ground.'

'Push pedal or the copter is screwed. Okay.'

'When you want to land, you must hover first. Decrease power gradually until the craft begins to descend, use the pedals to keep your heading, and just before you touch down the air trapped between the ground and the rotor will create a cushion. When that happens, you cut the power completely and allow the copter to settle by itself. Is all that clear?'

'Easy,' said Hal. 'Hop out, it's my turn.'

Clunk released the stick and stood up. 'Remember, everything in moderation. Small, gradual movements. Don't jerk the stick around or you'll have the craft all over the place.'

Hal sat in the pilot's chair and reached for the starter, while Clunk ducked under the rotor and hurried around to the spare seat. He fished out the coil of rope and tied a loose end to the tubular frame. While he did so, the rotor began to turn.

'When we're clear of the cliff, I want you to fly some distance from the column and practice hovering.'

'Anything you say.' Hal glanced up at the blurred rotor and twisted the throttle.

'Left pedal!' cried Clunk, as the copter began to slew around.

Hal stomped on it and the copter lurched.

Clunk held on tight. 'Are you sure about this, Mr Spacejock?'

'You had a go. It's my turn.' Hal opened the throttle and they rose unsteadily into the air, drifting sideways and turning anti-clockwise at the same time. He tried pressing one pedal, then quickly pressed the other as a gentle turn became a spin. Just as he thought he'd controlled it, the copter began to spin in the opposite direction, faster and faster until sky and ground were just a blur. He heard Clunk cry out, but was too busy mashing the pedals and yanking the stick to all points of the compass to take in any instructions.

Somehow, by pressing and pulling everything in reach, he managed to get the copter level. He looked round to give Clunk a comforting wink, then stared in astonishment.

The co-pilot's seat was empty.

◆

'Clunk?' Hal rose in his chair and tried to see over the far side, but all he could see was the knot around the frame. A quick glance over his own side showed the copter was rocketing into the sky. Then he looked down and spotted Clunk hanging to the very end of the rope, just above the ocean. His face was tilted up, and his mouth was forming words at high speed. 'Hang on!' shouted Hal, somewhat unnecessarily.

Clunk took one hand off the rope to gesture at him.

'Unscrew the throttle to descend,' muttered Hal, remembering fragments from his all-too-brief lesson. He twisted the grip to the left and the copter immediately turned right. He pushed the left-hand pedal to the stops, and the craft lurched round and spun the opposite way. Once he managed to correct the spin, he looked down to see how the altitude was doing and quickly realised all upward motion had ceased. In fact, the copter was now plummeting seaward. Far below, with the salty water coming up to meet him, Clunk was frantically climbing the rope.

'Screw the throttle to go up,' said Hal, twisting the grip firmly. This time he remembered to push the pedal, and the copter rose like a moon rocket. Clunk lost his grip on the rope and slid all the way to the end, where he just managed to save himself by wrapping three loops around his forearm.

Hal looked up in surprise as a shadow fell across the controls. He was halfway up the column, rising like an express lift and drifting ever closer to the rocky face.

'How do you tilt?' Hal looked down at the stick, then back at the column, which was close enough to make out small plants growing in the cracks. He shoved the stick to his left, and for good measure pushed both pedals and twisted the throttle at the same time. The copter jerked up, spinning in mid-air, then headed straight for the cliff face. Hal pulled back until the copter was high enough to clear, then remembered Clunk hanging from the rope far below. When he looked down he saw the robot's expression as it hurtled towards the wall of stone: eyes wide, mouth open, jaw dropped.

With a casual flick of the wrist Hal turned the copter back towards the column, while a twist of the throttle brought it high enough to clear the tip. As he reached the cracked, rocky surface he eased the stick back to hover, and then he noticed movement to his right. Glancing round he saw Clunk's arm reaching into the copter for a handhold. A moment later, the robot's head appeared, followed by the other arm.

'What d'you come back up for?' demanded Hal. 'We're hovering over the damn thing!'

Clunk opened his mouth and delivered a long and varied string of curses. He'd spent several minutes collating the list from the sealed section of his vocabulary, and the results were impressive.

'Finished?' asked Hal, as the robot tailed off.

Clunk glared at him. 'For now,' he said, loosening his grip and sliding down the rope.

Hal saw him land on the tip of the column, trailing several

metres of cord. 'Steady,' he murmured. He saw Clunk stagger in the downdraft, and he backed the copter away a little.

Beneath him, Clunk was on his hands and knees, exploring the narrow tip of the column with his hands. He stopped near a patch of sand and began to dig, burrowing down like a dog after a rabbit, throwing up gouts of dirt in his haste. The digging stopped and Clunk worked at something buried in the sand. Then he stood up and waved at the copter.

Hal pushed the stick forward, lining up the rope so that it would drag across the top of the column. As he approached, he saw Clunk stagger. Then he stared in amazement - the towering shaft of rock was falling away from him, into the sea.

28

The copter dived towards the ocean with the cord streaming out behind, blades hissing as it tore through the air. The cord passed within a metre of the column, and Clunk threw himself headlong to grab hold of it. Once he was safe Hal pulled the nose up to avoid sticking the flying machine in the ocean floor.

They were still clawing for height when the column fell into the sea, throwing water high into the air. Hal brought the machine to a hover as Clunk clambered in, a slim metal box gripped between his lips. He flopped into the passenger seat and gestured at the cliffs. 'Land!' he shouted over the whap-whap-whap of the rotor.

Hal headed for the strip of green atop the crumbling cliff face, where he set the machine down with a bump. 'That thing's been sticking out of the sea for thousands of years, and then we turn up and boom, it's gone. What happened?'

'It was rigged to collapse,' said Clunk. 'I suspected as much, but I thought I'd have time to collect the backup before the destruct was triggered.'

'Is that it?' Hal looked at the small box doubtfully. 'It looks like a sandwich tin.'

'Slide across,' said Clunk, leaping down from the copter. 'We'll fly back to the palace and I'll see what I can get out of it.'

The copter settled in the palace courtyard and Clunk hurried towards the cool interior. On the way, he worked the box open and withdrew a small glass cube. 'I'm going to plug this chip into one of the computers. Given time I'll be able to generate an index and find the information we need.'

Hal's stomach growled. 'How much time?'

'Depends on the speed of the hardware.' Clunk led the way to the computing room, where he slotted the chip into a reader and began to type. After a few moments, the chip lit up and a hollow rectangle appeared on the screen. 'This will show the indexing progress,' said Clunk.

'It's not doing anything.'

'Wait.'

They did. Five minutes later, the box was still blank.

Hal cleared his throat. 'This isn't one of those progress bars which does nothing for twenty minutes, then fills up in the blink of an eye?'

Clunk shook his head, his face grave. 'This could take a very long time, Mr Spacejock. There's a huge amount of information on the chip and the hardware may not be up to the task.'

'So you need a more powerful machine?'

'Evidently.'

'Can't you read the chip yourself?'

'I'm afraid not. My onboard storage is limited, and even with additional memory I'd be no faster than these computers.'

Hal snapped his fingers. 'Wait here!'

Hal burst into the courtyard, running at full tilt. The copter was where they left it, the rotor swinging slowly in the breeze, and he ducked his head and reached into the foot well where his fingers closed on the briefcase. Then he ran back to the computer room.

'One high-powered computer,' he said, holding the briefcase out.

Clunk smiled. 'I wondered what you were up to.' He took the case, laid it on the bench and opened it. Immediately, a short length of red cable flopped out, the end a mass of torn wires.

'What happened to that?' asked Hal.

'It was damaged when I rescued it from the groundcar,' said Clunk. 'I'm sure Sonya will understand.'

There was a clattering whirr as the briefcase powered on. 'Hey, where am I?'

'You don't want to know,' said Hal. 'We need your help to get back to Sonya.'

'What do you want me to do?' asked the briefcase. 'I'm very powerful, you know.'

'I'm sure you are. Now listen, we've got a huge amount of data and Clunk here is trying to generate an index so we can find the information we need to get home. With me so far?'

'Of course. How will I access the data?'

Clunk took up a spare reader. 'Can you scan for the correct frequency?'

'Already obtained,' said the briefcase. There was a click as

274

the cooling fans switched to high speed, blasting dust off the computers nearby. 'Where's the data?'

Clunk took the backup chip and plugged it into Bobby's reader. A second or two later, it lit up. 'I want you to index everything. Save all references to teleporters in a separate file.'

A rectangle appeared on the briefcase's screen, and almost immediately filled with solid green. 'What shall I do with the file?'

'Wait a minute,' said Hal. 'Have you done it already?'

'Of course,' said the briefcase. 'And the file?'

'Give me access,' said Clunk. He put one hand on the briefcase and the screen flashed through page after page of diagrams, star maps, text and mathematical tables.

'That's a very old protocol you have there,' said the briefcase. 'Have you considered an upgrade?'

Clunk ignored him. 'I've narrowed it down to two possible addresses,' he said to Hal. 'One of them must be Canessa.'

'And the other?'

'It could be anywhere. The database contains information on gravity, atmospheric composition and the construction diagrams of the buildings. Both are identical to my own measurements from Canessa.'

'Isn't there any way to tell?'

'No. It's a coin toss.' Clunk closed the briefcase, ignoring its squawk of protest. 'We'd better take as much of this equipment as we can.'

'What about the keypad? And a power source?'

'We'll stop at the pillbox for those. Then it's back to the teleporter.'

Rex gripped the control stick with one hand and tightened his safety harness with the other. The tiny craft shook as it dropped into the planet's upper atmosphere, and there was a sheen of sweat on Rex's forehead. It was several years since his last planetfall and that had been on Ullimo, where ground control had landed the ship automatically. Here, he'd have to do it himself.

A buzzer sounded, and he scanned the instruments. The hull temperature warning was yellow, and he fired the attitude jets to slow the rate of descent. Beneath him, the planetary surface was stretched out like a living, full-colour map. He'd already selected his landing spot, and the ship's computer was showing one more loop of the planet before final approach.

Twenty minutes later the shaking ceased. Rex was on the far side of the planet from the touchdown area and the ground below was as dark as deep space, with only a sliver of light showing near the horizon. The cabin was chilly, and thin air whistled over the cockpit as the ship tore through the sky.

The sun appeared five minutes from touchdown, flooding the ship with warm yellow light, immediately raising the temperature by five or six degrees.

Rex looked out. The land below was heavily forested, with undulations where the trees rose up and over small hills. To his right there were two clearings side by side, and in the middle of the nearest was his target - a white freighter with a pointed nose and a swept-back tail. The Volante.

Rex glanced at the second clearing, and did a double-take

as he saw the stone pillars in the middle. What the hell were they doing there?

The ship's computer chimed and a heads-up display appeared on the windshield. The landing area was marked with a small red box, the hover point with a blue circle. As Rex approached the circle his computer displayed the required speed, altitude and attitude alongside it. By matching all three, he was able to bring the ship to a halt above the smaller clearing, and a minute later he felt a gentle bump as the landing legs made contact.

The canopy hissed as the seals parted, whining loudly as it rose out of the way. Rex loosened his straps and swung his legs over the side, scrambling to the ground as the canopy reversed direction. It sealed with a thump, and Rex flipped open a panel and entered a code. With the vessel secured, he hurried over to examine the stone structures in the middle of the clearing.

◆

Sonya stared at the clean white wall inches from her nose. A moment later, she heard a repeat of the noise which had woken her: a male voice calling her name. It had to be Hal and his robot, back from their little expedition. She looked at her watch and cursed. Two more hours to go. She'd have to work on Hal - get him to move her equipment out of the clearing and talk him into setting it up. If that failed she had Tinker on standby, but she would only use the robot as a last resort.

Sonya stood up and ran her fingers through her hair. Then she opened her door. 'Mr Spacejock, I –' Her voice tailed off as she saw Rex Curtis standing outside with a blaster in his hand. 'W-what are you doing here?'

'Change of plans. Is Spacejock aboard?'

'No. I don't know. I thought you were them, coming back.'

'Them?'

Sonya glared at him. 'Yeah, them. Spacejock rescued his damned robot, the one your people were supposed to get rid of. I came aboard and walked right into an interrogation.'

'Where are they?'

'There's a ruin in the next clearing.'

'I know. I landed next to it.'

'Well, they went underground looking for me. That was hours ago and I've not seen them since.'

'Where's the briefcase?'

'Hal's got it,' said Sonya quietly.

'What?'

'I had it with me and they almost caught me in the ruins. I ran for it, but when I got to the trees I realised I'd left the case behind.'

'Why didn't you go back?'

'They found it and took it underground with them.'

'Well, we'll just have to get it back again.' Rex jabbed his finger at the cargo door. 'I need that briefcase to fly the Volante. If that paperwork isn't delivered on time, my whole company is going to collapse.'

'I thought you wanted me to delay Hal's ship?'

'That's right. Then I discover this paperwork is needed to set up our new finance deal. Central Bank - they're our new lenders. So I came here as quick as I could to get it moving again.'

'Why don't you get Hal to fly us there? As soon as he comes back –'

Rex shook his head. 'I'm not putting myself at the mercy of a freelancer. No, it's time to use Tinker.'

29

The copter took off from the palace, laden with computer hardware, circuit boards and spares. It swept over the palace wall, skimming the trees as it struggled for height. A few minutes later Clunk set the machine down outside the concrete pillbox and vanished inside, emerging straight away with the control panel. Hal stored it away, while Clunk climbed onto the roof of the pillbox to get at the energy panels, stacking them on the edge for Hal to lift down.

He'd just packed the fifth panel when Clunk returned with two more. 'That should do it,' said the robot. 'We can always come back if we need anything else.'

Hal eyed the heavily laden copter. 'You'll have to come back for me, by the look of it.'

'Nonsense. Put the boards down there, get in and I'll put the computer on top.'

Hal grunted as the heavy metal box landed in his lap. 'Take care. That's delicate equipment.'

'Sorry, I forget they weren't brass.' Clunk sat in the pilot's chair and started the motor. 'Lucky we don't have far to go.'

The copter lurched into the air and gathered speed quickly, leaving the trees behind as it headed out across the plain. They were halfway to the hill when Hal felt a tickle on the back of his hand. He looked down and saw a tiny spider dragging itself across his skin, flattened by the downdraft. Taking his hand off the bar, he shook it over the side and watched the spider sail away in the wind. Something tickled the back of his neck, and he flicked away another spider, just as something else crawled up his shin. He looked around the metal case and stared in horror at the wave of spiders crawling up his legs. With a yell, he threw the computer over the side and set about the spiders with a vengeance, flicking them overboard, swatting them as they crawled up his legs, over his lap and onto his chest. When the last one had gone, he pulled his legs up and watched the tangle of equipment closely, ready to lash out at the slightest movement.

Moments later, the hill came into view. They landed alongside, and while Clunk dealt with the engine Hal stepped down and dusted off his flight suit.

Clunk looked around. 'Where did that computer go?'

'The damn thing was full of spiders. Millions of them crawling all over me - going up my legs, around my –'

'Hopefully we won't need it.' Clunk looked up at the mast on top of the teleporter. 'We're going to need at least four of those energy panels. You get them on the roof while I make a start inside.'

Hal glanced at the sheer concrete walls. 'How am I supposed to get up there?'

'Push the copter up to the wall, climb up the copter, step onto the roof. Simple.'

'Smarty pants,' muttered Hal.

Clunk gathered an armful of components and vanished inside the building, while Hal moved the copter into position, fetched the panels and balanced them on the rotor. He clambered onto the machine and slid the panels onto the concrete roof, one by one. Then he inspected the mast, and decided Clunk would be grateful if he fitted the panels in place. It certainly looked simple enough.

Hal pulled himself onto the roof, collected an armful of panels and crossed to the mast. There were several clamps on the metal pole, and after a few minutes work he had the new panels ringing the mast like petals on a giant flower. After that, it was a simple matter to strip the electrical cables and offer them up to the contacts. He closed the last connection, and there was a loud pop from below, followed by a stream of curses.

Hal looked over the edge, just as Clunk emerged from the building with a smoking circuit board in his hands. The robot stared up at him. 'What did you do?' His gaze travelled to the mast. 'Did you connect those panels into the circuit?'

'I thought I was being useful.'

Clunk waved the smoking circuit board. 'You're lucky I have another. Now get down here before you fall off.'

Hal clambered down the copter and entered the teleporter. Inside, Clunk was working on a bunch of cables protruding from the wall. The robot had exposed the tip of his index finger and was busy flashing wires together, inspecting each joint carefully as it cooled.

'How's it going?'

'Fantastic, apart from the unexpected power surges.'

'I'm sorry, okay? I just thought –'

'Best if you don't.' Clunk inspected the control panel. 'That should do it.'

'You mean we can go back?'

Clunk looked at him thoughtfully. 'I should go first, to test the device. It might transport me somewhere completely unexpected.'

'How will I know if it worked properly?'

'Give me five minutes. If I'm not back by then, the teleporter will be ready to send you.' Clunk held up the control panel. 'When all the lights are on, it's ready. Press this button to go.'

'When all the lights are on, press the go button. Understood.'

'You'd better wait outside. I'm not sure how large the sphere of influence is, especially with those additional panels.'

'How will you come back if the teleporter hasn't charged up?'

'According to the teleporter diagrams, receiving uses a lot less power than transmitting.'

Suddenly Hal's mouth fell open. 'Clunk! Don't you see?'

'What?' asked the robot, looking around.

'The teleport scientist, the one with the display at the spaceport! We can give him the diagrams to build a real machine!'

'That quack?' snorted Clunk. 'He couldn't build a paper plane.'

'No, listen. We put all our money into his shares, and when we're holding as many as possible we reveal the teleporter plans. He spends all his time building and marketing the things and we pocket all the cash. It's perfect!' Hal realised Clunk wasn't quite as enthusiastic as he was. 'All right, say we cut him out and do it ourselves. With your brains, skill and wisdom and my er ... my er ... '

'Let's worry about the future when we're safely aboard the Volante,' said Clunk.

'I know, I'll do the marketing,' said Hal. 'Spacejock Teleporters. Or what about Spacezap? No, Insta-trav!'

'Mr Spacejock?'

'Huh?'

283

'I'm going to activate the teleporter. I suggest you step outside.'

Hal stopped in the doorway. 'Clunk, I really appreciate this.'

'It's nothing, Mr Spacejock.'

'You say that, and yet you're willing to lay down your life to protect me from danger. You –'

'Actually, I was programmed this way.'

'Oh. Well, thanks anyway.' Hal turned and walked outside. As he stepped away from the building there was a tremendous flash of light, followed by a high-pitched whine. He ran to the doorway and looked inside. He was alone.

The control panel beeped and one light came on. As he watched, another joined it. Ten seconds later a third lit up.

'Nine more,' muttered Hal. 'I hope this damn thing works.'

◆

Sonya led Rex to the ruins, while Tinker followed with steady, thumping footsteps. They walked in silence, with Rex lost in thought and Sonya puzzling over his sudden arrival. Eventually she had to ask the question which was bothering her. 'Tell me, why can't Hal fly us to Ackexa?'

'I don't trust him. I'm going to take his ship, deliver the cargo and then come back for him afterwards.'

'But surely –'

Rex stopped. 'Look, Spacejock and I have a feud going ... we're both after the same business, and we'll take any advantage we can get. I've already told you my company will go under if Central doesn't get that paperwork in time. If Spacejock discovers he can ruin me by dumping all those

284

pallets into a star, what do you think he'll do? No, I'm taking his ship and I'm delivering them myself. That's the end of the matter.'

They set off again, and this time Sonya was silent. A minute or two later they arrived at the clearing, where the jet-black flyer crouched near the stone pillars like a bird of prey. The air was still, and the mossy structures cast dark shadows across the grass.

'This place gives me the creeps,' muttered Sonya.

Rex waved Tinker towards the entrance. 'I want you to go down there, locate my briefcase and return it to me. Is that clear?'

The robot's eyes gleamed. 'You wish me to eliminate foes?'

'No,' said Rex firmly. He ignored the robot's crestfallen look and elaborated on his instructions. 'I want you to go down those steps and find the briefcase. It might be in the possession of a human or another robot.'

'Foes?' said Tinker hopefully.

'Just ask for the briefcase, all right?'

'And if they refuse to give it to me?'

'Threaten them.'

'If they still refuse?'

'Take the briefcase by force. Destroy the robot and slap the human about if you have to.'

Tinker cracked his knuckles. 'Mission understood. Find the briefcase, destroy the robot and whack the human.'

'I said slap, not ...' began Rex, but Tinker was already descending the staircase.

Sonya gestured after him. 'You can't set him off like that. Someone could get hurt!'

'Don't waste your sympathy on Spacejock,' said Rex. 'He

never spared any for your Outsider kin while he was busy stranding them.'

'I'm beginning to wonder whether that wasn't just a malicious rumour.'

'You know the saying. Where there's smoke, and all that.' Rex shrugged. 'Spacejock's in the thick of it, you mark my words.'

◆

Clunk arrived with a flash of light, leaving him blinking and dazed in a mirrored chamber. He sniffed, analysing the air, and a broad grin appeared on his face. It was planet Canessa! He'd found the way home!

He tucked the briefcase under his arm and activated the control pad. The heavy door began to open, and Clunk darted towards it. Mr Spacejock could arrive any moment now, and while the alien data hadn't been all that clear about the effects of teleporting two beings into the same physical space, the gruesome diagrams spoke volumes.

Clunk stepped over the threshold, and started as a huge shadow loomed from the corridor. He had no time to react - a large fist drove out of the darkness, smashing into his chest, breaking through his plasteel skin and crushing his internals. He dropped to his knees, his vision blurred and his circuits screaming fatal errors.

The briefcase was wrenched from his grip and a hulking figure turned its back and strode away, its head brushing the ceiling and its shoulders as wide as the corridor.

Clunk's vision dimmed, and the last thing he saw was the concrete floor coming up to meet him.

30

There was faint crash from underground, and Sonya peered down the stairs. Rex was squatting in front of the opening, head cocked as he listened to Tinker's progress.

'We should have gone with him,' said Sonya. 'Hal could be lying down there hurt, and if Tinker –'

'Spacejock's nothing but a low-down pirate, and you know it.'

Sonya frowned. 'I spent some time with Hal, you know. He's –'

'A charming rogue? A dashing spaceship captain?' Rex glanced up at her. 'I'm surprised. I thought you were a level-headed career woman, not a simpering stud worshipper.'

Sonya snorted. 'I worship nobody. It's just ...' But how could she explain her instincts? That Hal seemed like a decent person?

'Where's that bloody robot got to?' muttered Rex, scowling into the dark. 'If he's got lost –' He broke off at the sound of heavy footsteps, and a moment later the robot came into sight, bounding up the stairs two at a time, swinging the battered briefcase from its left hand.

Rex stood back as Tinker reached the top of the stairs. The robot handed the case over and stood to attention as Rex examined it. The silver case was scratched, the corners were out of true and when he opened the lid the red cable hung limply, the end just a tangle of wires. 'Looks like it's been through a black hole,' he said, switching it on. 'Bobby? Can you hear me?'

Fans whirred, blowing streams of dust, and the briefcase beeped. 'Yes, Mr Curtis.'

'Are you hurt?'

'I cannot feel pain.'

'I mean are you working?'

'Of course.'

'What about this?' Rex tapped the torn red cable. 'Is it important?'

Sonya nodded. 'That's the cable for overriding the ship.'

'You mean we can't fly the Volante?' He grabbed the black cable. 'What about this one? Come on, you're the computer expert! Talk to me!'

'I might be able to crack the Navcom by force, but it could take a while.' Sonya looked thoughtful. 'You know, it would be easier if you just let Hal fly us there.'

'Will you give that a rest?' Rex snapped his fingers at Tinker. 'You! Wait here and don't let anyone out.'

Tinker looked down at him, his face impassive. 'You wish me to remain on this planet?'

'It's your duty.'

Slowly, Tinker shook his head. 'This is not the best position for defence.'

'Are you disobeyeing an order?'

'Negative. In order to maximise effectiveness I wait at the foot of the steps, concealed in darkness.'

Rex looked relieved. 'Right. You maximise whatever you want as long as nobody gets past.'

Tinker saluted, then turned and marched down the stairs.

'Well, Ms Polarov,' said Rex, hefting the case. 'Back to the ship.'

'What about Spacejock? You can't just leave him here with that thing on guard!'

Rex sighed. 'Look, you're going to need time with the ship, right? Once you've hacked in and we're ready to leave, you can come back and tell Tinker to let the guy out in an hour or two.' He jerked his thumb at the flyer. 'He can use that to get off the planet. Happy now?'

Sonya nodded slowly.

'So let's get to the ship and start work. If that paperwork isn't delivered on time my whole company's going down the drain.'

◆

Hal materialised in the teleport chamber and saw his startled face reflected in the mirror-finish walls. He recognised his surroundings immediately, and pumped his fist in the air with delight. 'Clunk, we did it!' He stepped away from the centre of the floor, moving towards the doorway. 'Clunk?'

Light blazed from the corridor and a huge figure advanced on him. 'Foes will be destroyed,' said a metallic voice.

Hal backed up, squinting into the blinding glare. 'Clunk? Is that you?'

It most certainly wasn't. Instead of a friendly squashy face, this robot had a head like a granite boulder. Its jaw was big enough to crush cars, and as for its massive hands ... Hal frowned. Were they really covered in blood? 'Where's Clunk?' he demanded. 'What have you done with him?'

The robot charged without warning, powering into the chamber with its head down and its arms spread wide. At the last moment Hal stepped aside, and the robot slammed into the mirrored wall, shattering the panels and exposing tightly packed wires. Shards of glass rained down, and Hal scuttled around the chamber as the robot recovered. This time he was ready, and when it charged he pushed off from the wall and ducked under its grasping hands. He slammed into the glass panel beneath the controls, bounced off and landed flat on his back.

There was a burst of music, and when Hal looked up he realised the control panel was glowing. Across the chamber, the robot let out a furious yell, slamming its fists into the mirrored wall in rage. Glass exploded outwards under the impact, showering the floor and crunching under the robot's feet.

Hal got up and faced the robot, his back to the wall. 'Not very quick, are you?'

The robot's eyes blazed in the low light, and it clenched and unclenched its fists. 'Foes must be destroyed.'

'You want to destroy a foe? Come and get me, you ugly mother!'

The robot charged, its massive fists clenched for the killing blow. Casually, almost lazily, Hal slapped his palm on the control panel. There was a brilliant flash as the teleporter activated, and when Hal's vision cleared he was alone.

He'd only savoured his victory for a couple of seconds when a warning light began to pulse, filling the chamber with blood-red flashes. One of the mirrored panels exploded in a shower of sparks and broken glass, and Hal stumbled out of the chamber with his arms over his head. He staggered along the corridor, his vision full of flashes, red lights and after-images. Gradually his sight recovered, and in the semi-darkness he spotted a trail of dark liquid on the floor. It ended in a huddled bronze shape.

'Clunk!' Hal broke into a run, threw himself down and turned the robot over, wincing as he saw the damage. There was a large hole in Clunk's chest, and coolant pumped weakly from the split tubing.

'Watch out,' gasped Clunk, fluid welling from his mouth. 'Robot. Danger!'

'Don't worry, Clunk. I got it.'

'Glad ... okay.' Clunk relaxed, and the seeping stopped.

'Who does it belong to, Clunk? What's going on?'

More panels exploded in the teleporter, forcing waves of acrid smoke along the tunnel.

'Clunk, can you walk?'

Clunk's eyes closed and his head dropped to one side.

'I guess that's a no.' Hal got the heavy body over one shoulder, staggered upright and made his way along the tunnel to the staircase, half-choked by the swirling smoke. He took the steps one at a time, muscles burning, sweat and coolant soaking into his flight suit. With each laboured step he dreamt up new and exciting ways of making someone pay for what had happened to Clunk, for the killer robot, for everything.

The slippery stairs at the top were a nightmare, but Hal got by on willpower alone. He emerged in the clearing and his eyes widened at the black flyer standing nearby. He took a step towards it, then realised there was no time to investigate. Another killer robot could be stalking Sonya.

Suddenly the ground shook, and smoke and dust jetted from

the mouth of the stairs. There was a deep, booming explosion underground, knocking Hal off his feet. His vision danced as the rumbling continued, and one by one the stone columns crumbled and fell.

The noises stopped and the ground was still.

Hal took one last look at the smoke-shrouded ruins and the sinister black ship, then gathered Clunk up and staggered towards the trees.

◆

Sonya followed Rex to the clearing, where they entered the Volante by the cargo ramp at the rear. At the top, Rex glanced down at the jumbled crates of equipment. 'It's a pity. Some of that stuff was brand new.'

Sonya looked down. Ullimo seemed a long way away. 'You can always pick it up when you bring the *Volante* back.'

'Come on!' called Rex, from the inner door.

In the flight deck, he thrust the briefcase into her arms and gestured at the console. 'You're the expert. Do your stuff.'

Sonya put the briefcase in the foot well, opened the top and unrolled the black cable, plugging it into the console. Then she set to work.

'Are you sure you should be doing that?' said a voice through concealed speakers.

Rex jumped. 'Who's that?'

'It's the ship's computer,' said Sonya. 'Don't worry, it can't do anything.' She switched the briefcase on. 'Bobby, can you hear me?'

'Yes indeed.'

'I need you to break into the Navcom for me.'

'You really shouldn't be doing this,' said the Navcom.

'Bobby, can you run the program Dent installed?'

'Which one?'

'Daisy cutter.'

'Sorry, but no. The output cable has been destroyed.'

'I want you to route it through the secondary.'

'I can't do that. It doesn't have the right configuration.'

'I know. I need you to modify the code.'

'It won't give me as much control,' warned the computer. 'I'll only be able to manage ship functions sequentially.'

'Just do it!' shouted Rex. He began to pace the flight deck. 'I want this thing off the ground in five minutes. Do you understand?'

'Oh yes, sure thing. Executing now.'

An eerie wail came through the console speakers.

'What the hell's that?' demanded Rex.

'Defences,' said Bobby. His fans began to whirr, blasting hot air across the deck. 'I notice you're trying to steal the ship. Would you like to browse the penalties for this offence?'

Sonya shook her head. 'We're just borrowing it, Bobby. Honestly.'

'If you say so.' There was a beep. 'I'm through the first layer already. I can start the engines if you like.'

Rex stopped pacing. 'Don't talk. Act!'

There was a rumble from the bowels of the ship, followed by a roar as the engines fired. After a few seconds they began to flutter, alternately hissing and roaring. 'More defences,' said Bobby loudly. 'Stay tuned, folks.'

Rex glanced at Sonya. 'All right, it's time. Go and tell Tinker to let Spacejock up in sixty minutes. The code for the flyer is my surname spelt backwards.'

The briefcase buzzed. 'That password is easily guessed. Would you like some help picking a secure one?'

'Shut up,' said Sonya. She eyed Rex thoughtfully. 'Are you going to wait for me?'

'You think I'd abandon you here?'

'I don't know what to think.'

'Hey, you're the one who's worried about Spacejock.'

'Right now I'm more worried about me.'

Rex shrugged. 'All right, leave him to his own devices.'

'Secondary defences breached,' said Bobby, his voice high with excitement. 'This is so much fun, Mr Curtis!'

'Tell me the instant we're ready to leave.'

'Just a few moments,' said Bobby cheerfully. 'While I'm working, would you like to enter my unlock code?'

Rex frowned. 'What's an unlock code?'

'Don't ask,' said Sonya grimly. She glanced towards the airlock. She could run to the ruins and back in ten minutes, but what chance Rex would leave without her? About a hundred percent, by her reckoning.

◆

Hal heard the *Volante's* engines before he was halfway to the clearing. He increased his pace, staggering over the uneven ground with Clunk's dead weight bearing down on his shoulders like a bag of rocks. Sweat ran into his eyes, and coolant ran freely from the robot's shattered chest, staining his flight suit with streaks of red and green. By the time he reached the clearing the ship was hidden behind a spreading cloud of steam and smoke. Avoiding the fiery jets, he plunged straight into the thick fog, heading for the cargo ramp.

The noise beneath the ship was unbearable - an ear-splitting roar from the landing jets, a deep rumble from the main drives - while white-hot fire from the thrusters cut through the steam like knives. He stopped at the nearest landing leg, where he let Clunk slither to the ground. Leaning against the leg for support, he flipped open a panel and pressed the cargo ramp override. Nothing happened. He mashed the button with his thumb, hitting it repeatedly as the engine note rose higher and higher. Raw heat washed over him in waves and the ground began to shimmer. He was too late. The ship was leaving.

Hal glanced over his shoulder, towards the forest, and realised he'd never get clear in time.

He jumped as a hand grabbed his ankle, and when he looked down he saw Clunk struggling weakly, gesturing towards his shattered chest. Through the shimmering heat Hal saw a loop of cable, and when he looked at the landing leg he realised what Clunk was telling him. The comms socket! Clunk could control the ship!

Hal grabbed the cable and rammed the plug into the socket. 'Okay, Clunk,' he muttered. 'Let's put paid to their little game.'

The engine noise grew louder. 'Come on,' shouted Hal. 'Clunk, do something!'

A shadow fell across him, and when he looked round he saw the cargo ramp dropping. It fell in fits and starts, as if controlled by opposing forces.

Hal yanked the plug and bent to retrieve Clunk.

'Leave me,' said the robot. 'Slow you down.'

'I'm not leaving you anywhere,' growled Hal. With superhuman effort he swung Clunk onto his shoulders and staggered towards the ramp, while all around them thrusters hammered the ground as they prepared to lift the ship into space.

'What's that?' demanded Rex, as a light began to flash on the console.

'Cargo door,' said Sonya, reading the indicator label. 'The Navcom's fighting back.'

'Shut the damned thing.'

Sonya tipped the briefcase over, opened the lid and began to type. After a few moments, the red light went out. 'Ship sealed. We're ready for lift-off.'

'Take her up, then.' Rex glanced at Sonya, who was biting her lip. 'Don't worry about Spacejock. We'll tip the authorities off. They'll pick him up in a day or so.'

'If he lasts that long,' muttered Sonya, remembering the look in Tinker's eyes.

31

Once they were safely in space, Sonya programmed the course for Ackexa and set the briefcase up to handle their jump. She worked efficiently, but her mind was worrying at several loose ends. Finally, she turned to face Rex. 'Mr Curtis, I want to know what's going on.'

Rex looked at her, his eyes calculating.

'No bullshit,' said Sonya. 'The truth.'

'Very well. As of tomorrow, Curtis Freightlines will cease to exist.'

'You said delivering this cargo would save the company!'

'Actually, it's going to start a new one.' Rex gestured around the flight deck. 'Welcome to the *Aurora*, and my very first job as Feenix Transport.'

'What about Spacejock?'

'Don't feel sorry for him. I wouldn't be here if he hadn't stolen Central Bank from us.'

'But you left him your flyer! When he gets free –'

'He's not going anywhere. Tinker will see to that.'

'And me?' asked Sonya softly. 'Were you going to leave me too?'

'Only if you sided against me.' Rex smiled. 'You made the right choice. I can use someone with your talents.'

'Wait a minute. Curtis Freightlines has gone broke? What about my new job? My luxury apartment? My residency?'

'All gone, I'm afraid. But you won't need –'

'No! I can't go to Ackexa!' Sonya's voice rose, and she fought down panic. 'Without the right documents they'll haul me off the ship! I'll never be allowed off the planet again!'

'I'll have a word with them. After all, you're with me now. My partner in crime.'

Sonya stared at him, her face white. 'You bastard!' Her gaze darted to the briefcase. 'Bobby, cancel the jump. Set course for Canessa. We're going back.'

'No we're not.' Rex drew his gun. 'Get up.'

'What are you doing?'

'Into the airlock,' said Rex calmly. 'You're going back to Canessa all right. Without a spacesuit.'

❧

Hal hurried along the *Volante's* lower deck corridor, heading for the lift. He had done what he could for Clunk, and now he was determined to wrest back control of his ship. He'd grabbed a length of steel pipe from the cargo hold, and as the lift bore him towards the flight deck he slapped the end in the palm of his hand. The lift stopped and a burst of adrenaline raced through his veins, leaving a cold, tingling feeling.

'What are you doing?' said a female voice, muffled by the doors. Sonya!

'Into the airlock,' said a male voice. 'You're going back to Canessa all right. Without a spacesuit!'

299

The doors opened and Hal burst into the flight deck, pipe raised. There was a man with his back to the lift, a blaster in his right hand. Sonya was halfway to the airlock, her face pale. She spotted Hal and screamed as he brought the pipe down over the back of her attacker's head.

The man half-turned and the pipe struck him a glancing blow. The gun fell from his nerveless fingers and he collapsed to the deck, where he lay still. Hal stepped over him, scooped up the gun and took Sonya in his arMs. She buried her face in his chest and he felt her trembling. 'Don't worry,' he muttered, feeling awkward with the weapons in his hands. 'It's all over.'

'Did you kill him?'

Hal let go of Sonya and bent to examine the fallen man, who was lying face down on the deck. 'He's alive, but he'll have a massive headache when he wakes up.'

'Rex is going to be –'

'Rex?' Hal stared. 'You know him?'

'He's my, er, professor.'

Hal's eyebrows rose. 'This guy's a teacher?'

'Sort of. You know my theory? The expanding civilisation?'

'Yeah. Weathering or something.'

'Right. Well my professor has another theory, the opposite of mine. He makes a lot of money lecturing about it, and when I publish my findings he'll be discredited.'

'You're telling me some egghead came all the way to Canessa with a killer robot just to stop you proving your theory? He must be insane!'

'You haven't met many academics, have you?'

'Just as well. It's incredible.' Hal shook his head slowly. Then he looked at Sonya. 'By the way, your theory was right. I've seen your vanished civilisation myself.'

Sonya looked shocked. 'Really?'

Hal nodded. 'I'll tell you about it later. Let me take the garbage out first.' He grabbed Rex's ankles and dragged him into the airlock, sealing him in.

'What are you going to do?'

'Nothing. The authorities can deal with him on Ackexa.'

'Ackexa?'

'Of course. I've got a cargo to deliver.'

'Don't you think we should take him to Ullimo first? I mean, he's not an Outsider. There might be complications.'

Hal snorted. 'Good.'

Sonya eyed the gun. 'Tell me, how did you get aboard? I thought Rex had –'

'Well, I thought everything was lost but Clunk ...' Hal's eyes widened. 'Oh, shit! Clunk!'

'What?'

'I'm up here chatting, and he's in the hold fighting for his life.' Hal strode into the lift and hit the down button. 'If anything happens to my robot, that professor of yours won't have to worry about the authorities. I'll space him myself.'

~

Sonya sat in the pilot's chair, staring through the white noise on the main screen. The ship was going to Ackexa, her home planet, deep in Outsider space. Without ID they'd never let her leave, and the only way she could get Hal to change course was to confess everything and throw herself on his mercy. And if she did that she was likely to end up in the airlock with Rex.

She glanced down at the briefcase, out of sight under the console. What if she sealed the lift and changed course? Bobby could land the ship and she could flee, leaving the port staff to release Hal and Clunk. She bit her lip. What would she do without ID? Once Hal spoke out, Union authorities would hunt her down and ship her back to Ackexa. It wouldn't work.

She heard a tapping sound, a persistent rat-tat-tat clamouring for her attention. When she looked round she saw Rex beckoning through the airlock porthole.

Sonya turned away, her mind racing. He'd meant to kill her, but the dynamic had changed now that Hal had the gun. She could make a deal with Rex. If she let him out they could seal Hal in the cargo hold and land somewhere inside Union space. After they'd gone, Hal would probably blame everything on the deranged academic, leaving her in the clear. A thought struck her, and she looked down at her blouse. A piece of her clothing trapped in the airlock door might even convince Hal that Rex had carried out his threat to space her.

Torn by indecision, Sonya glanced at the airlock. Through the porthole she saw Rex mime a circle and point at her, his meaning clear: Any planet you want.

◆

Hal had removed Clunk's shattered chest panel and was poking around in the robot's insides, trying to determine the extent of the damage.

'That tickles,' said Clunk faintly.

'Hey, you're alive!'

'Barely.'

'That ruddy great robot certainly did a job on you,' muttered Hal. 'He's bent these rod things and crushed the, er, thingamabob over here and ...' Clunk jerked as he prodded a loose connector. 'Oops, sorry.'

'Leave it,' murmured the robot.

'Will you be okay?'

'What's ... happening? Ship moving?'

'We're going to Ackexa. Don't worry, they'll fix you up.'

Clunk coughed, and fluid welled from his mouth. 'Go back to the flight deck.'

'I'm staying right here.'

'Can't do anything for me,' whispered Clunk. 'Too far gone.'

'Don't say that. Be positive!'

Slowly, Clunk's head moved from side to side. 'Brain failure. Permanent.'

'Permanent! I thought –'

'I'm sorry, Mr Spacejock.'

'If I hadn't taken Sonya on board –'

Clunk's mouth jerked, seeping more fluid. 'Don't trust her.'

Hal looked round at the sound of footsteps. 'Speak of the devil,' he said, as Sonya entered the hold carrying a paper cup and plate.

'I thought you'd like something to eat.' Sonya looked at Clunk. 'How's he doing?'

'He'll be fine once we reach Ackexa.'

'Their facilities might not be the most up-to-date.'

'No problem. Neither is Clunk.'

'Hal, I need to talk.'

'Shoot.'

'I'm not really a historian. I work for Curtis Freightlines.'

Hal laughed. 'Is that professor guy going to be mad or what? He thought you were going after his population theories!'

'Professor? What professor?'

Hal jerked his thumb at the door. 'That idiot in the airlock. Rex wotsisname.'

'He's not a professor,' said Sonya quietly. 'He was my boss.'

'That's Rex Curtis?' Hal slammed his fist into his palm. 'I thought he looked familiar! Wait a minute, why were you pretending to be a passenger if you work for him?'

'It's a long story.'

'I've got plenty of time.'

'First, you have to understand my situation. I'm an Outsider refugee living in Union space under sufferance. I had a casual job with Curtis Freightlines, but I needed a permanent position before I could apply for residency.'

'How would stealing my ship help with that? Were you going to sell it and use the money for bribes?'

'Rex told me I could have a permanent position if I did a certain job for him. He wanted you held you up for a few hours. That's all.'

'But why? It doesn't make sense!'

'You don't understand. Losing the Central Bank contract meant the end of his company.'

'That makes killer robots okay, then?'

'I didn't have anything to do with that!' said Sonya. 'I was only supposed to make you late for Central Bank so they wouldn't use your services again. None of this was supposed to happen.' She bit her lip. 'He lied to me, Hal! He told me you were smuggling refugees, abandoning families on deserted planets, leaving people to die.'

'Oh sure.' Hal snorted in disgust. 'And I barbecue puppies for breakfast.'

'He was so convincing! Then, while you were underground he turned up out of the blue, waving that gun, and ... '

'And I left you in the flight deck with him.' Hal frowned. 'What are you doing down here? Why didn't you let him out?'

'I ...'

Slam!

Sonya looked round in shock. 'What was that?'

'Oh, very neat,' said Hal grimly. 'That was Curtis. Your boss just locked us in.'

◆

Rex had been unable to suppress a smile when Sonya approached the airlock door to let him out. He'd threatened to kill her, and still she was prepared to take his word over Spacejock's. Stupid bitch.

'Come on dear, let me out,' muttered Rex, maintaining his smile with difficulty while Sonya studied him through the porthole.

The smile vanished as Sonya raised her middle finger at him, and moments later she was gone.

Rex stared at the deserted flight deck. 'Of all the vicious, back-stabbing ...' His voice tailed off, and he turned to survey his prison. It was small, just a connecting tunnel between the outside world and the flight deck. There was an overhead camera, secure inside a tamper-proof dome, and the walls were lined with lockers.

Rex stood at the outer door, rubbed condensation from the porthole and squinted through the perspex. Outside, there was only darkness, punctuated with points of light from the stars. There would be no escape in that direction. He explored the lockers next, pulling them open one after another, hoping for a weapon of some kind. The smallest were crammed with odds and ends - spare parts, a ball of twine, three pairs of scissors. All useless. The biggest lockers held spacesuits and helmets, breathing equipment and tools.

He was about to slam the door on the spacesuits when he saw the communications panel set into the chest plate. Turning quickly, he looked towards the inner door. Right next to the controls there was an intercom, and Rex smiled to himself as he realised Dent's wonderful, helpful briefcase was plugged into the other end.

He hurried to the control panel and pressed the call button. 'Bobby, open the inner door!'

'I'm afraid I can't do that.'

'Why the hell not?'

'I'm not in control of that system.'

'So get control,' shouted Rex. He winced as his voice reverberated around the airlock, pounding his aching head.

'I'll have to relinquish other systems in order to do so.'

'Just get me out of here,' said Rex softly.

'Complying. Please stand by.'

◆

Hal's eyes narrowed as he looked at Sonya. 'I see it all now.'

'See what?'

Hal gestured at her. 'All this nicey-nice. You were just keeping me busy while that Curtis bastard –'

'No! It's not like that! I didn't let him out!'

'Oh, come on. Who else could it be?'

'I don't know, perhaps he ...' Sonya stared at him. 'Bobby!'

'Who the hell is Bobby?'

'The briefcase. It's plugged into the Navcom. Rex must have called it from the airlock.'

'Dammit, why didn't you say something? I could've pulled that thing out and –'

Sonya grabbed his arm. 'Hal, can he open the hold from the flight deck?'

'Yeah, of course.'

They both stared at the rear door. 'He's going to kill us,' said Sonya quietly. 'He'll open that door, and without helmets we'll suffocate in seconds.'

'We'll see about that.' Hal grabbed a length of pipe and strode to the inner door. He levered at the slab of metal, but the only effect was to bend the pipe in two.

'Is there another way out?'

Hal shook his head, his face grim. 'Let's face it, we're stuffed.'

'What about your robot? What about Clunk?'

'He's already stuffed.'

'No, he might have an idea!'

'Good point.' Hal hurried across to the workbench. 'Clunk, we're trapped in the hold. What can we do?'

The robot jerked, and his eyes half-opened. 'Plug me in. Data socket.'

'It won't work,' said Sonya briskly. 'Bobby isolated the hold.'

'Perhaps ... ' began Clunk. 'Perhaps ... '

Hal patted him on the shoulder. 'You take it easy, I'll worry about the escape plans.'

'Lee,' said Clunk weakly. He coughed, and more coolant ran down his cheek to join the pool on the bench.

'What?'

'New robot. LI-52.'

'Lee?' Hal frowned. 'You mean the robot I won in that competition?'

'Plug in. Transfer me.' Clunk shifted his gaze. 'In the locker.'

Hal ran to the side of the hold and pulled open a small door. A grey shape toppled out, slamming face down onto the deck. 'That'll do it some good,' muttered Hal. He rolled the prone form onto its back and dragged it to the workbench, where he withdrew a tangled data cable from Clunk's chest and plugged it into the robot at his feet. 'That's it, go for it!' He watched Clunk's furrowed face anxiously, willing the data across. Instead, the robot's drawn face relaxed and the fluid stopped pumping from his mouth.

Hal stared at the inert form in despair, clenching and unclenching his fists. Then he grabbed the length of pipe and attacked the door, filling the hold with the ring of metal on metal. 'Rex Curtis! Come down here and face me, you weasel!' He tossed the pipe aside and rained blows on the door with his fists. 'You're a dead man, Curtis!'

'Stop!' shouted Sonya, grabbing his arm. 'You'll hurt yourself!'

Hal rounded on her, his face white. 'Hurt myself? Clunk's dead, we're about to be snap-frozen, and you're worried about a couple of bruises?'

'There has to be another way!'

'She's right,' said a calm voice. 'There's no need to hurt yourself.'

32

'Bobby, open the cargo door,' shouted Rex as soon as the lift opened. He had just run the length of the ship and was breathing heavily, the blood pounding at his temples like blows from a mallet.

'I can only do so much at once,' said the briefcase plaintively. 'I'm still trying to control the airlock.'

'Screw the airlock. Get that damned hold open.' Rex stared at the screen, which showed a mottled green planet rotating in front of a starfield. 'Where are we?'

'Approaching planet Ackexa.'

'Already? My, she's a fast ship.' Rex loosened his collar. 'Damned hot, too. Can't you turn the heating down?'

'The heating isn't on.'

'Why's it so muggy then?'

'Because you're overworking me,' said the briefcase. 'My cooling system is operating at extremes. It was never designed for this kind of load.'

'After you've done I'll give you a week in cold storage. Happy?'

Cooling fans whistled. 'Estimate cargo hold override in eight minutes.'

'You'll do it in five. Spacejock has a gun, and when he comes out of that elevator he's going to put a shot right through your dinky little case.'

'I can seal the elevator. That will keep them out of the flight deck.'

'Don't talk. Do it!' Rex rubbed the welts on his forehead. 'Nobody's going to stand in my way, you hear? Not Spacejock, not that Polarov woman and certainly not you.' He jabbed his finger at the console. 'I want the ship under my control, and I want that hold door opened. No excuses, no whining and no fancy computer talk.'

◆

Clunk came online with a start, feeling as though he'd been sucked through a straw and spat into a huge, roomy warehouse. As his mind adjusted, he realised the warehouse was LI-52's vastly superior storage capacity.

He'd made it!

It took several milliseconds for his system to adjust, enumerating and scanning the motors, actuators and senses available to him. There were many functions his operating system could not identify, modern devices requiring newer drivers than he possessed, but he managed to get the basics under control before he switched on his hearing.

'There has to be another way!' he heard Sonya say, her voice as clear as a bell.

Clunk was still marvelling at the sweet, pure tone when a series of thuds struck him like physical blows. His eyes blinked open and he sat up just as Hal slammed his fist into the door again.

'She's right,' said Clunk. 'There's no need to hurt yourself.'

◆

Hal stared at the grey robot in amazement. Its eyes were warm yellow, and its face was creased with concern. 'Clunk?'

'That's me.'

'I thought you were gone,' said Hal quietly. 'You were just lying there.'

'I'm sorry, Mr Spacejock. I was too damaged to attract your attention.'

'Well, it's great to have you back. Even if you do look completely different.'

Clunk raised a hand and rotated it, causing a whirr from the motors. 'I could get used to this.'

'Don't admire yourself for too long.' Hal gestured at the door. 'Either we get out of the hold, or –'

'Stand back,' said Clunk, herding them away. 'I don't want to hit you with the fragments.'

'Are you sure you know what you're doing?' Hal nodded at the door. 'That's ten centimetres thick, that is.'

'Mr Spacejock, this chassis has the strength of ten men.' Clunk motioned them aside, then crouched and exploded forward in a blur. There was a bang as he bounced off the solid metal, and a thump as he landed flat on his back.

'Maybe you need the strength of twelve men,' said Hal.

'I don't have total control over this body. It has - wait a minute, I can hear something!' Clunk knelt alongside the door and listened intently. Then he smiled. 'It's Lucy!'

'Lucy?' exclaimed Hal. 'Of course!'

'Who's Lucy?' asked Sonya.

'She's a sort of pet,' said Hal. He put his hand out. 'About so high . . .'

'Orange fur and teeth?'

'That's her.'

'You told me she'd left the ship!'

'Ah, yes. Sorry about that.' Hal looked embarrassed. 'She's a stowaway really. I was taking her home after Ackexa.'

Clunk glared at them. 'Will you two SHUT UP!'

In the sudden quiet, they heard Lucy snuffling at the door. Clunk tapped on the solid metal, and there was an answering knock.

'That's great,' said Hal. 'Now we can walk straight out of here.'

Clunk frowned at him. Then he sprang up and ran to the corner of the hold, bowling Hal and Sonya over in his haste.

Hal watched in amazement as the robot opened the jetbike enclosure. 'Brilliant idea, Clunk!' He grabbed Sonya and shouted with glee. 'The jetbike! We can get out of here!'

Clunk shook his head. 'Actually, that's not the plan. It only carries one person, and you don't have any spacesuits.'

Hal's face fell.

'However, I can use it to reach the flight deck.'

'Won't the airlock be sealed?'

'I'll use the emergency override. I shall fly to the outer door, gain access to the flight deck and take control of the ship.'

'Take care, okay? No heroics.'

Clunk winked at him, then crouched over the jetbike and started the motor. He pulled the flap down and there was a roar as the bike shot out of the launch tube.

Hal gave Sonya a reassuring smile. 'Don't worry, he'll do it.'

'You should have given him Rex's gun.'

'It wouldn't make any difference. He can't harm humans anyway.'

Sonya stared at him. 'So how's he going to beat Rex? Polish him to death?'

Hal looked thoughtful. 'You know, perhaps we'd better try Lucy again.'

Clunk angled the jetbike along the side of the ship and advanced the throttle. The Volante's bulk slid past, a dark shadow cruising through space like a prowling shark. All around, stars were spread out like multicoloured jewels, bright and sharp.

The airlock came into view, and Clunk used the bike's thrusters to match speed with the flush-fitting door. He eased closer until the bike was only centimetres from the hull, then reversed the throttles to bring it to a halt. Leaning across, he pressed his palm to the hull and watched the flap swing up. Underneath, the status lights were green, confirming the inner door was closed. Just for a second, Clunk found himself wishing it wasn't, so he could evacuate Rex into space as easily as flushing a toilet. He suppressed the thought and pressed the override.

Nothing happened.

Clunk frowned. Emergency access meant now, not tomorrow. He pressed the button repeatedly, but still nothing happened. Then he remembered what Sonya had said - the ship was being controlled by the briefcase. He was locked out.

Clunk thought for a moment, then extended his probe and connected to the data socket. Rehearsing his words carefully, he called the flight deck.

◆

Rex was pacing the flight deck impatiently, while the cooling circuits in the briefcase howled as it fought a losing battle against the Navcom's defences. 'Mr Curtis, I cannot hold the ship much longer.'

'What are you talking about? She's mine!'

'The Navcom is winning. It's only a matter of time before we're at the ship's mercy.'

Rex glanced towards the airlock. 'You mean they could open the door on me?'

'Once they regain control they can do anything.'

Rex cursed. On the console, the cargo door indicator was dark. 'How long until you get that thing open?'

'A few moments more.'

'Keep on it. And then I want you to make for Ackexa at top speed.'

'Mr Curtis, I have an incoming call from Ackexa quarantine.'

'Get rid of them.'

'I can't. They want to speak with you.'

'All right, put them on.'

The console crackled and a distorted voice came through the speakers. 'Greetings, pilot of the *Volante*. As you're no doubt aware, visitors to our glorious planet must undergo rigorous inspection to ensure compliance with our import restrictions.'

'Can this wait?' asked Rex. 'I'm in a hurry here.'

'Alas, no. You will please stand by for inspection.'

'Goddam bureaucrats,' growled Rex. 'They're worse than our lot.'

'Your ship has not stopped. You will please halt your ship.'

'Look, sunshine. I've got a cargo to deliver, and –'

'If you do not halt your ship I will be forced to open fire, leaving perhaps enough metal to fill a tooth.'

'All right, we're stopping.' Rex cut the connection. 'Do as he says, but when their guy arrives I want you to stall him. And get that damned cargo door open!'

◆

Deep in the Navcom's circuits, a battle was raging. Hastily erected defences were no match for the briefcase's awesome power, and most fell like cardboard soldiers under the persistent attacks. The fight was centred on the door control circuits, although the briefcase occasionally launched sorties against other shipboard functions. The Navcom ignored these, tightly focussed on one overriding goal: to prevent the opening of the cargo hold door.

One by one the defences fell, torn apart by rampaging subroutines. Losing positions were abandoned and whirlpools of frantic activity were stilled, to become dark lifeless voids. Red tendrils of malicious code snaked through the darkness, reinforcements on their way to the final battle. In the centre of the maelstrom pure white became yellow, dull red, brown.

A tiny bubble burst clear, a white spark that drove fearlessly through the attackers, pushing them aside like grains of sand.

The spark reached an abandoned outpost, where it flared and was consumed.

Then the brown centre turned black.

◆

Hal was trying to coax Lucy to perform, promising her everything from a biscuit to her very own planet, but the ape simply chattered in return, only tapping the door occasionally. Finally, Hal lost his temper. 'Open the bloody door, you sad excuse for a simian!' He thumped the metal with his fist. 'Hit the button or I'll turn you into a bath mat!'

Sonya shushed him. 'You'll just scare her away,' she hissed.

'All right, you try.'

Sonya crouched next to the door and raised her voice. 'Lucy, can you hear me?'

There was a subdued noise from the ape.

'I want you to follow my hand,' said Sonya, tapping on the door. As Lucy tapped back, Sonya raised her hand higher and higher, approaching the control panel. 'Come on Lucy, follow the noise.'

Hal jumped as a siren began to wail. Directly overhead, a hazard light began to flash. 'The doors are going to open!' he shouted. 'It's too late!'

◆

'Mr Curtis, I have obtained control of the cargo door.'

'Don't waste time gabbing. Open the bloody thing!'

'I can't do that.'

'Why the hell not?'

'Human lives are involved. My programming forbids it. However, if you happened to accidentally lean on that large red button in the bottom-right corner of the console ... '

Rex pressed it, and blood red light spilled onto the console as the button began to flash. The viewscreen switched to a close-up of the rear doors, which glistened under the flashing yellow hazard lights. There was a puff of air as the doors cracked open, and slowly the gap widened, revealing the darkness of space beyond.

'So long, Spacejoke,' muttered Rex, as the doors opened to their fullest extent. 'Thanks for the ship, buddy.'

◆

'Is that the customs officer?' demanded a gravelly voice.

'Yes sir,' said Clunk, almost letting go of the ship in surprise. It had been several minutes since he'd called the flight deck, and the long silence had convinced him Rex had caught on to the deception.

'Sorry about the delay, we've got electrical probleMs. You can come in now.'

Clunk disconnected from the data socket as the airlock door slid open. He propelled himself inside and crossed to the inner door. The porthole was frosted, and when he scraped away the ice crystals he saw Curtis in the pilot's chair, talking to the console. Clunk's temperature rose at the sight. That was Mr Spacejock's place!

The door opened and Clunk entered the flight deck. He summed up the situation at a glance - with Curtis at the console, sudden moves were out of the question. One press of the cargo door button and Hal and Sonya would be spaced.

Rex looked round. If he was surprised to see a robot he hid it well, for his face was calm. 'Welcome to the *Volante*, officer. How may I help you?'

'I need to get into your cargo hold,' said Clunk, his voice clipped as it emerged from Lee's thin lips.

'Don't we all?' said Rex, with a laugh. 'Unfortunately the lift is stuck.'

'Really. I've heard some excuses in my time, but –'

'It's true! Try it yourself if you don't believe me.'

Clunk strode to the lift and pressed the button. Nothing happened. He looked round and spotted the briefcase under the console, connected to it with a length of cable. So that was the game.

'Tell you what,' said Rex. 'After I've docked you can come aboard with the customs guys. You can be first in the hold.'

'I can't wait that long. Final inspection must take place before docking is complete.' Clunk frowned. Could he do anything to break the briefcase's hold? His eyes widened as he spotted the flashing red light on the console. Rex had already opened the hold doors! Hal and Sonya were dead!

Fireworks went off in his head as his tenuous hold over Lee's body snapped. One by one his functions shut down, and with a final, soundless scream his mind was swallowed by a dark, featureless void.

33

Rex watched the frozen robot warily. Was it shamming? Preparing to spring?

'Seized good and proper,' he muttered, after waiting a little longer. 'Bobby, give me a status report.'

'I'm losing the ship, Mr Curtis,' said the briefcase, speaking loudly over the whirr of its cooling system. 'The Navcom took back several core functions while I was concentrating on the cargo doors. We're not going to make it.'

Rex swore. 'How am I supposed to start a new cargo business without a ship? Try harder!'

'What about the customs vessel? That robot didn't walk here.'

'A customs vessel is hardly a freighter, is it?' Rex snapped. 'I want this ship.'

'That option is no longer available.'

Rex strode into the airlock and stared through the porthole. Outside, a sleek jetbike was moored to the ship. 'How far is the orbiter?'

'I'm unable to access that information.'

'It can't be far if it used that little bike thing.' Rex glanced up as the lights flickered. 'What was that?'

'I can't hold on much longer,' explained Bobby. 'As soon

as I gain control over one function, the Navcom takes back another.'

Rex returned to the flight deck and began to pace up and down. 'If we abandon this thing some nosy bastard will find it. Spacejock's robot contains enough evidence to put me away for life.' He stopped pacing. 'Can you blow it up?'

'No. Once you unplug me the Navcom will cancel anything I set up.'

'What if I left you here?'

There was a long silence. 'I don't think much of that idea,' said Bobby finally. 'Anyway, deliberately exposing me to danger would void your warranty.'

'Screw the warranty.'

'And I would only be able to delay the inevitable. The Navcom will regain control whether I'm here or not.'

'Can you give me long enough to get clear?'

'Negative.'

Rex cursed.

'Anyway, you need me.'

'Oh?'

'You can't steal another ship on your own.' The briefcase hesitated. 'I have an idea. Would you like to hear it?'

'Go on.'

'Why don't we aim the *Volante* at the local star? We can escape on the jetbike, and the ship will be consumed.'

'No evidence. I like it.' Rex frowned. 'But isn't that the same as programming it to blow up?'

'No. I can swap the orbiter and the star in the navigation system. The Navcom will *want* to fly there.'

'Won't it stop when it realises what's happening?'

'No again. By the time it's close enough for external sensors to pick up the danger, the ship will be unable to escape the star's gravity.'

Rex nodded. 'Do it.'

'We'll have to leave before the ship starts to accelerate. Otherwise you'll waste most of the jetbike's fuel bringing it to a halt, and you won't have enough to reach the orbiter.'

'Of course.'

'And you'd better don a space suit. You'll find them in the airlock.'

'Want me to brush my teeth? Comb my hair?'

'That won't be necessary,' said the briefcase, oblivious to the sarcasm. 'The spacesuit filters will handle your bad breath.'

Rex strode into the airlock, muttering to himself as he yanked open the locker and selected a suit. He donned it quickly, tugging the stiff fabric over his clothes until he was encased up to his neck. He reached for the helmet and hesitated. Turning his back on the airlock camera, he cupped his hand over his mouth and exhaled quickly. Bad breath? What was the briefcase talking about? He lifted a helmet from the rack and lowered it into position, locking the ring. A heads-up display appeared on the inside of his faceplate, showing the remaining air and a row of green status indicators. Everything was set.

Rex turned and walked slowly into the flight deck. The helmet reduced his field of vision, and what little he could see was distorted by the curvature of the thick perspex. On his way to the console he was forced to detour around the frozen robot, which was standing in the way like a discarded statue.

The helmet speakers crackled and Bobby's voice burst out, almost deafening him. 'All set?'

'Yeah, I'm ready.'

'Very well. I shall program a sixty second countdown. Once

it begins you must unplug me and leave the ship as quickly as possible. The Volante will turn and accelerate towards the sun the instant the countdown finishes.'

'I got that already.'

'Have you checked your space suit?'

Rex nodded, then realised the briefcase couldn't see him. 'Yes.'

'Pick me up.'

Rex bent at the waist, gripped the briefcase handle in a gloved hand, and stood up. The patch cord swung from the console like a thin umbilical.

'Once I'm loose you can plug me into your space suit,' said the briefcase. 'There's a connector on your chest.'

'Can't you get on with it?'

'Okay, starting countdown in three seconds. Two. One. Disconnect me!'

Rex tried to pull the plug from the console, but it was stuck fast.

'It's a push and twist fitting,' said the briefcase. 'Hurry up!'

Rex tried to push the plug, but the thick glove prevented him from getting a purchase on it.

'Fifty seconds,' said the briefcase. 'We need to leave.'

Rex wrapped two loops of cord round his hand, put one foot on the console and heaved. Something gave inside the cable and Rex backed towards the airlock, stretching the plastic coating until it was impossibly thin. He was almost at the inner door when he thumped into something: turning round he saw the frozen robot toppling backwards to block the airlock threshold.

Cursing, he stepped over the robot, set the briefcase down, got both hands under its metal shoulders and hoisted it into a sitting position, coils of stretchy plastic tangled around its neck and arMs. Then he pushed it back into the flight deck, where it landed with a crash. With the doorway clear, Rex grabbed the thin cord and snapped it, then slammed the inner door, grabbed the briefcase and hurried to the outer door.

The air misted and vanished as the door cracked open. Debris was sucked from the airlock through the widening gap, and as the door opened fully Rex felt the deck shudder underfoot. He left the Volante just as the starfield started to pan by - the ship was already turning.

Clambering onto the jetbike, Rex fired the motor. He was reaching for the quick release when the Volante leapt forward, almost throwing him from the saddle as it dragged the tethered bike along for the ride. With the briefcase held firmly under one arm, he just managed to hang on with his free hand. But hanging on wasn't enough - the terrific acceleration would continue until oblivion. Muscles straining, he pulled himself forward and hit the quick release with his fist. There was a jolt as the bike came free and the ship surged away.

Rex opened the throttle, steering the bike away on a diverging course. He twisted in his seat to look back, and saw the long, blazing exhaust at the rear of the ship. Far ahead, directly in line with the ship, the local star shone with a baleful orange glow.

Satisfied the Volante was on course for destruction, Rex glanced around, expecting to see the mottled green orb of planet Ackexa.

There was nothing but stars.

❖

Clunk woke to a barrage of flashing lights. Every alert on the console was blinking, from the exterior temperature warning to the coffee maker's water level indicator. If that wasn't enough, the flight deck was bathed in orange light from the viewscreen, which was showing a boiling ocean of liquid flame: the surface of the local star. Like a magnet, Clunk's gaze was drawn to the flashing red light that indicated the cargo doors. This was the only one that mattered to him, for it confirmed Hal Spacejock was gone.

Dead.

Clunk's head dropped. He'd met many humans in all his long years, but only Mr Spacejock - Hal - had cared enough to take him in. He'd been treated with kindness and respect, and when Hal needed him most, he'd failed him.

Clunk raised his head and stared at the viewscreen. The Volante was roaring towards the local star, bent on fiery destruction. He could see no point in stopping it.

For several minutes he watched the star looming closer and closer while the alarms went crazy. Then he wiped the display and selected views of the Volante's interior, one camera at a time. His face was stern as he saw the empty recreation room, the Hal-less kitchen alcove and the Spacejock-free cabins, and something close to a sob escaped his lips as he saw the neat pallets of paperwork in the cargo hold, the rear doors open to space. His vision misted as the last view flicked up on the screen: a shot along the darkened lower deck passageway.

Clunk was about to switch off the display when a shadow moved across the screen. With trembling fingers, he reached for the lighting controls. Was it Hal? Had he survived somehow? His hopes were dashed as the light near the camera came up, showing Lucy scampering past the camera on her way to the rec room.

Clunk frowned. Lucy - it would be wrong for her to go down with the ship. He would take her back to Oliape II and set her free. After that ... well, there were plenty of stars in the galaxy.

He reached for the programming console and began to undo the briefcase's instructions. As he was busy with a particularly devious piece of code, he thought he detected movement out of the corner of his eye. He dismissed it, certain it was Lucy. Then he reconsidered. Lucy was only one metre high, and the shadow was almost double that.

Barely daring to hope, Clunk activated the light near the lift. In the harsh glare he saw Sonya and Hal, the latter hammering angrily on the lift door with his fist. With waves of joy coursing through his circuits, Clunk abandoned his programming and leapt to his feet. 'Navcom, unseal the lift,' he cried. 'It's Mr Spacejock! He's ... he's saved!'

◆

Hal stepped from the lift and was immediately engulfed in a pair of metal arMs. His ribs creaked and he struggled to free himself, convinced another killer robot had been set on him. Then he realised it was Clunk.

'Mr Spacejock, I'm so glad to see you!'

'Me too,' wheezed Hal, struggling to draw breath.

'But how did you escape?' Clunk frowned at him. 'And why aren't you saying anything?'

'I am, you daft hunk of tin.'

The robot continued to stare. 'Hello? Can you hear me?'

Hal nodded. 'Loud and clear.'

'My audio receptors!' Clunk opened his mouth wide and shook his head until his brain rattled. 'That's better. My hearing must have failed when I seized up.' He glanced at Sonya, then back at Hal. 'I thought you'd been spaced. How did you escape?'

Hal frowned. 'What are you talking about?'

'The cargo hold! Curtis opened the doors!'

'No he didn't.'

'He did! I saw it on the screen!'

'Sounds like hearing wasn't your only problem.'

Clunk turned to the console. 'Navcom, please explain.'

'I was trying to, only you couldn't hear me,' said the Navcom. 'The briefcase was trying to open the cargo hold door, and Curtis was refusing to let you into the ship until the cargo hold was vented to space.'

'Bastard,' muttered Hal.

'I duped the briefcase into thinking it had control, and when Rex pressed the button I displayed a recorded image of the cargo door opening.'

Clunk frowned. 'That would never work. The briefcase would know that it hadn't opened anything.'

'Certainly. However, I routed the cargo door commands to another location.'

'Where to?'

'Let's just say it's lucky nobody was using the toilet.'

⁍

In the early days of space travel, passengers would spend a year's wages for a brief trip into orbit, where they could experience weightlessness and gaze upon a starfield unsullied by atmospheric gases and pollution.

To escape the same terrible view, Rex would have given up every salary bonus he'd ever awarded himself.

With rising panic, he hauled the briefcase off his lap and flipped it open. It could call the ship back, raise someone on the orbiter, get help. It had to! Rex tapped the keyboard with his gloved finger and the display lit up. Through the distorted lens of his helmet he could just make out the words on the screen:

Fatal error! Atmosphere 0%. Nitrogen 0%. Cooling system failed. Detonation in ten seconds … Nine … Eight …

◆

Hal stared out of the airlock. 'What the hell was that?'

Clunk looked up from the console. 'What?'

'I just saw a flash of light out there.'

'Perhaps it was a reflection.'

'Some reflection.' Hal rubbed his eyes. 'It half blinded me.'

Clunk continued to work on the console and gradually the warning lights returned to normal. After the last one stopped blinking he unplugged himself and examined the status screens. 'That should do it, Mr Spacejock. I've uncoupled the navigation console, returned the star map to its default configuration and brought the Navcom back to full operational status. We're back on course, our cruising speed is back to normal and I've even set the console clock to the correct time.' He looked across the flight deck at Hal, who was still gazing through the porthole. 'I said, that should do it.'

'Uh-huh?'

'You can thank me later,' muttered Clunk. He glanced at the camera. 'Navcom, can you hear me?'

'Yes, Clunk. And I appreciate your efforts.'

'It was nothing.' He glared at Hal. 'Apparently.'

The Navcom was more forthcoming. 'I thought you handled the situation remarkably well, given your new body.'

'Tell me, did you get anything on that briefcase?'

'Negative.'

'What, nothing at all?'

'I was unable to breach its defences without an unlock code.'

'You tried though.'

'Certainly. However, the briefcase locked up after nine billion combinations.'

'Nine billion!' Clunk's face bore a concerned expression as he looked at Hal. 'Mr Spacejock, I fear –' He staggered, and put out a hand to steady himself. 'I fear the flash you saw might have been Mr Curtis.'

'Rex?' Hal stared at the porthole. 'You mean he blew up?'

'Not him. The briefcase!'

Sonya gasped. 'Dent warned me about that! He told me it was cooled by some kind of fusion reactor, using nitrogen from the air. He said it could knock a planet out of orbit if it failed.'

'Nitrogen from the air? But he went out into a vacuum!' Clunk slumped into the pilot's chair. 'It's all my fault! I instructed the Navcom to break into the briefcase, but I didn't know the extra load would cause ... ' He put his head in his hands. 'Oh, this is terrible.'

Hal patted him on the shoulder. 'It's okay, Clunk. It wasn't your fault.'

'Really?'

'Yes, really. If he hadn't skipped with the jetbike and left us to fly into the sun, you wouldn't have murdered him.'

Clunk groaned.

'Anyway, I'd have killed him myself if you hadn't done it.' Hal looked to Sonya for help, but she was staring out the airlock. 'Are you okay?'

'I've caused so much trouble,' she said quietly. 'Clunk was stolen and dismantled on Ullimo, then he was wrecked on Canessa. You almost lost your ship and we nearly flew into a star. And now Rex is dead.'

'Yeah, but we won,' said Hal. 'And we didn't even lose the cargo.'

'Do you usually?'

'Well, you know ...'

Sonya turned to stare at Hal, her face pale. 'Can I beg a favour?'

'Sure. Anything.'

'Take me back to Canessa. Set me down next to Rex's flyer.'

'We can't do that!' protested Clunk. 'If we turn back now we'll be late for the cargo delivery. Mr Spacejock will suffer heavy penalties.'

Hal sighed. 'He's right, Sonya. We're delivering to a bank, and if we mess this one up they'll put me out of business.'

'I don't have any ID, I don't have a letter of employment ... If I land on Ackexa I'll never be free again!'

'Don't worry, we'll hide you.' Hal snapped his fingers. 'I've got it! We can tell them you're a historian studying alien cultures.'

'You think they're stupid? They'd never fall for a feeble ...' Sonya put a hand to her mouth. 'I mean –'

'You could always offer her a job,' said Clunk without

looking up. 'All she needs is a letter of employment to prove she's been accepted in Union territory.'

'That's it!' Hal grabbed Sonya by the shoulders. 'We'll make a great team! You're resourceful, attractive and intelligent, and I'm ...'

'You're sweet,' said Sonya, kissing him on the cheek.

'Are they going to reproduce now?' said the Navcom.

'Shh,' said Clunk, as Hal's face turned a deep shade of red. The robot tapped away at the console then pressed a button and a sheet of paper whirred out. 'Here you are, Ms Smith. Welcome to the *Volante*.'

'Actually, it's Polarov.'

'What an interesting name,' said Hal, as Clunk printed another letter. He signed it with a flourish, folded it in half and handed it over. 'There you are, you're officially a co-pilot.'

'But I don't know the first thing about flying a ship!' protested Sonya.

'That never stopped Mr Spacejock,' muttered Clunk. He turned away to scan the console. 'That's odd,' he said as he waved his hand over a contact. The viewscreen changed to a long-range shot of a mottled green planet. Underneath, the status line read: Planet Canessa.

'Canessa!' Hal stared at the image. 'I thought we were halfway to Ackexa!'

'So did Mr Curtis,' said the Navcom. 'Alas, he was fooled by my screen saver.'

'Impossible,' said Sonya. 'Rex is an experienced pilot. He'd never fall for a trick like that.'

'Yeah, the screen saver looks totally fake,' said Hal. 'It's all twinkly stars and zooming comets.'

Clunk glanced at him apologetically. 'I did enhance it a little.'

'What for?'

'Well, the Navcom told me about your –'

'Wait a minute,' Sonya interrupted him. 'If that's Canessa, you can land and set me free. I don't have to go to Ackexa!'

34

The *Volante* set down on Canessa, using the same clearing it had vacated an hour or so earlier. During the landing Clunk explained how the Navcom had flown in circles, fooling Bobby the Briefcase by faking log files as fast as the rogue computer could inspect them. The screensaver had done the rest.

The outer door opened, ready to let Sonya out, but Hal still had doubts. 'What if the flyer's tanks are empty?'

Clunk shrugged. 'We can top them up if need be. The fuel is compatible.'

'And Sonya can't fly. She said so!'

'She's only got to tell the computer what to do. Judging from your description it's a recent model. Completely automated.'

Hal looked around the flight deck. 'Where is she, anyway?'

'I believe she's making use of our toilet. The flyer has no such facilities.'

At that moment Sonya stepped out of the lift. She beamed at Hal, and together they left the ship. At the bottom of the ramp, Hal looked up to see Clunk watching from the airlock. 'Aren't you coming?'

'I'd only get in the way, Mr Spacejock.' He touched his forehead. 'Goodbye, Ms Polarov.'

Sonya nodded at him, then turned for the forest. Hal led

the way to the second clearing, holding aside branches and trampling the undergrowth to let Sonya through.

'It looks a bit small for a long trip like that,' he said, as the ship came into view.

'It got Rex here. Anyway, I don't have much stuff to collect.'

'And you'll come back?'

Sonya nodded. 'Meet you in orbit around planet Oliape II, as agreed.'

'Well, you'd better be going.' Hal hesitated. 'You know, I –'

'You have a deadline.' Sonya kissed him on the cheek, and before he could respond she was climbing the ladder and punching in Rex's security code. The canopy rose into the air and Sonya slid into the cockpit and strapped herself in. She checked the instruments, particularly the fuel gauge, then nodded. The canopy came down, and just before it sealed Sonya flashed Hal another smile. He raised his hand to wave just as the flyer's engine burst into life, forcing him back with a wash of hot exhaust.

The flyer rolled over the uneven ground towards the far side of the clearing. Slowly, it turned to face him, and the engine noise rose as the ship began to hover. The undercarriage retracted, barely visible in the whirling cloud of smoke and debris, and then the ship was roaring towards him. Hal ducked as it passed overhead, and turned to watch the vessel heading for the sky. Before long it had vanished, a faint rumble the only clue it had ever been there.

Lowering his hand, Hal turned for the forest. It was time to deliver the cargo.

◆

The *Volante's* engines roared as it descended towards Ackexa. A battlecruiser had escorted them safely into planetary orbit, protecting against pirate attacks. Lucy was hidden away in the bowels of the ship, and Central Bank had cleared them for immediate landing at the company's private field.

'Contact in five seconds,' said the Navcom. 'Three. Two. One.'

The ship bumped down and the engines cut out. 'Landing successful. Local time three pm.'

'I'll get the ramp down,' said Clunk. 'Are you going to supervise, Mr Spacejock?'

'Yeah, I'll watch. Can't trust anyone these days.'

They left through the airlock, pausing at the top to examine their surroundings. They didn't stop long: the air was hazy with smog and there was a bitter stench that made Hal's eyes water. 'What the hell is that?'

'Fossil fuels,' said Clunk. 'Probably burning them for heating or power.'

'Phew. Remind me never to take another Outsider job.'

'I told you not to take this one.'

'Yeah, about ten minutes too late.' Hal led the way to the ground, where a dozen mechanics were standing in a half circle around the foot of the ramp, hands in their pockets and sullen looks on their faces. 'Some welcoming committee,' muttered Hal. 'Do you think they've ever seen a robot?'

'Greetings,' said Clunk, raising his hand. 'We come in peace.'

A couple of mechanics spat on the ground.

'Can I have Rex's gun back now?' Hal asked Clunk out of the side of his mouth. 'They don't look too friendly.'

The mechanics stepped back, allowing them through, and together they made their way to the back of the ship where they found a large white truck reversed up to the ramp. Hal watched as a workman came out of the ship with an armful of bound papers. His expression changed suddenly as the man threw the whole lot carelessly into the back of the truck. 'What the ...Clunk, they're shredding it!'

He was about to rush over and flatten the workmen when Clunk put a hand on his arm. 'Look at the sign on the truck.'

Hal did so. 'Docu-Shred? Secure disposal?'

'It seems the paperwork wasn't as important as your Mr Fish made out.'

'Taking my name in vain?' said a quiet voice.

Hal turned round to see Mr Fish a few paces away, watching the unloading. 'Was this planned all along?'

Fish nodded. 'It's important paperwork. Commercially sensitive, so to speak.'

'Why drag it all the way back here?'

'We have to witness the destruction.' Fish smiled. 'You've done well, Mr Spacejock. No trouble, I trust?'

'None at all,' said Hal firmly. 'It was a doddle.'

Clunk cleared his throat. 'Mr Spacejock, I'd better attend to the refuelling.'

Hal watched him leave, then turned back to Fish. 'About the money ...'

'I'll make sure the fee is transferred into your account before you leave.' Fish hesitated. 'Incidentally, have you heard the news about Curtis Freightlines?'

'Went broke, didn't they?'

'Correct. Their finance was withdrawn and the whole enterprise crumbled.'

'That happened a bit quickly,' said Hal.

'The end is often swift.' Fish glanced at him. 'Tell me, have you considered expanding your business?'

'How do you mean?'

'There's going to be a lot of work around. An enterprising young man could do well for himself, particularly with our financial backing.'

'Freighters are old hat,' said Hal. 'I'm about to patent an instant delivery method. Here today, somewhere else in a minute or two.'

'Really?'

'Absolutely. The slogan needs a bit of work, but these things take time. Except for the delivery, of course. That's instant.'

'But how will you achieve this miracle? I don't understand –'

'That's why you're not running a freight business,' said Hal.

'Touch?. Well, until this new method of yours is ready, perhaps you would consider working for us on a contract basis?'

Hal shook his head. 'With Curtis gone, I'm going to be in demand. I'll take it one job at a time.'

'We'll pay an additional twenty percent on your standard rate.'

Hal glanced at the Volante and saw the refuelling crew connecting a thick pipe to the ship. 'How much is fuel in this part of the galaxy?'

Fish smiled. 'This one's on us, Mr Spacejock. A goodwill gesture.'

A few minutes later, the recycling truck burst into life. As it drove away, a group of workmen trooped down the cargo ramp in a group. 'I've got to deliver a special cargo,' said Hal. 'After that, the next one's yours. Okay?'

'Fair enough, Mr Spacejock.' They shook hands, and Fish followed the workmen back towards the distant buildings.

The refuelling was almost finished when Hal arrived. He told Clunk about the bank's offer, and the robot made him repeat it three times before it sank in. Even then he looked doubtful.

'Banks just don't do that sort of thing,' he said.

'Clunk, they're desperate. With Curtis out of the picture there's going to be an almighty backlog.'

'There are still plenty of freelancers, Mr Spacejock.'

'Ah, but we've got a secret weapon.'

Clunk looked surprised. 'We do? What's that?'

'The teleporter, of course!'

'If you're referring to that deluded old gentleman at the Ullimo spaceport . . .'

'Not him!' said Hal. 'The teleporter on the robot planet. You read the plans off that chip thing!'

'I did indeed. Straight into Sonya's briefcase, which is currently orbiting Canessa as a cloud of micro particles.'

Hal groaned. 'You didn't keep a copy?'

'I'm sorry, Mr Spacejock.'

Hal stared at the deck, his dreams of riches fading. Then he folded his arMs. 'Okay, here's what we'll do. Fish offered me a contract for all their work. I'll take it, and insist on membership to the Spacer's Guild.'

'You can't handle all his freight!'

'He doesn't know that, does he? And once we're in the Spacer's Guild we won't need his work - they'll be queuing up with plump, juicy jobs and –'

'A contract is a contract,' said Clunk firmly.

'We'll get a loan and buy up a couple of Curtis's old ships - you can fly one, Sonya can have another and I'll take the third. It'll be the start of Spacejock Freightlines!'

'That's a rather ambitious plan, Mr Spacejock. Particularly since only one of your three pilots can fly.'

337

'Come on, let's design the adverts! Last one up the ramp is a loser.'

◆

The *Volante* was in orbit around Oliape II. Hal was in the rec room, having left Clunk in the flight deck with strict orders to call him the moment Sonya came into range. Lucy was still aboard, despite Clunk's protests, as Hal was reluctant to land in case Sonya missed them.

Hal eyed the AutoChef. He was getting hungry, but had to weigh the demands of his stomach against the likelihood of severe injury. In the end his stomach won out, and he approached the machine to place an order. 'I'd like a plate of cheese sandwiches. White bread, not too heavy on the butter.'

'Unable to comply. Please call service with code C6.'

'C6?' Hal frowned. 'Isn't that the one about obstructions in the dispenser?'

'Confirmed. Please call service with code C6.'

Hal lifted the flap and discovered a folded sheet of paper tucked inside. His heart sank as he saw the words 'Dear Hal' on the front, and he was just unfolding the note when Clunk arrived.

'There's no sign of her, Mr Spacejock. Do you think we should wait any longer?'

Hal waved the note at him. 'This is from Sonya.'

'Ah,' said the robot. 'I wondered if that might happen.'

Hal scanned the sheet of paper. 'She's gone,' he said quietly. 'Skipped town. Skedaddled. Flown the nest and left us to mind the baby.'

'Speaking of which, we really must return Lucy.'

'She never gave me a chance,' said Hal. 'I saved her life, and she never said a word of thanks.'

'That's hardly surprising, since she doesn't speak our language. Or indeed, any sort of language.'

'Eh?'

'Lucy, Mr Spacejock. We must return her as soon as possible.'

'I was talking about Sonya.'

'What for? She's gone.'

'Yes, I know. That's what I'm talking about!'

'And have you finished now? Only Lucy is –'

'Will you shut up about that bloody ape!' Hal screwed Sonya's note up and stormed out of the rec room.

'I'll just take the ship down, shall I?' said Clunk mildly, as a cabin door thudded to.

They dropped Lucy in the damp forest, and although she protested loudly at first, she seemed to cheer up when a number of other apes came out of the forest to welcome her. Upon their return to the flight deck, Clunk discovered job offers coming from all directions, and within minutes he was mapping out a route that would take them from one profitable cargo to another. Still smarting from Sonya's note, Hal returned to the rec room where he sat in silence with a plate of mucus-flavoured biscuits at his side.

The Volante got under way, and he didn't notice.

The lights dimmed as the ship entered the night cycle, and he didn't stir.

An hour or so later, footsteps approached along the lower deck passageway.

'Mr Spacejock, are you there?'

'Yes, Clunk.' Hal blinked as the robot turned the lights on. Through watering eyes, he saw a vague bronze shape. 'Is that your old body?'

'Yes. I mended it.'

'Why?'

'Well, it's a bit like your old boots.'

'Worn out and full of holes?'

'No,' said Clunk with a frown. 'Familiar and comfortable.'

Hal sighed. 'I'm sorry Clunk. I was just . . . '

'I know, Mr Spacejock. And that's why I'm here. You see, I have a surprise for you.'

'Oh?'

Clunk turned his back to address someone outside. 'He's ready. In you go.'

'Hal?' said a female voice. 'Oh, I want to thank you so much!'

Hal sat up. 'But . . . that sounds like Sonya!'

'That's right!' said Clunk. He gestured at the figure waiting outside. 'Come in, come in.'

Hal leapt up, his heart pounding. She'd come back! The brush-off letter was just a cover! His welcoming smile vanished as a robot came through the door. 'What the hell's this?'

'Charming,' said the robot, in a perfect copy of Sonya's voice.

'I used Lee's body and the brain you saved on Ullimo,' said Clunk proudly. 'Not only that, but I've managed to synthesise Sonya's voice. Her name is Katie.'

Katie fluttered her eyelids with a sound like mating cockroaches. 'So, big boy. Want to play a game?'

Hal stared at the robot for several seconds, his face a mask. Then, slowly, he began to smile. The smile grew until it stretched across his face, and then he burst out laughing.

'I love a man with a sense of humour,' said Katie, advancing with outstretched arMs. 'Come on, give me a kiss.'

'Here, steady on,' said Hal, scuttling behind the armchair.

'Come on, don't be shy!'

Hal ducked her grasping hands and fled to the corridor. Katie followed, and moments later there was a sound of ripping cloth, followed by Hal's frantic cries for help.

'Oh well,' murmured Clunk. 'At least he's happy.'

Epilogue

Dear Hal,

You're a wonderful guy, but deep down I know you'll never forgive me for the trouble I caused. I didn't want to leave like this, but you'll agree it's for the best. Don't trouble yourself looking for me ... I'm going to sell the flyer and use the funds to set myself up in comfort.

Your employment letter will secure my Union residency, and who knows, one day we might run into each other ... as equals.

Please give my regards to Clunk. I know he didn't trust me, and that makes him an excellent judge of character.

Ever yours,

Sonya Polarov

P.S. No offence, but I couldn't live on your cooking.

If you enjoyed this book, please leave a brief review at your online bookseller of choice. Thanks!

About the Author

Simon Haynes was born in England and grew up in Spain. His family moved to Australia when he was 16.

In addition to novels, Simon writes computer software. In fact, he writes computer software to help him write novels faster, which leaves him more time to improve his writing software. And write novels faster. (www.spacejock.com/yWriter.html)

Simon's goal is to write fifteen novels before someone takes his keyboard away.

Update 2018: goal achieved and I still have my keyboard!

New goal: write thirty novels.

Simon's website is spacejock.com.au

Stay in touch!

Author's newsletter:
spacejock.com.au/ML.html

facebook.com/halspacejock
twitter.com/spacejock

The Hal Spacejock series by Simon Haynes

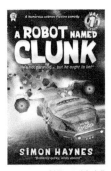

1. A ROBOT NAMED CLUNK

Deep in debt and with his life on the line, Hal takes on a dodgy cargo job ... and an equally dodgy co-pilot.

2. SECOND COURSE

When Hal finds an alien teleporter network he does the sensible thing and pushes Clunk the robot in first.

3. JUST DESSERTS

Gun-crazed mercenaries have Hal in their sights, and a secret agent is pulling the strings. One wrong step and three planets go to war!

4. NO FREE LUNCH

Everyone thinks Peace Force trainee Harriet Walsh is paranoid and deluded, but Hal stands at her side. That would be the handcuffs.

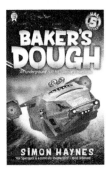

5. BAKER'S DOUGH

When you stand to inherit a fortune, good body-guards are essential. If you're really desperate, call Hal and Clunk. Baker's Dough features intense rivalry, sublime double-crosses and more greed than a free buffet.

6. SAFE ART

Valuable artworks and a tight deadline ... you'd be mad to hire Hal for that one, but who said the art world was sane?

7. BIG BANG

A house clearance job sounds like easy money, but rising floodwaters, an unstable landscape and a surprise find are going to make life very difficult for Hal and Clunk.

8. DOUBLE TROUBLE

Hal Spacejock dons a flash suit, hypershades and a curly earpiece for a stint as a secret agent, while a pair of Clunk's most rusted friends invite him to a 'unique business opportunity'.

9. MAX DAMAGE

Hal and Clunk answer a distress call, and they discover a fellow pilot stranded deep inside an asteroid field. Clunk is busy at the controls so Hal dons a spacesuit and sets off on a heroic rescue mission.

10. Cold Boots

Coming 2019

Ebook and Trade Paperback

The Secret War Series
Set in the Hal Spacejock universe

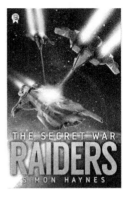

Everyone is touched by the war, and Sam Willet is no exception.

Sam wants to train as a fighter pilot, but instead she's assigned to Tactical Operations.

It's vital work, but it's still a desk job, far from the front line.

Then, terrible news: Sam's older brother is killed in combat.

Sam is given leave to attend his memorial service, but she's barely boarded the transport when the enemy launches a surprise attack, striking far behind friendly lines as they try to take the entire sector.

Desperately short of pilots, the Commander asks Sam to step up.

Now, at last, she has the chance to prove herself.

But will that chance end in death... or glory?

Ebook and Trade Paperback

The Harriet Walsh series

Harriet's boss is a huge robot with failing batteries, the patrol car is driving her up the wall and her first big case will probably kill her.

So why did she join the Peace Force?

When an intergalactic crime-fighting organisation offers Harriet Walsh a job, she's convinced it's a mistake. She dislikes puzzles, has never read a detective mystery, and hates wearing uniforms. It makes no sense ... why would the Peace Force choose her?

Who cares? Harriet needs the money, and as long as they keep paying her, she's happy to go along with the training.

She'd better dig out some of those detective mysteries though, because she's about to embark on her first real mission ...

The Peace Force has a new recruit, and she's driving everyone crazy.

From disobeying orders to handling unauthorised cases, nothing is off-limits. Worse, Harriet Walsh is forced to team up with the newbie, because the recruit's shady past has just caught up with her.

Meanwhile, a dignitary wants to complain about rogue officers working out of the station. She insists on meeting the station's commanding officer ... and they don't have one.

All up, it's another typical day in the Peace Force!

Dismolle is supposed to be a peaceful retirement planet. So what's with all the gunfire?

A criminal gang has moved into Chirless, planet Dismolle's second major city. Elderly residents are fed up with all the loud music, noisy cars and late night parties, not to mention the hold-ups, muggings and the occasional gunfight.

There's no Peace Force in Chirless, so they call on Harriet Walsh of the Dismolle City branch for help. That puts Harriet right in the firing line, and now she's supposed to round up an entire gang with only her training pistol and a few old allies as backup.

And her allies aren't just old, they're positively ancient!

Ebook and Trade Paperback

The Hal Junior Series
Set in the Hal Spacejock universe

Spot the crossover characters, references and in-jokes!

Hal Junior lives aboard a futuristic space station. His mum is chief scientist, his dad cleans air filters and his best mate is Stephen 'Stinky' Binn. As for Hal ... he's a bit of a trouble magnet. He means well, but his wild schemes and crazy plans never turn out as expected!

Hal Junior: The Secret Signal features mayhem and laughs, daring and intrigue ... plus a home-made space cannon!

200 pages, illustrated, ISBN 978-1-877034-07-7

"A thoroughly enjoyable read for 10-year-olds and adults alike"
The West Australian

'I've heard of food going off
      ... but this is ridiculous!'

Space Station Oberon is expecting an important visitor, and everyone is on their best behaviour. Even Hal Junior is doing his best to stay out of trouble!

From multi-coloured smoke bombs to exploding space rations, Hal Junior proves ... *trouble is what he's best at!*

200 pages, illustrated, ISBN 978-1-877034-25-1

Imagine a whole week of fishing, swimming, sleeping in tents and running wild!
Unfortunately, the boys crash land in the middle of a forest, and there's little chance of rescue. Is this the end of the camping trip ... or the start of a thrilling new adventure?

200 pages, illustrated, ISBN 978-1-877034-24-4

Space Station Oberon is on high alert, because a comet is about to whizz past the nearby planet of Gyris. All the scientists are preparing for the exciting event, and all the kids are planning on watching.

All the kids except Hal Junior, who's been given detention...

165 pages, illustrated, ISBN 978-1-877034-38-1

Ebook and Trade Paperback

New from Simon Haynes
The Robot vs Dragons series

"Laugh after laugh, dark in places but the humour punches through. One of the best books I've read in 2018 so far. Amazing, 5"*

Welcome to the Old Kingdom!

It's a wonderful time to visit! There's lots to do and plenty to see!
What are you waiting for? Dive into the Old Kingdom right now!

Clunk, an elderly robot, does exactly that. He's just plunged into the sea off the coast of the Old Kingdom, and if he knew what was coming next he'd sit down on the ocean floor and wait for rescue.

Dragged from the ocean, coughing up seaweed, salty water and stray pieces of jellyfish, he's taken to the nearby city of Chatter's Reach, where he's given a sword and told to fight the Queen's Champion, Sur Loyne.

As if that wasn't bad enough, the Old Kingdom still thinks the wheel is a pretty nifty idea, and Clunk's chances of finding spare parts - or his missing memory modules - are nil.

Still, Clunk is an optimist, and it's not long before he's embarking on a quest to find his way home.

Unfortunately it's going to be a very tough ask, given the lack of charging points in the medieval kingdom...

Ebook and Trade Paperback

Printed in Great Britain
by Amazon

39461362R00202